HANDLE WITH CARE

Handle with Care

JODI PICOULT

ISIS
LARGE PRINT
Oxford

First published in Great Britain 2009
by
Hodder & Stoughton
First published in Australia and New Zealand
by Allen & Unwin

Published in Large Print 2009 by ISIS Publishing Ltd.,
7 Centremead, Osney Mead, Oxford OX2 0ES
by arrangement with
Hodder & Stoughton
an Hachette Livre UK company,
and Allen & Unwin

British Library Cataloguing in Publication Data
Picoult, Jodi, 1966–
   Handle with care
   1. Osteogenesis imperfecta - - Patients - - Fiction.
   2. Mothers and daughters - - Fiction.
   3. Physicians - - Malpractice - - Fiction.
   4. Large type books.
   I. Title
   813.5'4–dc22

ISBN 978–0–7531–8424–0 (hb)
ISBN 978–0–7531–8425–7 (pb)

Printed and bound in Great Britain by
T. J. International Ltd., Padstow, Cornwall

For Marjorie Rose,
Who makes flowers bloom onstage,
Provides me with goss half a world away,
And knows you're never fully dressed
without a green bag
BFFAA

ACKNOWLEDGMENTS

It may be a cliché to say I didn't do this alone, but it's also true. First and foremost, I want to thank the parents of kids with OI who invited me into their lives for a little while — and the kids themselves, who made me laugh and reminded me daily that strength is far more than a physical measure of stamina: Laurie Blaisdell and Rachel, Taryn Macliver and Matthew, Tony and Stacey Moss and Hope, Amy Phelps and Jonathan. Thanks to my cracker-jack medical team: Mark Brezinski, David Toub, John Femino, E. Rebecca Schirrer, Emily Baker, Michele Lauria, Karen George, Steve Sargent; and my legal eagles: Jen Sternick, Lise Iwon, Chris Keating, Jennifer Sargent. I owe Debbie Bernstein for sharing her story about being adopted (and letting me steal huge parts of it). I am likewise indebted to Donna Branca, for revisiting memories that are painful and for being gracious and honest when I asked questions. Thanks to Jeff Fleury, Nick Giaccone, and Frank Moran for helping me create Sean's life as a police officer. For other expertise in their fields, thanks to Michael Goldman (who also let me use his fantastic T-shirt slogan), Steve Alspach, Stefanie Ryan, Kathy Hemenway, Jan Scheiner, Fonsaca Malyan, Kevin Lavigne, Ellen Wilber, Sindy Buzzell, and Fred Clow. It would be a gross oversight not to highlight the involvement that Atria Books has in making my books such successes; I am grateful to Carolyn Reidy, Judith Curr, David Brown, Kathleen Schmidt, Mellony Torres, Sarah Branham, Laura Stern, Gary Urda, Lisa Keim, Christine Duplessis, Michael Selleck, the whole of the fabulous sales force, and everyone else who has worked so hard to make my books leap off the shelves into the arms and hearts of readers. A special thanks goes to Camille McDuffie, my secret weapon/publicist extraordinaire. To Emily Bestler, who always makes me feel like a star (and makes sure everyone else seems to think I'm one, too). To Laura Gross, with whom I celebrated my twentieth anniversary this year — and who is the other half of a partnership I rank right up there with my marriage. To Jane Picoult, my mom, who believed I could do this long before anyone else, and who laughs and cries in all the right places.

In the interests of accuracy, I should state that, although there was an OI convention in Omaha, I've changed the date. Also, I've slightly amended the way juries are picked in New Hampshire — it's not by individual, as I've written, but it's a lot more interesting to read that way!

I have two special thank-yous. The first is to Katie Desmond, the sister I never had, who created the recipes I've attributed here to Charlotte O'Keefe. If you're ever lucky enough to be invited to her house for dinner, don't walk, run. The second is to Kara Sheridan, who is one of the most inspirational women I've ever met: she's a scholar studying body image and self-esteem for disabled teens. She's an athlete — a swimmer who's broken records. She's about to get married to a wonderful, adorable guy. And — oh, by the way, she also has Type III osteogenesis imperfecta. Thanks, Kara, for showing the world that barriers were meant to be broken, that no one can be defined by a disability, and that nothing's ever impossible.

Finally, I have to thank once again Kyle, Jake, and Sammy, for giving me something wonderful to come home to; and Tim, who is my happy ending.

And did you get what
you wanted from this life, even so?
I did.
And what did you want?
To call myself beloved, to feel myself
beloved on the earth.

— Raymond Carver, *Late Fragment*

PROLOGUE

Charlotte

February 14, 2002

Things break all the time. Glass, and dishes, and fingernails. Cars and contracts and potato chips. You can break a record, a horse, a dollar. You can break the ice. There are coffee breaks and lunch breaks and prison breaks. Day breaks, waves break, voices break. Chains can be broken. So can silence, and fever.

For the last two months of my pregnancy, I made lists of these things, in the hopes that it would make your birth easier.

Promises break.

Hearts break.

On the night before you were born, I sat up in bed with something to add to my list. I rummaged in my night-stand for a pencil and paper, but Sean put his warm hand on my leg. *Charlotte?* he asked. *Is everything okay?*

Before I could answer, he pulled me into his arms, flush against him, and I fell asleep feeling safe, forgetting to write down what I had dreamed.

It wasn't until weeks later, when you were here, that I remembered what had awakened me that night: fault lines. These are the places where the earth breaks apart. These are the spots where earthquakes originate, where volcanoes are born. Or in other words: the world is crumbling under us; it's the solid ground beneath our feet that's an illusion.

You arrived during a storm that nobody had predicted. A nor'easter, the weathermen said later, a blizzard that was supposed to blow north into Canada instead of working its way into a frenzy and battering the coast of New England. The news broadcasts tossed aside their features on high school sweethearts who met up again in a nursing home and got remarried, on the celebrated history behind the candy heart, and instead began to run constant weather bulletins about the strength of the storm and the communities where ice had knocked out the power. Amelia was sitting at the kitchen table, cutting folded paper into valentines as I watched the snow blow in six-foot drifts against the glass slider. The television showed footage of cars sliding off the roads.

I squinted at the screen, at the flashing blues of the police cruiser that had pulled in behind the overturned vehicle, trying to see whether the officer in the driver's seat was Sean.

A sharp rap on the slider made me jump. "Mommy!" Amelia cried, startled, too.

I turned just in time to see a volley of hail strike a second time, creating a crack in the plate glass no bigger than my fingernail. As we watched, it spread into a web of splintered glass as big as my fist. "Daddy will fix it later," I said.

2

That was the moment when my water broke.

Amelia glanced down between my feet. "You had an accident."

I waddled to the phone, and when Sean didn't answer his cell, I called Dispatch. "This is Sean O'Keefe's wife," I said. "I'm in labor." The dispatcher said that he could send out an ambulance, but that it would probably take a while — they were maxed out with motor vehicle accidents.

"That's okay," I said, remembering the long labor I'd had with your sister. "I've probably got a while."

Suddenly I doubled over with a contraction so strong that the phone fell out of my hand. I saw Amelia watching, her eyes wide. "I'm fine," I lied, smiling until my cheeks hurt. "The phone slipped." I reached for the receiver, and this time I called Piper, whom I trusted more than anyone in the world to rescue me.

"You can't be in labor," she said, even though she knew better — she was not only my best friend but also my initial obstetrician. "The C-section's scheduled for Monday."

"I don't think the baby got the memo," I gasped, and I gritted my teeth against another contraction.

She didn't say what we were both thinking: that I could not have you naturally. "Where's Sean?"

"I . . . don't . . . kno— oh, Piper!"

"Breathe," Piper said automatically, and I started to pant, *ha-ha-hee-hee*, the way she'd taught me. "I'll call Gianna and tell her we're on our way."

Gianna was Dr Del Sol, the maternal-fetal-medicine OB who had stepped in just eight weeks ago at Piper's request. "We?"

"Were you planning on driving yourself?"

Fifteen minutes later, I had bribed away your sister's questions by settling her on the couch and turning on *Blue's Clues*. I sat next to her, wearing your father's winter coat, the only one that fit me now.

The first time I had gone into labor, I'd had a bag packed and waiting at the door. I'd had a birthing plan and a mix tape of music to play in the delivery room. I knew it would hurt, but the reward was this incredible prize: the child I'd waited months to meet. The first time I had gone into labor, I'd been so excited.

This time, I was petrified. You were safer inside me than you would be once you were out.

Just then the door burst open and Piper filled all the space with her assured voice and her bright pink parka. Her husband, Rob, trailed behind, carrying Emma, who was carrying a snowball. "*Blue's Clues*?" he said, settling down next to your sister. "You know, that's my absolute favorite show . . . after *Jerry Springer*."

Amelia. I hadn't even thought about who would watch her while I was at the hospital having you.

"How far apart?" Piper asked.

My contractions were coming every seven minutes. As another one rolled over me like a riptide, I grabbed the arm of the couch and counted to twenty. I focused on that crack in the glass door.

Trails of frost spiraled outward from its point of origin. It was beautiful and terrifying all at once.

4

Piper sat down beside me and held my hand. "Charlotte, it's going to be okay," she promised, and because I was a fool, I believed her.

The emergency room was thick with people who'd been injured in motor vehicle accidents during the storm. Young men held bloody towels to their scalps; children mewed on stretchers. I was whisked past them all by Piper, up to the birthing center, where Dr Del Sol was already pacing the corridor. Within ten minutes, I was being given an epidural and wheeled to the operating room for a C-section.

I played games with myself: if there are an even number of fluorescent lights on the ceiling of this corridor, then Sean will arrive in time. If there are more men than women in the elevator, everything the doctors told me will turn out to be a mistake. Without me even having to ask, Piper had put on scrubs, so that she could fill in for Sean as my labor coach. "He'll be here," she said, looking down at me.

The operating room was clinical, metallic. A nurse with green eyes — that was all I could see above her mask and below her cap — lifted my gown and swabbed my belly with Betadine. I started to panic as they hung the sterile drape in place. What if I didn't have enough anesthesia running through the lower half of my body and I felt the scalpel slicing me? What if, in spite of all I'd hoped for, you were born and did not survive?

Suddenly the door flew open. Sean blew into the room on a cold streak of winter, holding a mask up to

5

his face, his scrub shirt haphazardly tucked in. "Wait," he cried. He came to the head of the stretcher and touched my cheek. "Baby," he said. "I'm sorry. I came as soon as I heard —"

Piper patted Sean on the arm. "Three's a crowd," she said, backing away from me, but not before she squeezed my hand one last time.

And then, Sean was beside me, the heat of his palms on my shoulders, the hymn of his voice distracting me as Dr Del Sol lifted the scalpel. "You scared the hell out of me," he said. "What were you and Piper thinking, driving yourselves?"

"That we didn't want to have the baby on the kitchen floor?"

Sean shook his head. "Something awful could have happened."

I felt a tug below the white drape and sucked in my breath, turning my head to the side. That was when I saw it: the enlarged twenty-seven-week sonogram with your seven broken bones, your fiddlehead limbs bowed inward. *Something awful already has happened*, I thought.

And then you were crying, even though they lifted you as if you were made out of spun sugar. You were crying, but not the hitched, simple cry of a newborn. You were screaming as if you'd been torn apart. "Easy," Dr Del Sol said to the OR nurse. "You need to support the whole —"

There was a pop, like a burst bubble, and although I had not thought it possible, you screamed even louder. "Oh, God," the nurse said, her voice a cone of hysteria.

"Was that a break? Did I do that?" I tried to see you, but I could only make out a slash of a mouth, the ruby furor of your cheeks.

The team of doctors and nurses gathered around you couldn't stop your sobbing. I think, until the moment I heard you cry, a part of me had believed that all the sonograms and tests and doctors had been wrong. Until the moment I heard you cry, I had been worried that I wouldn't know how to love you.

Sean peered over their shoulders. "She's perfect," he said, turning to me, but the words curled up at the end like a puppy's tail, looking for approval.

Perfect babies didn't sob so hard that you could feel your own heart tearing down the center. Perfect babies looked that way on the outside, and *were* that way on the inside.

"Don't lift her arm," a nurse murmured.

And another: "How am I supposed to swaddle her if I can't touch her?"

And through it all you screamed, a note I'd never heard before.

Willow, I whispered, the name that your father and I had agreed on. I had had to convince him. *I won't call her that*, he said. *They weep.* But I wanted to give you a prophecy to carry with you, the name of a tree that bends instead of breaking.

Willow, I whispered again, and somehow through the cacophony of the medical staff and the whir of machinery and the fever pitch of your pain, you heard me.

Willow, I said out loud, and you turned toward the sound as if the word was my arms around you. *Willow*, I said, and just like that, you stopped crying.

When I was five months pregnant, I got a call from the restaurant where I used to work. The pastry chef's mother had broken her hip, and they had a food critic coming in that night from the *Boston Globe*, and even though it was incredibly presumptuous and surely not a good time for me, could I possibly come in and just whip up my chocolate mille-feuille, the one with the spiced chocolate ice cream, avocado, and bananas brûlée?

I admit, I was being selfish. I felt logy and fat, and I wanted to remind myself that I had once been good for something other than playing Go Fish with your sister and separating the laundry into whites and darks. I left Amelia with a teenage sitter and drove to Capers.

The kitchen hadn't changed in the years since I'd been there, although the new head chef had moved around the items in the pantries. I immediately cleared off my work space and set about making my phyllo. Somewhere in the middle of it all, I dropped a stick of butter, and I reached down to pick it up before someone slipped and fell. But this time, when I bent forward, I was acutely aware of the fact that I could not jackknife at the waist anymore. I felt you steal my breath, as I stole yours. "Sorry, baby," I said out loud, and I straightened up again.

Now I wonder: Is that when those seven breaks happened? When I kept someone else from getting hurt, did I hurt *you*?

I gave birth shortly after three, but I didn't see you again until it was 8p.m. Every half hour, Sean left to get an update: *She's being X-rayed. They're drawing blood. They think her ankle might be broken, too.* And then, at six o'clock, he brought the best news of all: *Type III*, he said. *She's got seven healing fractures and four new ones, but she's breathing fine.* I lay in the hospital bed, smiling uncontrollably, certain that I was the only mother in the birthing center who had ever been delighted with news like this.

For two months now, we had known that you'd be born with OI — osteogenesis imperfecta, two letters of the alphabet that would become second nature. It was a collagen defect that caused bones so brittle they might break with a stumble, a twist, a sneeze. There were several types — but only two presented with fractures in utero, like we'd seen on my ultrasound. And yet the radiologist could still not conclusively say whether you had Type II, which was fatal at birth, or Type III, which was severe and progressively deforming. Now I knew that you might have hundreds more breaks over the years, but it hardly mattered: you would have a lifetime in which to sustain them.

When the storm let up, Sean went home to get your sister, so that she could meet you. I watched the Doppler weather scan track the blizzard as it moved south, turning into an icy rain that would paralyze the

9

Washington, D.C., airports for three days. There was a knock at my door, and I struggled to sit up a bit, even though doing so sent fire through my new stitches. "Hey," Piper said, coming into the room and sitting on the edge of my bed. "I heard the news."

"I know," I said. "We're so lucky."

There was only the tiniest hesitation before she smiled and nodded. "She's on her way down now," Piper said, and just then, a nurse pushed a bassinet into the room.

"Here's Mommy," she trilled.

You were fast asleep on your back, on the undulating foam egg crate with which they had lined the little plastic bed. There were bandages wrapped around your tiny arms and legs, your left ankle.

As you got older, it would be easier to tell that you had OI — people who knew what to look for would see it in the bowing of your arms and legs, in the triangular peak of your face and the fact that you would never grow much beyond three feet tall — but right then, even with your bandages, you looked flawless. Your skin was the color of the palest peach, your mouth a tiny raspberry. Your hair was flyaway, golden, your eyelashes as long as my pinkie fingernail. I reached out to touch you and — remembering — drew my hand away.

I had been so busy wishing for your survival that I hadn't given much thought to the challenges it would present. I had a beautiful baby girl, who was as fragile as a soap bubble. As your mother, I was supposed to protect you. But what if I tried and only wound up doing harm?

10

Piper and the nurse exchanged a glance. "You want to hold her, don't you?" she said, and she slid her arm as a brace beneath the foam liner while the nurse raised the edges into parabolic wings that would support your arms. Slowly, they placed the foam into the crook of my elbow.

Hey, I whispered, cradling you closer. My hand, trapped beneath you, felt the rough edge of the foam pad. I wondered how long it would be before I could carry the damp weight of you, feel your skin against mine. I thought of all the times Amelia had cried as a newborn; how I'd nurse her in bed and fall asleep with her in my embrace, always worried that I might roll over and hurt her. But with you, even lifting you out of the crib could be a danger. Even rubbing your back.

I looked up at Piper. "Maybe you should take her . . ."

She sank down beside me and traced a finger over the rising moon of your scalp. "Charlotte," Piper said, "she won't break."

We both knew that was a lie, but before I could call her on it, Amelia streaked into the room, snow on her mittens and woolen hat. "She's here, she's here," your sister sang. The day I had told her you were coming, she asked if it could be in time for lunch. When I told her she'd have to wait about five months, she decided that was too long. Instead, she pretended that you had already arrived, carrying around her favorite doll and calling her Sissy. Sometimes, when Amelia got bored or distracted, she would drop the doll on its head, and your father would laugh. *Good thing that's the practice version*, he'd say.

Sean filled the doorway just as Amelia climbed onto the bed, into Piper's lap, to pass judgment. "She's too small to skate with me," Amelia said. "And how come she's dressed like a mummy?"

"Those are ribbons," I said. "Gift wrapping."

It was the first time I lied to protect you, and as if you knew, you chose that moment to wake up. You didn't cry, you didn't squirm. "What happened to her eyes?" Amelia gasped, as we all looked at the calling card for your disease: the whites of your sclera, which instead flashed a brilliant, electric blue.

In the middle of the night, the graveyard shift of nurses came on duty. You and I were fast asleep when the woman came into the room. I swam into consciousness, focusing on her uniform, her ID tag, her frizzy red hair. "Wait," I said, as she reached for your swaddled blanket. "Be careful."

She smiled indulgently. "Relax, Mom. I've only checked a diaper ten thousand times."

But this was before I had learned to be your voice, and as she untucked the fold of the swaddling, she pulled too fast. You rolled to your side and started to shriek — not the whimper you'd made earlier, when you were hungry, but the shrill whistle I'd heard when you were born. "You hurt her!"

"She just doesn't like getting up in the middle of the night —"

12

I could not imagine anything worse than your cries, but then your skin turned as blue as your eyes, and your breath became a string of gasps. The nurse leaned over with her stethoscope. "What's the matter? What's wrong with her?" I demanded.

She frowned as she listened to your chest, and then suddenly you went limp. The nurse pressed a button behind my bed. *"Code Blue,"* I heard, and the tiny room was suddenly packed with people, even though it was still the middle of the night. Words flew like missiles: *hypoxemic . . . arterial blood gas . . . SO$_2$ of forty-six percent . . . administering FIO$_2$.*

"I'm starting chest compressions," someone said.

"This one's got OI."

"Better to live with some fractures than die without them."

"We need a portable chest film *stat —*"

"There were no breath sounds on the left side when this started —"

"No point waiting for the X-ray. There could be a tension pneumothorax —"

Between the shifting columns of their bodies, I saw the wink of a needle sinking between your ribs, and then moments later a scalpel cutting below it, the bead of blood, the clamp, the length of tubing that was fed into your chest. I watched them sew the tube into place, where it snaked out of your side.

By the time Sean arrived, wild-eyed and frantic, you had been moved to the NICU. "They cut her," I sobbed, the only words I could manage to find, and when he pulled me into his arms, I finally let go of all the tears I'd been too terrified to cry.

"Mr and Mrs O'Keefe? I'm Dr Rhodes." A man who looked young enough to be in high school poked his head into the room, and Sean's hand grabbed mine tightly.

"Is Willow all right?" Sean asked.

"Can we see her?"

"Soon," the doctor said, and the knot inside me dissolved. "A chest X-ray confirmed a broken rib. She was hypoxemic for several minutes, which resulted in an expanding pneumothorax, a resultant mediastinal shift, and cardiopulmonary arrest."

"English," Sean roared. "For God's sake."

"She was without oxygen for a few minutes, Mr O'Keefe. Her heart, trachea, and major vessels shifted to the opposite side of her body as a result of the air that filled her chest cavity. The chest tube will allow them to go back where they belong."

"No oxygen," Sean said, the words sticking in his throat. "You're talking about brain damage."

"It's possible. We won't know for a while."

Sean leaned forward, his hands clasped so tight that the knuckles stood out in bright white relief. "But her heart . . ."

"She's stable now — although there's a possibility of another cardio-vascular collapse. We're just not sure how her body will react to what we've done to save her this time."

I burst into tears. "I don't want her to go through that again. I can't let them do that to her, Sean."

14

The doctor looked stricken. "You might want to consider a DNR. It's a do not resuscitate order that's kept in her medical file. It basically says that if something like this occurs again, you don't want any extraordinary measures taken to revive Willow."

I had spent the last few weeks of my pregnancy preparing myself for the worst, and as it turned out, it wasn't anywhere close.

"Just something to think about," the doctor said.

Maybe, Sean said, *she wasn't meant to be here with us. Maybe this is God's will.*

What about my *will?* I asked. *I want her. I've wanted her all along.*

He looked up at me, wounded. *And you think I haven't?*

Through the window, I could see the slope of the hospital lawn, covered with dazzling snow. It was a knife-bright, blinding day; you never would have guessed that hours before there had been a raging blizzard. An enterprising father, trying to occupy his son, had taken a cafeteria tray outside. The boy was careening down the hill, whooping as a spray of snow arced out behind him. He stood up and waved toward the hospital, where someone must have been looking out from a window just like mine. I wondered if his mother was in the hospital, having another baby. If she was next door, even now, watching her son sled.

My daughter, I thought absently, *will never be able to do that.*

Piper held my hand tightly as we stared down at you in the NICU. The chest tube was still snaking out from between your battered ribs; bandages wrapped your arms and legs tight. I swayed a little on my feet. "Are you okay?" Piper asked.

"I'm not the one you need to worry about." I looked up at her. "They asked if we wanted to sign a DNR."

Piper's eyes widened. "Who asked that?"

"Dr Rhodes —"

"He's a *resident,*" she said, as distastefully as if she'd said "He's a Nazi." "He doesn't know the way to the cafeteria yet, much less the protocol for talking to a mother who's just watched her baby suffer a full cardiac arrest in front of her eyes. No pediatrician would recommend a newborn be DNR before there was brain testing that proved irreversible damage —"

"They cut her open in front of me," I said, my voice quivering. "I heard her ribs break when they tried to start her heart again."

"Charlotte —"

"Would you sign one?"

When she didn't answer, I walked to the other side of the bassinet, so that you were caught between us like a secret. "Is this what the rest of my life is going to be like?"

For a long time, Piper didn't respond. We listened to the symphony of whirs and beeps that surrounded you. I watched you startle, your tiny toes curling up, your arms open wide. "Not the rest of your life," Piper said. "Willow's."

16

Later that day, with Piper's words ringing in my ears, I signed the do not resuscitate order. It was a plea for mercy in black and white, until you read between the lines: here was the first time I lied, and said that I wished you'd never been born.

I

Most things break, including hearts. The lessons of life amount not to wisdom, but to scar tissue and callus.

— Wallace Stegner, *The Spectator Bird*

Tempering: to heat slowly and gradually.

Most of the time when we talk about a temper, we mean a quickness to anger. In cooking, though, tempering is about making something stronger by taking your time. You temper eggs by adding a hot liquid in small increments. The idea is to raise their temperature without causing them to curdle. The result is a stirred custard that can be used as a dessert sauce or incorporated into a complex dessert.

Here's something interesting: the consistency of the finished product has nothing to do with the type of liquid used to heat it. The more eggs you use, the thicker and richer the final product will be.

Or in other words, it's the substance you've got when you start that determines the outcome.

CRÈME PATISSERIE

2 cups whole milk
6 egg yolks at room temperature
5 ounces sugar
1½ ounces cornstarch
1 teaspoon vanilla

Bring the milk just to a boil in a non-reactive saucepan. In a stainless steel bowl, whisk the egg yolks, sugar, and cornstarch. Temper the yolk mixture with milk. Put the milk and yolk mixture back on the heat, whisking constantly. When the mixture starts to thicken, whisk faster until it boils, then remove from heat. Add vanilla and pour into a stainless steel bowl. Sprinkle with a bit of sugar, and place plastic wrap directly on top of the crème. Put in fridge and chill before serving. This can be used as a filling for fruit tarts, napoleons, cream puffs, éclairs, et cetera.

Amelia

February 2007

My whole life, I've never been on a vacation. I've never even left New Hampshire, unless you count the time that I went with you and Mom to Nebraska — and even *you* have to admit that sitting in a hospital room for three days watching really old *Tom and Jerry* cartoons while you got tested at Shriners was nothing like going to a beach or to the Grand Canyon. So you can imagine how excited I was when I found out that our family was planning to go to Disney World. We would go during February school vacation. We'd stay at a hotel that had a monorail running right through the middle of it.

Mom began to make a list of the rides we would go on. It's a Small World, Dumbo the Flying Elephant, Peter Pan's Flight.

"Those are for babies," I complained.

"Those are the ones that are safe," she said.

"Space Mountain," I suggested.

"Pirates of the Caribbean," she answered.

"Great," I yelled. "I get to go on the first vacation of my life, and I won't even have any fun." Then I stormed off to our room, and even though I wasn't downstairs anymore, I could pretty much imagine what our parents were saying: *There Amelia goes, being difficult again.*

It's funny, when things like this happen (which is, like, *always*), Mom isn't the one who tries to iron out the mess. She's too busy making sure you're all right, so the task falls to Dad. Ah, see, there's something else that I'm jealous about: he's your real dad, but he's only my stepfather. I don't know my real dad; he and my mother split up before I was even born, and she swears that his absence is the best gift he could ever have given me. But Sean adopted me, and he acts like he loves me just as much as he loves you — even though there's this black, jagged splinter in my mind that constantly reminds me this couldn't possibly be true.

"Meel," he said when he came into my room (he's the only one I'd ever let call me that in a million years; it makes me think of the worms that get into flour and ruin it, but not when Dad says it), "I know you're ready for the big rides. But we're trying to make sure that Willow has a good time, too."

Because when Willow's having a good time, we're all having a good time. He didn't have to say it, but I heard it all the same.

"We just want to be a family on vacation," he said.

I hesitated. "The teacup ride," I heard myself say.

Dad said he'd go to bat for me, and even though Mom was dead set against it — what if you smacked up against the thick plaster wall of the teacup? — he convinced her that we could whirl around in circles with you wedged between us so that you wouldn't get hurt. Then he grinned at me, so proud of himself for having negotiated this deal that I didn't have the heart to tell him I really couldn't care less about the teacup ride.

The reason it had popped into my head was because, a few years ago, I'd seen a commercial for Disney World on TV. It showed Tinker Bell floating like a mosquito through the Magic Kingdom over the heads of the cheery visitors. There was one family that had two daughters, the same age as you and me, and they were on the Mad Hatter's teacup ride. I couldn't take my eyes off them — the older daughter even had brown hair, like I do; and if you squinted, the father looked a lot like Dad. The family seemed so happy it made my stomach hurt to watch it. I knew that the people on the commercial probably weren't even a real family — that the mom and dad were probably two single actors, that they had most likely met their fake daughters that very morning as they arrived on set to shoot the commercial — but I *wanted* them to be one. I wanted to believe they were laughing, smiling, even as they were spinning out of control.

Pick ten strangers and stick them in a room, and ask them which one of us they feel sorrier for — you or me — and we all know who they'll choose. It's kind of hard to look past your casts; and the fact that you're the size of a two-year-old, even though you're five; and the funny twitch of your hips when you're healthy enough to walk. I'm not saying that you've had it easy. It's just that I have it worse, because every time I think my life sucks, I look at you and hate myself even more for thinking my life sucks in the first place.

Here's a snapshot of what it's like to be me:

Amelia, don't jump on the bed, you'll hurt Willow.

Amelia, how many times have I told you not to leave your socks on the floor, because Willow could trip over them?

Amelia, turn off the TV (although I've only watched a half hour, and you've been staring at it like a zombie for five hours straight).

I know how selfish this makes me sound, but then again, knowing something's true doesn't keep you from feeling it. And I may only be twelve, but believe me, that's long enough to know that our family isn't the same as other families, and never will be. Case in point: What family packs a whole extra suitcase full of Ace bandages and waterproof casts, just in case? What mom spends days researching the hospitals in Orlando?

It was the day we were leaving, and as Dad loaded up the car, you and I sat at the kitchen table, playing Rock Paper Scissors. "Shoot," I said, and we both threw scissors. I should have known better; you always threw scissors. "Shoot," I said again, and this time I threw rock. "Rock breaks scissors," I said, bumping my fist on top of your hand.

"Careful," Mom said, even though she was facing in the opposite direction.

"I win."

"You always win."

I laughed at you. "That's because you always throw scissors."

"Leonardo da Vinci invented the scissors," you said. You were, in general, full of information no one else knew or cared about, because you read all the time, or surfed the Net, or listened to shows on the History Channel that put me to sleep. It freaked people out, to come across a five-year-old who knew that toilets flush in the key of E-flat or that the oldest word in the English language is *town*, but Mom said that lots of kids with OI were early readers with advanced verbal skills. I figured it was like a muscle: your brain got used more than the rest of your body, which was always breaking down; no wonder you sounded like a little Einstein.

"Do I have everything?" Mom asked, but she was talking to herself. For the bazillionth time she ran through a checklist. "The letter," she said, and then she turned to me. "Amelia, we need the doctor's note."

It was a letter from Dr Rosenblad, saying the obvious: that you had OI, that you were treated by him at Children's Hospital — in case of emergency, which was actually pretty amusing since your breaks were one emergency after another. It was in the glove compartment of the van, next to the registration and the owner's manual from Toyota, plus a torn map of Massachusetts, a Jiffy Lube receipt, and a piece of gum that had lost its wrapper and grown furry. I'd done the inventory once when my mother was paying for gas.

"If it's in the van, why can't you just get it when we drive to the airport?"

"Because I'll forget," Mom said as Dad walked in.

"We're locked and loaded," he said. "What do you say, Willow? Should we go visit Mickey?"

You gave him a huge grin, as if Mickey Mouse was real and not just some teenage girl wearing a big plastic head for her summer job. "Mickey Mouse's birthday is November eighteenth," you announced as he helped you crawl down from the chair. "Amelia beat me at Rock Paper Scissors."

"That's because you always throw scissors," Dad said.

Mom frowned over her list one last time. "Sean, did you pack the Motrin?"

"Two bottles."

"And the camera?"

"Shoot, I took it out and left it on the dresser upstairs —" He turned to me. "Sweetie, can you grab it while I put Willow in the car?"

I nodded and ran upstairs. When I came down, camera in hand, Mom was standing alone in the kitchen turning in a slow circle, as if she didn't know what to do without Willow by her side. She shut off the lights and locked the front door, and I bounded over to the van. I handed the camera to Dad and buckled myself in beside your car seat, and let myself admit that, as dorky as it was to be twelve years old and excited about Disney World, I was. I was thinking about sunshine and Disney songs and monorails, and not at all about the letter from Dr Rosenblad.

Which means that everything that happened was my fault.

28

We didn't even make it to the stupid teacups. By the time our flight landed and we got to the hotel, it was late afternoon. We drove to the theme park and had just walked onto Main Street, U.S.A. — Cinderella's Castle in full view — when the perfect storm hit. You said you were hungry, and we turned into an old-time ice-cream parlor. Dad stood in line holding your hand while Mom brought napkins over to the table where I was sitting. "Look," I said, pointing out Goofy pumping the hand of a screaming toddler. At exactly the same moment that Mom let one napkin flutter to the ground and Dad let go of your hand to take out his wallet, you hurried to the window to see what I wanted to show you, and you slipped on the tiny paper square.

We all watched it in slow motion, the way your legs simply gave out from underneath you, so that you sat down hard on your bottom. You looked up at us, and the whites of your eyes flashed blue, the way they always do when you break.

It was almost like the people at Disney World had been expecting this to happen. No sooner had Mom told the man scooping ice cream that you'd broken your leg than two men from their medical facility came with a stretcher. With Mom giving orders, the way she always does around doctors, they managed to get you onto it. You weren't crying, but then, you hardly ever did when you broke something. Once, I had fractured my pinkie playing tetherball at school and I couldn't stop freaking out when it turned bright red and blew up like a balloon, but you didn't even cry the time you broke your arm right through the skin.

"Doesn't it hurt?" I whispered, as they lifted up the stretcher so that it suddenly grew wheels.

You were biting your lower lip, and you nodded.

There was an ambulance waiting for us when we got to the Disney World gate. I took one last look at Main Street, U.S.A., at the top of the metal cone that housed Space Mountain, at the kids who were running in instead of going out, and then I crawled into the car that someone had arranged so Dad and I could follow you and Mom to the hospital.

It was weird, going to an emergency room that wasn't our usual one. Everyone at our local hospital knew you, and the doctors all listened to what Mom told them. Here, though, nobody was paying any attention to her. They said this could be not one but *two* femur fractures, and that might mean internal bleeding. Mom went into the examination room with you for the X-ray, which left Dad and me sitting on green plastic chairs in a waiting room. "I'm sorry, Meel," he said, and I just shrugged. "Maybe it'll be an easy one, and we can go back to the park tomorrow." There had been a man in a black suit at Disney World who told my father that we would be comped, whatever that meant, if we wanted to return another day.

It was Saturday night, and the people coming into the emergency room were much more interesting than the TV program that was playing. There were two kids who looked like they were old enough to be in college, both bleeding from the same spot on their foreheads and laughing every time they looked at each other. There was an old man wearing sequined pants and holding the right side of his stomach, and a girl who spoke only Spanish and was carrying screaming twin babies.

Suddenly, Mom burst out of the double doors to the right, with a nurse running after her and another woman in a skinny pin-striped skirt and red high heels. "The letter," she cried. "Sean, what did you do with it?"

"What letter?" Dad asked, but I already knew what she was talking about, and just like that, I thought I might throw up.

"Mrs O'Keefe," the woman said, "please. Let's do this somewhere more private."

She touched Mom's arm, and — well, the only way I can really describe it is that Mom just folded in half. We were led to a room with a tattered red couch and a little oval table and fake flowers in a vase. There was a picture on the wall of two pandas, and I stared at it while the woman in the skinny skirt — she said her name was Donna Roman, and she was from the Department of Children and Families — talked to our parents. "Dr Rice contacted us because he has some concerns about the injuries to Willow," she said. "Bowing in her arm and X-rays indicate that this wasn't her first break?"

"Willow's got osteogenesis imperfecta," Dad said.

"I already told her," Mom said. "She didn't listen."

"Without a physician's statement, we have to look into this further. It's just protocol, to protect children —"

"I'd like to protect my child," Mom said, her voice sharp as a razor. "I'd like you to let me get back in there so I can do just that."

"Dr Rice is an expert —"

"If he was an expert, then he'd know I was telling the truth," Mom shot back.

"From what I understand, Dr Rice is trying to reach your daughter's physician," Donna Roman said. "But since it's Saturday night, he's having trouble making contact. So in the meantime, I'd like to get you to sign releases that will allow us to do a full examination on Willow — a full bone scan and neurological exam — and in the meantime, we can talk a little bit."

"The last thing Willow needs is more testing —" Mom said.

"Look, Ms. Roman," Dad interrupted. "I'm a police officer. You can't really believe I'd lie to you?"

"I've already spoken to your wife, Mr O'Keefe, and I'm going to want to speak to you, too . . . but first I'd like to talk to Willow's sister."

My mouth opened and closed, but nothing came out of it. Mom was staring at me as if she were trying to do ESP, and I looked down at the floor until I saw those red high heels stop in front of me. "You must be Amelia," she said, and I nodded. "Why don't we take a walk?"

As we left, a police officer who looked like Dad did when he went to work stepped into the doorway. "Split them up," Donna Roman said, and he nodded. Then she took me to the candy machine at the far end of the hallway. "What would you like? Me, I'm a chocolate fiend, but maybe you're more of a potato chip girl?"

She was so much nicer to me when my parents weren't sitting there — I immediately pointed to a Snickers bar, figuring that I'd better take advantage of this while I could. "I guess this isn't quite what you'd hoped your vacation would be?" she said, and I shook my head. "Has this happened to Willow before?"

"Yeah. She breaks bones a lot."

"How?"

For someone who was supposed to be smart, this woman sure didn't seem it. How do *anyone's* bones break? "She falls down, I guess. Or gets hit by something."

"She gets hit by something?" Donna Roman repeated. "Or do you mean some*one*?"

There had been one time in nursery school when a kid had run into you on the playground. You were pretty gifted at ducking and weaving, but that day, you hadn't been fast enough. "Well," I said, "sometimes that happens, too."

"Who was with Willow when she got hurt *this* time, Amelia?"

I thought back to the ice-cream counter, to Dad, holding your hand. "My father."

Her mouth flattened. She fed coins into another machine, and out popped a bottled water. She twisted the cap. I wanted her to offer it to me, but I was too embarrassed to ask.

"Was he upset?"

I thought of my father's face as we sped off toward the hospital following the ambulance. Of his fists, balanced on his thighs as we waited for word about Willow's latest break. "Yeah — really upset."

"Do you think he did this because he was angry at Willow?"

"Did what?"

Donna Roman knelt down so that she was staring me in the eye. "Amelia," she said, "you can tell me what really happened. I'll make sure he doesn't hurt you."

Suddenly, I realized what she thought I'd meant. "My dad wasn't mad at Willow," I said. "He didn't hit her. It was an accident!"

"Accidents like that don't have to happen."

"No — you don't understand — it's because of Willow —"

"*Nothing* kids do justifies abuse," Donna Roman muttered under her breath, but I could hear her loud and clear. By now she was walking back toward the room where my parents were, and even though I was yelling, trying to get her to hear me, she wasn't listening. "Mr and Mrs O'Keefe," she said, "we're putting your children into protective custody."

"Why don't we just go down to the station to talk?" the officer was saying to Dad.

Mom threw her arms around me. "Protective custody? What does that mean?"

With a firm hand — and the help of the police officer — Donna Roman tried to peel her away from me. "We're just keeping the children safe until we can get this all cleared up. Willow will be here overnight." She

34

started to steer me out of the room, but I grabbed at the doorframe.

"Amelia?" my mother said, frantic. "What did you say?"

"I tried to tell her the truth!"

"Where are you taking my daughter?"

"Mom!" I shrieked, and I reached for her.

"Come on, sweetheart," Donna Roman said, and she pulled at my hands until I had to let go, until I was being dragged out of the hospital kicking and screaming. I did this for five minutes, until I went totally numb. Until I understood why you didn't cry, even though it hurt: there are kinds of pain you couldn't speak out loud.

I'd seen and heard the words *foster home* before, in books that I read and television programs I watched. I figured that they were for orphans and inner-city kids, kids whose parents were drug dealers — not girls like me who lived in nice houses and got plenty of Christmas presents and never went to sleep hungry. As it turned out, though, Mrs Ward, who ran this temporary foster home, could have been an ordinary mom. I guess she had been one, judging from the photos that plastered every surface like wallpaper. She met us at the door wearing a red bathrobe and slippers that looked like pink pigs. "You must be Amelia," she said, and she opened the door a little wider.

I was expecting a posse of kids, but it turned out that I was the only one staying with Mrs Ward. She took me into the kitchen, which smelled like dishwashing detergent and boiled noodles. She set a glass of milk and a stack of Oreo cookies in front of me. "You're probably starving," she said, and even though I was, I shook my head. I didn't want to take anything from her; it felt like giving in.

My bedroom had a dresser, a small bed, and a comforter with cherries printed all over it. There was a television and a remote. My parents would never let me have a television in my room; my mother said it was the Root of All Evil. I told Mrs Ward that, and she laughed. "Maybe so," she said, "but then again, sometimes *The Simpsons* are the best medicine." She opened a drawer and took out a clean towel and a nightgown that was a couple of sizes too big. I wondered where it had come from. I wondered how long the last girl who'd worn it had slept in this bed.

"I'm right down the hall if you need me," Mrs Ward said. "Is there anything else I can get you?"

My mother.

My father.

You.

Home.

"How long," I managed, the first words I had said out loud in this house, "do I have to be here?"

Mrs Ward smiled sadly. "I can't say, Amelia."

"Are my parents . . . are they in a foster home, too?"

She hesitated. "Something like that."

"I want to see Willow."

"First thing tomorrow," Mrs Ward said. "We'll go up to the hospital. How's that?"

I nodded. I wanted to believe her, so bad. With this promise tucked into my arms like my stuffed moose at home, I could sleep through the night. I could convince myself that everything was bound to get better.

I lay down and tried to remember the useless bits of information you'd rattle off before we went to sleep, when I was always telling you to just shut up already: Frogs have to close their eyes to swallow. One pencil can draw a line thirty-five miles long. *Cleveland*, spelled backward, is *DNA level C*.

I was starting to see why you carried those stupid facts like other kids dragged around security blankets — if I repeated them over and over, it almost made me feel better. I just wasn't sure if that was because it helped to know something, when the rest of my life seemed to be a big question mark, or because it reminded me of you.

I was still hungry, or empty, I couldn't tell which. After Mrs Ward had gone to her own bedroom, I tiptoed out of bed. I turned the light on in the hallway and went down to the kitchen. There, I opened up the refrigerator and let the light and cold fall over my bare feet. I stared at lunch meat, sealed into plastic packages; at a jumble of apples and peaches in a bin; at cartons of orange juice and milk lined up like soldiers. When I thought I heard a creak upstairs, I grabbed whatever I could: a loaf of bread, a Tupperware of cooked spaghetti, a handful of those Oreos. I ran back to my room and closed the door, spread my treasure out on the sheets in front of me.

At first, it was just the Oreos. But then my stomach rumbled and I ate all the spaghetti — with my fingers, because I had no fork. I had a piece of bread and another and then another, and before I knew it only the plastic wrapper was left. *What is wrong with me?* I thought, catching my reflection in the mirror. *Who eats a whole loaf of bread?* The outside of me was disgusting enough — boring brown hair that frizzed with crummy weather, eyes too far apart, that crooked front tooth, enough fat to muffin-top my jeans — but the inside of me was even worse. I pictured it as a big black hole, like the kind we learned about in science last year, that sucks everything into its center. *A vacuum of nothingness,* my teacher had called it.

Everything that had ever been good and kind in me, everything people imagined me to be, had been poisoned by the part of me that had wished, in the darkest crack of the night, that I could have a different family. The real me was a disgusting person who imagined a life where you had never been born. The real me had watched you being loaded into an ambulance and had let myself wish, for a half a second, that I could stay behind at Disney World. The real me was a bottomless soul who could eat a whole loaf of bread in ten minutes and still have room for more.

I hated myself.

I could not tell you what made me go into the bathroom that was attached to my room — wallpaper spotted with pink roses, shaped soaps curled in dishes next to the sink — and stick my finger down my throat. Maybe it was because I could feel the toxic stuff seeping into my bloodstream, and I wanted it out. Maybe it was punishment. Maybe it was because I wanted to control one part of me that had been

38

uncontrollable, so the rest of me would fall into line. *Rats can't throw up*, you'd told me once; it popped into my head now. With one hand holding up my hair, I vomited into the toilet until I was flushed and sweating and empty and relieved to learn that, yes, I *could* do this one thing right, even if it made me feel worse than I had before. With my stomach cinching and bile bitter on the back of my tongue, I felt horrible — but this time there was a physical reason I could point to.

Weak and wobbly, I stumbled back to my borrowed bed and reached for the television remote. My eyes felt like sandpaper and my throat ached, but I could not fall asleep. Instead I flipped through the cable channels, through home decorating shows and cartoons and late-night talk shows and Iron Chef cooking contests. It was on Nick at Nite, twenty-two minutes into *The Dick Van Dyke Show*, that the old Disney World commercial came on — like a joke, a tease, a warning. It felt like a punch in the gut: there was Tinker Bell, there were the happy people; there was the family that could have been us on the teacup ride.

What if my parents never came back?

What if you didn't get better?

What if I had to stay here forever?

When I started to sob, I stuffed the corner of the pillow deep into my mouth so Mrs Ward wouldn't hear. I hit the mute button on the television remote, and I watched the family at Disney World going round in circles.

Sean

It's funny, isn't it, how you can be 100 percent sure of your opinion on something until it happens to you. Like arresting someone — people who aren't in law enforcement think it's appalling to know that, even with probable cause, mistakes are made. If that's the case, you unarrest the person and tell him you were just doing what you had to. Better that than take the risk of letting a criminal walk free, I've always said, and to hell with civil libertarians who wouldn't know a perp if he spit in their faces. This was what I believed, heart and soul, until I was carted down to the Lake Buena Vista PD on suspicion of child abuse. One look at your X-rays, at the dozens of healing fractures, at the curvature of your lower right arm where it should have been straight — and the doctors went ballistic and called DCF. Dr Rosenblad had given us a note years ago that should have served as a Get Out of Jail Free card, because lots of parents with OI kids are accused of child abuse when the case history isn't known — and

Charlotte's always carried it around in the minivan, just in case. But today, with everything we had to remember to pack for the trip, the letter was forgotten, and what we got instead was a trip to the police station for interrogation.

"This is bullshit," I yelled. "My daughter fell down *in public*. There were at least ten witnesses. Why aren't you dragging *them* in? Don't you guys have real cases to keep you busy around here?"

I'd been alternating between playing good cop and bad cop, but as it turned out, neither worked when you were up against another officer from an unfamiliar jurisdiction. It was nearly midnight on Saturday — which meant that it could be Monday before this was sorted out with Dr Rosenblad. I hadn't seen Charlotte since they'd brought us to the station to be questioned — in cases like this, we'd separate the parents so that they had less of a chance to fabricate a story. The problem was, even the truth sounded crazy. A kid slips on a napkin and winds up with compound fractures in both femurs? You don't need nineteen years on the job, like I have, to be suspicious of that one.

I imagined Charlotte was falling apart at the seams — being away from you while you were hurting would rip her to pieces, and then knowing that Amelia was God knows where was even more devastating. I kept thinking of how Amelia used to hate to sleep with the lights off, how I'd have to creep into her room in the middle of the night and turn them off when she'd fallen asleep. *Are you scared?* I'd asked her once, and she'd said she wasn't. *I just don't want to miss anything.* We lived in Bankton, New Hampshire — a small town where you could actually drive down the street and have people honk when they recognized your car; a place where if you forgot your credit card at the grocery store, the checkout girl would just let you take your food and come back to pay later. That's not to say that we didn't have our share of the seedy underbelly of life — cops get to see behind the white picket fences and polished doors, where there are all kinds of hidden nightmares: esteemed local bigwigs who beat their wives, honors students with drug addictions, schoolteachers with kiddie porn on their computers. But part of my goal, as a police officer, was to leave all that crap at the station and make sure you and Amelia grew up blissfully naïve. And what happens instead? You watch the Florida police come into the emergency room to take your parents away. Amelia gets carted off to a foster-care facility. How much would this lousy attempt at a vacation scar you both?

The detective had left me alone after two rounds of interrogation. This was his way, I knew, of hanging me out to dry — assuming that the information he was gathering between our little sessions would be enough to scare me into confessing that I'd broken your legs.

I wondered if Charlotte was in this building somewhere, in another interrogation room, or a lockup. If they wanted to keep us here overnight, they had to arrest us — and they had grounds for that. A new injury had occurred here in Florida — that, coupled with the old injuries on the X-ray, was probable cause, until someone could corroborate our explanations. But the hell with it — I was tired of waiting. You and your sister needed me.

I stood up and banged on the glass mirror that I knew the detective was watching me through.

He came back into the room. Skinny, redheaded, pimples — he couldn't have been thirty yet. I weighed 225 — all muscle — and stood six-three; for the past three years I'd won our department's unofficial weight-lifting challenge during annual fitness testing. I could have snapped him in half if I wanted to. Which made me remember why he was questioning me in the first place.

"Mr O'Keefe," the detective said. "Let's go through this again."

"I want to see my wife."

"That's not possible right now."

"Will you at least tell me if she's okay?"

My voice cracked on that last word, and it was enough to soften the detective. "She's fine," he said. "She's with another detective right now."

"I want to make a phone call."

"You're not under arrest," the detective said.

I laughed. "Yeah, right."

He gestured toward the phone in the middle of the desk. "Dial nine for an outside line," he said, and he leaned back in his chair and folded his arms, as if to make it clear that he wasn't giving me any privacy.

"You know the number for the hospital where my daughter's being kept?"

"You can't call her."

"Why not? I'm not under arrest," I repeated.

"It's late. No good parent would want to wake his kid up. But then you're not a good parent, are you, Sean?"

"No good parent would leave his kid alone at a hospital when she's scared and hurt," I countered.

"Let's get through what we need to here, and then maybe you'll be able to catch your daughter before she goes to bed."

"I'm not saying another word until I talk to her," I bargained. "Give me that number, and I'll tell you what really happened today."

He stared at me for a minute — I knew that technique, too. When you have been doing this as long as I have, you can ferret out truth by reading someone's eyes. I wonder what he saw in mine. Disappointment, maybe. Here I was, a police officer, and I hadn't even been able to keep you safe.

The detective picked up the phone and dialed. He asked for your room and talked quietly to a nurse who answered. Then he handed the receiver to me. "You have one minute," he said.

You were groggy, shaken awake by that nurse. Your voice sounded small enough for me to carry around in my back pocket. "Willow," I said. "It's Daddy."

"Where are you? Where's Mommy?"

"We're coming back for you, honey. We're going to see you tomorrow, first thing." I didn't know that this was true, but I wasn't going to let you think we'd abandoned you. "One to ten?" I asked.

It was a game we played whenever there was a break — I offered you a pain scale, you showed me how brave you were. "Zero," you whispered, and it felt like a punch.

Here's something you should know about me: I don't cry. I haven't cried since my father passed away, when I was ten. I've come close, let me tell you. Like when you were born, and almost died right afterward. Or when I saw the look on your face when, as a two-year-old, you had to learn how to walk again after being casted for five months with a hip fracture. Or today, when I saw Amelia being pulled away. It's not that I don't feel like breaking down — it's that someone's got to be the strong one, so that you all don't have to be.

So I pulled it together and cleared my throat. "Tell me something I don't know, baby."

It was another game between us: I'd come home, and you'd recite something you'd learned that day — honestly, I'd never seen a kid absorb information like you. Your body might betray you at every turn, but your brain picked up the slack.

"A nurse told me that a giraffe's heart weighs twenty-five pounds," you said.

"That's huge," I replied. How heavy was my own? "Now, Wills, I want you to lie down and get a good night's rest, so that you're wide awake when I come get you in the morning."

"You promise?"

I swallowed. "You bet, baby. Sleep tight, okay?" I handed the phone back to the detective.

"How touching," he said flatly, hanging it up. "All right, I'm listening."

I rested my elbows on the table between us. "We had just gotten into the park, and there was an ice-cream place close to the entry. Willow was hungry, so we decided we'd stop off there. My wife went to get napkins, Amelia sat down at a table, and Willow and I were waiting in line. Her sister saw something through the window, and Willow ran to go look at it, and she fell down and broke her femurs. She's got a disease called osteogenesis imperfecta, which means her bones are extremely brittle. One in ten thousand kids are born with it. What the fuck else do you want to know?"

"That's exactly the statement you gave an hour ago." The detective threw down his pen. "I thought you were going to tell me what happened."

"I did. I just didn't tell you what you wanted to hear."

The detective stood up. "Sean O'Keefe," he said. "You're under arrest."

By seven on Sunday morning, I was pacing in the waiting room of the police station, a free man, waiting for Charlotte to be released. The desk sergeant who let me out of the lockup shuffled beside me, uncomfortable. "I'm sure you understand," he said. "Given the circumstances, we were only doing our job."

My jaw tightened. "Where's my older daughter?"

"DCF is on their way here with her."

I had been told — professional courtesy — that Louie, the dispatcher at the Bankton PD who confirmed my claim to be an officer with the department, also told them you had a disease that caused your bones to break easily, but that DCF wouldn't release Willow until they had confirmation from a medical professional. So I'd prayed half the night — although I have to admit I give less credit for our release to Jesus than I do to your mother. Charlotte watched enough *Law & Order* to know that once her rights had been read to her she was allowed a phone call — and to my surprise, she didn't use it to contact you. Instead, she called Piper Reece, her best friend.

I like Piper, honestly, I do. God knows I love her for whatever connections she used to cold-call Mark Rosenblad at 3a.m. on a weekend and get him to phone the hospital where you were being treated. I even owe Piper for my marriage — she and Rob are the ones who introduced me to Charlotte. But all this being said, sometimes Piper is . . . just a little too *much*. She's smart and opinionated and frustratingly right most of the time. Most of the fights I've had with your mother have had their roots in something Piper got her thinking about. The thing is, where Piper can carry off that brashness and confidence, on Charlotte, it seems a little off — like a kid playing dress-up in her mom's closet. Your mother is quieter, more of a mystery; her strengths sneak up on you instead of smacking you front and center. If Piper's the one you notice when you walk into a room, with her boy-cut blond hair and forever legs and her wide smile, Charlotte's the one you find yourself thinking about long after you've left. But then again, that in-your-face fierceness that makes Piper so exhausting sometimes is also what got me out of the lockup in Lake Buena Vista. I suppose this means, in the grand cosmic tally, I have something else to thank her for.

Suddenly a door opened, and I could see Charlotte — dazed, pale, her brown curls tumbling out of her ponytail elastic. She was blistering the officer escorting her: "If Amelia isn't back here before I count to ten, I swear I'll —"

God, I love your mother. She and I think exactly alike, when it counts.

Then she noticed me and broke off. "Sean!" she cried, and ran into my arms.

I wish you could know what it feels like to find the missing piece of you, the thing that makes you stronger. Charlotte's that, for me. She's tiny, only five-two, but underneath her serpentine curves — the ones she's always stressing out about because she's not a size four like Piper — are muscles that would surprise you, developed from years of hauling flour when she was a pastry chef and — later — you and your equipment.

"You all right, baby?" I murmured against her hair. She smelled like apples and suntan lotion. She'd made us all put it on before we even left the Orlando airport. *To be safe*, she'd said.

She didn't answer, just nodded against my chest.

There was a cry from the doorway, and we both looked up in time to see Amelia barreling toward us. "I forgot," she sobbed. "Mom, I forgot to take the doctor's note. I'm sorry. I'm so sorry."

"It's not anyone's fault." I knelt down and brushed her tears away with my thumbs. "Let's get out of here."

48

The desk sergeant had offered to drive us to the hospital in a cruiser, but I asked him to call us a cab instead; I wanted them to stew in their own poor judgment instead of trying to make it up to us. As the taxi pulled up in front of the police department entrance, we three moved as a unit out the front door. I let Charlotte and Amelia slide into the cab before getting in myself. "To the hospital," I told the driver, and I closed my eyes and leaned my head back against the padded seat.

"Thank God," your mother said. "Thank God that's over."

I didn't even open my eyes. "It's not over," I said. "Someone is going to pay."

Charlotte

Suffice it to say that the trip home wasn't a pleasant one. You had been put into a spica cast — surely one of the biggest torture devices ever created by doctors. It was a half shell of plaster that covered you from knee to ribs. You were in a semireclined position, because that's what your bones needed to knit together. The cast kept your legs splayed wide so that the femurs would set correctly.

Here's what we were told:

1. You would wear this cast for four months.
2. Then it would be sliced in half, and you would spend weeks sitting in it like an oyster on the half shell, trying to rebuild your stomach muscles so that you could sit upright again.
3. The small square cutout of the plaster at your belly would allow your stomach to expand while you ate.
4. The open gash between your legs was left so you could go to the bathroom.

Here's what we were not told:

1. You wouldn't be able to sit completely upright, or lie completely down.
2. You couldn't fly back to New Hampshire in a normal plane seat.
3. You couldn't even lie down in the back of a normal car.
4. You wouldn't be able to sit comfortably for long periods in your wheelchair.
5. Your clothes wouldn't fit over the cast.

Because of all these things, we did not leave Florida immediately. We rented a Suburban, with three full bench seats, and settled Amelia in the back. You had the whole middle bench, and we padded this with blankets we'd bought at Wal-Mart. There we'd also bought men's T-shirts and boxer shorts — the elastic waists could stretch over the cast and be belted with a hair scrunchie if you pulled the extra fabric to the side, and if you didn't look too closely, they almost passed for shorts. They were not fashionable, but they covered up your crotch, which was left wide open by the position of the cast.

Then we started the long drive home.

You slept; the painkillers they'd given you at the hospital were still swimming through your blood. Amelia alternated between doing word search puzzles and asking if we were almost home yet. We ate at drive-through restaurants, because you couldn't sit up at a table.

Seven hours into our journey, Amelia shifted in the backseat. "You know how Mrs Grey always makes us write about the cool stuff we did over vacation? I'm going to talk about you guys trying to figure out how to get Willow onto the toilet to pee."

"Don't you dare," I said.

"Well, if I don't, my essay's going to be *really* short."

"We could make the rest of the trip fun," I suggested at one point. "Stop off in Memphis at Graceland . . . or Washington, D.C. . . ."

"Or we could just drive straight through and be done with it," Sean said.

I glanced at him. In the dark, a green band of light from the dashboard reflected like a mask around his eyes.

"Could we go to the White House?" Amelia asked, perking up.

I imagined the hothouse of humidity that Washington would be; I pictured us lugging you around on our hips as we climbed the steps to the Air and Space Museum. Out the window, the black road was a ribbon that kept unraveling in front of us; we couldn't manage to catch up to its end. "Your father's right," I said.

When we finally got home, word had already spread about what happened. There was a note from Piper on the kitchen counter, with a list of all the people who'd brought casseroles she'd stashed in the fridge and a rating system: five stars (eat this one first), three stars (better than Chef Boyardee), one star (botulism alert). I learned a long time ago with you that folks who are trying to be kind would rather do it with a macaroni-and-cheese bake than any personal involvement. You hand off a serving dish and you've done your job — no need to get personally involved, and your conscience is clean. Food is the currency of aid.

People ask all the time how I'm doing, but the truth is, they don't really want to know. They look at your casts — camouflage or hot pink or neon orange. They watch me unload the car and set up your walker, with its tennis-ball feet, so that we can creep across the sidewalk, while behind us, their children swing from monkey bars and play dodgeball and do all the other ordinary things that would cause you to break. They smile at me, because they want to be polite or politically correct, but the whole time they are thinking, *Thank God. Thank God it was her, instead of me.*

Your father says that I'm not being fair when I say things like this. That some people, when they ask, really do want to lend a hand. I tell him that if they really wanted to lend a hand, they wouldn't bring macaroni casseroles — instead they'd offer to take Amelia apple picking or ice skating so that she can get out of the house when you can't, or they'd rake the gutters of the house, which are always clogging up after a storm. And if they truly wanted to be saviors, they'd call the insurance company and spend four hours on the phone arguing over bills, so I wouldn't have to.

Sean doesn't realize that most people who offer their help do it to make themselves feel better, not us. To be honest, I don't blame them. It's superstition: if you give assistance to the family in need . . . if you throw salt over your shoulder . . . if you don't step on the cracks, then maybe you'll be immune. Maybe you'll be able to convince yourself that this could never happen to you.

Don't get me wrong; I am not complaining. Other people look at me and think: *That poor woman; she has a child with a disability*. But all I see when I look at you is the girl who had memorized all the words to Queen's *Bohemian Rhapsody* by the time she was three, the girl who crawls into bed with me whenever there's a thunderstorm — not because you're afraid but because I am, the girl whose laugh has always vibrated inside my own body like a tuning fork. I would never have wished for an able-bodied child, because that child would have been someone who wasn't you.

The next morning I spent five hours on the phone with the insurance company. Ambulance trips were not covered by our policy; however, the hospital in Florida would not discharge anyone in a spica cast unless he or she was traveling by ambulance. It was a catch-22, but I was the only one who could see it, and it led to a conversation that felt like theater of the absurd. "Let me get this straight," I said to the fourth supervisor I'd spoken with that day. "You're telling me I didn't have to take the ambulance; therefore you won't cover the cost."

"That's correct, ma'am."

On the couch, you were propped up on pillows, drawing stripes on your cast with markers. "Can you tell me what the alternative was?" I asked.

"Apparently you could have kept the patient in the hospital."

54

"You do understand this cast is going to stay on for months. Are you suggesting I keep my daughter hospitalized for that long?"

"No, ma'am. Just until transportation could be arranged."

"But the only transportation the hospital would allow us to leave in was an ambulance!" I said. By now your leg looked like a candy cane. "Would your policy have covered the additional stay?"

"No, ma'am. The maximum number of nights allowed for injuries like these is —"

"Yeah, we've been through that." I sighed.

"It seems to me," the supervisor said tartly, "that given the option of paying for additional nights in the hospital or an unauthorized ambulance trip, you don't have much to complain about."

I felt my cheeks flame. "Well, it seems to me that *you* are an enormous ass!" I yelled, and I slammed down the phone. I turned around and saw you, marker trailing out of your hand, precariously close to the fabric of the couch cushions. You were twisted like a pretzel, your lower half in the cast still facing forward, your head leaning back over your shoulder so that you could see out the window.

"Swear jar," you murmured. You had a canning jar that you'd covered with iridescent gift wrap, and every time Sean swore in front of you, you netted a quarter. Just this month alone, you were up to forty-two dollars — you'd kept count the whole way home from Florida. I took a quarter out of my pocket and put it into the jar on the table nearby, but you weren't looking; your attention was still focused outside, on a frozen pond at the edge of the lawn, where Amelia was skating.

Your sister had been ice skating since, well, since she was your age. She and Piper's daughter, Emma, took lessons together twice a week, and there was nothing you wanted more than to copy your sister. Skating, however, happened to be a sport you'd never, ever be allowed to try. Once, you'd broken your arm when you were pretending to skate on one foot across the kitchen linoleum in your socks.

"Between my foul language and your dad's, you're going to have enough cold, hard cash to buy a plane ticket out of here pretty soon," I joked, trying to distract you. "Where to? Vegas?"

You turned away from the window and looked at me. "That would be dumb," you said. "I can't play Blackjack till I'm twenty-one."

Sean had taught you how. Also Hearts, Texas Hold 'Em, and Five-Card Stud. I'd been horrified, until I realized that playing Go Fish for hours at a time might officially qualify as torture. "So the Caribbean, then?"

As if you would ever travel unimpeded, as if you would ever take a vacation without thinking about this last one. "I was thinking of buying some books. Like Dr Seuss stuff."

You read at a sixth-grade level, even though your peers were still sounding out the alphabet. It was one of the few perks of OI: when you had to be immobile, you'd pore over books, or get on the Internet. In fact, when Amelia wanted to rile you, she called you Wikipedia. "Dr Seuss?" I said. "Really?"

"They're not for me. I thought we could ship them to that hospital in Florida. The only thing they had to read was *Where's Spot?* and that gets really old after the fifth or sixth time."

That left me speechless. All I wanted to do was forget about that stupid hospital, to curse the insurance nightmare it had led to and the fact that you would be stuck in the four-month hell of a spica cast — and there you were, already past the pity party. Just because you had every right to feel sorry for yourself didn't mean you ever took the opportunity to do so. In fact, sometimes I was sure that the reason people stared at you with your crutches and wheelchair had nothing to do with your disabilities, and everything to do with the fact that you had abilities they only dreamed of.

The phone rang again — for the briefest of seconds I fantasized that it was the CEO of the health insurance company, calling to personally apologize. But it was Piper, checking in. "Is this a good time?"

"Not really," I said. "Why don't you call back in a few months?"

"Is she in a lot of pain? Did you call Rosenblad?" Piper asked. "Where's Sean?"

"Yes, no, and I hope earning enough to cover the credit card bills for the vacation we didn't get to have."

"Well, listen, I'll pick up Amelia for skating tomorrow, when I take Emma. One less thing for you to worry about."

Worry about it? I hadn't even *known* Amelia had practice. It wasn't just on the bottom of the totem pole; it wasn't even *on* the totem pole.

"What else do you need?" Piper asked. "Groceries? Gas? Johnny Depp?"

"I was going to say Xanax . . . but now I might take door number three."

"It figures. You're married to a guy who looks like Brad Pitt — with a better body — and you go for the long-haired artsy type."

"Grass is always greener, I guess." Absently I watched you reach for the old laptop computer beside you and try to balance it on your lap. It kept toppling over, because of the angle of your cast, so I grabbed a throw pillow and set it on your lap as a table. "Unfortunately, right now, my side of the fence is looking pretty grim," I told her.

"Oops, I've got to go. Apparently, my patient's crowning."

"If I had a dollar for every time I heard that one —"

Piper laughed. "Charlotte," she said. "Try taking down the fence."

I hung up. You were typing feverishly with two fingers. "What are you doing?"

"Setting up a Gmail account for Amelia's goldfish," you said.

"I highly doubt he needs one . . ."

"That's why he asked *me* to do this, instead of *you* . . ."

Take down the fence. "Willow," I announced, "shut down the laptop. You and I are going skating."

"You're kidding."

"Nope."

"But you said —"

"Willow, do you want to argue, or do you want to skate?" You beamed, a smile the likes of which I had not seen on you since before we left for Florida. I pulled on a sweater and my boots, then brought my winter coat in from the mudroom to cover your upper half. I wound blankets around your legs and hoisted you onto my hip. Without the cast, you were elfin, slight. With it, you weighed fifty-three pounds.

The one thing a spica cast was good for — practically *made* for — was balancing you on my hip. You leaned away from me a little bit, but I could still wrap one arm around you and maneuver us through the foyer and down the front steps.

When Amelia saw us coming, tortoise-slow, navigating hummocks of snow and patches of black ice, she stopped spinning. "I'm going skating," you sang, and Amelia's eyes flew to mine.

"You heard her."

"*You're* taking *her* skating. Aren't you the one who wanted Dad to fill in the skating pond? You called it cruel and unusual punishment for Willow."

"I'm taking down the fence," I said.

"*What* fence?"

I wrapped the blankets underneath your bottom and gently set you down on the ice. "Amelia," I said, "this is the part where I need your help. I want you to watch her — don't take your eyes off her — while I go grab my skates."

I sprinted back to the house, stopping only at the threshold to make sure that Amelia was still staring at you, just like I'd left her. My skates were buried in a boot bin in the mudroom — I couldn't tell you the last time I'd used them. The laces knotted them together like lovers; I slung them over my shoulder and then hoisted the computer desk chair with its rolling casters into my arms. Outside, I tipped it over, so that the seat was balanced on my head. I thought of African women in their bright skirts, with baskets of fruit and bags of rice set squarely on their heads as they walked home to feed their families.

When I got to the little pond, I set the chair on the ice. I adjusted the back and the arms so that they sloped and flared to accommodate your cast. Then I lifted you up and set you into the snug mesh seat.

I sat down to lace up my skates. "Hold on, Wiki," Amelia said, and you grabbed the arms of the chair. She stood behind you and started to move across the ice. The blankets around your legs ballooned, and I called out to your sister to be careful. But Amelia already was. She was leaning over the back of the chair so that one arm held you close in the seat while she skated faster and faster. Then she quickly reversed direction, so that she was facing you, pulling the arms of the chair as she skated backward.

You tilted your head back and closed your eyes as Amelia spun you in a circle. Amelia's dark curls streamed out from beneath her striped wool cap; your laugh fluted across the ice like a bright banner. "Mom," you called out. "Look at us!"

I stood up, my ankles wobbling. "Wait for me," I said, growing steadier with every step.

Sean

On my first day back at work, I came into the locker room to find a Wanted poster hanging near my dry-cleaned uniform. Written across the photo of my face, in bright red marker, was the word APPREHENDED. "Very funny," I muttered, and I ripped down the flyer.

"Sean O'Keefe!" said one of the guys, pretending to hold a microphone in his hand as he held it up to another cop. "You've just won the Super Bowl. What are you going to do next?"

Two fists, pumped in the air. "I'm going to *Disney World!*"

The rest of the guys cracked up. "Hey, your travel agent called," one said. "She's booked your tickets to Gitmo for your next vacation."

My captain hushed them all up and came to stand in front of me. "Seriously, Sean, you know we're just pulling your chain. How's Willow?"

"She's okay."

"Well, if there's anything we can do . . . " the captain said, and he let the rest of his sentence fade like smoke.

I scowled, pretending that this didn't bother me, that I was in on the joke instead of being the laughingstock.

"Don't you guys have something constructive to do? What do you think this is, the Lake Buena Vista PD?"

At that, everyone howled with laughter and dribbled out of the locker room, leaving me alone to dress. I smacked my fist into the metal frame of my locker, and it jumped open. A piece of paper fluttered out — my face again, with Mickey Mouse ears superimposed on my head. And on the bottom: "It's a Small World After All."

Instead of getting dressed, I navigated the hallways of the department to the dispatch office and yanked a telephone book from a stack kept on a shelf. I looked for the ad until I found the name I was looking for, the one I'd seen on countless late-night television commercials: "Robert Ramirez, Plaintiff's Attorney: Because you deserve the best."

I do, I thought. *And so does my family.*

So I dialed the number. "Yes," I said. "I'd like to make an appointment."

I was the designated night watchman. After you girls were fast asleep and Charlotte was showered and climbing into bed, it was my job to turn off the lights, lock the doors, do one last pass through the house. With you in your cast, your makeshift bed was the living room couch. I almost turned off the kitchen night-light before I remembered, and then I came closer and pulled the blanket up to your chin and kissed your forehead.

Upstairs, I checked on Amelia and then went into our room. Charlotte was standing in the bathroom with a towel wrapped around herself, brushing her teeth. Her hair was still wet. I stepped up behind her and put my hands on her shoulders, twirled a curl around one of my fingers. "I love the way your hair does that," I said, watching it spring back into the same spiral it had been a minute before. "It's got a memory of its own."

"Mind of its own is more like it," she said, shaking out her hair before she bent down to rinse out her mouth. When she straightened back up again, I kissed her.

"Minty fresh," I said.

She laughed. "Did I miss something? Are we filming a Crest commercial?"

In the mirror, our eyes met. I've always wondered whether she sees what I do when I look at her. Or for that matter, whether she notices the fact that my hair's gotten thinner on the top. "What do you want?" she asked.

"How do you know I want something?"

"Because I've been married to you for seven years?"

I followed her into the bedroom and watched as she dropped the towel and pulled on an oversize T-shirt to sleep in. I know you wouldn't want to hear this — what kid does? — but that was another thing that I loved about your mother. Even after seven years, she still sort of ducked when she changed in front of me, as if I did not know every inch of her by heart.

"I need you and Willow to come somewhere with me tomorrow," I said. "A lawyer's office."

Charlotte sank onto the mattress. "For what?"

I struggled to put into words the feelings that were my explanation. "The way we were treated. The arrest. I can't just let them get away with it."

She stared at me. "I thought you were the one who wanted to just get home and get on with our lives."

"Yeah, and you know what that meant for me today? The whole department thinks I'm some huge joke. I'm always going to be the cop who managed to get arrested. All I've got in my job is my reputation. And they ruined that." I sat down beside Charlotte, hesitating. I championed the truth every day, but I didn't always like speaking it, especially when it meant saying something that left me bare. "They took my family away. I was in that cell, thinking about you and Amelia and Willow, and all I wanted to do was hurt someone. All I wanted to do was turn into the person they already thought I was."

Charlotte lifted her gaze to mine. "Who's 'they'?"

I threaded my fingers through hers. "Well," I said, "that's what I hope the lawyer will tell us."

The waiting room walls of the law offices of Robert Ramirez were papered with the canceled settlement checks that he'd won for former clients. I paced with my hands clasped behind my back, leaning in to read a few. "Pay to the Order of $350,000." "$1.2 million." "$890,000." Amelia was hovering over the coffee machine, a nifty little thing that let you put in a single cup and push a button to get the flavor you wanted. "Mom," she asked, "can I have some?"

"No," Charlotte said. She was sitting next to you on the couch, trying to keep your cast from sliding off the stiff leather.

"But they have tea. And cocoa."

"No means no, Amelia!"

The secretary stood up behind her desk. "Mr Ramirez is ready to see you now."

I pulled you onto my hip, and we all followed the secretary down the hall to a conference room enclosed by walls of frosted glass. The secretary held the door open, but even so, I had to tilt you sideways to get your legs through the clearing. I kept my eyes on Ramirez; I wanted to watch his reaction when he saw you. "Mr O'Keefe," he said, and he held out a hand.

I shook it. "This is my wife, Charlotte, and my girls, Amelia and Willow."

"Ladies," Ramirez said, and then he turned to his secretary. "Briony, why don't you get the crayons and a couple of coloring books?"

From behind me, I heard Amelia snort — I knew she was thinking that this guy didn't have a clue, that coloring books were for little kids, not ones who were already wearing training bras.

"The hundred billionth crayon made by Crayola was Periwinkle Blue," you said.

Ramirez raised his brows. "Good to know," he replied, and then he gestured toward a woman standing nearby. "I'd like to introduce you to my associate, Marin Gates."

She looked the part. With black hair pulled back in a clip and a navy suit, she could have been pretty, but there was something off about her. Her mouth, I decided. She looked like she'd just spit out something that tasted awful.

"I've invited Marin to sit in on this meeting," Ramirez said. "Please, take a seat."

Before we could, though, the secretary reappeared with the coloring books. She handed them to Charlotte, black-and-white pamphlets that said ROBERT RAMIREZ, ESQUIRE across the top in block letters. "Oh, look," your mother said, shooting a withering glance in my direction. "Who knew they'd invented personal injury coloring books?"

Ramirez grinned. "The Internet is a wondrous place."

The seats in the conference room were too narrow to accommodate your spica cast. After three abortive attempts to sit you down, I finally hauled you back onto my hip again and faced the lawyer.

"How can we help you, Mr O'Keefe?" he asked.

"It's Sergeant O'Keefe, actually," I corrected. "I work on the Bankton, New Hampshire, police force; I have for the past nineteen years. My family and I just got back from Disney World, and that's what brought me here today. I've never been treated so poorly in my whole life. I mean, what's more normal than a trip to Disney World, right? But no, instead, my wife and I wind up arrested, my kids are taken away from me and put into protective custody, my youngest daughter is alone by herself in a hospital, scared out of her mind . . ." I drew in my breath. "Privacy's a

66

fundamental right, and the privacy of my family was violated beyond belief."

Marin Gates cleared her throat. "I can see that you're still very upset, Officer O'Keefe. We're going to try to help you . . . but we need you to back up a bit and slow down. Why did you go to Disney World?"

So I told her. I told her about your OI, and the ice cream, and how you fell. I told her about the men in black suits who led us out of the theme park and arranged for the ambulance, as if the sooner they got rid of us the better. I told her about the woman who'd taken Amelia away from us, about the interrogations that went on for hours at the police station, about the way no one there believed me. I told her about the jokes that had been made about me at my own station.

"I want names," I said. "I want to sue, and I want to do it fast. I want to go after someone at Disney World, someone at the hospital, and someone at DCF. I want people's jobs, and I want money out of this to make up for the hell we went through."

By the time I finished, my face felt hot. I couldn't look at your mother; I didn't want to see her face after what I'd said.

Ramirez nodded. "The type of case you're suggesting is very expensive, Sergeant O'Keefe. Any lawyer that takes it on would do a cost-benefit analysis first, and I can tell you right away that, even though you're seeking a money judgment, you're not going to get one."

"But those checks in the waiting room . . ."

"Were for cases where the plaintiff had a valid complaint. From what you've described to us, the people who worked at Disney World and the hospital and DCF were just doing their jobs. Doctors have a legal responsibility to report suspicions of child abuse. Without the letter from your hometown doctor, the police had probable cause to make the arrest in the state of Florida. DCF has an obligation to protect children, particularly when the child in question is too young to give a detailed account of her own health issues. As an officer of the law, I'm sure if you step back and remove the emotion from the facts here, you'll see that, once the health-care information was received from New Hampshire, your kids were immediately turned over to you; you and your wife were released . . . sure, it made you feel awful. But embarrassment isn't a just cause of action."

"What about emotional damages?" I blustered. "Do you have any idea what that was like for me? For my kids?"

"I'm sure it was nothing compared to the emotional burden of living day in and day out with a child who has these particular health problems," Ramirez said, and beside me, Charlotte lifted her gaze to his. The lawyer smiled sympathetically at her. "I mean, it must be quite challenging." He leaned forward, frowning a little. "I don't know much about — what's it called? Osteo . . ."

"Osteogenesis imperfecta," Charlotte said softly.

"How many breaks has Willow had?"

"Fifty-two," you said. "And did you know that the only bone that hasn't been broken by a person in a skiing accident yet is one in the inner ear?"

"I did not," Ramirez said, taken aback. "She's something else, huh?"

I shrugged. You were Willow, pure and simple. There was nobody else like you. I knew it the moment I first held you, wrapped in foam so that you wouldn't get hurt in my arms: your soul was stronger than your body, and in spite of what the doctors told me over and over, I always believed that was the reason for the breaks. What ordinary skeleton could contain a heart as big as the whole world?

Marin Gates cleared her throat. "How was Willow conceived?"

"Ugh," Amelia said — until then, I'd forgotten she was with us — "that's totally gross." I shook my head at her, a warning.

"We had a hard time," Charlotte said. "We were about to try in vitro when I found out I was pregnant."

"Grosser," Amelia said.

"*Amelia!*" I passed you over to your mother and pulled your sister up by the hand. "You can wait outside," I said under my breath.

The secretary looked at us as we entered the waiting room again, but she didn't say anything. "What are you going to talk about next?" Amelia challenged. "Your personal experience with hemorrhoids?"

"That's enough," I said, trying hard not to lose my temper in front of the secretary. "We'll be out soon."

While I headed back down the hall, I heard the secretary's high heels clicking as she walked toward Amelia. "Want a cup of cocoa?" she asked.

When I entered the conference room again, Charlotte was still talking. ". . . but I was thirty-eight years old," she said. "You know what they write on your charts, when you're thirty-eight? 'Geriatric pregnancy.' I was worried about having a Down syndrome child — I never had even *heard* of OI."

"Did you have amnio?"

"Amnio won't tell you automatically that a fetus has OI; you'd have to be looking for it because it's already shown up in your family. But Willow's case was a spontaneous mutation. It wasn't inherited."

"So you didn't know before Willow was born that she had OI?" Ramirez asked.

"We knew when Charlotte's second ultrasound showed a bunch of broken bones," I answered. "Look, are we done here? If you don't want this case, I'm sure I can find —"

"Do you remember that weird thing at the first ultrasound?" Charlotte said, turning to me.

"What weird thing?" Ramirez asked.

"The tech thought the picture of the brain looked too clear."

"There's no such thing as too clear," I said.

Ramirez and his associate exchanged a glance. "And what did your OB say?"

"Nothing." Charlotte shrugged. "No one even mentioned OI until we did another ultrasound at twenty-seven weeks, and saw all the fractures."

Ramirez turned to Marin Gates. "See if it's ever diagnosed in utero that early," he ordered, and then he turned back to Charlotte. "Would you be willing to release your medical records to us? We'll have to do some research on whether or not you have a cause of action —"

"I thought we didn't have a lawsuit," I said.

"You might, Officer O'Keefe." Robert Ramirez looked at you as if he was memorizing your features. "Just not the one you thought."

Marin

Twelve years ago I was a senior in college, going nowhere fast, when I sat down at the kitchen table and had a talk with my mother (more on that later). "I don't know what I want to be," I said.

This was hugely ironic for me, because I didn't really know what I had *been*, either. Since I was five, I've known that I was adopted, which is a politically correct term for being clueless about one's own origins.

"What do you like to do?" my mother had asked, taking a sip of her coffee. She took it black; I took mine light and sweet. It was one of thousands of discrepancies between us that always led to unspoken questions: Had my birth mother taken her coffee light and sweet, too? Did she have my blue eyes, my high cheekbones, my left-handedness?

"I like to read," I said, and then I rolled my eyes. "This is stupid."

"And you like to argue."

I smirked at her.

"Reading. Arguing. Honey," my mother said, brightening, "you were meant to be a lawyer."

Fast-forward nine years: I'd been called back to the doctor's office because of an abnormal Pap smear. While I was waiting for the gynecologist to come in, the life I didn't have flashed before my eyes: the kids I'd put off having because I was too busy in law school and building my career; the men I hadn't dated because I wanted to make law review instead; the house in the country I didn't buy because I worked such long hours I never would have been able to enjoy that expansive teak deck, that mountain view. "Let's go over your family medical history," my doctor said, and I gave my standard answer: "I'm adopted; I don't know my family medical history."

Even though I turned out to be fine — the abnormal results were a lab error — I think that was the day I decided to search for my birth parents.

I know what you're thinking: wasn't I happy with my adoptive parents? Well, the answer was yes — which is why I hadn't even entertained the thought of searching until I was thirty-one. I'd always been happy and grateful that I got to grow up with my family; I didn't need or want a new one. And the very last thing I wanted to do was break their hearts by telling them I was mounting a search.

But even though I knew my whole life that my adoptive parents desperately wanted me, somewhere in my mind, I knew that my birth parents didn't. My mom had given me the party line about them being too young and not ready to have a family — and logically I understood that — but emotionally, I felt like I'd been tossed aside. I guess I wanted to know why. So after a talk with my adoptive parents — one during which my mother cried the whole time she promised to help me — I tentatively waded into the search that I'd been toying with for the past six months.

Being adopted felt like reading a book that had the first chapter ripped out. You might be enjoying the plot and the characters, but you'd probably also like to read that first line, too. However, when you took the book back to the store to say that the first chapter was missing, they told you they couldn't sell you a replacement copy that was intact. What if you read that first chapter and realized you hated the book, and posted a nasty review on Amazon? What if you hurt the author's feelings? Better just to stick with your partial copy and enjoy the rest of the story.

Adoption records weren't open — not even for someone like me, who knew how to pull strings legally. Which meant that every step was Herculean, and that there were far more failures than successes. I'd spent the first three months of my search paying a private investigator over six hundred dollars to tell me that he had turned up absolutely nothing. That, I figured, I could have done myself for free.

The problem was that my real job kept interfering.

As soon as we finished showing the O'Keefes out of the law office, I rounded on my boss. "For the record? This kind of lawsuit is completely unpalatable to me," I said.

"Will you still say that," Bob mused, "if we wind up with the biggest wrongful birth payout in New Hampshire?"

"You don't know that —"

He shrugged. "Depends on what her medical records turn up."

A wrongful birth lawsuit implies that, if the mother had known during her pregnancy that her child was going to be significantly impaired, she would have chosen to abort the fetus. It places the onus of responsibility for the child's subsequent disability on the ob-gyn. From a plaintiff's standpoint, it's a medical malpractice suit. For the defense, it becomes a morality question: who has the right to decide what kind of life is too limited to be worth living?

Many states had banned wrongful birth suits. New Hampshire wasn't one of them. There had been several settlements for the parents of children who'd been born with spina bifida or cystic fibrosis or, in one case, a boy who was profoundly retarded and wheelchair-bound due to a genetic abnormality — even though the illness had never been *diagnosed* before, much less noticed in utero. In New Hampshire, parents were responsible for the care of disabled children their whole lives — not just till age eighteen — which was as good a reason as any to seek damages. There was no question Willow O'Keefe was a sad story, with her enormous body cast, but she'd smiled and answered questions when the father left the room and Bob chatted her up. To put it bluntly: she was cute and bright and articulate — and therefore a much tougher hardship case to sell to a jury.

"If Charlotte O'Keefe's provider didn't meet the standard of care," Bob said, "then she *should* be held liable, so this doesn't happen again."

I rolled my eyes. "You can't play the conscience card when you stand to make a few million, Bob. And it's a slippery slope — if an OB decides a kid with brittle bones shouldn't be born, what's next? A prenatal test for low IQ, so you can scrap the fetus that won't grow up and get into Harvard?"

He clapped me on the back. "You know, it's nice to see someone so passionate. Personally, whenever people start talking about curing *too* many things with science, I'm always glad bioethics wasn't an issue during the time polio, TB, and yellow fever were running rampant." We were walking toward our individual offices, but he suddenly stopped and turned to me. "Are you a neo-Nazi?"

"*What?*"

"I didn't think so. But if we were asked to defend a client who was a neo-Nazi in a criminal suit, could you do your job — even if you found his beliefs disgusting?"

"Of course, and that's a question for a first-year law student," I said immediately. "But this is totally different."

Bob shook his head. "That's the thing, Marin," he replied. "It really isn't."

I waited until he'd closed the door to his office and then let out a groan of frustration. Inside my office, I kicked off my heels and stomped to my desk to sit down. Briony had brought in my mail, neatly bound in an elastic band. I sifted through it, sorting envelopes into case-by-case piles, until I came to one that had an unfamiliar return address.

A month ago, after I'd fired the private investigator, I had sent a letter to the court in Hillsborough County to get my adoption decree. For ten dollars, you could get a copy of the original document. Armed with that, and the fact that I had been born at St. Joseph Hospital in Nashua, I planned to do some legwork and ferret out the first name of my birth mother. I was hoping for a court intern who might not know what he or she was doing and would forget to white out my birth name on the document. Instead, I wound up with a clerk named Maisie Donovan, who'd worked at the county court since the dinosaurs died out — and who had sent me the envelope I now held in my shaking hands.

COUNTY COURT OF HILLSBOROUGH, NEW HAMPSHIRE IN RE: ADOPTION OF BABY GIRL
FINAL DECREE

AND NOW, July 28, 1973, upon consideration of the within Petition and of the hearing and thereon, and the Court having made an investigation to verify the statements of the Petition and other facts to give the Court full knowledge as to the desirability of the proposed adoption;

The Court, being satisfied, finds that the statements made in the Petition are true, and that the welfare of the person proposed to be adopted will be promoted by this adoption; and directs that BABY GIRL, the person proposed to be adopted, shall have all the rights of a child and heir of Arthur William Gates and Yvonne Sugarman Gates, and shall be subject to all the duties

of such child; and shall hereafter assume the name of
MARIN ELIZABETH GATES.

I read it a second time, and a third. I stared at the
judge's signature — Alfred something-or-other. For ten
dollars I had been given the earth-shattering information that:

1. I am female
2. My name is Marin Elizabeth Gates

Well, what had I expected? A Hallmark card from my
birth mother and an invitation to this year's family
reunion? With a sigh, I opened my filing cabinet and
dropped the decree into the folder that I'd marked
PERSONAL. Then I took out a new manila folder and
wrote O'KEEFE across the tab. "Wrongful birth," I
murmured out loud, just to test the words on my
tongue; they were (no surprise) bitter as coffee grains. I
tried to turn my attention to a lawsuit with the thinly
veiled message that there are some children who should
never be born, and winged a silent thank-you to my
birth mother for not feeling the same way.

Piper

Technically, I was your godmother. Apparently, that meant that I was responsible for your religious education, which was sort of a colossal joke since I never set foot in a church (blame that healthy fear of the roof bursting into flames), while your mother rarely missed a weekend Mass. I liked to think of my role, instead, as the fairy-tale version. That one day, with or without the help of mice wearing tiny overalls, I'd make you feel like a princess.

To that end, I rarely showed up to your house empty-handed. Charlotte said I was spoiling you, but I wasn't draping you in diamonds or giving you the keys to a Hummer. I brought magic tricks, candy bars, kiddie videotapes that Emma had outgrown. Even when I visited directly from a stint at the hospital, I'd improvise: a rubber glove, knotted into a balloon. A hair net from the OR. "The day you bring her a speculum," Charlotte used to say, "your welcome is officially rescinded."

"Hello," I yelled as I walked through the front door. To be honest, I can't remember a time I ever knocked. "Five minutes," I said, as Emma tore up the stairs to find Amelia. "Don't even take your coat off." I wandered through the hallway into Charlotte's living room, where you were propped up in your spica cast, reading.

"Piper!" you said, and your face lit up.

Sometimes, when I looked at you, I didn't see the compromised twist of your bones or the short stature that came part and parcel with your illness. Instead, I remembered your mother crying when she told me that she had failed to get pregnant yet another month; I remembered her taking the Doptone out of my ears at an office visit so that she could listen to your hummingbird heartbeat, too.

I sat down beside you on the couch and took your gift du jour out of my coat pocket. It was a beach ball — believe me, it wasn't easy finding one of those in February. "We didn't get to go to the beach," you said. "I fell down."

"Ah, but this isn't just a beach ball," I corrected, and I inflated it until it was as firm and round as the belly of a woman in her ninth month. Then I pushed it between your knees, the ball wedged tight against the plaster, and began to strike the top of it with an open palm. "This," I said, "is a bongo drum."

You laughed, and began to smack the plastic surface, too. The sound brought Charlotte into the room. "You look like hell," I said. "When was the last time you slept?"

"Gee, Piper, it's really great to see you, too . . ."

"Is Amelia ready?"

"For what?"

80

"Skating?"

She smacked her forehead. "I totally forgot. *Amelia!*" she yelled, and then to me: "We just got home from the lawyer's."

"And? Is Sean still on a rampage to sue the world?"

Instead of answering, she rapped her hand against the beach ball. She didn't like it when I ragged on Sean. Your mother was my best friend in the world, but your father could drive me crazy. He got an idea in his head, and that was the end of that — you couldn't budge him. The world was utterly black-and-white for Sean, and I guess I've always been the kind of person who prefers a splash of color.

"Guess what, Piper," you interrupted. "I went skating, too."

I glanced at Charlotte, who nodded. She was usually terrified about the pond in the backyard and its constant temptation; I couldn't wait to hear the details of this story. "I suppose if you forgot about skating, you forgot about the bake sale, too?"

Charlotte winced. "What did you make?"

"I made brownies," I told her. "In the shape of skates. With frosting for the laces and blades. Get it? Ice skates with frosting?"

"You made *brownies?*" Charlotte said, and I followed her as she headed toward the kitchen.

"From scratch. The rest of the moms already blacklisted me because I missed the spring show for a medical conference. I'm trying to atone."

"So you whipped these up when? While you were stitching an episiotomy? After being on call for thirty-six hours?" Charlotte opened her pantry and rummaged through the shelves, finally grabbing a package of Chips Ahoy! and spilling them onto a serving platter. "Honestly, Piper, do you always have to be so damn *perfect*?"

With a fork, she was attacking the edges of the cookies. "Whoa. Who peed in your Cheerios?"

"Well, what do you expect? You waltz in here and tell me I look like crap, and then you make me feel completely inadequate —"

"You're a *pastry chef*, Charlotte. You could bake circles around — What on earth are you doing?"

"Making them look homemade," Charlotte said. "Because I'm not a pastry chef, not anymore. Not for a long time."

When I'd first met Charlotte, she had just been named the finest pastry chef in New Hampshire. I'd actually read about her in a magazine that lauded her ability to take unlikely ingredients and come up with the most remarkable confections. She used to never come empty-handed to my house — she'd bring cupcakes with spun-sugar icing, pies with berries that burst like fireworks, puddings that acted like balms. Her soufflés were as light as summer clouds; her chocolate fondant could wipe your mind clean of whatever obstacles had littered your day. She told me that, when she baked, she could feel herself coming back to center, that everything else fell away, and she remembered who she was supposed to be. I'd been jealous. I had a vocation — and I was a damn good doctor — but Charlotte had a *calling*. She dreamed of

82

opening a patisserie, of writing her own best-selling cookbook. In fact, I never imagined she would find anything she loved more than baking, until you came along.

I moved the platter away. "Charlotte. Are you okay?"

"Let's see. I was arrested last weekend; my daughter's in a body cast; I don't even have time to take a shower — yup, I'm just fantastic." She turned to the doorway and the staircase upstairs. "Amelia! Let's *go*!"

"Emma's gone selectively deaf, too," I said. "I swear she ignores me on purpose. Yesterday, I asked her eight times to clear the kitchen counter —"

"You know what," Charlotte said wearily. "I really don't care about the problems you're having with your daughter."

No sooner had my jaw dropped — I had always been Charlotte's confidante, not her punching bag — than she shook her head and apologized. "I'm sorry. I don't know what's wrong with me. I shouldn't be taking this out on you."

"It's okay," I said.

Just then the older girls clattered down the stairs and skidded past us in a flurry of whispers and giggles. I put my hand on Charlotte's arm. "Just so you know," I said firmly. "You're the most devoted mother I've ever met. You've given up your whole life to take care of Willow."

She ducked her head and nodded before looking up at me. "Do you remember her first ultrasound?"

I thought for a second, and then I grinned. "We saw her sucking her thumb. I didn't even have to point it out to you and Sean; it was clear as day."

"Right," your mother repeated. "Clear as day."

Charlotte

March 2007

What if it was someone's fault?

The idea was just the germ of a seed, carried in the hollow beneath my breastbone when we left the law offices. Even when I was lying awake next to Sean, I heard it as a drumbeat in my blood: *what if, what if, what if*. For five years now I had loved you, hovered over you, held you when you had a break. I had gotten exactly what I so desperately wished for: a beautiful baby. So how could I admit to anyone — much less myself — that you were not only the most wonderful thing that had ever happened to me ... but also the most exhausting, the most overwhelming?

I would listen to people complain about their kids being impolite or surly or even getting into trouble with the law, and I'd be jealous. When those kids turned eighteen, they'd be on their own, making their own mistakes and being held accountable. But you were not the kind of child I could let fly in the world. After all, what if you fell?

And what would happen to you when I wasn't around to catch you anymore?

After one week went by and then another, I began to realize that the law offices of Robert Ramirez were just as disgusted by a woman who would harbor these secret thoughts as I was. Instead, I threw myself into making you happy. I played Scrabble until I knew all the two-letter words by heart; I watched programs on Animal Planet until I had memorized the scripts. By now, your father had settled back into his work routine; Amelia had gone back to school.

This morning, you and I were squeezed into the downstairs bathroom. I faced you, my arms under yours, balancing you over the toilet so that you could pee. "The bags," you said. "They're getting in the way!"

With one hand, I adjusted the trash bags that were wrapped around your legs while I grunted under the weight of you. It had taken a series of failed attempts to figure out how one went to the bathroom while wearing a spica cast — another little tidbit the doctors don't share. From parents on online forums I had learned to wedge plastic garbage bags under the lip of the cast where it had been left open, a liner of sorts so that the plaster edge would stay dry and clean. Needless to say, a trip to the bathroom for you took about thirty minutes, and after a few accidents, you'd gotten very good at predicting when you had to go, instead of waiting till the last minute.

"Forty thousand people get hurt by toilets every year," you said.

I gritted my teeth. "For God's sake, Willow, just concentrate before you make it forty thousand and one."

"Okay, I'm done."

With another balancing act, I passed you the roll of toilet tissue and let you reach between your legs. "Good work," I said, leaning down to flush and then gingerly backing out of the narrow bathroom door. But my sneaker caught on the edge of the rug, and I felt myself going down. I twisted so that I'd land first, so that my body would cushion your blow.

I'm not sure which of us started to laugh first, and when the doorbell and phone rang simultaneously, we started to laugh even harder. Maybe I would change my message. *Sorry, I can't come to the phone right now. I'm holding my daughter, in her fifty-pound cast, over the toilet bowl.*

I levered myself on my elbows, pulling you upright with me. The doorbell rang again, impatient. "Coming," I called out.

"Mommy!" you screeched. "My pants!"

You were still half naked after our bathroom run, and getting you into your flannel pajama bottoms would be another ten-minute endeavor. Instead, I grabbed one of the trash bags still tucked into your cast and wrapped it around you like a black plastic skirt.

On the front porch stood Mrs Dumbroski, one of the neighbors who lived down the road. She had twin grandsons your age, who had visited last year, stolen her glasses when she fell asleep, and set a pile of raked leaves on fire that would have spread to her garage if the mailman hadn't come by at just the right moment. "Hello, dear," Mrs Dumbroski said. "I hope this isn't a bad time."

"Oh no," I answered. "We were just . . ." I looked at you, wearing the trash bag, and we both started to laugh again.

"I was looking for my dish," Mrs Dumbroski said.

"Your dish?"

"The one I baked the lasagna in. I do hope you've had a chance to enjoy it."

It must have been one of the meals that had been waiting for us on our return home from the hell that was Disney World. To be honest, we'd eaten only a few; the rest were getting freezer burn even as I stood there. There was only so much mac and cheese and lasagna and baked ziti that a human could stomach.

It seemed to me that if you made a meal for someone who was sick, it was pretty cheeky to ask whether or not she'd finished it so you could have your Pyrex back.

"How about I try to find the dish, Mrs Dumbroski, and have Sean drop it off at your house later?"

Her lips pursed. "Well," she said, "then I suppose I'll have to wait to make my tuna casserole."

For just a moment I entertained the thought of stuffing you into Mrs Dumbroski's chicken-wing arms and watching her totter under the weight of you while I went to the freezer, found her stupid lasagna, and threw it onto the ground at her feet — but instead I just smiled. "Thanks for being so accommodating. I've got to get Willow down for a nap now," I said, and I closed the door.

"I don't take naps," you said.

"I know. I just said that to make her leave, so I wouldn't kill her." I twirled you into the living room and positioned a legion of pillows behind your back and under your knees, so that you could sit comfortably. Then I reached for your pajama bottoms and leaned over to tap the blinking button on the answering machine. "Left leg first," I said, sliding the wide waistband over your cast.

You have one new message.

I slipped your right leg into the pants and shimmied them over the plaster at your hips.

Mr and Mrs O'Keefe . . . this is Marin Gates from the Law Offices of Robert Ramirez. We've got something we'd like to discuss with you.

"Mom," you whined as my hands stilled at your waist.

I gathered the extra fabric into a knot. "Yes," I said, my heart racing. "Almost done."

This time, Amelia was in school, but we still had to bring Willow to the lawyer's office. And this time, they were ready: beside the coffee machine were juice packs; next to the glossy architectural magazines was a small stack of picture books. When the secretary brought us back to meet the lawyers, we were not led to the conference room. Instead she opened the door to an office that was a hundred different shades of white: from the pickled wood floor to the creamy wall paneling to the pair of pale leather sofas. You craned your neck, taking this all in. Was it supposed to look like heaven? And if so, what did that make Robert Ramirez?

"I thought the couch might be more comfortable for Willow," he said smoothly. "And I also thought she might like to watch a movie instead of listening to the grown-ups talk about all this boring stuff." He held up the DVD of *Ratatouille* — your favorite, although he couldn't have known that. After we'd watched it for the first time, we'd cooked the real deal for dinner.

Marin Gates brought over a portable DVD player and a very swanky pair of Bose headphones. She plugged it in, settled you on the couch, turned on the DVD, and popped the straw into a juice pack.

"Sergeant O'Keefe, Mrs O'Keefe," Ramirez said. "We thought it would be better to discuss this without Willow in the room, but we also realized that might be a physical impossibility given her condition. Marin's the one who came up with the idea of the DVD. She's also been doing a great deal of work these past two weeks. We reviewed your medical records, and we gave them to someone else to review. Does the name Marcus Cavendish ring a bell?"

Sean and I looked at each other and shook our heads.

"Dr Cavendish is Scottish. He's one of the foremost experts on osteogenesis imperfecta in the world. And according to him, it appears that you have a good cause of action of medical malpractice against your obstetrician. You remembered your eighteen-week ultrasound being too clear, Mrs O'Keefe . . . That's significant evidence that your obstetrician missed. She should have been able to recognize your baby's condition then, long before broken bones were visible at the later ultrasound. And she should have presented that information to you at a time in your pregnancy . . . that might have allowed you to change the outcome."

My head was spinning, and Sean looked utterly confused. "Wait a second," he said. "What kind of lawsuit is this?"

Ramirez glanced at you. "It's called wrongful birth," he said.

"And what the hell does that mean?"

The lawyer glanced at Marin Gates, who cleared her throat. "A wrongful birth lawsuit entitles the parents to sue for damages incurred from the birth and care of a severely disabled child," she said. "The implication is that if your provider had told you earlier on that your baby was going to be impaired, you would have had choices and options as to whether or not to continue with the pregnancy."

I remembered snapping at Piper weeks ago: *Do you always have to be so damn perfect?*

What if the one time she *hadn't* been perfect was when it came to you?

I was as rooted to my seat as you were; I couldn't move, couldn't breathe. Sean spoke for me: "You're saying my daughter never should have been born?" he accused. "That she was a *mistake*? I'm not listening to this bullshit."

I glanced at you: you had taken off your headphones and were hanging on every word.

90

As your father stood up, so did Robert Ramirez. "Sergeant O'Keefe, I know how horrible it sounds. But the term *wrongful birth* is just a legal one. We don't wish your child wasn't born — she's absolutely beautiful. We just think that, when a doctor doesn't meet the standard of care a patient deserves, someone ought to be held responsible." He took a step forward. "It's medical malpractice. Think of all the time and money that's gone into taking care of Willow — and *will* go into taking care of her in the future. Why should *you* pay for someone else's mistake?"

Sean towered over the lawyer, and for a second, I thought he might swat Ramirez out of his way. But instead he jabbed one finger into the lawyer's chest. "I *love* my daughter," Sean said, his voice thick. "I *love* her."

He pulled you into his arms, yanking the headphone jack out so that the DVD player overturned, knocking over the juice box onto the leather couch. "Oh," I cried, digging in my purse for a tissue to blot the stain. That gorgeous, creamy leather; it would be ruined.

"It's all right, Mrs O'Keefe," Marin murmured, kneeling beside me. "Don't worry about it."

"Daddy, the movie's not done," you said.

"Yes it is." Sean pulled the headphones off you and threw them down. "Charlotte," he said, "let's get the hell out of here."

He was already striding down the hall, volcanic, as I mopped up the juice. I realized that both lawyers were staring at me, and I rocked back on my heels.

"Charlotte!" Sean's voice rang from the waiting room.

"Um . . . thank you. I'm really sorry that we bothered you." I stood up, crossing my arms, as if I were cold, or had to hold myself together. "I just . . . there's one thing . . ." I looked up at the lawyers and took a deep breath. "What happens if we win?"

II

Sling me under the sea.
Pack me down in the salt and wet.
No farmer's plow shall touch my bones.
No Hamlet hold my jaws and speak
How jokes are gone and empty is my mouth.
Long, green-eyed scavengers shall pick my eyes,
Purple fish play hide-and-seek,
And I shall be song of thunder, crash of sea,
Down on the floors of salt and wet.
Sling me . . . under the sea.

— Carl Sandburg, *Bones*

Folding: a gentle process in which one mixture is added to another, using a large metal spoon or spatula.

Most of the time when you talk about folding, it involves an edge. You fold laundry, you fold notes in half. With batter, it's different: you bring two diverse substances together, but that space between them doesn't completely disappear — a mixture that's been folded the right way is light, airy, the parts still getting to know each other.

It's a combination on the cusp, as one mixture yields to the other. Think of a bad hand of poker, of an argument, of any situation where one party simply gives in.

CHOCOLATE RASPBERRY SOUFFLÉ

1 pint raspberries, pureed and strained
8 eggs, separated
4 ounces sugar
3 ounces all-purpose flour
8 ounces good-quality bittersweet chocolate, chopped
2 ounces Chambord liqueur
2 tablespoons melted butter
Sugar for dusting ramekins

Heat the raspberry puree to lukewarm in a heavy saucepan. Whisk the egg yolks with 3 ounces of sugar in large mixing bowl; whisk in the flour and raspberry puree, and return the mixture to the saucepan.

Cook over medium-low heat, stirring constantly, until the custard is thick. Do not allow it to boil. Remove from heat, and stir in the chocolate until it is completely melted. Mix in the liqueur. Cover the base mixture with plastic to prevent a skin from forming.

Meanwhile, butter six ramekins and dust with sugar. Preheat the oven to 425 degrees F.

Whip the egg whites to stiff peaks with the remaining ounce of sugar. And here is the part where you will see it — the coming together of two very different mixtures — as you fold the egg whites into the chocolate. Neither one will be willing to give up its substance: the darkness of the chocolate will become part of the foam of the egg whites, and vice versa.

Spoon the mixture into the ramekins, just ¼ inch shy of the rim. Bake immediately. The soufflés are done when they are well risen, golden brown on top, with edges that appear dry — about 20 minutes. But do not be surprised if, when you remove them from the oven, they sink under the weight of their own promise.

Charlotte

April 2007

You can't live a life without impact. It was one of the first things doctors told us when they began explaining the catch-22 that was osteogenesis imperfecta: be active, but don't break, because if you break, you can't be active. The parents who kept their kids sedentary, or had them walk on their knees so that they would be less likely to fall and suffer a fracture, also ran the risk of never having their children's muscles and joints develop enough to protect the bones.

Sean was the risk taker when it came to you. Then again, he wasn't the one who was home most often when you had a break. But he'd spent years convincing me that a few casts was small price to pay for a real life; maybe now I could convince him that two silly words like *wrongful birth* meant nothing when compared to the future they might secure for you. In spite of Sean's exit from the lawyer's office, I kept hoping they might call me again. I fell asleep thinking about what Robert Ramirez had said. I woke up with an unfamiliar taste in my mouth, part sweet and part sour; it took me days to realize this was simply hope.

You were sitting in a hospital bed with a blanket thrown over your spica cast, reading a trivia book while we waited for your pamidronate infusion. At first, you'd come in every two months; now we only had to make biannual treks down to Boston. Pamidronate wasn't a cure for OI, just a treatment — one that made it possible for Type IIIs like you to walk at all, instead of being wheelchair-bound. Before this, even stepping down could cause microfractures in your feet.

"You wouldn't believe it, looking at her femur breaks, but her Z score's much better," Dr Rosenblad said. "She's at minus three."

When you were born and had a Dexascan reading for bone density, your score was minus six. Ninety-eight percent of the population fell between plus and minus two. Bone constantly makes new bone and absorbs old bone; pamidronate slowed down the rate at which your body would absorb the bone; it allowed you to move enough to build up strength in your bones. Once, Dr Rosenblad had explained it to me by holding up a kitchen sponge: bone was porous, the pamidronate filled in the holes a little.

You'd had over fifty fractures in five years with the treatment; I couldn't imagine what life would have been like without it.

"I've got a good fact for you today, Willow," Dr Rosenblad said. "In a pinch, if you need a substitute for blood plasma, you can use the goop inside coconuts."

Your eyes widened. "Have you ever *done* that?"

"I was thinking of trying it today . . ." He grinned at you. "Just joking. Got any questions for me before we get the show on the road?"

You slipped your hand into mine. "Two sticks, right?"

"That's the rule," I said. If a nurse couldn't get the IV inserted in your vein in two tries, I'd make her get someone else to do it.

It's funny — when I went out with Sean and another cop and his wife, I was the shy one. I was never the life of the party; I didn't strike up conversations with people standing in the grocery line behind me. But put me in a hospital setting, and I would fight to the death for you. I would be your voice, until you learned to speak up for yourself. I had not always been like this — who doesn't want to believe a doctor knows best? But there are practitioners who can go an entire career without ever running across a case of OI. The fact that people told me they knew what they were doing did not mean I would trust them.

Except Piper. I had believed her when she told me that there was no way we could have known any sooner that you would be born this way.

"I think we're good to go," Dr Rosenblad said.

The treatments were four hours each, for three days in a row. After two hours of multiple nurses and residents coming in to get your vitals (honestly, did they think that your weight and height changed in the span of a half hour?), Dr Rosenblad would be called in, and then you'd give a urine sample. After that came the blood draw — six vials while you clutched my hand so hard you left tiny half-moons with your fingernails on the canvas of my skin. Finally, the nurse would administer the IV — the part you resisted the most. As soon as I heard her footsteps in the hall, I tried to distract you by pointing out facts in your book.

Flamingo tongues were eaten in ancient Rome as a delicacy.

In Kentucky, it's illegal to carry ice cream in your back pocket.

"Hey, sugar," the nurse said. She had a cloud of unnaturally yellow hair and wore a stethoscope with a monkey clipped to the side of it. She was carrying a small plastic tray with an IV needle, alcohol wipes, and two strips of white tape.

"Needles suck," you said.

"Willow! Watch your language!"

"But *suck* isn't a swear word. Vacuums suck."

"Especially if you're the one doing the housecleaning," the nurse murmured, swabbing your arm. "Now, Willow, I'm going to count to three before I stick you. Ready? One . . . two!"

"Three," you yelped. "You lied!"

"Sometimes it's easier to not be expecting it," the nurse said, but she was lifting the needle again. "That wasn't a good one. Let's give it another try —"

"No," I interrupted. "Is there another nurse on the floor who can do this?"

"I've been putting in IVs for thirteen years —"

"But not in my daughter."

Her face frosted over. "I'll get my supervisor."

100

She closed the door behind us. "But that was only the first stick," you said.

I sank down beside you on the bed. "She was sneaky. I'm not taking any chances."

Your fingers ruffled the pages of your book, as if you were reading Braille. One factoid jumped out at me: *The safest year of life, statistically, is age ten.*

You were halfway there.

The nice part about your being kept overnight in the hospital was that I didn't have to worry whether you'd wind up there, courtesy of a slip in the tub or an arm hooked on the sleeve of your jacket. As soon as they had finished the first infusion and flushed the IV and you were sleeping deeply, I crept out of the darkened room and went to the bank of pay phones near the elevators so that I could call home.

"How is she?" Sean asked as soon as he picked up the phone.

"Bored. Fidgety. The usual. How's Amelia?"

"She got an A on her math quiz and threw a fit when I told her she had to wash the dishes after dinner."

I smiled. "The usual," I repeated.

"Guess what we had for dinner?" Sean said. "Chicken cordon bleu, roasted potatoes, and stir-fried green beans."

"Yeah, right," I said. "You can't even boil an egg."

"I didn't say I cooked. The take-out counter at the grocery store was just particularly well stocked tonight."

"Well, Willow and I had a culinary feast of tapioca pudding, chicken noodle soup, and red Jell-O."

"I want to call her before I go to work tomorrow. What time will she get up?"

"Six, for the nurses' shift change," I said.

"I'll set my alarm," Sean answered.

"By the way, Dr Rosenblad asked me about doing the surgery again."

This was — no pun intended — a bone of contention for Sean and me. Your orthopedic surgeon wanted to rod your femurs after you were out of your spica cast, so that, even if there were future breaks, they wouldn't displace. Rodding also prevented bowing, since OI bone grows spirally. As Dr Rosenblad said, it was the best way to manage OI, since you can't cure OI. But although I was gung ho about doing anything and everything that might save you some pain in the future, Sean looked at the here and now — and the fact that a surgery meant you'd be incapacitated once again. I could practically hear him digging in his heels. "Didn't you print out some article about how rodding stunts growth in OI kids —"

"You're thinking of the spinal rods," I said. "Once they put them in to combat the scoliosis, Willow won't get any taller. This is different. Dr Rosenblad even said the rods have gotten so sophisticated, they'll grow with her — they telescope out."

"What if she doesn't have any more femur breaks? Then she's having the surgery for nothing."

The chances of you not having another leg break were about as good as those of the sun not rising tomorrow morning. That was the other difference between Sean and me — I was the resident pessimist. "Do you really want to have to deal with another spica cast? If she winds up in one when she's seven or ten or twelve, who's going to be able to lift her then?"

Sean sighed. "She's a kid, Charlotte. Shouldn't she be able to run around for a while before you take that away again?"

"*I'm* not taking anything away," I said, stung. "The fact is, she's going to fall. The fact is, she's going to break. Don't cast me as the villain, Sean, just because I'm trying to help her in the long run."

There was a hesitation. "I know how hard it is," he said. "I know how much you do for her."

It was as close as he could come to alluding to the disastrous visit in the lawyer's office. "I wasn't complaining —"

"I never said you were. I'm just saying . . . we knew it wouldn't be easy, right?"

Yes, we'd known that. But I guess I also hadn't realized it would ever be quite this hard. "I have to go," I said, and when Sean said he loved me, I pretended I had not heard.

I hung up and immediately dialed Piper. "What's wrong with men?" I asked.

In the background, I could hear the water running, dishes clattering in the sink. "Is that a rhetorical question?" she said.

"Sean doesn't want Willow to have rodding surgery."

"Hang on. Aren't you in Boston for pamidronate?"

"Yes, and Rosenblad brought it up today when we saw him," I said. "He's been urging us to do it for a year now, and Sean keeps putting it off, and Willow keeps breaking."

"Even though she'll be better off in the long run?"

"Even though."

"Well," Piper said, "then I have one word for you: *Lysistrata*."

I burst out laughing. "I've been sleeping with Willow on the living room couch for the past month. If I told Sean I was going to stop having sex with him, it would be a pretty empty threat."

"There's your answer, then," Piper said. "Bring on the candles, oysters, negligee, the whole nine yards . . . and when he's blissed out in a hedonistic coma, ask him again." I heard a voice in the background. "Rob says that'll work like a charm."

"Thank him for the vote of confidence."

"Hey, by the way, tell Willow that a person's thumb is as long as his nose."

"Really?" I wedged my hand up to my face to check. "She'll love that."

"Oh, shoot, that's my call waiting. Why can't babies get born at nine in the *morning*?"

"Is that a rhetorical question?" I said.

"And we come full circle. Talk to you tomorrow, Char."

After I hung up, I stared at the receiver for a long moment. *She'll be better off in the long run*, Piper had said.

Did she believe that, unconditionally? Not just about a rodding surgery but about any action that a good mother would undertake?

I didn't know if I could even muster the courage to sue for wrongful birth. Saying abstractly that there were some children who shouldn't be born was hard enough, but this went one step further. This meant saying one particular child — *my* child — shouldn't have been born. What kind of mother would face a judge and a jury, and announce that she wished her child had never existed?

Either the kind of mother who didn't love her daughter at all . . . or the kind of mother who loved her daughter too much. The kind of mother who would say anything and everything if it meant you'd have a better life.

But even if I came to terms with that moral conundrum, the additional wrinkle here was that the person on the other end of the lawsuit was not a stranger — she was my best friend.

I thought of the foam pad we had once used to line your car bed and your crib, how sometimes, when I lifted you out of it, I could still see the impression you'd made, like a memory, or a ghost. And then, like magic, it would disappear. The indelible mark I'd left on Piper, the indelible mark she'd left on *me* — well, maybe they weren't permanent. For years, I'd believed Piper when she said tests wouldn't have told us any earlier that you had OI, but she had been talking about blood tests. She'd never even alluded to the fact that *other* prenatal testing — like ultrasounds — might have picked up your OI. Had she been making excuses for me, or for herself?

It won't affect her, a voice in my head murmured. *That's what malpractice insurance is for.* But it would affect *us*. In order to make sure you could rely on me, I would lose the friend I'd relied on since before you were born.

Last year, when Emma and Amelia were in sixth grade, the gym teacher had come up behind Emma and squeezed her shoulders while she waited on the sidelines of a softball game. Innocuous, most likely, but Emma had come home saying that it creeped her out. *What do I do?* Piper had asked me. *Give him the benefit of the doubt, or be a helicopter parent?* Before I could even offer her my opinion, she'd made up her mind. *It's my daughter,* she said. *If I don't go in and open up my mouth, I may live to regret it.*

I loved Piper Reece. But I would always love you more.

With my heart pounding, I took a business card out of my back pocket and dialed the number before I could lose my nerve.

"Marin Gates," said a voice on the other end.

"Oh," I stumbled, surprised. I had been anticipating an answering machine this late at night. "I wasn't expecting you to be there . . ."

"Who is this?"

"Charlotte O'Keefe. I was in your office a couple of weeks ago with my husband about —"

"Yes, I remember," Marin said.

I twisted the metal snake of the phone cord around my arm, imagined the words I would funnel into it, send into the world, make real.

"Mrs O'Keefe?"

"I'm interested in . . . taking legal action."

There was a brief silence. "Why don't we schedule a time for you to come in and meet with me? I can have my secretary call you tomorrow."

"No," I said, and then shook my head. "I mean, that's fine, but I won't be home tomorrow. I'm in the hospital with Willow."

"I'm sorry to hear that."

"No, she's fine. Well, she's *not* fine, but this is routine. We'll be home Thursday."

"I'll make a note."

"Good," I said, my breath coming in a rush. "Good."

"Give my best to your family," Marin replied.

"I've just got one question," I said, but she had already hung up the phone. I pressed the mouthpiece against my lips, tasted the bitter metal. "Would you do this?" I whispered out loud. "Would you do this, if you were me?"

If you'd like to make a call, said the mechanical voice of an operator, *please hang up and try again.*

What would Sean say?

Nothing, I realized, because I wouldn't tell him what I'd done.

I walked back down the hall toward your room. On the bed, you were snoring softly. The video you'd been watching when you fell asleep cast a reflection over your bed in reds and greens and golds, an early rush of autumn. I lay down on the narrow cot that had been converted from one of the guest chairs by a helpful nurse; she'd left me a threadbare blanket and a pillow that crackled like polar ice.

The mural on the far wall was an ancient map, with a pirate ship sailing off its borders. Not long ago, sailors believed that the seas were precipitous, that compasses could point out the spots where, beyond, there'd be dragons. I wondered about the explorers who'd sailed their ships to the end of the world. How terrified they must have been when they risked falling over the edge; how amazed to discover, instead, places they had seen only in their dreams.

Piper

I met Charlotte eight years ago, in one of the coldest rinks in New Hampshire, when we were dressing our four-year-old daughters as shooting stars for a forty-five-second performance in the club's winter skating show. I was waiting for Emma to finish lacing up her skates while other mothers effortlessly yanked their daughters' hair into buns and tied the ribbons of the shimmering costumes around their wrists and ankles. They chatted about the Christmas wrapping paper sale the skating club was doing for fund-raising and complained about their husbands, who hadn't charged the video camera batteries long enough. In contrast to this offhanded competence, Charlotte sat alone, off to one side, trying to coax a very stubborn Amelia into tying back her long hair. "Amelia," she said, "your teacher won't let you onto the ice like that. Everyone has to match."

She looked familiar, although I didn't remember meeting her. I thrust a few bobby pins at Charlotte and smiled. "If you need them," I said, "I also have superglue and marine varnish. This isn't our first year with the Nazi Skating Club."

Charlotte burst out laughing and took the pins. "They're four years old!"

"Apparently, if you don't start young, they'll have nothing to talk about in therapy," I joked. "I'm Piper, by the way. Proudly defiant skating parent."

She held out a hand. "Charlotte."

"Mom," Emma said, "that's Amelia. I told you about her last week. She just moved here."

"We came because of work," Charlotte said.

"For you or your husband?"

"I'm not married," she said. "I'm the new pastry chef over at Capers."

"That's where I know you from. I read about you in that magazine article."

Charlotte blushed. "Don't believe everything in print . . ."

"You ought to be proud! Me, I can't even bake a Betty Crocker mix without screwing it up. Luckily, that's not part of my job description."

"What do you do?"

"I'm an obstetrician."

"Well, that beats what I do, hands down," Charlotte said. "When I deliver, people gain weight. When you deliver, they lose it."

Emma poked a finger into a hole in her costume. "Mine's going to fall off because you don't know how to sew," she accused.

"It won't fall off," I sighed, then turned to Charlotte. "I was too busy suturing to sew a costume, so I hot-glued the seams."

110

"Next time," Charlotte told Emma, "I'll sew yours when I do Amelia's."

I liked that — the idea that she was already counting on us being friends. We were destined to be partners in crime, subversive parents who didn't care what the establishment thought. Just then, the teacher stuck her head inside the locker room door. "Amelia? Emma?" she snapped. "We're all *waiting* for you out here!"

"Girls, you'd better hurry. You heard what Eva Braun said."

Emma scowled. "Mommy, her name's *Miss Helen*."

Charlotte laughed. "Break a leg!" she said as they hurried into the rink. "Or does that only work if the stage isn't made of ice?"

I don't know whether you can look at your past and find, woven like the hidden symbols on a treasure map, the path that will point to your final destination, but I have thought back to that moment, to Charlotte's good-luck phrase, many times. Do I remember it because of the way you were born? Or were you born because of the way I remember it?

Rob was braced over me, his leg moving between mine as he kissed me. "We can't," I whispered. "Emma's still awake."

"She won't come in here . . ."

"You don't know that —"

Rob buried his face in my neck. "She knows we have sex. If we didn't, she wouldn't be here."

"Do *you* like to imagine your parents having sex?"

Grimacing, Rob rolled away from me. "Okay, *that* effectively killed the mood."

I laughed. "Give her ten minutes to fall asleep and I'll get the fire going again."

He pillowed his head on his arms, staring up at the ceiling. "How many times a week do you think Charlotte and Sean do it?"

"I don't know!"

Rob glanced at me. "Sure you do. Girls talk about that kind of thing."

"Okay, first of all, no we don't. And second of all, even if we did, I don't sit around wondering how often my best friend has sex with her husband."

"Yeah, right," Rob said. "So you've never looked at Sean and wondered what it would be like to sleep with him?"

I came up on an elbow. "Have *you?*"

He grinned. "Sean's not my type . . ."

"Very funny." My gaze slid toward him. "Charlotte? *Really?*"

"Well . . . you know . . . it's just a curiosity. Even Gordon Ramsay's got to think about Big Macs once or twice in passing."

"So I'm the high-maintenance gourmet meal and Charlotte's fast food?"

"It was a bad metaphor," Rob admitted.

Sean O'Keefe was tall, strong, physically fierce — orthogonal to Rob's slight runner's frame, his careful surgeon's hands, his addiction to reading. One of the reasons I'd fallen for Rob was that he seemed to be more impressed with my mind than with my legs. If I'd ever considered what it would be like to roll around with someone like Sean, the impulse must have been quickly squashed: after all these years, and all these conversations with Charlotte, I knew him too well to find him attractive.

But Sean's intensity also carried over into his parenting — he was crazy about his little girls; he was deeply private and protective of Charlotte. Rob was cerebral, not visceral. What would it feel like to have so much raw passion focused on you at once? I tried to picture Sean in bed. Did he wear pajama pants, like Rob? Or go commando?

"Huh," Rob said. "I didn't know you could blush way down to your —"

I yanked the sheets up to my chin. "To answer your question," I said, "I'm not even sure it's once a week. Between Willow and Sean's work schedule, they're probably not even in the same room at night most of the time."

It was odd, I realized, that Charlotte and I had *not* discussed sex. Not because I was her friend but because I was her doctor — part of my medical questioning involved whether or not a patient was having any problems during intercourse. Had I asked her that? Or had I skipped over it because it seemed too personal to ask that of a friend instead of a stranger? Back then, sex was a means to an end: a baby. But what about now? Was Charlotte happy? Did she and Sean lie in bed, comparing themselves to me and Rob?

"Well, go figure. You and I *are* in the same room at night." Rob leaned over me. "How about we maximize that potential?"

"Emma —"

"Is lost in her dreams by now." Rob pulled my pajama top over my head and stared at me. "As a matter of fact, so am I . . ."

I wrapped my arms around his neck and kissed him slowly. "Still thinking about Charlotte?"

"Charlotte who?" Rob murmured, and he kissed me back.

Once a month, Charlotte and I went to a movie and then to a seedy bar called Maxie's Pad — a place whose name absolutely cracked me up, given the gynecological connotation, although I'm quite sure that was lost on Maxie himself, a grizzled old Maine fisherman who, when we first ordered Chardonnay, had told us it wasn't on tap. Even when the only films playing were really awful slasher flicks or teen comedies, I'd drag Charlotte out for the night. If I didn't, there were stretches of time when she'd never have left the house.

The best thing about Maxie's was his grandson, Moose, a linebacker who'd been kicked out of college in the middle of a cheating scandal. He'd started bartending for his grandpa three years ago, when he was back home evaluating his options, and he'd never left. He was six-six, blond, brawny, and had the mental acuity of a spatula.

114

"Here you go, ma'am," Moose said, sliding a pale ale toward Charlotte, who barely even flicked a glance at him.

There was something wrong with Charlotte tonight. She'd tried to back out of our standing date, but I wouldn't allow it, and for the past few hours she'd been distant and distracted. I attributed it to concern over you — with the pamidronate treatment and the femur breaks and the rodding surgery, she had plenty on her mind — and I was determined to divert her attention. "He winked at you," I announced as soon as Moose turned away to help another customer.

"Oh, get out," Charlotte said. "I'm too old to be flirted with."

"Forty-four is the new twenty-two."

"Yeah, well, talk to me when you're my age."

"Charlotte, I'm only two years younger than you!" I laughed and took a sip of my own beer. "God, we're pathetic. He's probably thinking, *Those poor middle-aged women; the least I can do is make their day by pretending I find them even remotely sexy.*"

Charlotte lifted her mug. "Here's to *not* being married to a guy too young to rent a car from Hertz."

I was the one who'd introduced your mother and your father. I think it's human nature that those of us who are married cannot rest easy until we find mates for our single friends. Charlotte had never been married — Amelia's father had been a drug addict who'd tried to clean up his act during Charlotte's pregnancy, failed miserably, and moved to India with a seventeen-year-old pole dancer. So when I was pulled over for speeding by a really good-looking cop who wasn't wearing a wedding band, I invited him to dinner so that he could meet Charlotte.

"I don't do blind dates," your mother told me.

"Then google him."

Ten minutes later she called me, frantic, because Sean O'Keefe was also the name of a recently paroled child molester. Ten months later, she married the *other* Sean O'Keefe.

I watched Moose stack glasses behind the bar, the light playing over his muscles. "So how goes it with Sean?" I asked. "Have you managed to convince him to do it yet?"

Charlotte startled, nearly knocking over her beer. "To do what?"

"The rodding surgery for Willow. Hello?"

"Right," Charlotte said. "I forgot I'd told you about that."

"Charlotte, we talk every day." I looked at her more carefully. "Are you sure you're okay?"

"I just need a good night's sleep," she replied, but she was looking down into her beer, running one finger along the rim of the glass until it sang to us. "You know, I was reading something at the hospital, some magazine. There was an article in there about a family who sued the hospital after their son was born with cystic fibrosis."

I shook my head. "That pass-the-buck mentality drives me crazy. Pin the blame on someone else to make yourself feel better."

"Maybe someone else really *was* at fault."

"It's the luck of the draw. You know what an obstetrician would say if a couple had a newborn with CF? 'Oh, they got a bad baby.' It's not a judgment call, it's just a statement of fact."

"A bad baby," Charlotte repeated. "Is that what you think happened to me?"

Sometimes, I let myself run on without thinking — like right now, when I remembered too late that Charlotte's interest in this subject was more than theoretical. I felt heat flood my face. "I wasn't talking about Willow. She's —"

"Perfect?" Charlotte challenged.

But you *were*. You did the funniest Paris Hilton impression I'd ever seen; you could sing the alphabet backward; your features were delicate, elfin, fairy-tale. Those brittle bones were the least important part of you.

Suddenly Charlotte folded. "I'm sorry. I shouldn't have said that."

"No, honestly, my mouth shouldn't be able to function unless my brain's engaged."

"I'm just exhausted," Charlotte said. "I ought to call it a night."

When I started to get up off my stool, she shook her head. "Stay here, finish your beer."

"Let me walk you out to the car —"

"I'm a big girl, Piper. Really. Just forget I even said anything."

I nodded. And, stupid me, I did.

Amelia

So there I was in the school library, one of the few places where I could pretend my life wasn't totally ruled by your OI, when I stumbled across it: a photograph in a magazine of a woman who looked just like you. It was weird, like one of those FBI photos where they artificially age a kid who's been kidnapped ten years, so that you might be able to recognize him on the street. There was your flyaway silk hair, your pointy chin, your bowed legs. I'd met other OI kids before and knew you all had similar features, but this was really ridiculous.

Even more weird was the fact that this lady was holding a baby, and was standing next to a giant. He had his arm around her and was grinning out of the photo with a really heinous overbite.

"Alma Dukins," the text below it read, "is only 3'2"; her husband, Grady, is 6'4"."

"Whatcha doing?" Emma said.

She was my best friend; we'd been best friends for, like, ever. After the whole Disney nightmare, when kids in school found out I'd been shipped off to a foster home overnight, she (a) didn't treat me like a leper, and

(b) threatened to deck anyone who did. Right now, she'd come up behind my chair and notched her chin over my shoulder. "Hey, that woman looks like your sister."

I nodded. "She's got OI, too. Maybe Wills was switched at birth."

Emma sank into the empty chair beside me. "Is that her husband? My dad could totally fix his teeth." She peered at the magazine. "God, how do they even *do* it?"

"That's disgusting," I said, although I had been wondering the same thing.

Emma blew a bubble with her gum. "I guess everyone's the same height when you're lying down doing the nasty," she said. "I thought Willow couldn't have kids."

I kind of thought that, too. I guess no one had ever really discussed it with you, because you were only five, and believe me I didn't want to think about anything as repulsive as this, but if you could break a bone coughing, how would you ever get a baby out of you, or a you-know-what *in*?

I knew if I wanted rugrats, I'd be able to have them one day. If *you* wanted kids, though, it wouldn't be easy, even if it was possible. It wasn't fair, but then again, what *was* when it came to you?

You couldn't skate. You couldn't bike. You couldn't ski. And even when you *did* play a game that was physical — like hide-and-seek — Mom used to insist that you get an extra count of twenty. I pretended to be bent out of shape by this so you wouldn't feel like you were getting special treatment, but deep down I knew it

119

was the right thing to do — you couldn't get around as fast as I could, with your braces or crutches or wheelchair, and it took you longer to wiggle into a hiding spot. *Amelia, wait up!* you always said when we were walking somewhere, and I would, because I knew there were a million other ways I would leave you behind.

I would grow up, while you'd stay the size of a toddler.

I would go to college, move away from home, and not have to worry about things like whether I could reach the gas pump or the buttons on the ATM.

I'd maybe find a guy who didn't think I was a total loser and get married and have kids and be able to carry them around without worrying that I'd get microfractures in my spine.

I read the finer print of the magazine article.

Alma Dukins, 34, gave birth on March 5, 2008, to a healthy baby girl. Dukins, who has osteogenesis imperfecta Type III, is 3'2" tall and weighed 39 pounds before her pregnancy. She gained 19 pounds during her pregnancy and her daughter, Lulu, was delivered by C-section at 32 weeks, when Alma's small body could not accommodate the enlarging uterus. She weighed four pounds, six ounces, and was 16½ inches long at birth.

You were at the stage when you played with dolls. Mom said I used to do that, too, although I only remember dismembering mine and cutting off all their hair. Sometimes I would catch Mom watching you wrap your fake baby's arm in a cast, and it was like a storm cloud passed over her face — she was probably thinking that chances were you'd never have a real baby, mixed with feeling relief that you wouldn't have to know what it was like to watch your own kid break a million bones, like she did.

But in spite of what my mother thought, here was proof that someone with OI could have a family. This Alma woman was Type III, like you. She didn't walk like you could — she was wheelchair-bound. And yet she'd managed to find a husband, goofy smile and all, and have a baby of her own.

"You ought to show Willow," Emma said. "Just take it. Who's going to know?"

So I checked to see if the librarian was still on her computer, ordering clothes from Gap.com (we'd done our share of spying on her), and then I faked a coughing fit. I doubled over and tucked the magazine inside my jacket. I smiled weakly as the librarian glanced at me to make sure I wasn't hacking out a lung on the floor or anything.

Emma expected me to keep the magazine for you, to show you or even Mom that one day you could grow up and get married and have a kid. But I had stolen it for a completely different reason. See, this year, you were starting kindergarten. And one day you'd be a seventh grader, like me. And you might be sitting in this library and come across this stupid magazine and see what I had seen when I looked at it: the space between Alma and her husband, that baby, too huge in her arms.

To me, this didn't look like a happy family. It was a circus freak show, minus the big top. Why else would it be in a magazine? Normal families didn't make the news.

In English class I asked to go to the bathroom. There, I tore the page out of the magazine and ripped the picture into the tiniest pieces I could. I flushed them down the toilet, the best I could do to protect you.

Marin

People think of the law as a virtual hallowed hall of justice, but the truth is that my job more closely resembles a bad sitcom. I once represented a woman who was carrying a frozen turkey out of her local Stop-n-Save grocery store the day before Thanksgiving, when the turkey slipped through the plastic bag and fractured her foot. She sued the Stop-n-Save, but we also included the company that made the plastic bags, and she walked away — without crutches, mind you — several hundred thousand dollars richer.

Then there was the case that involved a woman driving home at 2a.m. on a back road at eighty miles per hour, who collided with a lost tractor trailer that had backed up across the road to turn around. She was killed instantly, and her husband wanted to sue the tractor-trailer company because they didn't have lights along the side of the truck so that his wife could have seen it. We brought a wrongful death suit against the driver of the truck, citing loss of consortium — asking for millions to make up for the fact that the husband had lost his beloved wife's company. Unfortunately, during the case, the defendant's attorney uncovered the

123

fact that my client's wife had been on her way home from a rendezvous with her lover.

You win some, you lose some.

Looking at Charlotte O'Keefe, who was sitting in my office with her cell phone clutched in her hands, I was pretty sure which way this case was going to go. "Where's Willow?" I asked.

"Physical therapy," Charlotte said. "She's there till eleven."

"And the breaks? They're healing well?"

"Fingers crossed," Charlotte replied.

"You're expecting a call?"

She looked down, as if she was surprised to find herself holding her phone. "Oh, no. I mean, I hope not. I just have to be available if Willow gets hurt."

We smiled politely at each other. "Should we . . . wait a little longer for your husband?"

"Well," she said, coloring. "He's not going to be joining us."

To be honest, when Charlotte had called me to set up a meeting and talk about representation, I'd been surprised. Sean O'Keefe had made his feelings pretty damn clear when he'd stormed out of Bob's office. Her phone call indicated that he'd calmed down enough to pursue litigation, but now — looking at Charlotte — I was starting to get a sinking feeling. "But he *does* want to file a lawsuit, right?"

She shifted on her chair. "I don't understand why I can't do this on my own."

"Besides the obvious answer — that your husband's bound to find out sooner or later — there's a legal reason. You and your husband are both responsible for the care and raising of Willow. Let's say you hire a lawyer by yourself and settle with the doctor, and then you get hit by a car and die. Your husband can go back and sue the doctor on his own, because he wasn't a party to your settlement and didn't release the doctor from future liability. Because of this, any defendant is going to insist that any settlement that's reached or judgment in a trial include both of the parents. Which means that, even if Sergeant O'Keefe doesn't want to be part of this lawsuit, he's going to be impleaded — that is, brought into the lawsuit — so that it won't be litigated again in the future."

Charlotte frowned. "I understand."

"Is that going to be a problem?"

"No," she said. "No, it's not. But . . . we don't have money to hire a lawyer. We're barely scraping by as it is, with everything Willow needs. That's why . . . that's why I'm here today to talk about the lawsuit."

Every plaintiff mill firm — Bob Ramirez included — began a case with a cost-benefit analysis. It's what had taken us so long to contact the O'Keefes between meetings: I would review a claim with experts, I would do due diligence to ascertain other suits like this and what the payouts had been. Once I knew that the estimated settlement would at least cover the costs of our time and the experts' fees, I'd call the prospective clients and tell them they had a valid complaint. "You don't have to worry about attorney's fees," I now said smoothly. "That would become part of the settlement. However, realistically, you do need to know that most wrongful birth suits settle out of court for less money than a jury would award, because malpractice insurance companies don't want the press. Of the cases that do go to court, seventy-five percent find in favor of the defendant. Your particular case, which hinges on a misread sonogram, might not sway the jury — sonograms don't make the most convincing evidence at a trial. And there will be considerable public scrutiny. There always is, when someone brings a wrongful birth suit."

She looked up at me. "You mean people will think I'm in it for the money."

"Well," I said simply. "Aren't you?"

Charlotte's eyes welled with tears. "I'm in it for Willow. I'm the one who brought her into this world, so it's up to me to make sure that she suffers as little as possible. That doesn't make me a monster." She pressed her fingers to the corners of her eyes. "Or does it?"

I gritted my teeth and passed her a box of Kleenex. Well, wasn't that the $64,000 question?

It was probable that, by the time this lawsuit got to court, you would be old enough to fully understand the ramifications of what your mother was doing — just like I had, one day, when I was told about my adoption. I knew what it was like to feel as if your own mom didn't want you. In fact, I'd spent my whole childhood inventing excuses for her. Daydream 1: She was desperately in love with a boy who'd gotten her pregnant, and her family couldn't bear the stain of shame, so they sent her to Switzerland and told everyone she was at boarding school when, instead, she was having me. Daydream 2: She was headed off to the Peace Corps to save the world when she found herself pregnant — and realized she had to put the needs of others above her own desire for a baby. Daydream 3: She was an actress, America's sweetheart, who would lose her family-values midwest audience if they learned that she was a single mom. Daydream 4: She and my father were poor, struggling dairy farmers who wanted their baby to have a better life than they could offer.

I figured there was one seminal moment when a woman realized what it meant to be a mother. For my birth mom, maybe it was when she passed me to a nurse and said goodbye. For the mother who'd raised me, it was when she sat me down at the kitchen table and told me that I had been adopted. For your mother, it was making the decision to file this lawsuit in spite of the public and private backlash. Being a good mother, it seemed to me, meant you ran the risk of losing your child.

"I wanted another baby so much," Charlotte said quietly. "I wanted to experience that, with Sean. I wanted us to take her to the park and push her on the swings. I wanted to bake cookies with her and go to her school plays. I wanted to teach her how to ride a horse and water-ski. I wanted her to take care of me when I got old," she said, looking up at me. "Not the other way around."

I felt the hair stand up on the back of my neck. I didn't want to believe that a person who had brought a baby into this world would quit so easily when the going got tough. "I think most parents know there's going to be some bad to go with the good," I said evenly.

"I wasn't naïve — I already had a daughter. I knew I'd take care of Willow when she was hurt. I knew I'd have to get up in the middle of the night when she had nightmares. But I didn't know she was going to be hurt for weeks at a time, for years at a time. I didn't know I'd be up with her every night. I didn't know that she would never get better."

I looked down, pretending to straighten some papers. What if the reason my mother had given me away was that I didn't measure up to what she had hoped for? "What about Willow?" I said, bluntly playing devil's advocate. "She's a smart kid. How do you think she'll handle her mother saying she should never have been born?"

Charlotte flinched. "She knows that's not the truth," she said. "I could never imagine my life without her in it."

A red flag went up in my mind. "Stop right there. Don't say that. You can't even *hint* at it. If you file this lawsuit, Mrs O'Keefe, you have to be able to swear — under oath — that if you'd known about your daughter's illness earlier, if you'd been given the choice, you would have terminated the pregnancy." I waited until her gaze met mine. "Is that going to be a problem?"

Her eyes slid away, focusing on something outside my window. "Can you miss a person you've never known?"

There was a knock at the door, and the receptionist popped her head in. "Sorry to interrupt, Marin," Briony said, "but your eleven o'clock is here."

"Eleven?" Charlotte said, jumping to her feet. "I'm late. Willow's going to panic." She grabbed her purse, slung it over her shoulder, and hurried out of my office.

"I'll be in touch," I called after her.

It wasn't until that afternoon, when I began to think about what Charlotte O'Keefe had said to me, that I realized she'd answered my question about abortion with another question.

Sean

At ten o'clock on Saturday night, it became clear to me that I was going to hell.

Saturday nights were the ones that made you remember every sleepy picture-postcard New England town had a split personality, that the healthy, smiling guys you saw featured in *Yankee* magazine might pass out drunk at the local bar. On Saturday nights, lonely kids tried to hang themselves from the closet racks in their dorm rooms and high school girls got raped by college boys.

Saturday nights were also when you'd catch someone bobbing and weaving so bad in a car that it was only a matter of time before the drunk rammed into someone else. Tonight I was pulled over behind a bank parking lot when a white Camry crawled by, practically on the dotted yellow line. I flicked on my blues and followed the driver, waiting for the car to pull onto the shoulder.

I stepped out and approached the driver's window. "Good evening," I said, "do you know why —" But before I could finish asking the driver to tell me why he thought I'd pulled him over, the window rolled down and I found myself staring at our priest.

"Oh, Sean, it's you," Father Grady said. He had a shock of white hair that Amelia called his Einstein-do, and he was wearing his clerical collar. His eyes were glassy and bright.

I hesitated. "Father, I'm going to have to see your license and registration . . ."

"Not a problem," the priest said, digging in his glove compartment. "You're just doing your job." I watched him fumble, dropping his license three times before he managed to hand it to me. I glanced inside the car but didn't see any bottles or cans.

"Father, you were all over the road there."

"Was I?"

I could smell alcohol on his breath. "You have any drinks tonight, Father?"

"Can't say that I have . . ."

Priests couldn't lie, could they? "You mind stepping out of the car for me?"

"Sure, Sean." He stumbled out of the door and leaned against the hood of his Camry, his hands in his pockets. "Haven't seen your family at Mass lately . . ."

"Father, do you wear contact lenses?"

"No . . ."

This was the beginning of the test for horizontal gaze nystagmus, an involuntary jerking of the eyeball that could suggest drunkenness. "I'm just going to ask you to follow this light," I said, taking a penlight out of my pocket and holding it several inches away from his face, a bit above eye level. "Follow it only with your eyes — keep your head still," I added. "Understand?"

131

Father Grady nodded. I checked his equal pupil size and tracking as he followed the beam, marking down a lack of smooth pursuit, and an end-point nystagmus as I moved the beam toward his left ear.

"Thanks, Father. Now, can you stand on your right foot for me, like this?" I demonstrated, and he lifted his left foot. He wobbled but stayed upright. "Now the left," I said, and this time, he pitched forward.

"Okay, Father, one last thing — can you walk for me, heel to toe?" I showed him how and then watched him trip over his own feet.

Bankton was so tiny we didn't ride with partners. I could have probably let Father Grady go; no one would have been the wiser, and maybe he'd even put a good word in to heaven for me. But letting him go also meant I would be lying to myself — and surely that was just as grievous a sin. Who might be driving on the roads that led to his house . . . a teenager, coming home from a date? A dad flying back from a business trip out of town? A mom with a sick kid, headed to the hospital? It wasn't Father Grady I was trying to rescue, it was the people he might hurt in his condition.

"I hate to do this, Father, but I'm going to have to arrest you for driving under the influence." I Mirandized him and gently led the priest into the back of the cruiser.

"What about my car?"

"It'll be towed. You can get it tomorrow," I said.

"But tomorrow's *Sunday!*"

We were only about a half mile from the station, which was a blessing, because I didn't think I could stand to make small talk with my priest after I'd arrested him. At the station, I went through the rigmarole of implied consent and told Father Grady I wanted him to take a Breathalyzer test. "You have the right to have a similar test or tests done by a person of your choosing," I said. "You'll be given the opportunity to request this additional test, if you want. If you do not permit a test at the direction of the law enforcement officer, you may lose your license for a period of one hundred and eighty days, not concurrent with any loss of license if found guilty of the charge of DUI."

"No, Seanie, I trust you," Father Grady said.

It didn't surprise me when he blew a .15.

Since my shift was ending, I offered to take him back home. The road snaked in front of me as I passed the church and drove up a hill to the little white house that served as the rectory. I parked in the driveway and helped him walk a relatively straight line to the door. "I was at a wake tonight," he said, turning his key in the lock.

"Father," I sighed. "You don't have to explain."

"It was a boy — only twenty-six. Motorcycle accident last Tuesday, you probably know all about it. I knew I'd be driving home. But there was the mother, sobbing her heart out, and the brothers, completely shattered — and I wanted to leave them with a tribute, instead of with all that loss."

I didn't want to listen. I didn't need to borrow anyone else's problems. But I found myself nodding at the priest all the same.

"So it was a few toasts, a few shots of whiskey," Father Grady said. "Don't you lose sleep over this, Sean. I know perfectly well that doing the right thing for someone else occasionally means doing something that feels wrong to you."

The door swung open in front of us. I'd never been inside the rectory before — it was homey and small, with framed psalms hanging on the walls for decoration, a crystal bowl of M&M's on the kitchen table, and a Patriots banner behind the couch. "I'm just going to lie down," Father Grady murmured, and he stretched out on the couch.

I took off his shoes and covered him with a blanket I found in a closet. "Good night, Father."

His eyes opened a crack. "See you tomorrow at Mass?"

"You bet," I said, but Father Grady had already started to snore.

When I had told Charlotte that I wanted to go to church the next morning, she asked if I was feeling all right. Usually, she had to drag me to Mass, but part of me had wanted to know if Father Grady was going to do a sermon about our encounter last night. *Sins of the fathers, that's what he could call it*, I thought now, and I snickered. Beside me, in the pew, Charlotte pinched me. "Sssh," she mouthed.

One of the reasons I didn't like going to church was the stares. *Piety* and *pity* were a little too close to each other for my tastes. I'd listen to a blue-haired old lady tell me she was praying for you, and I'd smile and say thanks, but inside, I was ticked off. Who'd asked her to pray for you? Didn't she realize I did enough of that on my own?

Charlotte said that an offer to help was not a comment on someone else's weakness, and that a police officer ought to know that. But hell, if you wanted to know what I was really thinking when I asked a lost out-of-towner if he needed directions or gave a battered wife my card and told her to call me if she needed assistance, it was this: pull yourself up by your bootstraps and figure a way out of the mess you've gotten yourself into. There was a big difference, the way I saw it, between a nightmare you woke up in unexpectedly and a nightmare of your own making.

Father Grady winced as the organist started a particularly rousing version of a hymn, and I tucked away my grin. Instead of leaving the poor guy a glass of water last night, I should have mixed him up a hangover remedy.

Behind us, a baby started to wail. As mean-spirited as it was of me, it felt good to have everyone focused on a family other than ours. I heard the furious whispers of the parents deciding who would be the one to take the baby out of the church.

Amelia was sitting on my other side. She elbowed me and mimed for a pen. I reached into my pocket and handed her a ballpoint. Turning over her palm, she drew five tiny dashes and a hangman's noose. I smiled and traced the letter *A* on her thigh.

She wrote: –A–A–

M, I wrote with my finger.

Amelia shook her head.

T?

–ATA–

I tried L, P, and R, but no luck. S?

Amelia beamed and scribbled it into the puzzle: SATA–

I laughed out loud, and Charlotte looked down at us, her eyes flashing a warning. Amelia took the pen and filled in the N, then held up her hand so I could see. Just then, loud and clear, you said, "What's Satan?" and your mother turned bright red, hauled you into her arms, and hurried outside.

A moment later, Amelia and I followed. Charlotte was sitting with you on the steps of the church, holding the baby who'd been screaming during the whole Mass. "What are you doing out here?" she asked.

"Thought we'd be safer when the lightning struck." I smiled down at the baby, who was stuffing grass into his mouth. "Did we pick up an extra along the way?"

"His mother's in the bathroom," Charlotte said. "Amelia, watch your sister and the baby."

"Do I get paid for it?"

"I cannot believe you'd have the nerve to ask me that after what you just did during Mass." Charlotte stood up. "Let's take a walk."

I fell into step beside her. Charlotte had always smelled of sugar cookies — later I learned that it was vanilla, which she would rub on her wrists and behind her ears, perfume for a pastry chef. It was part of why I loved her. Here's a news flash for the ladies: for every one of you who thinks we all want a girl like Angelina

136

Jolie, all skinny elbows and angles, the truth is, we'd rather curl up with someone like Charlotte — a woman who's soft when a guy wraps his arms around her; a woman who might have a smear of flour on her shirt the whole day and not notice or care, not even when she goes out to meet with the PTA; a woman who doesn't feel like an exotic vacation but is the home we can't wait to come back to. "You know what?" I said genially, wrapping an arm around her. "Life is great. It's a gorgeous day, I'm with my family, I'm not sitting in that cave of a church . . ."

"And I'm sure Father Grady enjoyed hearing Willow's little outburst, too."

"Believe me, Father Grady's got bigger problems on his plate," I said.

We had crossed the parking lot, heading toward a field overrun with clover. "Sean," Charlotte said, "I've got a confession to make."

"Maybe you ought to take that inside, then."

"I went back to the lawyer."

I stopped walking. "You *what?*"

"I met with Marin Gates, about filing a wrongful birth lawsuit."

"Jesus Christ, Charlotte —"

"Sean!" She threw a glance toward the church.

"How could you do that? Just go behind my back like my opinion doesn't matter?"

She folded her arms. "What about *my* opinion? Doesn't that matter to *you?*"

"Of course it does — but some bloodsucking lawyer's opinion, I don't give a shit about. Don't you see what they're doing? They want money, pure and simple. They don't give a damn about you or me or Willow; they don't care who's screwed during the process. We're just a means to an end." I took a step closer to her. "So Willow's got some problems — who doesn't? There's kids with ADHD and kids who sneak out at night to smoke and drink and kids who get beat up at school for liking math — you don't see those parents trying to blame someone else so they can get cash."

"How come you were perfectly willing to sue Disney World and half of the public service system in Florida for cash? What's different here?"

I jerked my chin up. "They played us for fools."

"What if the doctors did, too?" Charlotte argued. "What if Piper made a mistake?"

"Then she made a mistake!" I shrugged. "Would it have changed the outcome? If you'd known about all the breaks, all the trips to the ER, all we'd have to do for Willow, would you have wanted her any less?"

She opened her mouth, and then resolutely clamped it shut.

That scared the hell out of me.

"So what if she winds up in a lot of casts?" I said, reaching for Charlotte's hand. "She also knows the name of every bone in the freaking body and she hates the color yellow and she told me last night she wants to be a beekeeper when she grows up. She's our little girl, Charlotte. We don't need help. We've handled this for five years; we'll keep handling it ourselves."

138

Charlotte drew away from me. "Where's the *we*, Sean? You go off to work. You go out with the guys for poker night. You make it sound like you're with Willow twenty-four/seven, but you have no idea what that's like."

"Then we'll get a visiting nurse. An aide . . ."

"And we'll pay her with what?" Charlotte snapped. "Come to think of it, how are we going to afford a new car big enough to carry Willow's chair and walker and crutches, since ours is going on two hundred thousand miles? How are we going to pay off her surgeries, the parts insurance won't cover? How are we going to make sure her house has a handicapped ramp and a kitchen sink low enough for a wheelchair?"

"Are you saying I can't provide for my own kid?" I said, my voice escalating.

Suddenly, all the bluster went out of Charlotte. "Oh, Sean. You're the best father. But . . . you're not a mother."

There was a shriek, and — instinct kicking in — both Charlotte and I sprinted across the parking lot, expecting to find Willow twisted on the pavement with a bone breaking through her skin. Instead, Amelia was holding the crying baby at arm's length, a stain streaking the front of her shirt. "It barfed on me!" she wailed.

The baby's mother came hurrying out of the church. "I'm so sorry," she said, to us, to Amelia, as Willow sat on the ground, laughing at her sister's bad luck. "I think he might be coming down with something . . ."

Charlotte stepped forward and took the baby from Amelia. "Maybe a virus," she said. "Don't worry. These things happen."

She stood back as the woman gave a wad of Baby Wipes to Amelia to clean herself off. "This conversation is over," I murmured to Charlotte. "Period."

Charlotte bounced the baby in her arms. "Sure, Sean," she said, too easily. "Whatever you say."

By six o'clock that night, Charlotte had caught whatever the baby had, and was sick as a dog. Vomiting like crazy, she'd sequestered herself in the bathroom. I was supposed to work the night shift, but it was blatantly clear that wasn't going to happen. "Amelia needs help with her science homework," Charlotte murmured, patting her face with a damp towel. "And the girls need dinner . . ."

"I'll take care of it," I said. "What else do you need?"

"To die?" Charlotte moaned, and she shoved me out of the way to kneel in front of the toilet again.

I backed out of the bathroom, closing the door behind me. Downstairs, you were sitting on the living room couch eating a banana. "You're gonna spoil your appetite," I said.

"I'm not eating it, Daddy. I'm fixing it."

"Fixing it," I repeated. On the table in front of you was a knife, which you weren't supposed to have — I made a mental note to yell at Amelia for getting you one. There was a slice down the center of the banana.

You popped open the lid of a mending kit we'd taken from the hotel room in Florida, pulled out a

140

prethreaded needle, and started to sew up the wound in the banana skin.

"Willow," I said. "What are you doing?"

You blinked up at me. "Surgery."

I watched you for a few stitches, to make sure you didn't poke yourself with the needle, and then shrugged. Far be it from me to stand in the way of science.

In the kitchen, Amelia was sprawled across the table with markers, glue, and a piece of poster board. "You want to tell me why Willow's out there with a paring knife?" I said.

"Because she asked for one."

"If she asked for a chain saw, would you have gotten it out of the garage?"

"Well, that would kind of be overkill for cutting up a banana, don't you think?" Looking down at her project, Amelia sighed. "This totally sucks. I have to make a board game about the digestive system, and everyone's going to make fun of me because we all know where the digestive system *ends*."

"Funny you should use that word," I said.

"G-R-O-double-S, Dad."

I started pulling pots and pans out from beneath the counter and set out a frying pan. "What do you say to pancakes for dinner?" Not that they had a choice; it was the only thing I knew how to cook, except for peanut butter and jelly sandwiches.

"Mom made pancakes for breakfast," Amelia complained.

141

"Did you know that dissolvable stitches are made out of animal guts?" you called out.

"No, and now I kind of wish I didn't . . ."

Amelia rubbed a glue stick over her poster board. "Is Mom better yet?"

"No, baby."

"But she promised me she'd help draw the esophagus."

"I can help," I said.

"You can't draw, Dad. When we play Pictionary you always make a house, even when that has nothing to do with the answer."

"Well, how hard can an esophagus be? It's a tube, right?" I rummaged for a box of Bisquick.

There was a thump; the knife had rolled under the couch. You were twisting uncomfortably. "Hang on, Wills, I can get that for you," I called.

"I don't need it anymore," you said, but you hadn't stopped squirming.

Amelia sighed. "Willow, stop being such a baby before you pee in your pants."

I looked from your sister to you. "Do you have to go to the bathroom?"

"She's making that face she makes when she's trying to hold it in —"

"Amelia, enough." I walked into the living room and crouched down beside you. "Honey, you don't have to be embarrassed."

You flattened your lips together. "I want Mom to take me."

"Mom's not here," Amelia snapped.

I hoisted you off the couch to carry you into the downstairs bathroom. I'd just wrangled your awkwardly cast legs into the doorframe when you said, "You forgot the garbage bags."

Charlotte had told me how she'd line them inside your cast before you went to the bathroom. In all the time you'd been in your spica, I hadn't been pressed into duty for this — you were wildly self-conscious about having me pull down your pants. I reached around the doorframe to the dryer, where Charlotte had stashed a box of kitchen trash bags. "Okay," I said. "I'm a novice, so you have to tell me what to do."

"You have to swear you won't peek," you said.

"Cross my heart."

You untied the knot that was holding up the gigantic boxer shorts we'd pulled over your spica, and I lifted you up so that they would pool at your hips. As I pulled them off, you squealed. "Look up here!"

"Right." I resolutely fixed my eyes on yours, trying to maneuver the shorts off you without seeing what I was doing. Then I held up the garbage bag, which would have to be tucked in along the crotch line. "You want to do this part?" I asked, blushing.

I held you under the armpits while you struggled to line the cast with the plastic. "Ready," you said, and I positioned you over the toilet.

"No, back more," you said, and I adjusted you and waited.

And waited.

"Willow," I said, "go ahead and pee."

"I can't. You're listening."

143

"I'm not listening —"

"Yes you are."

"Your mother listens . . ."

"That's different," you said, and you burst into tears.

Once the floodgates opened, they opened universally. I glanced down at the bowl of the toilet, only to hear you cry louder. "You said you wouldn't peek!"

I snapped my eyes north, juggled you into my left arm, and reached for the toilet paper with the right.

"Dad!" Amelia yelled. "I think something's burning . . ."

"Oh shit," I muttered, giving only a passing thought to the swear jar. I stuffed a wad of paper into your hand. "Hurry up, Willow," I said, and then I flushed the toilet.

"I h-have to w-wash my hands," you hiccuped.

"Later," I bit out, and I carried you back to the couch, tossing your shorts into your lap before racing to the kitchen.

Amelia stood in front of the stove, where the pancakes were charring. "I turned off the burner," she said, coughing through the smoke.

"Thanks." She nodded and reached around me onto the counter for . . . Were those what I thought they were? Sure enough, Amelia sat down and picked up the hot glue gun. She'd affixed about thirty of my good clay poker chips around the edge of her poster board.

"Amelia!" I yelled. "Those are my poker chips!"

"You have a whole bunch. I just needed a few . . ."

"Did I *tell* you you could use them?"

"You didn't tell me I *couldn't*," Amelia said.

"Daddy," you called out from the living room, "my hands!"

"Okay," I said under my breath. "Okay." I counted to ten, and then carried the pan to the trash to scrape out its contents. The metal lip grazed my wrist and I dropped the pan. "Sonofabitch," I cried, and I switched on the cold-water faucet, thrusting my arm beneath it.

"I want to wash *my* hands," you wailed.

Amelia folded her arms. "You owe Willow a quarter," she said.

By nine o'clock, you girls were asleep and the pots had been washed and the dishwasher was humming in the kitchen. I went around the house, turning out the lights, then crept into the dark bedroom. Charlotte was lying down with one arm thrown over her head. "You don't have to tiptoe," she said. "I'm awake."

I sank down beside her. "You feeling any better?"

"I'm down a dress size. How are the girls?"

"Fine. Although I'm sorry to say Willow's patient didn't survive."

"Huh?"

"Nothing." I rolled onto my back. "We had peanut butter and jelly for dinner."

She patted my arm absently. "You know what I love about you?"

"Hmm?"

"You make me look *so* good by comparison . . ."

I propped my arms behind my head and stared up at the ceiling. "You don't bake anymore."

"Yeah, but I don't burn the pancakes," Charlotte said, smiling a little. "Amelia ratted you out when she came in to say good night."

"I'm serious. Remember how you used to make crème brûlée and petit fours and chocolate éclairs?"

"I guess other things became more important," Charlotte answered.

"You used to say you'd have your own bakery one day. You wanted to call it Syllable —"

"Syllabub," she corrected.

I may not have remembered the name right, but I knew what it meant, because I'd asked you: syllabub was the oldest English dessert, made when dairymaids would shoot warm milk straight from the cow into a pail that held cider or sherry. It was like eggnog, you told me, and you promised me you'd make me some to try, and the night you did you dipped a finger in the sweet cream and traced a trail down my chest that you kissed clean.

"That's what happens to dreams," Charlotte said. "Life gets in the way."

I sat up, picking at a stitch on the quilt. "I wanted a house, a backyard, a bunch of kids. A vacation every now and then. A good job. I wanted to coach softball and take my girls skiing and not know every fucking doctor in the Portsmouth Regional Hospital emergency room by name." I turned to her. "I may not be with her all the time, but when she breaks, Charlotte, I feel it. I swear I do. I'd do anything for her."

She faced me. "*Would* you?"

146

I could feel its weight on the mattress: the lawsuit, the elephant in the room. "It feels . . . ugly. It feels like we're saying we didn't love her, because she's . . . the way she is."

"It's *because* we want her, *because* we love her, that I'd ever think about this in the first place," Charlotte said. "I'm not stupid, Sean. I know people are going to talk, and say I'm after a big settlement. I know they're going to think I'm the worst mother in the world, the most selfish, you fill in the blank. But I don't care what they say about me — I care about Willow. I want to know that she'll be able to go to college and live on her own and do everything she dreams of. Even if that means that the whole world thinks I'm horrible. Does it really matter what everyone else says if *I* know why I'm doing it?" She faced me. "I'm going to lose my best friend because of this," she said. "I don't want to lose you, too."

In her previous life as a pastry chef, I'd always been amazed to watch tiny Charlotte hauling fifty-pound bags of flour around. There was strength in her that went far beyond my own size and force. I saw the world in black and white; it was why I was a career cop. But what if this lawsuit and its uncomfortable name *was* only a means to an end? Could something that looked so wrong on the outside turn out to be undeniably right?

My hand crept across the quilt to cover hers. "You won't," I said.

Charlotte

Late May 2007

Your first seven breaks happened before you entered this world. The next four happened minutes after you were born, as a nurse lifted you out of me. Another nine, when you were being resuscitated in the hospital, after you coded. The tenth: when you were lying across my lap and suddenly I heard a pop. Eleven was when you rolled over and your arm hit the edge of the crib. Twelve and thirteen were femur fractures; fourteen a tibia; fifteen a compression fracture of the spine. Sixteen was jumping down from a stoop; seventeen was a kid crashing into you on a playground; eighteen was when you slipped on a DVD jacket lying on the carpet. We still don't know what caused number nineteen. Twenty was when Amelia was jumping on a bed where you were sitting; twenty-one was a soccer ball that hit your left leg too hard; twenty-two was when I discovered waterproof casting materials and bought enough to supply an entire hospital, now stocked in my garage. Twenty-three happened in your sleep; twenty-four and twenty-five were a fall forward in the snow

148

that snapped both forearms at once. Twenty-six and twenty-seven were nasty fractures, fibula and tibia tenting through the skin at a nursery school Halloween party, where, ironically, you were wearing a mummy's costume whose bandages I used to splint the breaks. Twenty-eight happened during a sneeze; twenty-nine and thirty were ribs you broke on the edge of the kitchen table. Thirty-one was a hip fracture that required a metal plate and six screws. I stopped keeping track after that, until the ones from Disney World, which we had not numbered but instead named Mickey, Donald, and Goofy.

Four months after you were put in the spica cast, it was bivalved. This meant that it was cut in half and secured with low-budget clips that broke within hours, so I replaced them with bright strips of Velcro. Gradually, we'd remove the top, so that you could practice sitting up like a clam on the half shell, and you could strengthen the stomach and calf muscles that had deteriorated. According to Dr Rosenblad, you'd have a couple of weeks in the bottom of the shell; then you'd graduate to just sleeping in it. Eight weeks later you'd stand with a walker; four weeks after that, you'd be moving to the bathroom on your own.

The best part, though, was that you could go back to pre-school. It was a private school, held for two hours each morning in the basement of a church. You were a year older than other kids in the class, but you'd missed so much school because of breaks that we'd decided to repeat the year — you could read at a sixth-grade level, but you needed to be around other kids your age for socialization. You didn't have many friends — children were either frightened by your wheelchair and walker or, oddly, jealous of the casts that you'd come to school wearing. Now, driving to the church, I glanced into the rearview mirror. "So what are you going to do first?"

"The rice table." Miss Katie, whom you ranked somewhere just shy of Jesus on the adoration scale, had set up an enormous sandbox full of colored rice grains, which kids could pour into different size containers. You loved the noise it made; you told me it sounded like rain. "And the parachute."

This was a game where one child ran under a brightly colored round of silk while the rest held on to its edges. "You're going to have to wait a while for that, Wills," I said, and I pulled into the parking lot. "One day at a time."

I unloaded your wheelchair from the back of the van and settled you into it, then pushed you up the ramp that the school had added this past summer, after you'd enrolled. Inside, other students were hanging their coats in their cubbies; moms were rolling up dried finger paintings that were hanging on a clothes rack. "You're back!" one woman said, smiling down at you. Then she looked up at me. "Kelsey had her birthday party last weekend — she saved a goody bag for Willow. We would have invited her, but, well, it was at the Gymnastics Hut, and I figured she might feel left out."

As opposed to not being invited? I thought. But instead, I smiled. "That was very thoughtful."

150

A little boy touched the edges of your spica cast. "Wow," he breathed. "How do you pee in that thing?"

"I don't," you said, without cracking a smile. "I haven't gone in four months, Derek, so you'd better watch out 'cause I could blow like a volcano any minute."

"Willow," I murmured, "no need to be snarky."

"*He* started it . . ."

Miss Katie came into the hallway as she heard the commotion of our arrival. She did the slightest double take when she saw you in the bivalved cast but quickly recovered. "Willow!" she said, getting down on her knees to your level. "It is so nice to see you!" She summoned her assistant, Miss Sylvia. "Sylvia, can you keep an eye on Willow while her mom and I have a talk?"

I followed her down the hallway past the bathrooms with their impossibly squat toilets to the area that doubled as music room and gymnasium. "Charlotte," Kate said, "I must have misunderstood. When you called to tell me Willow was coming, I thought she was out of that body cast!"

"Well, she will be. It's a gradual thing." I smiled at her. "She's really excited to be back here."

"I think you're rushing things —"

"It's fine, really. She needs the activity. Even if she breaks again, a break after a few weeks of really great play is better for her body than just sitting around at home. And you don't have to worry about the other kids hurting her, beyond the usual. We wrestle with her. We tickle her."

"Yes, but you do all that at *home*," the teacher pointed out. "In a school environment . . . Well, it's riskier."

I stepped back, reading her loud and clear: *we're liable when she's on our grounds*. In spite of the Americans with Disabilities Act, I routinely read on online OI forums of private schools who kindly suggested that a healing child be kept at home, ostensibly for the child's best interests but more likely because of their own rising insurance premiums. It created a catch-22: legally, you had clear grounds to sue for discrimination, but once you did, you could bet that, even if you won your case, your child would be treated differently when she returned.

"Riskier for *whom*?" I said, my face growing hot. "I paid tuition to have my daughter here. Kate, you know damn well you can't tell me she's not welcome."

"I'm happy to refund you tuition for the months she's missed. And I would never tell you that Willow's not welcome — we love her, and we've missed her. We just want to make sure she's safe." She shook her head. "Look at it from our point of view. Next year, when Willow's in kindergarten, she'll have a full-time aide. We don't have that resource here."

"Then *I'll* be her aide. I'll stay with her. Just let her" — my voice snapped like a twig — "let her feel like she's normal."

Kate looked up at me. "Do you think being the only child with a parent in the classroom is going to make her feel that way?"

Speechless — *fuming* — I strode down the hall to where Miss Sylvia was still waiting with you, watching you show off the cast's Velcro straps. "We have to go," I said, blinking back tears.

"But I want to play at the rice table . . ."

"You know what?" Kate said. "Miss Sylvia will get you your own bag to take home! Thanks for coming to say hello to all your friends, Willow."

Confused, you turned to me. "Mommy? Why can't I stay?"

"We'll talk about it later."

Miss Sylvia returned with a Ziploc full of purple rice grains. "Here you go, pumpkin."

"Tell me this," I said, eyeing each of the teachers in turn. "What good is a life if she doesn't get to live it?"

I pushed you out of the school, still so angry that it took me a moment to realize you were deathly silent. When we reached the van, you had tears in your eyes. "It's okay, Mom," you said, with a resignation in your voice that no five-year-old ought to have. "I didn't want to stay anyway."

That was a lie; I knew how much you had been looking forward to seeing your friends.

"You know how, when there's a rock in the water, the water just moves around the sides if it's not there?" you said. "That's kind of how the other kids acted when you were talking to Miss Katie."

How could those teachers — or those other kids — not see how easily you bruised? I kissed you on the forehead. "You and I," I promised, "are going to have so much fun this afternoon, you aren't going to know what hit you." I leaned down to hoist you out of your wheelchair, but one of the Velcro straps on the cast popped open. "Shoot," I muttered, and as I jostled you to one hip to fix it, you dropped your Ziploc bag.

"My rice!" you said, and you instinctively twisted in my arms to reach it, which is exactly the moment I heard the snap: like a branch breaking, like the first bite of an autumn apple.

"Willow?" I said, but I already knew: the whites of your eyes had flashed, blue as lightning, and you were slipping away from me into the sleepy trance that would overcome you when it was a particularly bad fracture.

By the time I settled you in the back of the van, your eyes were nearly closed. "Baby, tell me where it hurts," I begged, but you didn't answer. Starting at the wrist, I gently felt up your arm, trying to find the tender spot. I had just hit a divot beneath your shoulder when you whimpered. But you had broken bones in the arm before, and this one wasn't stuck through the skin or twisted at a ninety-degree angle or any of the other hallmarks I associated with the kind of severe break that made you slip into a stupor. Had the bone pierced an organ?

I could have gone back into the school and asked them to call 911, but there was nothing an EMT could do for you that I didn't know how to do myself. So I rummaged in the back of the van and found an old *People* magazine. Using it as an immobilizer, I wrapped an Ace bandage around your upper arm. I winged a prayer that you wouldn't have to be casted — casts made bone density drop, and each place a cast ended was a new weak point for a future break. You could get away with a Wee Walker boot or an Aircast or a splint most of the time — except for hip fractures, and vertebrae, and femurs. Those breaks were the ones that made you go still and quiet, like now. Those breaks were the ones that had me driving straight to the ER, because I was too scared to handle them on my own.

At the hospital, I pulled into a handicapped spot and carried you into triage. "My daughter has osteogenesis imperfecta," I told the nurse. "She's broken her arm."

The woman pursed her lips. "How about you do the diagnosis *after* you get a medical degree?"

"Trudy, is there a problem?" A doctor who looked too young to even be shaving was suddenly standing in front of us, peering down at you. "Did I hear you say OI?"

"Yes," I said. "I think it's her humerus."

"I'll take care of this one," the doctor said. "I'm Dr Dewitt. Do you want to put her in a wheelchair —"

"We're good," I said, and I hoisted you higher in my arms. As he led us down the hall to Radiology, I gave him your medical history. He stopped me only once — to sweet-talk the technician into giving up a room quickly. "Okay," the doctor said, leaning over you on the X-ray table, his hand on your forearm. "I'm just going to move this the tiniest bit . . ."

"No," I said, stepping forward. "You can move the machine, can't you?"

"Well," Dr Dewitt said, nonplussed. "We don't usually."

"But you *can?*"

He looked at me again and then made adjustments to the equipment, draping the heavy lead vest over your chest. I moved to the rear of the room so the film could be taken. "Good job, Willow. Now just one more of your lower arm," the doctor said.

"No," I said.

The doctor looked up, exasperated. "With all due respect, Mrs O'Keefe, I really need to do my job."

But I was doing mine, too. When you broke, I tried to limit the number of X-rays that were done; sometimes I had them skipped altogether if they weren't going to change the outcome of the treatment. "We already know she's got a break," I reasoned. "Do you think it's displaced?"

The doctor's eyes widened as I spoke his own language to him. "No."

"Then you don't really have to X-ray the tibia and fibula, do you?"

"Well," Dr Dewitt admitted. "That depends."

"Do you have any idea how many X-rays my daughter will have to get in the course of her lifetime?" I asked.

He folded his arms. "You win. We really *don't* need to X-ray the lower arm."

While we waited for the film to develop, I rubbed your back. Slowly, you were returning from wherever it was that you went when you had a break. You were fidgeting more, whimpering. Shivering, which only made you hurt more.

I stuck my head out of the room to ask a technician if she had a blanket I might wrap around you and found Dr Dewitt approaching with your X-rays. "Willow's cold," I said, and he whipped off his white coat and settled it over your shoulders as soon as he stepped into the room. "The good news," he said, "is that Willow's other break is healing nicely."

What other break?

I didn't realize I'd said it aloud until the doctor pointed to a spot on your upper arm. It was hard to see — the collagen defect left your bones milky — but sure enough, there was the ridge of callus that suggested a healing fracture.

I felt a stab of guilt. When had you hurt yourself, and how could I not have known?

"Looks like it's about two weeks old," Dr Dewitt mused, and just like that, I remembered: one night, when I carried you to the bathroom in the middle of the night, I had nearly dropped you. Although you'd insisted you were fine, you had only been lying for my sake.

"I am amazed to report, Willow, that you've broken one of the bones that's hardest to break in the human body — your shoulder blade." He pointed to the second image on the light board, to a crack clear down the middle of the scapula. "It moves around so much, it's hardly ever fractured on impact."

"So what do we do?" I asked.

"Well, she's already in a spica cast . . . Short of mummification, the best thing is probably going to be a sling. It's going to hurt for a few days — but the alternative seems like cruel and unusual punishment."

He bandaged your arm up against your chest, like the broken wing of a bird. "That too tight?"

You looked up at him. "I broke my clavicle once. It hurt more. Did you know that clavicle means 'little key' — not just because it looks like one but because it connects all the other bones in the chest?"

Dr Dewitt's jaw dropped. "Are you some kind of Doogie Howser prodigy?"

"She reads a lot," I said, smiling.

"Scapula, sternum, and xiphoid," you added. "I can spell them, too."

"Damn," the doctor said softly, and then he blushed. "I mean, *darn*." His gaze met mine over your head. "She's the first OI patient I've had. It must be pretty wild."

"Yes," I said. "Wild."

"Well, Willow, if you want to come work here as an ortho resident, there's a white coat with your name on it." He nodded at me. "And if *you* ever need someone to talk to . . ." He took a business card out of his breast pocket.

I tucked it into my back pocket, embarrassed. This probably wasn't goodwill as much as it was preservation for Willow — the doctor had evidence of my own incompetence, two breaks up there in black and white. I pretended to be busy rummaging for something in my purse, but really, I was just waiting for him to leave. I heard him offer you a lollipop, say goodbye.

How could I claim to know what was best for you, what you deserved, when at any moment I might be thrown a curveball — and learn that I hadn't protected you as well as I should have? Was I considering this lawsuit because of you, or to atone for all the things I'd done wrong up to this point?

Like wishing for a baby. Each month when I'd realized that Sean and I had again not conceived, I used to strip and stand in the shower with the water streaming down my face, praying to God; praying to get pregnant, no matter what.

I hoisted you into my arms — my left hip, since it was your right shoulder that had broken — and walked out of the examination room. The doctor's card was burning a hole in my back pocket. I was so distracted, in fact, that I nearly ran over a little girl who was walking in the door of the hospital just as we were walking out. "Oh, honey, I'm sorry," I said, and backed up. She was about your age, and she held on to her mother's hand. She wore a pink tutu and mud boots with frog faces on the toes. Her head was completely bald.

You did the one thing you hated most when it happened to you: you stared.

The little girl stared back.

You'd learned early on that strangers would stare at a girl in a wheelchair. I'd taught you to smile at them, to say hello, so that they'd realize you were a person and not just some curiosity of nature. Amelia was your fiercest protector — if she saw a kid gawking at you, she'd walk right up and tell him that was what would happen if he didn't clean his room or eat his vegetables. Once or twice, she'd made a child burst into tears, and

I almost didn't reprimand her because it made you smile and sit up straighter in your wheelchair, instead of trying to be invisible.

But this was different; this was an equal match.

I squeezed your waist. "Willow," I chided.

The girl's mother looked up at me. A thousand words passed between us, although neither of us spoke. She nodded at me, and I nodded back.

You and I walked out of the hospital into a late spring day that smelled of cinnamon and asphalt. You squinted, tried to raise your arm to shield your eyes, and remembered that it was bound tight against your body. "That girl, Mommy," you said. "Why did she look like that?"

"Because she's sick, and that's what happens when she takes her medicine."

You considered this for a moment. "I'm so lucky . . . my medicine lets me have hair."

I was careful not to cry around you, but this time I could not help it. Here you were, with three out of four extremities broken. Here you were, with a healing fracture I hadn't even known occurred. Here you were, period. "Yes, we're lucky," I said.

You put your hand against my cheek. "It's okay, Mom," you said. And just as I'd done for you in the ER, you patted my back, the very same spot you'd broken in your own body.

Sean

"Stop, goddammit!" I yelled as I sprinted across the empty park, holding the can of spray paint. The kid still had a lead on me, not to mention the benefit of being thirty years younger, but I wasn't going to let him get away. Not even if it killed me, which, judging from the stitch in my side, it just might.

It had been one of those unseasonably warm spring days that made me remember what it felt like to be a kid, listening to the slap of girls' flip-flops as they walked past you at the town pool. I admit, during my lunch break, I'd put on some running shorts and taken a quick dip. We wouldn't be swimming for a while — out of solidarity with you, since you couldn't go into a pool until you were out of your spica cast. There was nothing you wanted to do more than swim — something you'd never really learned to do because of various breaks. Even after Charlotte had discovered fiberglass casts — which were waterproof and wicked expensive — you somehow managed to miss the swim-lesson season for one reason or another. When Amelia was being a particularly nasty preadolescent, she'd lord over you the fact that she was headed to a

161

pool party or out to the beach. Then you'd spend the whole day sulking or, in one memorable case, getting on the Internet and submitting a bid request for an inground pool — something we had neither the land nor the money for. Sometimes I thought you were obsessed with water — frozen in the winter or chlorinated in the summer; all you wanted was exactly what you couldn't have.

Sort of like the rest of us, I guess.

Now, my hair was still wet; I smelled of chlorine — and I was trying to figure out how I could mask that from you when I got home. The car windows were rolled down as I cruised by the local park, where a Little League game had recently broken up. And then I noticed a kid spray-painting graffiti on the dugout in broad daylight.

I don't know what frustrated me more — the fact that this boy was defacing public property or the fact that he was doing it right under my nose, without even the pretense of hiding. I parked far away and sneaked up behind him. "Hey," I called. "You want to tell me what you're doing?"

He turned around, caught in the act. He was tall and whip-thin, with stringy yellow hair and a sad attempt at a mustache crawling over his upper lip. His gaze met mine, clear and defiant, and then he dropped the spray can and started running.

I took off, too. The boy darted away from the park's borders and crossed beneath an overpass, where his sneaker slipped in a puddle of mud. He stumbled, which gave me just enough time to throw my weight into him and shove him up against the concrete wall, with my arm pushing into his throat. "I asked you a question," I grunted. "What the fuck were you doing?"

He clawed at my arm, choking, and suddenly I saw myself through his eyes.

I wasn't one of those cops who liked to use my position to bully people. So what had set me off so quickly? As I fell back, I figured it out: it wasn't the fact that the boy had been spray-painting the dugout, or that he hadn't shown remorse when I first arrived on the scene. It was that he'd run. That he *could* run.

I was angry at him because you, in this situation, couldn't have escaped.

The kid was bent over, coughing. "Jesus fucking Christ!" he gasped.

"I'm sorry," I said. "Really sorry."

He stared at me like an animal that had been cornered. "Get it over with, already. Arrest me."

I turned away. "Just go. Before I change my mind."

There was a beat of silence and then, again, the sound of running footsteps.

I leaned against the wall of the overpass and closed my eyes. These days, it felt like anger was a geyser inside of me, destined to explode at regular intervals. Sometimes that meant a kid like this one was on the receiving end. Sometimes it was my own child — I'd find myself yelling at Amelia for something inconsequential, like leaving her cereal bowl on top of the television, when it was an infraction I was just as likely to commit myself. And sometimes it was Charlotte I complained to — for cooking meat loaf when I'd wanted chicken cutlets, for not keeping the kids quiet when I was sleeping after a late-night shift, for not knowing where I'd left my keys, for making me think there might be someone to be angry with in the first place.

I was no stranger to lawsuits. I'd sued Ford, once, after riding around in a cruiser gave me a herniated disk. And okay, maybe it was their fault and maybe it wasn't, but they settled and I used the money to buy a van so we could move your wheelchairs and adaptive equipment around — and I'm quite sure that Ford Motor Company never even blinked when they cut the check for twenty thousand dollars in damages. But this was different; this wasn't a lawsuit that blamed something that had happened to you — it was a lawsuit to blame the fact that you were here. Although I could easily earmark what we could do for you with a big settlement, I couldn't wrap my head around the fact that, in order to get it, I'd have to lie.

For Charlotte, this didn't seem to be a problem. And that got me thinking: What else was she lying about, even now, that I didn't realize? Was she happy? Did she wish she could have started over, without me, without you? Did she love me?

What kind of father did it make me if I refused to file a lawsuit that might net you enough money to live comfortably for the rest of your life, instead of scraping money here and there and taking on extra shifts at high school basketball games and proms so that we'd have enough to buy you a memory-foam mattress, an electric wheelchair, an adapted car to drive? Then again, what kind of father did it make me if the only

164

way to net those rewards was to pretend I didn't want you here?

I leaned my head back against the concrete, my eyes closed. If you had been born without OI, and wound up in a car crash that left you paralyzed, I would have gone to an attorney's office and had them look up every accident report the involved that make and model car to see if there was something faulty with the vehicle, something that might have led to the crash — so that the people responsible for hurting you would pay. Was a wrongful birth lawsuit really all that different?

It was. It was, because when I even whispered the words to myself in front of the mirror while I was shaving, it made me feel sick to my stomach.

My cell phone began to ring, reminding me that I'd been away from the cruiser longer than I'd intended. "Hello?"

"Dad, it's me," Amelia said. "Mom never picked me up."

I glanced down at my watch. "School ended two hours ago."

"I know. She's not home, and she's not answering her cell phone."

"I'm on my way," I said.

Ten minutes later, a sullen Amelia swung into the cruiser. "Great. I just *love* being driven home in a cop car. Imagine the rumor mill."

"Lucky for you, Drama Queen, that the whole town knows your father's a policeman."

"Did you talk to Mom?"

I had tried, but like Amelia said, she wasn't answering any phone. The reason why became crystal clear when I pulled into our driveway and saw her carefully extricating you from the backseat — not just confined by your spica cast but sporting a new bandage that bound your upper arm to your body.

Charlotte turned as she heard us drive up, and winced. "Amelia," she said. "Oh, God. I'm sorry. I totally forgot —"

"Yeah, so what else is new?" Amelia muttered, and she stalked into the house.

I took you out of your mother's arms. "What happened, Wills?"

"I broke my scapula," you said. "It's really hard to do."

"The shoulder blade, can you believe it?" Charlotte said. "Clear down the middle."

"You didn't answer your phone."

"My battery died."

"You could have called from the hospital."

Charlotte looked up. "You can't actually be angry with me, Sean. I've been a *little* busy —"

"Don't you think I deserve to know if my daughter gets hurt?"

"Could you keep your voice down?"

"Why?" I demanded. "Why not let everyone listen? They're going to hear it all anyway, once you file —"

"I refuse to discuss this in front of Willow —"

"Well, you'd better get over that fast, sweetheart, because she's going to hear every last ugly word of it."

166

Charlotte's face turned red, and she took you out of my arms and carried you into the house. She settled you on the couch, handed you the television remote, then walked into the kitchen, expecting me to follow. "What the *hell* is the matter with you?"

"With *me*? You're the one who left Amelia sitting for two hours after school —"

"It was an accident —"

"Speaking of accidents," I said.

"It wasn't a serious break."

"You know what, Charlotte? It looks pretty fucking serious to me."

"What would you have done if I called you, anyway? Left work early again? That would be one less day you were getting paid, which means we'd be doubly screwed."

I felt the skin on the back of my neck tighten. Here was the underlying message in that goddamn lawsuit, the invisible ink that would show up between the lines of every court document: *Sean O'Keefe doesn't make enough money to take care of his daughter's special needs . . . which is why it's come to this.*

"You know what I think?" I said, trying to keep my voice even. "That if the shoe was on the other foot — if I'd been with Willow when she got hurt — and I didn't call you, you'd be furious. And you know what else I think? The reason you didn't call me has nothing to do with my job or with your cell phone battery. It's that you've already made up your mind. You're going to do whatever the hell you want, whenever the hell you want, no matter what I say." I stormed out of the house to my cruiser, still idling in the driveway, because God forbid I left my shift early.

I smacked my hand on the steering wheel, inadvertently honking the horn. The noise brought Charlotte to the window. Her face was tiny and white, an oval whose features were blurred at this distance.

I had asked Charlotte to marry me with petit fours. I went to a bakery and had them write a letter in icing on top of each one: MARRY ME, and then I mixed them up and served them on a plate. It's a puzzle, I told her. You have to put them in order.

ARMY REM, she wrote.

Charlotte was still at the window, watching me with her arms crossed. I could barely see in her the girl I'd told to try again. I could no longer picture the look on her face when, the second time, she got it right.

Amelia

When Mom called me down to dinner that night, I moved with all the wild and crazy enthusiasm of a death row prisoner heading to an execution. I mean, it didn't take a rocket scientist to know that nobody in this household was happy, and that it had something to do with the lawyer's office we'd gone to. My parents had not done much to mask their voices when they were yelling at each other. In the three hours since Dad had left and returned again, since Mom had cried into the mixing bowl while whipping up her meat loaf, you'd been whimpering. So I did what I always did when you were in pain: I stuck my iPod headphones in my ears and cranked the volume.

I didn't do it for the reason you'd think — to drown out the noise you were making. I knew that's what my parents thought: that I was totally unsympathetic. I wasn't about to try to explain it to them, either, but the truth was, I *needed* that music. I needed to distract myself from the fact that, when you were crying, there was nothing I could do to stop it, because that just made me hate myself even more.

Everyone — even you, in the bottom half of your spica cast, with your arm strapped up against your chest — was already sitting at the dinner table when I got there. Mom had cut your meat loaf into tiny squares, like postage stamps. It made me think of when you were little, sitting in your high chair. I used to try to play with you — rolling a ball or pulling you in a wagon — and every time I was told the same thing: *Be careful*.

Once, you were sitting on the bed and I was bouncing on it, and you fell off. One minute we were astronauts exploring the planet Zurgon, and the next, your left shin was bent at a ninety-degree angle and you were doing that freaky zoning-out thing you did when you had a bad break. Mom and Dad went out of their way to say this wasn't my fault, but who did they think they were kidding? I was the one who'd been jumping, even if it had been your idea in the first place. If I'd never been there, you wouldn't have gotten hurt.

I slid into my chair. We didn't have assigned seats, like some families did, but we all took the same ones for every meal. I was still wearing my headphones, with my music turned up loud — emo stuff, songs that made me feel like there were people with even crappier lives than mine. "Amelia," my father said. "Not at the table."

Sometimes I think there's a beast that lives inside me, in the cavern that's where my heart should be, and every now and then it fills every last inch of my skin, so that I can't help but do something inappropriate. Its breath is full of lies; it smells of spite. And just at this moment, it chose to rear its ugly head. I blinked at my father, cranked the volume, and said — too loudly, "Pass the potatoes."

I sounded like the biggest brat on earth, and maybe I wanted to be: like Pinocchio, if I acted like a self-centered teenager, eventually I'd become one, and everyone would notice me and cater to me instead of hand-feeding you your meat loaf and watching you to make sure you weren't slipping in your chair. Actually, I'd just settle for having someone notice I was even a *member* of this family.

"Wills," my mother said, "you have to eat *something*."

"It tastes like feet," you answered.

"Amelia, I'm not going to ask you again," Dad said. "Five more bites . . ."

"Amelia!"

They didn't look at each other; as far as I knew they hadn't spoken since this afternoon. I wondered if they realized that they could be on opposite sides of the globe right now, and still be having this dinner conversation, and it wouldn't make a difference.

You squirmed away from the fork Mom was waving in front of your face. "Stop treating me like a baby," you said. "Just because I broke my shoulder doesn't mean you have to treat me like I'm two years old!" To illustrate this, you reached for your glass with your free arm, but you knocked it over. Milk landed in part on the tablecloth and mostly smack in the middle of Dad's plate. "Goddammit!" he yelled, and he reached toward me and ripped the headphones out of my ears. "You're

171

part of this family, and you'll act that way at the dinner table."

I stared at him. "You first," I said.

His face turned a steamy red. "Amelia, go to your room."

"*Fine!*" I shoved my chair back with a screech and ran upstairs. With tears leaking out of my eyes and my nose running, I locked myself in the bathroom. The girl in the mirror was someone I didn't know: her mouth twisted, her eyes dark and hollow.

These days, it seemed as if everything pissed me off. I got pissed off when I woke up in the morning and you were staring at me like I was some zoo animal; I got pissed off when I went to school and my locker was near the French classroom when Madame Riordan had made it her personal mission to make my life horrible; I got pissed off when I saw a gaggle of cheerleaders, with their perfect legs and their perfect lives, who worried about things like who would ask them to the next dance and whether red nail polish looked trampy, instead of whether their moms would remember to pick them up from school or be otherwise occupied at the emergency room. The only times I wasn't pissed off, I was hungry — like right now. Or at least I thought it was hunger. Both felt like I was being consumed from the inside out; I couldn't tell the difference anymore.

The last time my parents had been fighting — which was, like, yesterday — you and I were in our bedroom, and we could hear them loud and clear. Words slipped under the door, even though it was closed: *wrongful birth . . . testimony . . . deposition.* At one point I

172

heard the mention of television: *Don't you think reporters would get wind of this? Is that what you really want?* Dad said, and for a moment I thought how cool it would be to be on the news, until I remembered that being a poster child for dysfunctional family life wasn't really how I wanted to spend my fifteen minutes of fame.

They're mad at me, you said.

No. They're mad at each other.

Then we both heard Dad say, *Do you really think Willow wouldn't figure this out?*

You looked at me. *Figure* what *out?*

I hesitated, and instead of answering, I reached for the book you had in your lap and told you I'd read out loud.

Normally you didn't like that — reading was just about the only thing you could do brilliantly, and you usually wanted to show it off, but you probably felt like I did at that moment: like there was a big Brillo pad in your stomach, and every time you moved, it grated your insides. I had friends whose parents had divorced. Wasn't this the way it all started?

I opened to a random page of facts and began to read out loud to you about unlikely and gruesome deaths. There was a Brink's car guard who was killed when fifty thousand dollars' worth of quarters fell out of a truck and crushed him. A gust of wind pushed a man's car into a river near Naples, Italy, so he broke the window and climbed out and swam to shore, only to be killed by a tree that blew over and crushed him. A man who went over Niagara Falls in a barrel in 1911 and broke nearly every bone in his body later on slipped on a banana peel in New Zealand and died from the fall.

You liked that last one best, and I'd gotten you to smile again, but inside, I was still miserable: how could anyone ever win when the world beat you down at every turn?

That was when Mom came into the room and sat down on the edge of your bed. "Do you and Daddy hate each other?" you asked.

"No, Wills," she said, smiling, but in a way that made her skin look like it was stretched too tightly over the edges of her face. "Everything's absolutely fine."

I stood up, my hands on my hips. "When are you going to tell her?" I demanded.

My mother's gaze could have cut me in half, I swear. "Amelia," she said in a tone that brooked no argument, "there is nothing to tell."

Now, sitting on the edge of the bathtub, I realized what a total liar my mother was. I wondered if that was what I was destined for, if you could inherit that tendency the same way she had passed me the ability to double-joint my elbows, to tie a cherry stem into a knot with my tongue.

I leaned over the toilet bowl, stuck my finger down my throat, and vomited, so that this time when I told myself I was empty and aching, I would finally be telling the truth.

Blind Baking: the process of baking a pie crust without the filling.

Sometimes, when you're dealing with a fragile dough, it will collapse in spite of your best intentions. For this reason, some pie crusts and tart shells must be baked before the filling is added. The best method is to line the tart pan or pie plate with the rolled-out dough and place it in the fridge for at least 30 minutes. When you are ready to bake, prick the crust in several spots with a fork, line the pie plate or tart shell with foil or parchment paper, and fill it with rice or dried beans. Bake as directed, then carefully remove the foil and the beans — the shell will have retained its form because of them. I like seeing how a substance that weighs heavily can, in the end, be lifted; I like the feel of the beans, like trouble that slips through your fingers. Most of all, I like the proof in the pastry: it is the things we have to bear that shape us.

SWEET PASTRY DOUGH

1 ⅓ cups all-purpose flour
Pinch of salt
1 tablespoon sugar
½ cup + 2 tablespoons cold unsalted butter, cut into small pieces

1 large egg yolk
1 tablespoon ice water

In a food processor, combine the flour, salt, sugar, and butter. Pulse until coarse. In a small bowl, whisk the egg yolk and ice water. With the processor running, add the yolk mixture to the flour and butter until a ball forms. Remove the dough, wrap it in plastic, flatten to a disk, and chill for 1 hour.

Roll the dough out on a lightly floured surface and place it in a tart pan with a removable bottom. Chill before baking.

Preheat the oven to 375 degrees F. Remove the tart pan from the fridge, prick the crust all over with a fork, line the shell with foil, and fill with dried beans. Bake for 17 minutes, remove the foil and beans, and continue baking for another 6 minutes. Cool completely before filling.

APRICOT TART

Sweet Pastry Dough tart shell — blind baked
2–3 apricots
2 egg yolks
1 cup heavy cream
¾ cup sugar
1½ tablespoons flour
¼ cup chopped hazelnuts

Peel the apricots, slice, and arrange in the bottom of a blind-baked tart shell.

Combine the egg yolks, cream, sugar, and flour. Pour over the apricots and sprinkle with the hazelnuts. Bake in a preheated 350 degree F oven for 35 minutes.

When you taste this one, you can still sense the heaviness left behind. It's the shadow under the sweet, the question on the tip of your tongue.

Marin

June 2007

Facebook is supposed to be a social network, but the truth is, most people I know who use it — me included — spend so much time online tweaking our profiles and writing graffiti on other people's walls or poking them that we never leave our computers to actually socially interact. Perhaps it was bad form to check one's Facebook in the middle of the workday, but once, I'd walked in on Bob Ramirez tooling around with his MySpace page and I realized that there was very little he could say to me without being a hypocrite.

These days I used Facebook to join groups — Birth Mothers and Adoptees Searching, Adoption Search Registry. Some members actually found the people they were looking for. Even if that hadn't happened to me, there was a nice comfort to logging on and reading the posts that proved I wasn't the only one frustrated by this whole process.

I logged in and checked my mini-feed. I'd been poked by a girl from high school who'd asked me to be her friend a week ago but whom I hadn't seen in fifteen years. I had been dared to take a quiz on Flixster by my cousin in Santa Barbara. I'd been voted by my other friends as the person you'd most prefer to be stuck in handcuffs with.

I glanced at the information just above this, my profile.

NAME: Marin Gates
NETWORKS: Portsmouth, NH/UNH Alumni/NH Bar Association
SEX: Female
INTERESTED IN: Men
RELATIONSHIP STATUS: Single

Single?

I reloaded the page. For the past four months on my Facebook page that line had read: *In a relationship with Joe McIntyre*. I clicked on the home page and scrolled through the news feed. There it was: a picture of his face and a status update: *Joe McIntyre and Marin Gates have ended their relationship*.

My jaw dropped open; I felt like I'd been sucker-punched.

I grabbed my coat and stormed into the reception area. "Wait!" Briony said. "Where are you going? You've got a conference call at —"

"Reschedule it," I snapped. "My boyfriend just dumped me via Facebook."

It was not like Joe McIntyre was the One. I'd met him at a Bruins game with clients; he passed me in the aisle and spilled his beer down the front of my shirt.

Not an auspicious beginning, but he had indigo eyes and a smile that contributed to global warming, and before I knew it, I'd not only promised that he could pay my dry-cleaning bill but also given him my phone number. On our first date, we found out that we worked less than a block away from each other — he was an environmental lawyer — and that we'd both graduated from UNH. On our second date, we went back to my place and didn't get out of bed for two straight days.

Joe was six years younger than me, which meant that at twenty-eight he was still playing the field and that at thirty-four I had traded in my wristwatch for a biological clock. I expected this fling to be a little fun: someone to go to a movie with on a Saturday night and get flowers from on Valentine's Day. I wasn't banking on forever; I fully figured that I would tell him sometime in the next few months that we were looking for different things in our lives right now.

But I sure as hell wouldn't have broken the news to him on Facebook.

I strode around the corner and walked into the reception area of the law firm where he worked. It was much less grandiose than Bob's, but then again, we were a plaintiff's attorney, we weren't trying to save the world. The receptionist smiled. "Can I help you?"

"Joe's expecting me," I said, and I headed down the hall.

When I opened the door to his office, he was dictating into a digital recorder. "Furthermore, we

180

believe it's in the best interests of Cochran and Sons to — Marin? What are you doing here?"

"You broke up with me on *Facebook*?"

"I was going to send a text, but I thought that would be worse," Joe said, jumping up to close the door as a colleague wandered by. "C'mon, Marin. You know I'm not good at the touchy-feely stuff." Then he grinned. "Well, the *metaphorical* touchy-feely stuff . . ."

"You are such an insensitive troll," I said.

"This was a lot more civilized, if you ask me. What was the alternative? Some big argument where you tell me to fuck off and die?"

"Yes!" I said, and then I took a deep breath. "Is there someone else?"

"There's something else," Joe said soberly. "For God's sake, Marin. You've blown me off the past three times I've tried to get together. What did you expect me to do? Just sit around waiting for you to have time for me?"

"That's not fair," I said. "I was reading marriage license applications —"

"Exactly," Joe replied. "You don't want to go out with me. You want to go out with your birth mother. Look, at first, I thought it was kind of hot — you know, you were so passionate when you talked about finding her. Except it turns out you're not passionate about anything *but* that, Marin." He slid his hands into his pockets. "You're so busy living in the past, you've got nothing to give right now."

I could feel my neck heating up beneath the collar of my suit. "Do you remember those two amazing days —

and nights — at my house?" I said, leaning toward him until we were a breath away. I watched his pupils dilate.

"Oh yeah," he murmured.

"I faked it. Every time," I said, and I walked out of Joe's office with my head high.

My birthday is January 3, 1973. I've known this, obviously, my whole life. The adoption decree I'd gotten from Hillsborough County was dated in late July, because of the six-month waiting period to finalize an adoption and the time it takes to schedule the hearing. There's a lot of debate about that six-month period, in the adoptive community. Some people feel it should be longer, to give the birth mom time to change her mind; some people feel it should be shorter, to give the adoptive parents peace of mind that their newborn won't be taken away. Where you fall on the spectrum, of course, depends on whether you have a baby to give away or one to receive.

I was a few days late. My father used to say that he was counting on me being his little tax deduction, but then I foiled that by arriving in the new year. On the slip of paper that came home from the hospital with me, saved in my baby book, was a bassinet card with my name torn off — but I could still make out a loop in the middle of the last name that hadn't been ripped away: a cursive *y* or *g* or *j* or *q*. I knew this about my former self, and I knew that my birth parents had lived in Hillsborough County, and that my mother had been seventeen. In the seventies, there was still a good chance that a seventeen-year-old would marry the father of her baby, and that had led me to the records room.

Using a due date calculator on a pregnancy website, I figured out that I must have been conceived sometime around April tenth in order to be due on New Year's Eve. (April tenth. A high school spring formal dance, I imagined. A midnight car ride to the shore. The waves on the sand, the sun breaking like a yolk over the ocean at dawn, he and she, sleeping in each other's arms.) At any rate, if she found out she was pregnant a month later, that meant getting married in the early summer of 1972.

In 1972, Nixon went to China. Eleven Israeli athletes were killed at the Munich Olympic games. A stamp cost eight cents. The Oakland As won the World Series, and *M*A*S*H* premiered on CBS.

On January 22, 1973, nineteen days after I was born and living with the Gates family, the U.S. Supreme Court ruled on *Roe v. Wade*.

Did my mother hear about that and curse her bad timing?

A few weeks ago I had started scouring the records of Hillsborough County for marriage certificates from the summer of 1972. If my mother was seventeen, there must have been a parental consent form attached, too. Surely that would limit the numbers I had to wade through.

I had blown Joe off for two consecutive weekends while I waded through over three thousand marriage certificate applications, and learned incredibly creepy things about my home state (like that a girl between

183

thirteen and seventeen, and a boy between fourteen and seventeen, could marry with parental consent), and yet, I didn't find an application that looked like it might belong to my birth parents.

The truth is, even before Joe dumped me, I had resigned myself to giving up my search.

I went back to work after I left his office, and somehow phoned in a performance the rest of the day. That night, I came back to my house, opened a bottle of wine and a tub of Ben & Jerry's Coffee Heath Bar Crunch, and faced the truth: I had to decide if I really wanted to find my birth mother. Presumably, she had gone through significant moral contortions deciding whether or not to give me up; surely I owed her the same self-assessment in deciding whether or not to find her. Curiosity wasn't good enough; neither was a medical scare that had left me wondering about my origins. Once I had a name: then what? Knowing where I came from did not necessarily mean I was brave enough to hear why I had been given away. If I was going to do this, I was going to be opening the door for a relationship that would change both of our lives.

I reached for the phone and dialed my mother. "What are you doing?" I asked.

"Trying to figure out how to TiVo *The Colbert Report*," she said. "What are *you* doing?"

I glanced down at the melting ice cream, the half-empty bottle of wine. "Embarking on a liquid diet," I said. "And you have to push the red button to get the right menu on the screen."

"Oh, there it is. Good. Your father gets cranky when I watch the show and he falls asleep."

"Can I ask you something?"

"Sure."

"Am I passionate?"

She laughed. "Things must be really bad if you're asking *me* that."

"I don't mean romantically. I mean, you know, about life. Did I have hobbies when I was little? Did I collect Garbage Pail Kids cards or beg to be on a swim team?"

"Honey, you were terrified of the water till you were twelve."

"Okay, maybe that wasn't the best example." I pinched the bridge of my nose. "Did I stick with things, even when they were hard? Or did I just give up?"

"Why? Did something happen at work?"

"No, not at work." I hesitated. "If you were me, would you look for your birth parents?"

There was a bubble of silence. "Wow. That's a pretty loaded question. And I thought we'd already had this discussion. I said that I'd support you —"

"I know what you said. But doesn't it hurt you?" I asked bluntly.

"I'm not going to lie, Marin. When you first started asking questions, it did. I guess a part of me felt like, if you loved me enough, you wouldn't need to find any other answers. But then you had the whole scare at the gynecologist's, and I realized this wasn't about me. It was about *you*."

"I don't *want* to hurt you."

"Don't worry about me," she said. "I'm old and tough."

That made me smile. "You're not old, and you're a softy." I drew in my breath. "I just keep thinking, you know, this is a really big deal. You dig up the box, and maybe you find buried treasure, but maybe you find something rotting."

"Maybe the person you're afraid of hurting is yourself."

Leave it to my mother to hit the nail on the head. What if, for example, I turned out to be related to Jeffrey Dahmer or Jesse Helms? Wouldn't that be information I'd be better off not knowing?

"She got rid of me over thirty years ago. What if I barge into her life and she doesn't want to see me?"

There was a soft sigh on the other end of the phone. It was, I realized, the sound I associated most with growing up. I'd heard it running into my mother's arms when a kid had pushed me off the swing at the playground. I'd heard it during an embrace before my newly minted prom date and I drove off to the dance; I'd heard it when she stood at the threshold of my college dorm, trying not to cry as she left me on my own for the first time. In that sound was my whole childhood.

"Marin," my mother said simply, "who *wouldn't* want you?"

Honestly, I am not the kind of person who believes in ghosts and karma and reincarnation. And yet, the very next day I found myself calling in sick to work so that I could drive to Falmouth, Massachusetts, to talk to a psychic about my birth mother. I took another swig of my Dunkin' Donuts coffee and imagined what the meeting would be like; whether I would come out of it with information that would send me in the right direction for my adoption search, like the woman who'd recommended Meshinda Dows and her prophecies in the first place.

The previous night I had joined ten adoption support groups online. I created a name for myself (Separ8tedatbirth@yahoo.com) and made lists from the websites in an empty Moleskine notebook.

1. USE STATE REGISTRIES.
2. REGISTER WITH ISRR — the Index of Search and Reunion Resources, the biggest registry there is.
3. REGISTER WITH THE WORLD WIDE REGISTRY.
4. TALK TO YOUR ADOPTIVE PARENTS ... AND COUSINS, UNCLES, OLDER SIBLINGS ...
5. FIGURE OUT YOUR CONDUIT. In other words, who arranged the adoption? A church, a lawyer, a physician, an agency? They might be a source of information.
6. FILE A WAIVER OF CONFIDENTIALITY, so if your birth mom comes looking for you, she knows that you want to be contacted.
7. POST YOUR INFO REGULARLY. There are people who really do forward all over in the hope that your info gets to the right place!

8. PLACE ADS IN THE PRIMARY NEWSPAPERS OF YOUR BIRTH CITY.
9. ABOVE ALL ELSE, IGNORE ANY SEARCH COMPANY YOU SEE ON TV ADS OR TALK SHOWS! THEY ARE SCAMS!

At two in the morning, I was still online in an adoption search chat room, reacting to horror stories from people who wanted to save me the trouble of making the same mistakes. There was RiggleBoy, who had contacted a 1–900 search number and given them his credit card information, only to be socked with a bill for $6500 at the end of one month. There was Joy4Eva, who'd found out that she was taken away from her birth family for neglect and abuse. AllieCapone688 gave me a list of three books that she used when she was getting started — which cost less than all she'd spent on private investigators. Only one woman had a happy ending: she'd gone to a psychic named Meshinda Dows, who had given her such accurate information that she found her birth mom in a week's time. *Try it*, FantaC suggested. *What have you got to lose?*

Well, my self-respect, for one. But all the same, I found myself Googling Meshinda Dows. She had one of those websites that takes forever to load, because there was a music file attached — in this case, an eerie mix of chimes and humpback whale songs. *Meshinda Dows*, the home page read, *Certified psychic counselor*.

Who certified psychic counselors? The U.S. Department of Snake Oil and Charlatans?

Serving the Cape Cod community for 35 years.

Which meant she was within driving distance from my home in Bankton.

Let me be your bridge to the past.

Before I could chicken out, I clicked on the email link and sent her a message explaining my search for my birth mom. Within thirty seconds of sending it, I got a reply:

Marin, I think I can be of great help to you. Are you free tomorrow afternoon?

I did not question why this woman was online at three in the morning. I didn't let myself wonder why a successful psychic would have an opening so quickly. Instead, I agreed to the sixty-dollar consultation fee and printed out the driving directions she gave me.

Five hours after I'd left my house that morning, I pulled into Meshinda Dows's driveway. She lived in a tiny house that was painted purple with red trim. She was easily in her sixties, but her hair was dyed jet black and reached her waist. "You must be Marin," she said.

Wow, already she was one for one.

She led me into a room that was divided from the foyer with a curtain made of silk scarves. Inside were two couches facing each other across a square white ottoman. On the ottoman were a feather, a fan, and a deck of cards. The shelves in the room were covered with Beanie Babies, each sealed in a small plastic bag with a heart-shaped tag protector. They looked like they were all suffocating.

Meshinda sat down, and I followed suit. "I take the money up front," she said.

"Oh." I dug in my purse and pulled out three twenty-dollar bills, which she folded and stuck into her pocket.

"Why don't we start with you telling me why you're here?"

I blinked at her. "Shouldn't you *know* that?"

"Psychic gifts don't always work that way, hon," she said. "You're a little nervous, aren't you?"

"I suppose."

"You shouldn't be. You're protected. You have spirits around you," she said. She closed her eyes and squinted. "Your . . . grandfather? He wants you to know he's breathing better now."

My jaw dropped open. My grandfather had died when I was thirteen, of complications from lung cancer. I had been terrified to visit him in the hospital and see him wasting away.

"He knew something important about your birth mother," Meshinda said.

Well, that was convenient, since Grandpa couldn't confirm or deny that now.

"She's thin and has dark hair," the psychic continued. "She was very young when it happened. I'm getting an accent . . ."

"Southern?" I asked.

"No, not Southern . . . I can't quite place it."
Meshinda looked at me. "I'm also getting some names.
Strange ones. Allagash . . . and Whitcomb . . . no, make
that Whittier."

"Allagash Whittier is a law firm in Nashua," I said.

"I think they have information. It might have been a
lawyer there who handled the adoption. I'd contact
them. And Maisie. Someone named Maisie has some
information, too."

Maisie was the name of the clerk of the Hillsborough
County court who'd sent me my adoption decree. "I'm
sure she does," I said. "She's got the whole file."

"I'm talking about another Maisie. An aunt or a
cousin . . . she adopted a baby from Africa."

"I don't have an aunt or a cousin named Maisie," I
said.

"You do," Meshinda insisted. "You haven't met her
yet." She wrinkled up her face, as if she was sucking on
a lemon. "Your birth father is named Owen. He has
something to do with the law."

I leaned forward, intrigued. Was that why I'd been
attracted to the career?

"He and your birth mom have had three more
children."

Whether or not that was true, I felt a pang in my
chest. How come those three got to stay, but I was
given away? The old adage I'd been told over and over
— that my birth parents loved me but couldn't take
care of me — had never quite rung true. If they loved
me so much, why had I been dispensable?

191

Meshinda touched a hand to her head. "That's it," she said. "Nothing else coming through." She patted my knee. "That lawyer," she advised. "That's the place to start."

On the way back home, I stopped off at McDonald's to eat something and sat outside at the human Habitrail playspace that was filled with toddlers and their caregivers. I called 411 and was connected to Allagash Whittier. By telling them I was an associate with Robert Ramirez, I was able to sweet-talk my way past the paralegals to a lawyer on staff. "Marin," the woman said, "what can I do for you?"

On the small bench where I sat, I curled a little closer into myself, to make the conversation more private. "It's sort of a strange request," I said. "I'm trying to find some information about a client your firm may have had in the early seventies. It would have been a young woman, around sixteen or seventeen?"

"That shouldn't be hard to find — we don't get too many of those. What's the last name?"

I hesitated. "I don't have a last name, exactly."

The line went silent. "Was this an adoption case?"

"Well. Yes. Mine."

The woman's voice was frosty. "I'd suggest you try the courthouse," she said, and she hung up.

I clutched the cell phone between my hands and watched a little boy shriek his way down a curved purple slide. He was Asian, his mother was not. Was he adopted? One day, would he be sitting here like I was, facing a dead end?

I dialed 411 again, and a moment later was connected to Maisie Donovan, the adoption search administrator for Hillsborough County. "You probably don't remember me," I said. "A few months ago, you sent me my adoption decree . . ."

"Name?"

"Well, that's what I'm looking for . . ."

"I meant *your* name," Maisie said.

"Marin Gates." I swallowed. "It's the craziest thing," I said. "I saw a psychic today. I mean, I'm not one of those nutcases who goes to psychics or anything . . . not that I have a problem with that if it's something, you know, you like to do every now and then . . . but anyway, I went to this woman's house and she told me that someone named Maisie had information about my birth mother." I forced a laugh. "She couldn't give me much more detail, but she got *that* part right, huh?"

"Ms. Gates," Maisie said flatly, "what can I do for you?"

I bowed my head toward the ground. "I don't know where to go from here," I admitted. "I don't know what to do next."

"For fifty dollars, I can send you your nonidentifying information in a letter."

"What's that?"

"Whatever's in your file that doesn't give away names, addresses, phone numbers, birth date —"

"The unimportant stuff," I said. "Do you think I'll learn anything from it?"

"Your adoption wasn't through an agency; it was a private one," Maisie explained, "so there wouldn't be much, I imagine. You'd probably find out that you're white."

I thought of the adoption decree she'd sent me. "I'm about as sure of that as I am that I'm female."

"Well, for fifty dollars, I'm happy to confirm it."

"Yes," I heard myself say. "I'd like that."

After I wrote the address where I needed to send my check on the back of my hand, I hung up and watched the children bouncing around like molecules in a heated solution. It was hard for me to imagine ever having a child. It was impossible to imagine giving one up.

"Mommy!" one little girl cried out from the top of a ladder. "Are you watching?"

Last night on the message boards, I had first seen the labels *a-mom* and *b-mom*. They weren't rankings, as I'd first thought — just shorthand for adoptive mom and birth mom. As it turned out, there was a huge controversy over the terminology. Some birth mothers felt the label made them sound like breeders, not mothers, and wanted to be called *first mother* or *natural mother*. But by that logic, *my* mom became the *second mother*, or the *unnatural mother*. Was it the act of giving birth that made you a mother? Did you lose that label when you relinquished your child? If people were measured by their deeds, on the one hand, I had a woman who had chosen to give me up; on the other, I had a woman who'd sat up with me at night when I was sick as a child, who'd cried with me over boyfriends, who'd clapped fiercely at my law school graduation. Which acts made you more of a mother?

Both, I realized. Being a parent wasn't just about bearing a child. It was about bearing witness to its life.

Suddenly, I found myself thinking of Charlotte O'Keefe.

Piper

The patient was about thirty-five weeks into her pregnancy and had just moved to Bankton with her husband. I hadn't seen her for any routine obstetric visits, but she'd been slotted into my schedule during my lunch break because she was complaining of fever and other symptoms that seemed to me like red flags for infection. According to the nurse who'd done the initial history, the woman had no medical problems.

I pushed open the door with a smile on my face, hoping to calm down what I was sure would be a panicking mother-to-be. "I'm Dr Reece," I said, shaking her hand and sitting down. "Sounds like you haven't been feeling too well."

"I thought it was the flu, but it wouldn't go away . . ."

"It's always a good idea to get something like that checked out when you're pregnant anyway," I said. "The pregnancy's been normal so far?"

"A breeze."

"And how long have you been having symptoms?"

"About a week now."

"Well, I'll give you a chance to change into a robe, and then we'll see what's going on." I stepped outside and reread her chart while I waited a few moments for her to change.

I loved my job. Most of the time when you were an obstetrician, you were present at one of the most joyous moments of a woman's life. Of course, there were incidents that were not quite as happy — I'd had my share of having to tell a pregnant woman that there'd been a fetal demise; I'd had surgeries where a placenta accreta led to DIC and the patient never regained consciousness. But I tried not to think about these; I liked to focus instead on the moment when that baby, slick and wriggling like a minnow in my hands, gasped its way into this world.

I knocked. "All set?"

She was sitting on the examination table, her belly resting on her lap like an offering. "Great," I said, fitting my stethoscope to my ears. "We'll start by listening to your chest." I huffed on the metal disk — as an OB I was particularly sensitive to cold metal objects being placed anywhere on a person — and set it gently against the woman's back. Her lungs were perfectly clear; no rasping, no rattles. "Sounds fine," I said. "Now let's check out your heart."

I slid aside the neckline of the gown to find a large median sternotomy scar — the vertical kind that goes straight down the chest. "What's that from?"

"Oh, that's just my heart transplant."

I raised my brows. "I thought you told the nurse that you didn't have any medical problems."

"I don't," the patient said, beaming. "My new heart's working great."

Charlotte didn't start seeing me as a patient until she was trying to get pregnant. Before that, we were still just moms who made fun of our daughters' skating coaches behind their backs; we'd save seats for each other at school parent nights; occasionally we'd get together with our spouses for dinner at a nice restaurant. But one day, when the girls were playing up in Emma's room, Charlotte told me that she and Sean had been trying to get pregnant for a year, and nothing had happened.

"I've done it all," she confided. "Ovulation predictors, special diets, Moon Boots — you name it."

"Have you seen a doctor?" I asked.

"Well," she said. "I was thinking about seeing *you*."

I didn't take on patients I knew personally. No matter what anyone said, you couldn't be an objective physician if it was someone you loved lying on your operating table. You could argue that the stakes for an OB were always high — and there's no question I gave 100 percent every time I walked into a delivery — but the stakes were just that tiny bit higher if the patient was personally connected to you. If you failed, you were not just failing your patient. You were failing your friend.

"I don't think that's the greatest idea, Charlotte," I said. "It's a tough line to cross."

"You mean the whole you've-got-your-hand-up-my-cervix-now-so-how-can-you-look-me-in-the-eye-when-we-go-shopping part?"

I grinned. "Not that. Seen one uterus, seen them all," I said. "It's just that a physician should be able to keep her distance, instead of being personally involved."

"But that's exactly why you're perfect for me," Charlotte argued. "Another doctor would try to help us conceive but wouldn't really give a damn. I want someone who cares beyond the point of professional responsibility. I want someone who wants me to have a baby as much as I want to."

Put that way, how could I deny her? I called Charlotte every morning so that we could dissect the letters to the editor in the local paper. She was the first one I ran to when I was fuming at Rob and needed to vent. I knew what shampoo she used, which side of her car the gas tank was on, how she took her coffee. She was, simply, my best friend. "Okay," I said.

A smile exploded on her face. "Do we start now?"

I burst out laughing. "No, Charlotte, I'm not going to do a pelvic exam on my living room floor while the girls are playing upstairs."

Instead, I had her come to the office the following day. As it turned out, there was no medical reason that she and Sean were having trouble getting pregnant. We talked about how eggs decline in quality after women hit their thirties, which meant it might take longer to happen — but *could* still happen. I got her started on folic acid and on tracking her basal body temperature. I

199

told Sean (in what had to have been his favorite conversation with me to date) that they should have sex more often. For six months, I tracked Charlotte's menstrual calendar in my own appointment book; I'd call on the twenty-eighth day and ask if she'd started her period — and for six months, she had. "Maybe we should talk about fertility drugs," I suggested, and the next month, just before her appointment with a specialist, Charlotte got pregnant the old-fashioned way.

Considering how long it took, the pregnancy itself was uneventful. Charlotte's blood tests and urine cultures always came back clean; her blood pressure was never elevated. She was nauseated round the clock, and she'd call me after throwing up at midnight to ask why the hell it was called morning sickness.

At her eleventh week of pregnancy, we heard the heartbeat for the first time. At the fifteenth, I did a quad screen on her blood to check for neural defects and Down syndrome. Two days later, when her results came in, I drove to her house during my lunch break. "What's wrong?" she asked, when she saw me standing at the door.

"Your test results. We have to talk."

I explained that the quad screen wasn't foolproof, that the test was designed specifically to have a 5 percent screen positive rate, which means that 5 percent of all women who took the test were going to be told that they had a higher than average risk of having a Down syndrome baby. "Based on your age alone, your risk is one in two hundred and seventy of having a baby with Down," I said. "But the blood test came back saying that, actually, your risk is higher than average — it's one in one hundred and fifty."

Charlotte folded her arms across her chest.

"You've got a few options," I said. "You're scheduled for an ultrasound in three weeks anyway. We can take a look during that ultrasound and see if anything is a red flag. If it does show something, we can send you for a level two ultrasound. If not, we can reduce your odds again to one in two hundred and fifty, which is nearly average, and assume the test was a false reading. But just remember — the ultrasound isn't one hundred percent peace of mind. If you want absolute answers, you'll have to have amniocentesis."

"I thought that could cause a miscarriage," Charlotte said.

"It can. But the risk of that is one in two hundred and seventy — right now, less than the chance that the baby has Down syndrome."

Charlotte rubbed a hand down her face. "So this amniocentesis," she said. "If it turns out that the baby has . . ." Her voice trailed off. "Then what?"

I knew Charlotte was Catholic. I also knew, as a practitioner, that it was my responsibility to give everyone all the information I had whenever possible. What they chose to do with it, based on their personal beliefs, was up to them. "Then you can decide whether or not to terminate," I said evenly.

She looked up at me. "Piper, I worked too hard to have this baby. I'm not going to give it up that easily."

"You should talk this over with Sean —"

"Let's do the ultrasound," Charlotte decided. "Let's just take it from there."

For all of these reasons, I remember very clearly the first time we saw you on the screen. Charlotte was lying down on the examination table; Sean was holding her hand. Janine, the ultrasound tech who worked at my practice, was taking the measurements before I went in to read the results myself. We would be looking for hydrocephalus, an endocardial cushion defect or abdominal wall defect, nuchal fold thickening, a short or absent nasal bone, hydronephrosis, echogenic bowel, shortened humeri or femurs — all markers used in the ultrasound diagnosis of Down syndrome. I made sure that the machine we used was one that had only recently arrived, brand-new, the ultimate technology at the time.

Janine came into my office as soon as she finished the scan. "I'm not seeing any of the usual suspects for Down," she said. "The only abnormality is the femurs — they're in the sixth percentile."

We got readings like that all the time — a fraction of a millimeter for a fetus might look much shorter than normal and, at the next sonogram, be perfectly fine. "That could be genetics. Charlotte's tiny."

Janine nodded. "Yeah, I'm going to just mark it down as something to keep an eye on." She paused. "There *was* something weird, though."

My head snapped up from the file I was writing in. "What?"

"Check out the pictures of the brain when you're in there."

I could feel my heart sink. "The brain?"

"It looks anatomically normal. But it's just incredibly . . . clear." She shook her head. "I've never seen anything like it."

So the ultrasound machine was exceptionally good at its job — I could see why Janine would be over the moon, but I didn't have time to rhapsodize about the new equipment. "I'm going to tell them the good news," I said, and I went into the examination room.

Charlotte knew; she knew as soon as she saw my face. "Oh, thank God," she said, and Sean leaned over to kiss her. Then she reached for my hand. "You're sure?"

"No. Ultrasound isn't an exact science. But I'd say the odds of having a normal, healthy baby just increased dramatically." I glanced at the screen, a frozen image of you sucking your thumb. "Your baby," I said, "looks perfect."

In my office, we did not advocate recreational ultrasounds — in layman's terms, that means ultrasounds beyond those medically necessary. But sometime in Charlotte's twenty-seventh week, she came to pick me up to go to a movie, and I was still delivering a baby at the hospital. An hour later, I found her in my office with her feet propped on the desk as she read a recent medical journal. "This is fascinating stuff," she said. "'Contemporary Management of Gestational Trophoblastic Neoplasia.' Remind me to take one of these the next time I can't fall asleep."

"I'm sorry," I said. "I didn't think I'd be this late. She made it to seven centimeters and then stopped dead."

"It's no big deal. I didn't really want to see a movie anyway. The baby's been dancing on my bladder all afternoon."

"Future ballerina?"

"Or placekicker, if you believe Sean." She looked up at me, trying to read my face for clues about the baby's sex.

Sean and Charlotte had chosen not to find out in advance. When parents told us that, we wrote it in their files. It had taken a Herculean effort for me to *not* peek during the ultrasound, so that I wouldn't inadvertently give away the secret.

It was seven o'clock; the receptionist had gone home for the day; the patients were all gone. Charlotte had been allowed to wait for me only because everyone knew we were friends. "We wouldn't have to tell him that we know," I said.

"Know what?"

"The baby's sex. Just because we missed the movie doesn't mean we can't catch another one . . ."

Charlotte's eyes widened. "You mean an ultrasound?"

"Why not?" I shrugged.

"Is it safe?"

"Absolutely." I grinned at her. "Come on, Charlotte. What have you got to lose?"

Five minutes later, we were in Janine's ultrasound suite. Charlotte had hiked her shirt up beneath her bra, and her pants were pushed down low on her abdomen.

204

I squirted gel onto her belly, and she squealed. "Sorry," I said. "Cold." Then I picked up the transducer and moved it over her skin.

The picture of you rose on the screen like a mermaid coming up to the water's surface: black one moment, and then slowly solidifying into an image we could recognize. There was a head, a spine, your tiny hand.

I swept the transducer to a point between your legs. Instead of the crossed bones of a fetus cramped inside the womb, your soles touched each other, your legs practically forming a circle. The first break I saw was the femur. It was angulated, bent acutely, instead of being straight. On the tibia I could see a line of black, a new fracture.

"So?" Charlotte said happily, craning her neck to see the screen. "When do I get to see the family jewels?"

I swallowed, moving the transducer up to see the barrel of your chest and the beaded ribs. There were five healing fractures here.

The room started spinning around me. Still holding the transducer, I leaned forward, settling my head between my knees. "Piper?" Charlotte said, coming up on her elbows.

I had learned about osteogenesis imperfecta in medical school, but I had never actually seen a case. What I remembered about it were pictures of fetuses with in vitro fractures like yours. Fetuses that died at birth or shortly after.

"Piper?" Charlotte repeated. "Are you okay?"

Pulling myself upright, I drew in a deep breath. "Yes," I said, my voice breaking. "But Charlotte . . . your daughter's not."

Sean

The very first time I heard the words *osteogenesis imperfecta* was after Piper drove Charlotte home, hysterical, from that off-the-cuff ultrasound in Piper's office. With Charlotte sobbing in my arms, I tried to make sense of the words Piper was lobbing at me like missiles: collagen deficiency, bones angulated and thickened, beaded ribs. She had already called a colleague, Dr Del Sol, who was a high-risk maternal-fetal-medicine physician at the hospital. We had an appointment for another ultrasound at 7:30a.m.

I had just come home from work — a construction detail that had been hellish because it had rained the entire afternoon and evening. My hair was still damp from the shower, my shirt sticking to the damp skin of my back. Amelia was upstairs watching TV in our bedroom, and I had been holding a container of ice cream, eating right out of it with a spoon, when Piper and Charlotte came into the house. "Damn," I said. "You caught me right in the act." Then I realized that Charlotte was crying.

It never failed to amaze me how the most ordinary day could be catapulted into the extraordinary in the blink of an eye. Take the mother who was handing a toy to her toddler in the backseat one moment, and in a massive motor vehicle accident the next. Or the frat boy who was chugging a beer on the porch as we drove up to arrest him for sexually assaulting another student. The wife who opened the door to find a police officer bearing the news of her husband's death. In my job, I'd often been present at the transition when the world as you knew it became the disaster you never expected — but I had not been on the receiving end before.

My throat felt like it had been lined with cotton. "How bad?"

Piper looked away. "I don't know."

"This osteopatho— "

"Osteogenesis imperfecta."

"How do you fix it?"

Charlotte had drawn back from me, her face swollen, her eyes red. "We can't," she said.

That night, after Piper had left and Charlotte had finally fallen into a fitful sleep, I got on the Internet and googled OI. There were four types, plus three more that had recently been identified, but only two of them showed fractures in utero. Type II infants would die before birth, or shortly after. Type III infants would survive but could have rib fractures that caused life-threatening breathing problems. Bone abnormalities would get worse and worse. These children might never walk.

Other words started jumping off the screen:

Wormian bones. Codfish vertebrae. Intramedullary rodding.

Short stature — some people grow only three feet tall.

Scoliosis. Hearing loss.

Respiratory failure is the most frequent cause of death, followed by accidental trauma.
Because OI is a genetic condition, it has no cure.

And

When diagnosed in utero, the majority of these pregnancies end in pregnancy interruption.

Below this was a photograph of a dead infant who'd had Type II OI. I could not tear my eyes away from the knotted legs, the shifted torso. Was this what our baby looked like? If so, wasn't it better to be stillborn?

At that thought, I squeezed my eyes shut, and prayed to God that He hadn't been listening. I would have loved you if you'd been born with seven heads and a tail. I would have loved you if you never drew breath or opened your eyes to see me. I *already* loved you; that didn't stop just because there was something wrong with the way your bones were made.

I quickly cleared the search history so that Charlotte wouldn't accidentally bring up the photograph when she was surfing the Net, and moved upstairs quietly. I stripped in the dark and slid into bed beside your mother. When I wrapped my arms around her, she shifted closer to me. I let my hand fall over the swell of her belly just as you kicked, as if to tell me not to worry, not to believe a word I read.

The next day, after another ultrasound and an X-ray, Dr Gianna Del Sol met us in her office to go over the report. "The ultrasound showed a demineralized skull," she explained. "Her long bones are three standard deviations off the mean, and they're angulated and thickened in a way that shows both healing fractures and new ones. The X-ray gave us a better picture of the rib fractures. All of this indicates that your baby has osteogenesis imperfecta."

I felt Charlotte's hand slip underneath mine.

"Based on the fact that we're seeing multiple fractures, it seems like we're talking about Type II or Type III."

"Is one worse than the other?" Charlotte asked. I looked into my lap, because I already knew the answer to that.

"Type IIs normally do not survive after birth. Type IIIs have significant disabilities and sometimes early mortality."

Charlotte burst into tears again; Dr Del Sol passed her a box of tissues.

"It's very hard to tell whether an infant has Type II or Type III. Type II can sometimes be diagnosed by ultrasound at sixteen weeks, Type III at eighteen. But every case is different, and your earlier ultrasound didn't reveal any fractures. Because of that, we can't give you an entirely accurate prognosis — beyond the fact that the best-case scenario is going to be severe, and the worst case will be lethal."

I looked at her. "So even when you think it's Type II, and that a baby has no chance of survival, it might beat the odds?"

"It's happened," Dr Del Sol said. "I read a case study about parents who were given a lethal prognosis yet chose to continue the pregnancy and wound up with an infant with Type III. However, Type III kids are still severely disabled. They'll have hundreds of breaks over the course of their lives. They may not be able to walk. There can be respiratory issues and joint problems, bone pain, muscle weakness, skull and spinal deformities." She hesitated. "There are places that can help you, if termination is something you want to consider."

Charlotte was twenty-seven weeks into her pregnancy. What clinic would do an abortion at twenty-seven weeks?

"We're not interested in termination," I said, and I looked at Charlotte for confirmation, but she was facing the doctor.

"Has there ever been a baby born here with Type II or Type III?" she asked.

Dr Del Sol nodded. "Nine years ago. I wasn't here at the time."

"How many breaks did *that* baby have when it was born?"

"Ten."

Charlotte smiled then, for the first time since last night. "Mine only has seven," she had said. "So that's already better, right?"

Dr Del Sol hesitated. "That baby," she said, "didn't survive."

One morning, when Charlotte's car was being serviced, I took you to physical therapy. A very nice girl with a gap between her teeth whose name was Molly or Mary (I always forgot) made you balance on a big red ball, which you liked, and do sit-ups, which you didn't. Every time you curled up on the side of your healing shoulder blade, your lips pressed together, and tears would streak from the corners of your eyes. I don't even think you knew you were crying, really — but after watching this for about ten minutes, I couldn't stand it anymore. I told Molly/Mary that we had another appointment, a flat lie, and I settled you in your wheelchair.

You hated being in the chair, and I couldn't say I blamed you. A good pediatric wheelchair was best when it was fitted well, because then you were comfortable, safe, and mobile. But they cost over $2800, and insurance would pay for one only every five years. The wheelchair you were riding in these days had been fitted to you when you were two, and you'd grown considerably since then. I couldn't even imagine how you'd squeeze into it at age seven.

On the back of it, I had painted a pink heart and the words HANDLE WITH CARE. I pushed you out to the car and lifted you into your car seat, then folded the wheelchair into the back of the van. When I slid into the driver's seat and checked you in the rearview mirror, you were cradling your sore arm. "Daddy," you said, "I don't want to go back there."

"I know, baby."

Suddenly I knew what I would do. I drove past our exit on the highway, to the Comfort Inn in Dover, and paid sixty-nine dollars for a room I had no plans to use. Strapped in your wheelchair, I pushed you to the indoor pool.

It was empty on a Tuesday morning. The room smelled heavily of chlorine, and there were six chaise lounges in various states of disrepair scattered around. A skylight was responsible for the dance of diamonds on the surface of the water. A stack of green and white striped towels sat on a bench beneath a sign: SWIM AT YOUR OWN RISK.

"Wills," I said, "you and I are going swimming."

You looked at me. "Mom said I can't, until my shoulder —"

"Mom isn't here to find out, is she?"

A smile bloomed on your face. "What about our bathing suits?"

"Well, that's part of the plan. If we stop off home to *get* our suits, Mom'll know something's up, won't she?" I stripped off my T-shirt and sneakers, and stood before you in a pair of faded cargo shorts. "I'm good to go."

You laughed and tried to get your shirt over your head, but you couldn't lift your arm high enough. I helped, and then shimmied your shorts down your legs so that you were sitting in the wheelchair in your underpants. They said THURSDAY on the front, although it was Tuesday. On the butt was a yellow smiley face.

After four months in the spica cast, your legs were thin and white, too reedy to support you. But I held you under the armpits as you walked toward the water and then sat you down on the steps. From a supply bin against the far wall, I took a kid's life jacket and zipped it onto you. I carried you in my arms to the middle of the pool.

"Fish can swim at sixty-eight miles an hour," you said, clutching at my shoulders.

"Impressive."

"The most common name for a goldfish is Jaws." You wrapped your arm around my neck in a death grip. "A can of Diet Coke floats in a pool. Regular Coke sinks . . ."

"Willow?" I said. "I know you're nervous. But if you don't close your mouth, a lot of water's going to go into it." And I let go.

Predictably, you panicked. Your arms and legs started pinwheeling, and the combined force flipped you onto your back, where you splashed and stared up at the ceiling. "Daddy! Daddy! I'm drowning!"

"You're not drowning." I lifted you upright. "It's all about those stomach muscles. The ones you didn't want to work on today at therapy. Think about moving slowly and staying upright." More gently this time, I released you.

You bobbled, your mouth sinking under the water. Immediately, I lunged for you, but you righted yourself. "I can do it," you said, maybe to me and maybe to

214

yourself. You moved one arm through the water, and then the other, compensating for the shoulder that was still healing. You bicycled your legs. And incrementally, you came closer to me. "Daddy!" you shouted, although I was only two feet away. "Daddy! Look at me!"

I watched you moving forward, inch by inch. "Look at you," I said, as you paddled under the weight of your own conviction. "Look at you."

"Sean," Charlotte said that night, when I thought she might have already fallen asleep beside me, "Marin Gates called today."

I was on my side, staring at the wall. I knew why the lawyer had phoned Charlotte: because I hadn't answered the six messages she'd left on my cell, asking me whether I had returned the signed papers agreeing to file a wrongful birth lawsuit — or if they'd somehow gotten lost in the mail.

I knew exactly where those papers were: inside the glove compartment of my car, where I'd shoved them after Charlotte handed them to me a month ago. "I'll get around to it," I said.

Her hand lighted on my shoulder. "Sean —"

I rolled onto my back. "You remember Ed Gatwick?" I asked.

"Ed?"

"Yeah. Guy I graduated from the academy with? He was on the job in Nashua. Responded to a call last week about suspicious activity at a residence, made by a neighbor. He told his partner he had a bad feeling about it, but he went inside, just in time for the meth lab in the kitchen to blow up in his face."

"How awful —"

"My point being," I interrupted, "that you should always listen to your gut."

"I am," Charlotte said. "I did. You heard what Marin said. Most of these cases settle out of court anyway. It's money. Money that we could put to good use for Willow."

"Yeah, and Piper becomes the sacrificial lamb."

Charlotte got quiet. "She has malpractice insurance."

"I don't think that protects her against backstabbing by her best friend."

She drew the sheet around her, sitting up in bed. "She would do it if it was *her* daughter."

I stared at her. "I don't think she would. I don't think *most* people would."

"Well, I don't care what other people think. Willow's opinion is the only one that counts," Charlotte said.

That, I realized, was the reason that I hadn't signed those damn papers. Like Charlotte, I was only thinking of you. I was thinking of the moment you realized that I wasn't a knight in shining armor. I knew it would happen eventually — that's what growing up is all about. But I didn't want to rush it. I wanted to be your champion for as long as I could keep you believing in me.

"If Willow's opinion is the only one that counts," I said, "how are you going to explain to her what you're doing? I mean, you want to lie on the witness stand —

216

say you would have aborted her — that's up to you. But to Willow, it might sound a hell of a lot like the truth."

Tears sprang to Charlotte's eyes. "She's smart. She'll understand that it doesn't matter what it looks like on the surface. She'll know deep down that I love her."

It was a catch-22. My refusal to sign those papers didn't mean Charlotte wouldn't try to proceed without me. If I refused to sign those papers, the rift between the two of us would hurt you, too. But what if Charlotte's prediction came true — that the money we'd get as a payout would go a long way toward justifying whatever wrong we'd done to get it? What if this lawsuit made it possible for you to have any adaptive aid you needed, any therapy not covered by insurance?

If I really wanted what was best for you, how could I sign those papers?

How could I *not?*

Suddenly, I wanted to make Charlotte see how this was tearing me up inside. I wanted her to feel the same sick knot that I felt every time I opened up my glove compartment and saw that envelope. It was like Pandora's box — she had opened it, and what had flown out but a solution to a problem we never imagined could be solved. Closing the lid now wouldn't change anything; we couldn't unlearn what we now knew to be possible.

I guess, if I was being honest, I wanted to punish her for putting me into this situation, where there was no black and white but a thousand shades of gray.

She was surprised when I grabbed her and kissed her. She backed away at first, looking at me, and then leaned into my body, trusting me to take her down a dizzy road where I'd taken her a thousand times before. "I love you," I said. "Do you believe that?"

Charlotte nodded, and as soon as she did, I tightened my fingers in her hair, forcing her head back and pinning her to the mattress. "Sean, you're crushing me," she whispered, and I covered her mouth with one hand and roughly ripped aside her pajama bottoms with the other. I forced my way inside her, even as she fought against me, even as I watched her back arch with surprise and maybe pain, even as her eyes filled with tears. "Doesn't matter what it looks like on the surface," I whispered, her own words striking her like a whip. "You know deep down that I love you."

I had started this wanting to make Charlotte feel like crap, but somehow, I wound up feeling like crap myself. So I rolled off her, yanking up my boxers. Charlotte turned away, curling into a ball. "You bastard," she sobbed. "You fucking bastard."

She was right; I *was* one. I had to be, or I wouldn't have been able to do what I did next: walk out to the car and get those papers from the glove compartment. Sit in the dark in the kitchen the whole of the night, staring at them, as if the words might rearrange themselves into something more acceptable. Knock down a shot of whiskey for each of the lines where Marin Gates had placed a little yellow Post-it arrow, pointing to the space where my signature was supposed to be.

I fell asleep at the kitchen table, waking before the sun did. When I tiptoed into the bedroom, Charlotte was still sleeping. She was on her side curled like a snail, the sheet and comforter balled at the bottom of the bed. I pulled them over her gently, the way I sometimes did for you when you'd kicked your blankets loose.

I left the papers, signed in all the right places, on the pillow beside her. With a note paper-clipped to the top. *I'm sorry*, I had written. *Forgive me.*

Then I drove to work, wondering the whole time whether that message had been intended for Charlotte, for you, or for myself.

Amelia

Late August 2007

Let's just say right off the bat that we lived in the sticks, and although my parents seemed to think this was going to be a huge benefit to me later in life (Why? Because I'd know what green grass smelled like first-hand? Because we didn't have to lock our front door?), I for one wished I'd had a vote when it came to settling down. Do you have any idea what it's like not to be able to get a cable modem when even Eskimos have them? Or to go shopping for school clothes at Wal-Mart because the nearest mall is an hour and a half away? Last year in social studies, when we were studying cruel and unusual punishment, I wrote a whole essay about living where the retail opportunities were somewhere between zero and nil, and although everyone in my class totally agreed with me, I only got a B, because my teacher was the kind of Birkenstock-granola hippie who thought Bankton, New Hampshire, was the best place on earth.

Today, though, all the planets must have aligned, because my mother had agreed to road-trip to Target with you and Piper and Emma.

It had been Piper's idea — right before the school year started she occasionally decided to do a mother-daughter shopping extravaganza. My mother usually had to be persuaded to come along, because we never seemed to have enough cash. Inevitably, Piper would wind up buying things for me, and my mother would feel guilty and swear she was never going shopping with Piper again. *What's the big deal?* Piper would say. *I like making the girls happy.* What's the big deal indeed? If Piper wanted to pad my wardrobe, I wasn't about to deny her that one small joy.

When Piper called this morning, though, I thought my mother would jump at the opportunity. You had once again managed to outgrow a pair of shoes without ever wearing them. Usually it was just one or the other — the left one got used while the right foot was stuck in a cast for a few months — but with the spica you'd worn this spring, both your feet had managed to grow a whole size, and the soles of your old shoes were barely even scuffed. Now — six months later, when you were officially learning to walk again — it had taken my mother a week to figure out that the reason you winced every time she made you use the walker to get to the bathroom by yourself had nothing to do with pain in your legs but actually with your feet being stuffed into too-tight sneakers.

To my surprise, my mother didn't want to go. She had been in a really weird mood; she had practically leapt out of her skin when I came up behind her while she was drinking a cup of coffee and reading some legal papers that looked totally boring and full of words like

IN RE and *WHOSOEVER*. And when Piper called and I handed her the phone, Mom dropped it twice. "I can't," I heard her tell Piper. "I've got some really important errands to run."

"Please, Mom?" I said, dancing around in front of her. "I promise, I won't even take a stick of gum from Piper. Not like last time."

Something I said must have struck a chord, because she looked down at those papers and then up at me. "Last time," she repeated absently, and the next thing I knew, we were on our way to Concord, to go shopping. My mother was still a little out of it, but I didn't notice. Piper's van had a DVD system, and you and Emma and I had wireless headphones on so that we could listen to *13 Going on 30*, which is the best movie ever. The last time I'd watched it had been at our house, and Piper had done the whole "Thriller" dance along with Jennifer Garner, leading Emma to proclaim that she just wanted to die of embarrassment on the spot, even though I secretly thought it was really cool that Piper could remember all the steps.

Two hours later, Emma and I were running through the juniors' section. Even though most of the styles seemed to have been made by Skanky Ho Enterprises, with V-necks that reached down to the belly button and pants so low-rise they could have been kneesocks, it was exciting to shop in an area that wasn't the kids' section. Across the aisle, Piper was pushing your wheelchair, navigating aisles that were completely *not* made for disabled people. Meanwhile, my mother — whose mood had deteriorated, if possible — kept kneeling down to try shoes on your feet. "Did you know those plastic thingies on the ends of the shoelaces are called aglets?" you asked.

"As a matter of fact I did," she said, exasperated, "because you told me the last time we did this."

I watched Emma reach up on her tiptoes to take down a blouse that would, as my mother would say, show the entire world your business. "Emma!" I said. "You've got to be kidding!"

"You wear it with a *camisole*," she said, and I pretended I had known that all along. The truth is that Emma could probably put that on and look like she was sixteen, because she was already five-five, and tall and thin like her mother. I didn't wear camisoles. It was just too depressing to know that the roll at my belly stuck out farther than my boobs.

I slipped my hand into the pocket of my sweatshirt. Inside was a plastic Ziploc bag. I'd been carrying them around for the past week. Twice now I'd made myself sick in places that weren't bathrooms — once behind the gym at school, once in Emma's kitchen, when she was upstairs looking for a CD. I'd do it when it got to the point where it was all I could think about — *Would I be found out? Would it stop the ache in my belly?* — and the only way to make it go away was to just give in and do it already, except after it happened, I hated myself for not holding out.

"This would look good on you," Emma said, holding up a pair of sweatpants big enough for an elephant.

"I don't like yellow," I said, and I wandered across the aisle.

223

Piper and my mother were in the middle of a conversation. Well, that's not really accurate. Piper was in the middle of a conversation and my mother was physically present in the same general space. She was zoned out, nodding at the right times but not really listening. She thought she could fool people, but she wasn't that great an actress. Take you, for example. How many fights had she had with Dad about whether or not to hire a lawyer, while you were sitting in the next room? And then, when you asked why they were arguing, she'd insist they weren't. Did she really think you were so incredibly involved in *Drake & Josh* episodes that you weren't hanging on every word?

I *wished* she'd listen. I wished she could hear the things you asked me when we were lying in bed at night, before we fell asleep: *Amelia, will we all live here forever? Amelia, will you help me brush my teeth, so I don't have to ask Mom to do it? Amelia, can your parents ever send you back to the place you came from?*

Was it any wonder that I found myself staring in the mirror at my disgusting face and even more disgusting body? My mother was going to a lawyer to sue over a kid who had turned out less than perfect.

"Where's Emma?" Piper asked.

"In the juniors' section, scoping out tops."

"Decent ones, or the tight kind that look like ads for porn?" Piper asked. "Some of the clothing they make for kids your age must be illegal."

I laughed. "Emma could always hire a lawyer. We know a good one."

224

"Amelia!" my mother cried out. "Look what you made me do!" But she said this *before* she managed to knock over the entire display of blouses.

"Oh, shoot," Piper said, hurrying to fix the racks. Over her head, my mother gave me a tight-lipped shake of her head.

She was angry at me, and I didn't even know why. I slipped through the forest of girls' clothing, my hands spread to brush against the vines of pant legs and sleeves. I ducked my head as I passed by Emma again. What had I done wrong?

Then again, what *didn't* I do wrong?

It was almost like she was mad I had brought up the lawyer in front of Piper. But Piper was her best friend. This legal thing was front and center in our house, like a dinosaur at the dinner table that we all pretended wasn't sticking its big, slimy face into the mashed potatoes. She couldn't have forgotten to mention it to Piper, could she?

Unless . . . she very intentionally *hadn't.*

Was this why she hadn't wanted to go shopping with Piper? Why we hadn't recently dropped by Piper's house when we were in the neighborhood, the way we used to? When my mother talked about damages and getting enough money to really take care of you the way that would help you the most, I hadn't really given much thought to the person who'd be on the receiving end of the lawsuit.

If it was the doctor she had been seeing when she was pregnant . . . well, that was Piper.

Suddenly I wasn't the only person in my mother's life who had turned out to be a disappointment. But instead of feeling let off the hook, I just felt sick.

I stood up, turning corners blindly, until I found myself standing in the lingerie section. I was crying by then, and just my luck, the only Target employee who was on the floor instead of the cash registers happened to be standing right in front of me. "Hon?" she asked. "Are you okay? Are you lost?"

As if I were five years old and had been separated from my mother. Which, actually, was not all that far off the mark.

"I'm fine," I said, ducking my head. "Thanks." I pushed past her, heading through the bras, even as one got caught on my sleeve. It was pink and silky, with brown polka dots. It looked like the kind of thing Emma would wear.

Instead of putting it back on its hanger, I stuffed it into my pocket, next to my Ziploc bags. I curled my fingers around it and checked to see whether the employee had been watching. The satin was cold between my fingers. I could swear it was pulsing, a secret heartbeat.

"Are you sure you're okay?" the woman asked again.

"Yes," I said, the lie coming easily, reminding me that, even as much as I hated her right now, I was my mother's daughter.

Piper

September 2007

I've always said that the best part of my job is that I don't do the work: that's up to the prospective mother, and I basically monitor what's going on and keep it running smoothly.

"Okay, Lila," I said, removing my hand from between her legs. "We're at ten centimeters. Almost there. You've got to push for me now."

She shook her head. "*You* do it," she muttered.

She'd been in labor for nineteen hours; I completely understood why she wanted to pass the buck. "You are so beautiful," her husband crooned, holding up her shoulders.

"You are so full of shit," Lila snarled, but as a contraction settled over her like a net, she bore down and pushed. I could see the fetal head swelling closer, and I held up my hand to keep it from popping out too fast and tearing the perineum. "Again," I urged. This time, the fetal head rushed forward like a tide, and as the mouth and nose broke the seal of Lila's skin, I suctioned them. The rest of the head was delivered, and I slipped the cord over it, supporting it as I turned the baby to control the shoulders. Five seconds later, the baby was balanced in the scale of my hands. "It's a boy," I said, as he announced, with a healthy cry, his own presence.

The cord was clamped, and Lila's husband cut it. "Oh, baby," he said, kissing her on the mouth.

"Oh, baby," Lila echoed, as her newborn son was settled in her arms by the labor nurse.

I smiled and resumed my position at the foot of the birthing chair. Now came the unceremonious part of the happy event: waiting around for the placenta to present itself like a late houseguest; checking the vagina, cervix, and vulva for lacerations and repairing them if necessary; doing a digital rectal exam. To be honest, the parents were usually so engrossed in the newest addition to their family, some women didn't even notice what was going on below their waists anymore.

Ten minutes later I congratulated the couple, stripped off my gloves, washed my hands, and headed outside to begin filling out the mountain of paperwork. I had barely taken two steps outside the patient's door, though, when a man wearing jeans and a polo shirt approached. He looked lost, like a father who was staggering into the birthing pavilion to locate his wife. "Can I help you?" I asked.

"Are you Dr Reece? Dr Piper Reece?"

"Guilty as charged."

He reached into his back pocket and pulled out what looked like a folded blue brochure, which he handed to me. "Thanks," he said, and he turned on his heel.

I opened the document and saw the words *WRONGFUL BIRTH ACTION.*

Birth of an unhealthy child.

Parents' right to recover is based on the defendant's negligent deprivation of the parents' right not to conceive a child or to prevent the child's birth.

Medically negligent.

Defendant failed to exercise due care.

Plaintiffs suffered injury or loss.

I had never been sued before, although, like every other obstetrician, I had medical malpractice insurance. On some level, I'd known that my lack of lawsuits was sheer luck — that it would happen sooner or later. I just hadn't expected it to feel like such a personal affront.

There had certainly been tragedies during my career — babies that were stillborn, mothers whose complications during childbirth led to excessive bleeding and even brain death. I carried those incidents with me, every day; I didn't need a lawsuit to make me revisit them over and over, and wonder what could have been done differently.

Which disaster had precipitated this? My eyes scanned to the top of the page again, reading the plaintiffs' names, which I'd somehow missed the first time around.

SEAN AND CHARLOTTE O'KEEFE v. PIPER REECE.

Suddenly I couldn't see. The space between my eyes and the paper was washed red, like the blood that was pounding so loudly in my ears that I did not hear a nurse ask if I was all right. I staggered down the hall to the first door I could find — into a supply closet filled with gauze and linens.

My best friend was suing me for medical malpractice.

For wrongful birth.

For not telling her earlier about your disease, so that she would have had the chance to abort the child she'd begged me to help her conceive.

I sank down onto the floor and cradled my head in my hands. One week ago, we'd driven down to Target with the girls. I'd treated her to lunch at an Italian bistro. Charlotte had tried on a pair of black pants and we'd laughed about low-rise waistbands and how there should be support thongs for women over forty. We'd bought Emma and Amelia matching pajamas.

We'd spent seven hours together in close quarters, and not once had she managed to mention that she was in the process of suing me.

I pulled my cell phone out of the clip at my waist and speed-dialed her — number 3, outranked only by Home and Rob's office. "Hello?" Charlotte answered.

It took me a moment to find my voice. "What is this?"

"Piper?"

"How *could* you? Everything was fine for five years, and all of a sudden out of nowhere you slap a lawsuit on me?"

"I really don't think we should be talking on the phone —"

"For God's sake, Charlotte. Do I deserve this? What did I ever do to you?"

There was a beat of silence. "It's what you *didn't* do," Charlotte said, and the line went dead.

Charlotte's medical records were back at my office, a ten-minute drive from the hospital birthing pavilion. As I entered, my receptionist glanced up. "I thought you were at a delivery," she said.

"It's over." I walked past her, into the records room, and pulled Charlotte's file, then headed back outside to my car.

I sat in the driver's seat with the file in my lap. *Don't think of this as Charlotte*, I told myself. *This is just any other patient.* But when I tried to bring myself to open the manila folder with the bright tabs on the edge, I couldn't do it.

I drove to Rob's practice. He was the only orthodontist in Bankton, New Hampshire, and pretty much had a monopoly on the adolescent market there, but he still went out of his way to make the dental experience something kids would enjoy. In one corner of the office was a projection TV, where a generic teen comedy was currently playing. There was a pinball machine and a computer station where patients could play video games. I walked up to his receptionist, Keiko. "Hi, Piper," she said. "Wow, I don't think we've seen you here in a good six months —"

"I need to see Rob," I interrupted. "Now." I grasped the file in my hands more tightly. "Can you tell him I'll meet him in his office?"

Unlike my office, which was all the colors of the sea and designed to put a woman at ease, in spite of the plaster models of fetal development that dotted the shelves like little Buddhas, Rob's was luxurious, paneled, masculine. He had an enormous desk, mahogany bookshelves, Ansel Adams prints on the wall. I sat down in his tufted leather chair and spun it around once. I felt small here. Inconsequential.

I did the one thing I'd wanted to do for two hours now: burst into tears.

"Piper?" Rob said as he came in to find me sobbing. "What's the matter?" He was at my side in a second, smelling of toothpaste and coffee as he folded me into his embrace. "Are you okay?"

"I'm being sued," I managed. "By Charlotte."

He drew back. "What?"

"Med mal. For Willow."

"I don't get it," Rob said. "You weren't even *at* the delivery."

"This is about what happened before." I glanced down at the file, still on the desk. "The diagnosis."

"But you *did* diagnose it. You referred her to the hospital when you found out."

"Apparently, Charlotte thinks I should have been able to tell her earlier — because then she could have had an abortion."

Rob shook his head. "Okay, that's ridiculous. They're die-hard Catholics. Remember that time you and Sean started arguing about *Roe v. Wade* and he left the restaurant?"

"That doesn't matter. I have other patients who are Catholic. You counsel termination no matter what, if it's an option. You don't make the decision *for* the couple, based on your own assumptions about them."

Rob hesitated. "Maybe this is about money."

"Would you ruin your best friend's reputation as a doctor just to get a settlement?"

Rob glanced down at the file. "If I know you, you documented every last detail of Charlotte's pregnancy in there, right?"

"I don't remember."

"Well, what does it say in the file?"

"I . . . can't open it. You do it, Rob."

"Sweetheart, if you don't remember, it's probably because there's nothing *to* remember. This is crazy. Just look through the file, and turn it over to the malpractice carrier. That's what you have insurance for, right?"

I nodded.

"Do you want me to stay with you?"

I shook my head. "I'm okay," I said, even though I didn't believe it. As the door closed behind him, I took a deep breath and opened the manila folder. I started at the very beginning, with Charlotte's medical history.

Not to be confused, I thought to myself, with our personal history.

HEIGHT: 5'2"
WEIGHT: 145
Patient has been trying unsuccessfully to conceive for a year.

I flipped the page — lab results that confirmed pregnancy; the blood tests for HIV, syphilis, hep B, anemia; urinalysis that screened for bacteria, sugar, protein. All had been normal, until the quad screen, and the elevated risk for Down syndrome.

The eighteen-week ultrasound had been part of routine pregnancy care, but I'd also been looking to confirm Down syndrome. Had I been so focused on that one task I never thought to look for any other anomalies? Or had they simply not been there?

I pored over the ultrasound report, scrutinized the pictures for any inkling of a break that I might have missed. I stared at the spine, at the heart, at the ribs, at the long bones. A fetus with OI might have had breaks at that point in time, but the collagen defect in the bones would have made them even more difficult to see. You couldn't really fault a physician for not red-flagging something that appeared, for all intents and purposes, normal.

The last image on the ultrasound report was of the fetal skull.

I flattened my hands on either side of the page, pinning down a picture of the brain that was sharp and focused.

Crystal clear.

Not because of the quality of our new equipment, as I'd assumed at the time, but because of a demineralized calvarium, a skull that had not ossified correctly.

As physicians, we're taught to look for things that are abnormal — not things that are too perfect.

Had I known back then, long before I knew you and your illness, that a demineralized calvarium was a hallmark of OI? *Should* I have known? Had I pushed down gently on Charlotte's belly, to see if the fetal skull gave way to the pressure? I couldn't remember. I couldn't remember anything, except telling her that her baby didn't seem to have Down syndrome.

I couldn't remember if I'd taken measures that I could point to, now, that could be used to prove this wasn't my fault.

I reached into my pocketbook and took out my wallet. Buried in the very bottom, among the gum wrappers and the pens from pharma companies, was a rubber-banded stack of business cards I had accumulated. I shuffled through them until I found the one I was looking for. Picking up Rob's phone, I dialed the law firm's number.

"Booker, Hood and Coates," the receptionist said.

"I'm one of your medical malpractice clients," I replied. "And I think I need your help."

★   ★   ★

That night, I could not sleep. I went into the bathroom and stared at myself in the mirror, trying to see if I already looked different than I had when the day had begun. Could you see doubt written on a face? Did it settle in the fine lines around the eyes, the bracket of the mouth?

Rob and I had decided not to tell Emma what had happened, at least not until there was something concrete to tell. It occurred to me that Amelia might mention something now that school had started up again — but then, maybe Amelia didn't know what her parents were doing, either.

I sat down on the toilet seat and looked at the moon. Full, orange, it seemed to be balanced on the windowsill. The light spilled into the bathroom and across the tile floor, pooling in the bowl of the tub. It wouldn't be long before dawn, and then I would be expected to go to work and take care of patients who were pregnant or trying to become pregnant, when I could no longer be sure of my own judgment.

The few times I'd been so upset that I couldn't sleep — like after my father died, and when my office manager stole several thousand dollars from the practice — I'd called Charlotte. Although I was the one who was used to being phoned in the middle of the night for an emergency, she hadn't complained. She'd acted as if she'd been expecting me to call, and even though I knew she had a thousand things to do the next day with Willow or Amelia, she'd stay up with me for hours, talking about everything and nothing, until my mind stopped racing long enough for me to relax.

236

I was licking my wounds, and I wanted to call my best friend. Except this time, she was the one who'd caused them.

A daddy longlegs was crawling up the wall. It left me almost breathless. Everything I knew about physics and gravity told me that it should be tumbling to the ground. The closer it got to the ceiling, the more I was riveted. It tucked two legs around the curl at the top of the wallpaper, where the strip had begun peeling off.

I'd asked Rob to fix it a thousand times; he'd ignored me. But now that I was looking at it — really looking — I realized I didn't like this wallpaper at all. What we needed was a fresh start. A good, new coat of paint.

I stood on the lip of the tub, reached up with my right hand, and in one swift pull, tore away a long tongue of wallpaper.

Most of the strip, though, was still affixed to the wall.

What did I know about removing wallpaper?

What did I know about *anything?*

I needed a steamer. But at three in the morning, I wasn't going to get one, so I turned on the hot-water faucets in the bath and the sink, letting steam cloud the room. I tried to curl my fingernails under the edges, to scrape the strip free.

There was a sudden rush of cold air. "What the hell are you doing?" Rob asked, bleary, standing in the doorway.

"Stripping the wallpaper."

"In the middle of the night? Piper," he sighed.

"I couldn't sleep."

He turned off the taps. "You have to try." Rob led me by the hand back to bed, where I lay down and drew the covers over me. I curled onto my side, and he fitted his arm around my waist.

"I could redo the bathroom," I whispered when his even breathing told me he was asleep again.

Charlotte and I had spent one day last summer reading every kitchen and bath makeover magazine in the Barnes & Noble racks. *Maybe you should go minimalist*, Charlotte had suggested, and then, turning the page, *French provincial?*

Get an air tub, she'd suggested. *A TOTO toilet. A heated towel rack.*

I'd laughed. *A second mortgage?*

When I met with Guy Booker at the law firm, would he take inventory of this house? Of our mutual funds and retirement accounts and Emma's college savings and all the other assets that could be taken away in a settlement?

Tomorrow, I decided, I would get one of those steamers. And whatever other tools I needed to strip wallpaper. I would fix it all myself.

"I think I dropped the ball," I admitted as I sat across from Guy Booker at a gleaming, imposing conference table.

My lawyer reminded me of Cary Grant — white hair with a raven's wing of color at the temples, tailored suit, even that little divot in his chin. "Why don't you let me be the judge of that?" he said.

He had told me that we had twenty days to file an answer to the complaint I'd been served — a formal pleading for the court. "You say that osteogenesis imperfecta can be diagnosed by a woman's twentieth week of pregnancy?" he asked.

"Yes — the lethal kind, anyway, by ultrasound."

"Yet the patient's daughter survived."

"Right," I said. *Thank God.*

I liked that he was referring to Charlotte as "the patient." It made it feel more clinical. It was one step farther away.

"So she's got the severe type — Type III."

"Yes."

He flipped through the file again. "The femur was in the sixth percentile?"

"Right. That's documented."

"But it's not a definitive marker for OI."

"It can mean all sorts of things. Down syndrome, skeletal dysplasia . . . or a short parent, or the fact that we took a bad measurement. A lot of fetuses with standard deviations like Willow's at eighteen weeks go on to be perfectly healthy. It's not until a later ultrasound, when that number falls off the charts, that we know we're dealing with some abnormality."

"So your advice would have been to wait and see, regardless?"

I stared at him. Put that way, it didn't seem like I'd made a mistake. "But the skull," I said. "My technician pointed it out —"

"Did she say to you that she thought there might be a medical issue?"

"No, but —"

"She said it was a very clear picture of the brain." He looked up at me. "Yes, your ultrasound technician called attention to something unusual — but not necessarily symptomatic. It might have been a technical issue with the machine, or the position of the transducer, or just a damn good scan."

"But it wasn't," I said, feeling tears claw at the back of my throat. "It was OI, and I missed it."

"You're talking about a procedure that isn't a conclusive test for the presence of OI. Or in other words, had the patient been seeing another physician instead of you, the same thing would have happened. That's not malpractice, Piper. That's sour grapes, on the part of the parents." Guy frowned. "Do you know of any physician who would have diagnosed OI based on the eighteen-week ultrasound of a demineralized calvarium, a shortened femur, and no obvious skeletal fractures?"

I glanced down at the table. I could nearly see my own reflection. "No," I admitted. "But they would have sent Charlotte for further testing — a more advanced ultrasound, and a CVS."

"You'd already suggested further testing once to the patient," Guy pointed out. "When her quad screen came back with a greater chance of having a Down syndrome baby."

I met his gaze.

"You advised amniocentesis then, didn't you? And what was her response?"

For the first time since I'd been handed that little blue folder, I felt the knot in my chest release. "She was going to have Willow no matter what."

"Well, Dr Reece," the lawyer said. "That sure as hell doesn't sound to me like wrongful birth."

Charlotte

I started lying all the time.

At first it was just tiny white lies: responses to questions like "Ma'am, are you okay?" when the dental receptionist called my name three times and I didn't hear her; or when a telemarketer phoned and I said that I was too busy to do a survey, when in fact I'd been sitting at the kitchen table staring into space. Then I began to lie in earnest. I'd cook a roast for dinner, completely forget it was in the oven, and tell Sean as he sawed through the blackened char that it clearly was the shoddy cut of meat the market had started stocking. I'd smile at neighbors and tell them, when they asked, that we were all doing well. And when your kindergarten teacher called me up and asked me to come to school because there had been an *incident*, I acted as if I had no idea what might have upset you in the first place.

When I arrived, you were sitting in the empty classroom in a tiny chair beside Ms. Watkins's desk. The transition to public school had been less divine than I'd expected it to be. Yes, you had a full-time aide paid for by the state of New Hampshire, but I had to argue every last right for you — from the ability to go to the bathroom by yourself to the chance to interact in gym class when the play wasn't too strenuous and you weren't in danger of suffering a break. The good news was that this took my mind off the lawsuit. The bad news was that I wasn't allowed to stay and make sure you were doing all right. You were in a classroom with new kids who didn't know you — and who didn't know about OI. When I asked you after your first day what you did in school, you told me how you and Martha played with Cuisenaire rods, how you were on the same team for Capture the Flag. I'd been thrilled to hear about this new friend and asked if you wanted to invite her over to the house. "I don't think she can, Mom," you told me. "She has to cook dinner for her family."

As far as I knew, the only friend you'd made in this class was your aide.

Your eyes flickered toward me when I shook the teacher's hand, but you didn't speak. "Hi, Willow," I said, sitting down beside you. "I hear you had a little trouble today."

"Do you want to tell your mom what happened, or should I?" Ms. Watkins asked.

You folded your arms and shook your head.

"Willow was invited to participate in some imaginary play with two children this morning."

My face lit up. "But — that's terrific! Willow loves to pretend." I turned to you. "Were you being animals? Or doctors? Space explorers?"

"They were playing house," Ms. Watkins explained. "Cassidy was role-playing the mom; Daniel was the dad —"

"And they wanted me to be the baby," you exploded. "I'm *not* a baby."

"Willow's very sensitive about her size," I explained. "We like to say she's just space-efficient."

"Mom, they kept saying that because I was littlest I had to be the baby, but I didn't want to be the baby. I wanted to be the dad."

This, I could tell, was news to Ms. Watkins, too. "The dad?" I said. "How come you didn't want to be the mom?"

"Because moms go into the bathroom and cry and turn on the water so no one can hear them."

Ms. Watkins looked at me. "Mrs O'Keefe," she said, "why don't you and I talk for a moment outside?"

For five whole minutes we drove in silence. "It is *not* okay for you to trip Cassidy when she walks by you for snack." Although I did have to give you some credit for ingenuity — there wasn't much you could do to hurt someone without also hurting yourself, and this was a pretty clever, if diabolical, tactic. "The last thing you want, Willow, is for Ms. Watkins to think you're a troublemaker after one week of school."

I did not tell you that, when we had gone into the hall and Ms. Watkins asked if there was something going on at home that might lead to you acting out in school, I had flat-out lied. "No," I said, after pretending to think a minute. "I can't imagine where she got that from. But then again, Willow's always had a remarkable imagination."

244

"Well?" I prompted, still waiting for some recognition from you that you'd crossed a line you shouldn't have. "Do you have something you want to say?"

I glanced in the rearview mirror for your response. You nodded, your eyes full of tears. "Please don't get rid of me, Mommy."

If I hadn't been paused at a stoplight, I probably would have crashed into the car in front of me. Your narrow shoulders were shaking; your nose was running. "I'll be better," you said. "I'll be perfect."

"Oh, Willow, honey. You *are* perfect." I felt trapped by my seat belt, by the ten seconds it took for the light to change. As soon as it did, I pulled into the first side street I could. I turned off the ignition and slipped into the backseat to take you out of your car seat. It had been adapted, like your infant car bed — this was upright but foam lined the straps, because otherwise even braking could cause a fracture. I gently untangled you and rocked you in my arms.

I had not talked to you about the lawsuit. I told myself that I was trying to keep you blissfully ignorant for as long as possible — much the same reason I hadn't told Ms. Watkins about it. But the longer I put off this conversation, the greater the likelihood you'd find out about it from a classmate, and I couldn't let that happen.

Had I really been trying to protect you? Or had I just been protecting myself? Would this be the moment I'd point to, months from now, as the beginning of the unraveling between us: *yes, we were sitting on*

Appleton Lane, under a sugar maple, the moment that my daughter started to hate me.

"Willow," I said, my throat suddenly so dry that I could not swallow. "If anyone's been bad, it's me. Do you remember when we went to visit that lawyer after your breaks at Disney World?"

"The man or the lady?"

"The lady. She's going to help us."

You blinked. "Help us do what?"

I hesitated. How was I supposed to explain the legal system to a five-year-old? "You know how there are rules?" I said. "At home, and at school? What happens if someone breaks those rules?"

"They get a time-out."

"Well, there are rules for grown-ups, too," I said. "Like, you can't hurt someone. And you can't take something that's not yours. And if you break the rules, you get punished. Lawyers can help you if someone breaks a rule and hurts you in the process. They make sure that the person who did something wrong takes responsibility."

"Like when Amelia stole my glitter nail polish and you made her buy me another one with her babysitting money?"

"Exactly like that," I said.

Your eyes welled up again. "I broke the rules in school and the lawyer's going to make me move out of the house," you said.

"No one is moving," I said firmly. "Especially not you. You didn't break the rules. Someone else did."

246

"Is it Daddy?" you asked. "Is that why he doesn't want you to get a lawyer?"

I stared at you. "You heard us talking about that?"

"I heard you *yelling* about it."

"It wasn't Daddy. And it wasn't Amelia." I took a deep breath. "It was Piper."

"*Piper* stole something from our house?"

"This is where it gets complicated," I said. "She didn't steal a *thing*, like a television or a bracelet. She just didn't tell me something that she should have. Something very important."

You looked down at your lap. "It was something about me, wasn't it?"

"Yes," I said. "But it's nothing that would ever change the way I feel about you. There's only one Willow O'Keefe on this planet, and I was lucky enough to get her." I kissed the top of your head, because I wasn't brave enough to look you in the eye. "It's a funny thing, though," I said, my voice knotting around a rope of tears. "In order for this lawyer to help us, I have to play a game. I have to say things I don't really mean. Things that might hurt if you heard them and didn't know I was really just acting."

Now I watched your face carefully to see if you were following me. "Like when someone gets shot on TV but not in real life?" you said.

"Right," I said. *They're fake bullets, so why do I still feel like I'm bleeding out?* "You're going to hear things, and maybe read things, and you'll think to yourself, *My mom would never say that*. And you'd be right. Because when I'm in court, talking to that lawyer, I'm pretending to be someone else, even though I look the same and my voice sounds the same. I might fool everyone else in the world, but I don't want to fool you."

You blinked up at me. "Can we practice?"

"What?"

"So I can tell. If you're acting or not."

I drew in my breath. "Okay," I said. "You were absolutely right to trip Cassidy today."

You stared at me fiercely. "You're lying. I wish you weren't, but you're lying."

"Good girl. Ms. Watkins needs to pluck her unibrow."

A smile fluted across your face. "That's a trick question, but you're still lying, because even if she really does look like there's a caterpillar between her eyes, that's something Amelia would say out loud but not you."

I burst out laughing. "Honestly, Willow."

"True!"

"But I didn't say anything yet!"

"You don't have to say *I love you* to say *I love you*," you said with a shrug. "All you have to do is say my name and I know."

"How?"

When I looked down at you, I was struck by how much of myself I could see in the shape of your eyes, in the light of your smile. "Say Cassidy," you instructed.

"Cassidy."

"Say . . . Ursula."

"Ursula," I parroted.

"Now . . . " and you pointed to your own chest.

"Willow."

"Can't you hear it?" you said. "When you love someone, you say their name different. Like it's safe inside your mouth."

"Willow," I repeated, feeling the pillow of the consonants and the swing of the vowels. Were you right? Could it drown out everything else I would have to say? "*Willow, Willow, Willow,*" I sang; a lullaby, a parachute, as if I could cushion you even now from whatever blows were coming.

Marin

October 2007

You have never seen anything like the amount of time and dead trees that go into a civil lawsuit. Once, during a suit brought against a priest for sexual assault, I had sat through a deposition of a psychiatrist that went on for three days. The first question was: *What is psychology?* The second: *What is sociology?* The third: *Who was Freud?* The expert was getting paid $350 an hour and wanted to make damn sure he took his time. I think we lost three stenographers to carpal tunnel syndrome before we finally got his answers on record.

It was eight months since I'd first met with Charlotte O'Keefe and her husband, and we were still in the learning phase. Basically, it involved the clients going about their everyday lives and, every now and then, getting a call from me saying that I needed this document or that information. Sean was promoted to lieutenant. Willow started full-day kindergarten. And Charlotte spent the seven hours that Willow was in school waiting for the phone to ring, in case her daughter had another break.

Part of getting ready for the depositions involved questionnaires called interrogatories that help lawyers like me see the strengths and weaknesses of the case, and whether or not it should settle. Discovery is aptly named: you are meant to find out if your case is a loser, and where the black holes are, before you're sucked into them.

Piper Reece's interrogatory had landed in my inbox this morning. I'd heard, through the grapevine, that she had taken a leave of absence from her practice and had her mentor come out of retirement to cover for her.

This entire lawsuit was predicated on the assumption that she had not told Charlotte about her baby's medical condition early on — had not given her information that might have led to terminating the pregnancy. And there was a little piece of me that wondered if it had been an oversight on the obstetrician's part or a subconscious slip. Were there obstetricians who — instead of recommending abortions — suggested adoption? Had one of them taken care of my own mother?

I had finally received my nonidentifying letter from Maisie in the Hillsborough County Court Records Office. *Dear Ms. Gates*, the letter had read.

The following information has been compiled from the court record of your adoption. Information in the record indicates the birth mother's obstetrician contacted his attorney seeking advice for a patient who was considering adoption. The attorney was aware

251

of the Gateses' interest in adopting. The attorney met with the birth parents after you were born and made arrangements for the adoption.

You were born in a Nashua hospital at 5:34p.m. on January 3, 1973. You were discharged from the hospital on January 5, 1973, into the care of Arthur and Yvonne Gates. Their adoption of you became final on July 28, 1973, in Hillsborough County Court.

Information recorded on the original birth certificate indicates the birth mother was seventeen when she gave birth to you. She was a Hillsborough County resident at the time. She was Caucasian, and her occupation was Student. The birth father was not identified on the birth certificate. At the time of the adoption, she was living in Epping, NH. The adoption petition identifies your religious affiliation as Roman Catholic. The birth mother and maternal grandmother signed a consent to your adoption.

Please feel free to contact me if I can be of any additional assistance.

Sincerely, Maisie Donovan

I realized that the point of the nonidentifying letter was to give information that wasn't specific — but there were so many other things I wanted to know instead. Had my father and mother broken up during the pregnancy? Had my mother been scared, in that hospital by herself? Had she held me even once, or just let the nurse take me away?

I wondered if my adoptive parents, who had raised me decidedly Protestant, had known I was born Catholic.

I wondered if Piper Reece had figured that, if Charlotte O'Keefe didn't want to raise a child like Willow, someone else might be more than happy to have the chance.

Clearing my head, I picked up the interrogatory she'd filled out and flipped through the pages to read her side of the story. My questions had begun generically and then gotten more medically specific at the end of the document. The first one, in fact, had been a complete softball: *When did you first meet Charlotte O'Keefe?*

I scanned the answer and blinked, certain I'd read that wrong.

Picking up the phone, I called Charlotte. "Hello?" she said, breathless.

"It's Marin Gates," I said. "We need to talk about the interrogatories."

"Oh! I'm so glad you called. There must be a mistake, because we got one with Amelia's name on it."

"That's not a mistake," I explained. "She's listed as one of our witnesses."

"Amelia? No, that's impossible. There is no way she's testifying in court," Charlotte said.

"She can describe the quality of life in your family, and how OI has affected her. She can talk about the trip to Disney World, and how traumatic it was to be taken out of your custody and put in a foster home —"

"I don't want her having to relive that —"

"She'll be a year older by the time the trial starts," I said. "And she may not *need* to be called as a witness. She's listed just in case, as protocol."

"Maybe I shouldn't even tell her, then," Charlotte murmured, which reminded me why I had called in the first place.

"I need to talk to you about Piper Reece's interrogatory," I said. "On it, I asked her when she first met you, and she said that you had been best friends for eight years."

There was a silence on the other end of the line.

"Best friends?"

"Well," Charlotte said. "Yes."

"I've been your lawyer for eight months," I said. "We've met half a dozen times in person and talked three times that much on the phone. And you never thought it might be the *tiniest* bit important to give me that little detail?"

"It has nothing to do with the case, does it?"

"You lied to me, Charlotte!" I said. "That has a hell of a lot to do with the case!"

"You didn't ask me if I was friends with Piper," Charlotte argued. "I didn't lie."

"It's a lie of omission."

I picked up Piper's interrogatory and read out loud. "'In all of the years we've been friends, I never had any indication that Charlotte felt this way about her prenatal care. In fact, we had been shopping together

254

with our daughters a week before I got served with what I feel is a baseless lawsuit. You can imagine how shocked I was.' You went *shopping* with this woman the week before you sued her? Do you have any idea how cold-blooded that's going to look to a jury?"

"What else did she say? Is she doing all right?"

"She's not working. She hasn't worked for two months," I said.

"Oh," Charlotte said, her voice small.

"Look, I'm a lawyer. I'm well aware that my job requires destroying the lives of people. But you apparently have a personal connection to this woman, in addition to a professional one. It's not going to make you sympathetic."

"Neither is telling a court that I didn't want Willow," Charlotte said.

Well, I couldn't argue with that.

"You may get what you want out of this lawsuit, but it's going to come at a great cost."

"You mean everyone's going to think I'm a bitch," Charlotte said. "For screwing my best friend. And for using my child's illness to get money. I'm not stupid, Marin. I know what they're going to say."

"Is that going to be a problem?"

Charlotte hesitated. "No," she said firmly. "No, it's not."

She'd already confessed to having problems getting her husband on board with this lawsuit. Now I'd found out that she had a hidden history with the defendant. What you didn't tell someone was just as debilitating as what you did; I only had to look as far as my stupid nonidentifying letter to feel it first-hand.

"Charlotte," I said, "no more secrets."

The purpose of a deposition is to find out what happens to a person when he or she is thrown into the trenches of a courtroom. Conducted by the opposing party's lawyer, it involves trying to impeach a potential witness's credibility based on statements in the interrogatories. The more honest — and unflappable — a person is, the better your case begins to look.

Today, Sean O'Keefe was being deposed, and it scared me to death.

He was tall, strong, handsome — and a wild card. Of all the face-to-face meetings I'd had with Charlotte to prepare, he'd come to only one. "Lieutenant O'Keefe," I had asked, "are you committed to this lawsuit?"

He had glanced at Charlotte, and an entire conversation had unraveled between them in utter silence. "I'm here, aren't I?" he had said.

It was my belief that Sean O'Keefe would rather be drawn and quartered than led to a witness stand for this trial, which should not really have been my problem — except it was. Because he was Willow's father, and if he screwed up on the stand, my case would be ruined. For this suit to succeed, the malpractice lawyers needed to believe that, when it came to wrongful birth, the O'Keefes presented a united front.

Charlotte, Sean, and I rode up in the elevator together. I had specifically scheduled the deposition during the hours you were in school, so child care wasn't an issue. "Whatever you do," I said, last-minute quarterbacking, "don't relax. They're going to lead you down the path to hell. They'll twist your words."

He grinned. "Go ahead, make my day."

"You can't play Dirty Harry with these guys," I said, panicking. "They've seen it before, and they'll trap you with your own bravado. Just remember to keep calm, and to count to ten before you answer anything. And —"

The elevator doors opened before I could finish my sentence. We stepped into the luxurious offices, where a paralegal in a fitted blue suit was already waiting. "Marin Gates?"

"Yes," I said.

"Mr Booker's expecting you." She led us down the hall to the conference room, a panorama of floor-to-ceiling windows that looked out toward the golden dome of the Statehouse. Tucked into one corner was the stenographer. Guy Booker was deep in conversation, his silver head bent. He stood up as we approached, revealing his client.

Piper Reece was prettier than I expected. She was blond, lanky, with dark circles underneath her eyes. She wasn't smiling; she stared at Charlotte as if she'd just been run through with a sword.

Charlotte, on the other hand, was doing everything possible *not* to look at her.

"How *could* you?" Piper accused. "How could you do this?"

257

Sean narrowed his eyes. "You'd better stop right there, Piper —"

I stepped between them. "Let's just get this over with, all right?"

"You have nothing to say?" Piper continued, as Charlotte settled herself at the table. "You don't even have the decency to look me in the eye and tell me off to my face?"

"Piper," Guy Booker said, putting a hand on her arm.

"If your client is going to be verbally abusive to mine," I announced, "we'll walk out of here right now."

"She wants abusive?" Sean muttered. "I'll show her abusive . . ."

I grabbed his arm and pulled him down into a chair. "Shut *up*," I whispered.

It was perhaps the first and only time in my life that I would ever have anything in common with Guy Booker — neither one of us relished being present at this deposition. "I'm quite sure my client can *restrain herself*," he said, facing Piper as he stressed the last two words. He turned to the stenographer. "Claudia, you ready to get started?"

I looked at Sean and mouthed the word *calm*. He nodded and cracked his neck on each side, like a prizefighter readying to head into the ring.

That snap, that audible pop: it made me think of you, breaking a bone.

Guy Booker opened a leather folder. It was buttery, most likely Italian. Part of the reason Booker, Hood & Coates won so many cases was the intimidation factor

— they *looked* like winners, from their opulent offices to their Armani suits and their Waterman pens. They probably even had their legal pads hand-made and water-marked with their corporate seal. Was it any wonder that half the opponents threw in the towel after a single glance?

"Lieutenant O'Keefe," he said. His voice was smooth, no friction between the words. *I'm your pal, I'm your buddy*, his tone suggested. "You believe in justice, don't you?"

"It's why I'm a police officer," Sean answered proudly.

"Do you think lawsuits can bring about justice?"

"Sure," Sean said. "It's the way this country works."

"Would you consider yourself particularly litigious?"

"No."

"I guess you must have had good reason, then, to sue Ford Motor Company in 2003?"

Shocked, I turned toward Sean. "You sued Ford?"

He was scowling. "What does that have to do with my daughter?"

"You received a settlement, didn't you? Of twenty thousand dollars?" He leafed through his leather folder. "Can you explain the nature of the complaint?"

"I slipped a disk in my back, sitting in the cruiser seat the whole day. Those things are designed for crash test dummies, not real humans doing their jobs."

I closed my eyes. *It would have been really nice*, I thought, *if either of my clients had been honest with me.*

"About Willow," Guy said. "How many hours per day would you say you spend with her?"

"Maybe twelve," he said.

"Of those twelve hours, how many is she asleep?"

"I don't know, eight, if it's a good night."

"If it's not a good night, how many times would you say you have to get up with her?"

"It depends," Sean said. "Once or twice."

"So the amount of time you're with her, and not trying to get her back to sleep — that's probably about four or five hours a day?"

"Sounds fair."

"During those hours, what do you and Willow do?"

"We play Nintendo. She beats the pants off me at Super Mario. And we play cards . . ." He blushed a little. "She's a natural at Five-Card Stud."

"What's her favorite TV show?" Guy asked.

"*Lizzie McGuire*, this week."

"Favorite color?"

"Magenta."

"What kind of music does she listen to?"

"Hannah Montana and the Jonas Brothers," Sean said.

I could remember sitting on the couch with my mother and watching *The Cosby Show*. We'd make a bowl of microwave popcorn and eat the entire thing. It had never been the same after Keshia Knight Pulliam had gotten too old and had been supplanted by Raven-Symone. If I had been raised by my birth mother, would my childhood have been colored differently? Would we have been hooked on soap operas, PBS documentaries, *Dynasty*?

"I hear Willow goes to kindergarten now."

"Yeah, she just started two months ago," Sean said.

"Does Willow have a good time in school?"

"It's hard for her sometimes, but I'd say she enjoys it."

"No one's denying that Willow is a child with disabilities," Guy said, "but those disabilities don't prevent her from having a positive educational experience, do they?"

"No."

"And they don't prevent her from sharing good times with your family, do they?"

"Absolutely not."

"In fact, would you say as Willow's father that you've done a good job making sure she has a good, rich life?"

Oh, no, I thought.

Sean sat up a little straighter, proud. "Damn right I have."

"Then why," Guy asked, going in for the kill, "are you saying that she should never have been born?"

The words went through Sean like a bullet. He jerked forward, flattening his hands on the table. "Don't you put words in my mouth. I never said that."

"Actually, you did." Guy took a copy of the complaint from his folder and slid it across the table toward Sean. "Right here."

"No." Sean set his jaw.

"Your signature on this document represents the truth, Lieutenant."

"Hey, listen, I love my daughter."

"You love her," Guy repeated. "So much that you think she'd be better off dead."

Sean reached for the complaint and crumpled it in his hand. "I'm not doing this," he said. "I don't want this; I never wanted this."

"Sean . . ." Charlotte stood up and grabbed his arm, and he rounded on her.

"How can you say this won't hurt Willow?" he said, the words torn from his throat.

"She knows these are only words, Sean, words that don't mean anything. She knows we love her. She knows that's why we're here."

"Guess what, Charlotte," he said. "Those are only words, too." And with that, he strode out of the conference room.

Charlotte stared after him, and then at me. "I-I have to go," she said. I stood up, not sure if I was supposed to follow her out or stay and try to patch up the damage with Guy Booker. Piper Reece was red-faced, staring into her lap. Charlotte's low heels sounded like gunshots as she hurried down the hallway.

"Marin," Guy said, leaning back in his chair. "You can't possibly think you've got a viable case here."

I could feel a bead of sweat running between my shoulder blades. "Here's what I know," I said, with much more conviction than I actually possessed. "You just saw first-hand how this illness has ripped their family apart. Seems to me a jury will see that, too."

I gathered my notes and my briefcase and walked down the hall with my head high, as if I actually

262

believed what I'd said. And only when I was in the elevator alone, and the doors had shut behind me, did I close my eyes and admit that Guy Booker was right.

My cell phone started to ring.

"Shit," I muttered, wiping my eyes, digging in my briefcase to answer it. Not that I wanted to: it was either Charlotte, apologizing for what had to be the biggest debacle of my career so far, or Robert Ramirez, firing me because bad news travels fast. But no number flashed on the screen; it was a private caller. I cleared my throat. "Hello?"

"Is this Marin Gates?"

"Speaking."

The elevator doors opened. On the far side of the lobby, I could see Charlotte pleading with Sean, who was shaking his head.

For a moment I almost forgot I was still on the phone. "This is Maisie Donovan," a reedy voice said. "I'm the clerk of —"

"I know who you are," I said quickly.

"Ms. Gates," she replied, "I have your birth mother's current address."

Amelia

I had been waiting for the bomb to drop. The best part of the stupid lawsuit was that it had been filed just as school was starting, when who was hooking up with whom was far more interesting than some random legal battle, so the news hadn't spread through the halls like electricity through a conductor. We'd been back for two months now, studying vocabulary and slogging through assemblies on boring topics by boring people and sitting for the NECAP tests, and every day when the last bell rang I marveled at the fact that I'd somehow gotten another reprieve.

Needless to say, Emma and I hadn't been hanging out. On the first day of school, I'd cornered her when we were headed into the gym. "I don't know what my parents are doing," I'd said. "I always said they were aliens, and this only proves it." Normally that would have made Emma laugh, but instead she just shook her head. "Yeah, that's really funny, Amelia," she said. "Remind me to crack jokes the next time someone *you* trust screws you over."

After that, I'd been too embarrassed to say anything to her. Even if I told her that I was on her side, and that

I thought it was ridiculous my parents were suing her mother, why would she believe me? If I were in her shoes, I'd assume that I was spying, and that anything I said could be used against me. She didn't tell people what had gone wrong between us — after all, that would embarrass her, too — so I figured she just said that we'd had a huge fight. And here's what I learned when I kept my distance from Emma: that the people I had always assumed were my friends actually had been Emma's, and just suffering my presence. I can't say it surprised me to find this out, but that didn't mean I wasn't hurt when I was holding my lunch tray and walked by the table where they were all sitting, without anyone making room. Or when I took out my PB and J sandwich, which had as usual gotten crushed by my math textbook in my locker so that the jelly was oozing through like blood on a crime victim's clothing, and didn't have Emma to say, *Here, have half of my tuna fish*.

After a few weeks, I had nearly gotten used to being invisible. In fact, I'd gotten quite skilled at it. I would sit in class so quiet and still that sometimes I could get flies to land on my hands; I slouched at the back of the bus so low that, one day, the driver headed back toward the school without even bothering to pull over at my stop. But one morning, I walked into homeroom and immediately knew something was different. Janet Efflingham's mother worked as a receptionist at a law firm and had told everyone about a big stinking fight my parents had had in a conference room there during a deposition. The whole school knew that my mother was suing Emma's.

I would have thought this put Emma and me right back into the same sorry, pathetic lifeboat, but I had forgotten that the best defense is a good offense. I was sitting in math class, which was the hardest one for me, because my chair was behind Emma's and we used to pass notes back and forth (*Doesn't Mr Funke look hotter now that he's getting divorced? Did Veronica Thomas get breast implants over the long Columbus Day weekend or what?*), when Emma decided to go public — and take the collective sympathy of the school with her.

Mr Funke had a transparency up on the screen. "So if we're talking about twenty percent of Millionaire Marvin's earnings, and he's made six millon dollars this year, what's the amount of alimony he has to pay to Whining Wanda?"

That's when Emma said, "Ask Amelia. She knows all about being a gold digger."

Somehow, Mr Funke seemed oblivious to the comment — although everyone else started snickering, and I could feel my cheeks burning. "Maybe it would help if your asshole mother learned how to do her stupid job," I shot back.

"Amelia," Mr Funke said sharply. "Go down to Ms. Greenhaus."

I stood up and grabbed my backpack — but the front pocket where I kept my pencils and my lunch money was still open, and a rain of pennies and quarters and dimes scattered over the floor in front of my desk. I almost knelt down to pick them up but then figured everyone would find that even more hilarious — a money-grubber's daughter grubbing money? — and instead I just left all the coins behind and fled.

I had no intention of going to the principal's office. Instead, I turned right when I should have turned left and walked toward the gym. During the day, the phys ed staff left the double doors open for ventilation. I panicked for only a moment about a teacher seeing me leave the school, then remembered that no one noticed me. I wasn't important enough.

Outside, I slung my backpack over my shoulders and started running. I ran across the soccer field and through the trees that lined the neighborhood closest to the school. I ran until I came to the main road that cut through town, and then I finally let myself slow down.

The CVS pharmacy was the last building you came to if you were heading out of town, and don't think I hadn't considered it. I wandered through the aisles. I slipped a Snickers bar into my pocket. And then I saw something even better.

The only problem with being invisible in school was that, when I came home, I could still see myself. I could run hard and fast and never escape that.

My parents, they didn't seem to want the kids they had. So maybe I'd just offer up one who was completely different.

Charlotte

"I was on a website this morning," I argued, "and a girl with Type III broke her wrist trying to lift up a half gallon of milk, Sean. How can you say that Willow's not going to need some kind of special care or live-in help? And where's that money going to come from?"

"So she buys two quarts of milk instead," Sean said. "We always said we weren't going to let her define herself by her disability — but here you are, doing just that."

"The ends justify the means."

Sean pulled into our driveway. "Yeah. Tell that to Hitler." He turned off the ignition; in the back, I could hear the soft sound of your snoring; whatever you'd done in school today had completely knocked you out. "I don't know you," he said quietly. "I don't understand the person who's doing this."

I had tried to calm him down after the deposition at Piper's lawyer's office — the deposition that never actually happened — but he was having none of it. "You say you'd do anything for Willow, but if you can't do this, then you're lying to yourself," I said.

"*I'm* lying," Sean repeated. "*I'm* lying? *You're* lying. Or at least you say you are, and that Willow will understand that all those awful things you say in front of a judge, well, you never meant them. Or at least I hope to God you're lying, because otherwise you lied to *me* all those years ago about wanting to keep the baby."

We both got out of the car; I slammed the door harder than I had to. "It's so damn convenient to be high and mighty when you're living in the past, isn't it? What about ten years from now? You're telling me that when Willow's got a state-of-the-art wheelchair, and she's enrolled in a summer camp for Little People, when she's got a pool in the backyard so she can build up her bone mass and muscles and a car adapted for her to drive like other kids her age, when it doesn't matter if the insurance company refuses to pay for another set of braces because we can always cover it ourselves without you having to work double shifts — you're telling me that she's going to remember what was said in a courtroom when she was just a baby?"

Sean stared at me. "Yeah. Actually, I am."

I took a step away from him. "I love her too much to let this opportunity go."

"Then you and I," Sean said, "have very different ways of showing love."

He reached into the back and unbuckled your car seat. Your face was flushed; you slowly swam out of your dreams. "I'm out, Charlotte," Sean said simply as he carried you into the house. "You do what you have to, but don't drag me down with you."

I thought, not for the first time, that, under any other circumstance, a fight like this would have led me directly to Piper. I would have called her and given her my side of the story and not Sean's. I would have felt better, knowing she'd listened.

And I would have done what I learned directly from you: let time heal the break that had somehow come between your father and me, a fracture that hurt no matter which way we turned.

"What the hell?" Sean asked, and I glanced up to find Amelia standing in the front hallway.

She was eating an apple, and her hair had been dyed an unnatural electric blue. She smirked at me. "Rock on," she said.

You stared at her. "Why does Amelia have cotton candy on her head?"

I sucked in my breath. "I can't do this now," I said, "I just can't." And I walked up the stairs as if each step was made of glass.

During the last eight weeks of my pregnancy, there were three seconds every morning that were perfect. I'd float to the surface of consciousness, and for those few blissful moments, I would have forgotten. I'd feel the slow roll of you, the snare drum of your kicks, and I'd think everything was going to be fine.

Reality always dropped like a curtain: that kick might have fractured your leg yet again. That turn you'd completed inside me could have hurt you. I'd lie very still on my pillow and wonder if you would die during delivery, or moments after. Or whether we would be lucky enough to win the jackpot: you'd survive, and be severely disabled. It was no small irony, I thought, that if your bones broke, so did my heart.

Once, I had a nightmare. I had given birth and no one would talk to me, tell me what was going on. Instead, the obstetrician and the anesthesiologist and the nurses all turned their backs on me. "Where's my baby?" I demanded, and even Sean shook his head and backed away. I struggled to a sitting position until I could look down between my legs and see it: what should have been a baby was just a pile of shattered crystal; between the shards I could see your tiny fingernails, a bloom of brain, an ear, a loop of intestine.

I had woken up, screaming; it took hours to fall back asleep. That next morning, when Sean woke me up, I said I could not get out of bed. And I meant it: I was certain that the very act of living, for me, would be a threat to your survival. With every step I took you might be jarred; by contrast, with care, I might keep you from breaking apart.

Sean had called Piper, who showed up at the house and talked to me about the logistics of pregnancy the way she'd describe them to a small child: the amniotic sac, the fluid, the cushion between my body and yours. I knew all this, of course, but then again, I thought I'd known other things that had turned out to be wrong: that bones grew stronger, not weaker; that a fetus not having Down syndrome must mean it was otherwise healthy. She told Sean maybe I just needed a day to sleep this off, and she'd check back in with me later.

But Sean was still worried, and after calling in sick to work, he phoned our priest.

Father Grady, apparently, made house calls. He sat down on a chair that Sean brought into the bedroom. "I hear you're a little worried."

"That's an understatement," I said.

"God doesn't give people burdens they can't handle," Father Grady pointed out.

That was all very well and good, but what had my baby done to piss Him off? Why would she have to prove herself by being hurt, before she even got here?

"I've always believed that He saves truly special babies for parents He trusts," Father Grady said.

"My baby might die," I said flatly.

"Your baby might not stay in this world," he corrected. "Instead, she'll get to be with Jesus."

I felt tears in my eyes. "Well, let Him have someone else's baby."

"Charlotte!" Sean said.

Father Grady looked down at me with wide, warm eyes. "Sean thought maybe it would help if I came over to bless the baby. Do you mind?" He lifted his hand, left it hovering over my abdomen.

I nodded; I was not about to turn down a blessing. But as he prayed over the hill of my belly, I silently said my own prayer: *Let me keep her, and you can take everything else I have.*

He left me with a holy card propped on my nightstand and promised to pray for us. Sean walked him back downstairs, and I stared at that card. Jesus was stretched across the crucifix. He had suffered pain,

272

I realized. He knew what it was like to feel a nail breaking through your skin, shattering the bone.

Twenty minutes later, dressed and showered, I found Sean sitting at the kitchen table cradling his head in his hands. He looked so beaten, so helpless. I was so busy worrying about this baby myself, I had not seen what he was going through. Imagine making a career out of protecting people, and then not being able to rescue your own unborn child. "You're up," he said the obvious.

"I thought maybe I'd go for a little walk."

"Good. Fresh air. I'll come with you." He stood too quickly, rattling the table.

"You know," I said, trying to smile, "I need to be by myself."

"Oh — right. No problem," he said, but he looked a little wounded. I could not understand the physics of this situation: we were in the thickest, most suffocating mess together; how could we possibly feel so far apart?

Sean assumed I needed to clear my head, think, reflect. But Father Grady's visit had gotten me wondering about a woman who'd stopped going to our church a year ago. She lived a half mile down the street, and from time to time I saw her putting out her garbage. Her name was Annie, and all I knew about her was that she'd been pregnant, and then one day she wasn't, and after that, she never came to Mass again. The rumor was that she'd had an abortion.

I had grown up Catholic. I had been taught by nuns. There were girls who'd gotten pregnant, but they either disappeared from the class rosters or left for a semester abroad, returning quieter and skittish. But in spite of this, I'd voted Democratic ever since I turned eighteen. It might not be my personal choice, but I thought women ought to have one.

These days, though, I was wondering if it wasn't my personal choice because I was Catholic, or simply because I had never been forced to make it in practice, instead of theory.

Annie's house was yellow, with fairy-tale trim and gardens that were full of day lilies in the summertime. I walked up to the front door and knocked, wondering what I would say to her if she answered. *Hi, I'm Charlotte. Why did you do it?*

It was a relief when no one answered; this was feeling more and more like a stupid idea. I'd started back down the driveway when suddenly I heard a voice behind me. "Oh, hi. I *thought* I heard someone on the porch." Annie was wearing jeans, a sleeveless red shirt, and gardening gloves. Her hair was caught up in a knot on the back of her head, and she was smiling. "You live up the road, don't you?"

I looked at her. "There's something wrong with my baby," I blurted.

She folded her arms across her chest, and the smile vanished from her face. "I'm sorry," she said woodenly.

"The doctors told me that if she lives — *if* — she's going to be so sick. So, so sick. And I'm not supposed to think about it, but I don't understand why it's a sin if you love something and want to keep it from having to suffer." I wiped my face with my sleeve. "I can't tell

274

my husband. I can't tell him I've even thought about this."

She scuffed at the ground with her sneaker. "My baby would have been two years, six months, and four days old today," she said. "There was something wrong with her, something genetic. If she lived, she would have been profoundly retarded. Like a six-month-old, forever." She took a deep breath. "It was my mother who talked me into it. She said, *Annie, you can barely take care of yourself. How are you going to take care of a baby like that?* She said, *You're young. You'll have another one.* So I gave in, and my doctor induced me at twenty-two weeks." Annie turned away, her eyes glittering. "Here's what no one tells you," she said. "When you deliver a fetus, you get a death certificate, but not a birth certificate. And afterward, your milk comes in, and there's nothing you can do to stop it." She looked up at me. "You can't win. Either you have the baby and wear your pain on the outside, or you don't have the baby, and you keep that ache in you forever. I know I didn't do the wrong thing. But I don't feel like I did the right thing, either."

There are legions of us, I realized. The mothers who have broken babies, and spend the rest of our lives wondering if we should have spared them. And the mothers who have let their broken babies go, who look at our children and see instead the faces of the ones they never met.

"They gave me a choice," Annie said, "and even now, I wish they hadn't."

Amelia

That night, I let you brush my hair and stick scrunchies all over it. Usually, you just made massive knots and annoyed me, but you loved doing it — your arms were too short for you to manage even a ponytail yourself, so when other girls your age were playing around with their hair and putting in ribbons and braids, you were stuck at the mercy of Mom, whose braiding experience was limited to challah. Don't go thinking I'd suddenly developed a conscience or anything — I just felt bad for you. Mom and Dad had been yelling about you as if you weren't there ever since they'd come home. I mean, for God's sake, your vocabulary was better than mine half the time — they couldn't possibly think this had all gone over your head.

"Amelia?" you asked, finishing off a braid that hung right over my nose. "I like your hair this color."

I scrutinized myself in the mirror. I didn't look like a cool punk chick, in spite of my best intentions. I looked more like Grover the Muppet.

"Amelia? Are Mom and Dad going to get a divorce?"

I met your gaze in the mirror. "I don't know, Wills."

I was already anticipating the next question: "Amelia?" you asked. "Is it my fault?"

"No," I said fiercely. "Honest." I pulled the barrettes and scrunchies out of my hair and started unraveling the knots. "Okay, enough. I'm not beauty queen material. Go to bed."

Everyone had forgotten to tuck you in tonight — not that I was expecting any better, with the pathetic level of parenting skills I was witnessing these days. You crawled into your bed from the open end — it still had bars on either side of the mattress, which you hated, because you said they were for babies even if they did keep you safe. I leaned down and tucked you in. Awkwardly, I even kissed your forehead. "'Night," I said, and I jumped under my own covers and turned off the light.

Sometimes, in the dark, the house felt like it had a heartbeat. I could hear it pulsing, *waa waa waa*, in my ears. It was even louder now. Maybe my new hair was some kind of superconductor. "You know how Mom always says that I can be anything when I grow up?" you whispered. "That's a lie."

I came up on one elbow. "Why?"

"I couldn't be a boy," you said.

I smirked. "Ask Mom about that sometime."

"And I couldn't be Miss America."

"How come?"

"You can't wear leg braces in a pageant," you said.

I thought about those pageants, girls too beautiful to be real, tall and thin and plastic-perfect. And then I thought of you, short and stubby and twisted, like a root growing wrong from the trunk of a tree, with a banner draped across your chest.

MISS UNDERSTOOD.

MISS INFORMED.

MISS TAKE.

That made my stomach hurt. "Go to sleep already," I said, more harshly than I meant to, and I counted to 1036 before you started snoring.

Downstairs, I tiptoed into the kitchen and opened the refrigerator. There was absolutely no food in this house. I would probably have to eat ramen for breakfast. It was getting to the point, honestly, where if my parents didn't go to the grocery store, they could be called to task for child abuse.

Been there, done that.

I rummaged through the fruit drawer and unearthed a fossilized lemon and a knob of ginger.

I slammed the refrigerator door shut and heard a moan.

Terrified — did people who broke into houses rape girls with blue hair? — I crept toward the kitchen doorway and looked into the living room. As my eyes adjusted to the darkness again, I saw it: the quilt draped across the back of the couch, the pillow my father had pulled over his head when he rolled over.

I felt the same pang in my stomach that I had felt when you were talking about beauty queens. Moving back through the kitchen as silent as snow, I trailed my fingers along the countertop until they closed over the hilt of a carving knife. I carried it upstairs with me into the bathroom.

The first cut stung. I watched the blood rise like a tide and spill down into my elbow. Shit, what had I done? I ran the cold water, held my forearm underneath it until the blood slowed.

Then I made another parallel cut.

They weren't on my wrists, don't think I was trying to kill myself. I just wanted to hurt, and understand exactly why I was hurting. This made sense: you cut, you felt pain, period. I could feel everything building up inside of me like steam heat, and I was just turning a valve. It made me think of my mother, when she made her pie crusts. She'd prick little holes all over the place. *So it can breathe*, she said.

I was just *breathing*.

I closed my eyes, anticipating each thin cut, feeling that wash of relief when it was done. God, it felt so good — that buildup, and the sweet release. I would have to hide these marks, because I would rather die than let anyone know I'd done this. But I was also proud of myself, a little bit. Crazy girls did this — the ones who wrote poetry about their organs being filled with tar and who wore so much black eyeliner they looked Egyptian — not good girls from good families. That meant either I was not a good girl or I did not come from a good family.

Take your pick.

I opened the tank of the toilet and stuck the knife inside. Maybe I would need it again.

I stared at the cuts, which were pulsing now, just like the rest of the house, *waa waa waa*. They looked like the ties of railroad tracks. Like a tower of stairs you'd find on a stage. I pictured a parade of ugly people like me, we beauty queens who could not walk without braces. I closed my eyes, and I imagined where those steps would lead.

III

In this abundant earth no doubt
Is little room for things worn out:
Disdain them, break them, throw them by!
And if before the days grew rough
We once were lov'd, us'd — well enough,
I think, we've far'd, my heart and I.

— Elizabeth Barrett Browning,
My Heart and I

Hardball: one of the stages of sugar syrup in the preparation of candy, which occurs at 250 to 266 degrees Fahrenheit.

Nougat, marshmallows, rock candy, gummies — these are all cooked to the hardball stage, when the sugar concentration is very high and syrup will form thick ropes when dripped from a spoon. (Be careful. Sugar burns long after it comes into contact with your skin; it's easy to forget that something so sweet can leave a scar.) To test your solution, drop a bit of it into cold water. It's ready if it forms a hard ball that doesn't flatten when fished out but whose shape can still be changed with significant pressure.

Which, of course, leads to the more colloquial definition of hardball: ruthless, aggressive, competitive behavior; the kind that's designed to mold someone else's thinking to match your own.

DIVINITY

2½ cups sugar
½ cup light corn syrup
½ cup water
Pinch of salt
3 large egg whites
1 teaspoon vanilla

½ cup chopped pecans
½ cup dried cherries, blueberries, or cranberries

I've always found it interesting that a candy with a name such as Divinity requires so much brutality to create.

In a 2-quart saucepan, mix the sugar, corn syrup, water, and salt. Using a candy thermometer, heat to the hardball stage, stirring only until the sugar is dissolved. Meanwhile, beat the egg whites to stiff peaks. When the syrup reaches 260 degrees F, add it gradually to the egg whites while beating at high speed in a mixer. Continue to beat until the candy takes shape — about 5 minutes. Stir in the vanilla, nuts, and dried fruit. Quickly drop the candy from a teaspoon onto waxed paper, finishing each piece with a swirl, and let it cool to room temperature.

Hardball, beating, beating again. Maybe this candy should have been called Submission.

Charlotte

January 2008

It had started as a stain in the outline of a stingray on the ceiling in the dining room — a watermark, an indication that there was something wrong with the pipes in the upstairs bathroom. But the watermark spread, until it no longer looked like a stingray but a whole tide, and half the ceiling seemed to have been steeped in tea leaves. The plumber fussed around under the sinks and beneath the front panel of the tub for about an hour before he reappeared in the kitchen, where I was boiling down spaghetti sauce. "Acid," he announced.

"No . . . just marinara."

"In the pipes," he said. "I don't know what you've been flushing down there, but it's eroding them."

"The only stuff we've been flushing is what everyone else flushes. It's not like the girls are doing chemistry experiments in the shower."

The plumber shrugged. "I can replace the pipes, but unless you fix the problem, it's just going to happen again."

It was costing me $350 just for this visit, by my calculation — we couldn't afford it, much less a second visit. "Fine."

It would be another thirty dollars for paint to cover the ceiling, and that was if we did it ourselves. And yet here we were eating pasta for the third time this week, because it was cheaper than meat, because you had needed new shoes, because we were effectively broke.

It was nearly six o'clock — the time Sean usually walked through the door. It had been almost three months since his disastrous deposition, not that you would have known it had ever happened, from our conversations. We talked about what the police chief had said to a local newspaper about an act of vandalism at the high school, about whether Sean should take the detectives' exam. We talked about Amelia, who had yesterday gone on a word strike and insisted on pantomiming. We talked about how you had walked all the way around the block today without me having to run back and get your chair because your legs were giving out.

We did not talk about this lawsuit.

I had grown up in a family where, if you didn't discuss a crisis, it didn't exist. My mother had breast cancer for months before I realized it, and by then it was too late. My father lost three jobs during my childhood, but it wasn't a topic of conversation — one day he'd just put on a suit again and head to a new office, as if there had been no interruption in the routine. The only place we were supposed to turn with our fears and worries was the confessional; the only comfort we needed was from God.

I had sworn that, when I had my own family, all the cards would be on the table. We wouldn't have hidden agendas and secrets and rose-colored glasses that kept us from seeing all the knots and snarls of an ordinary family's affairs. I had forgotten one critical element, though: people who didn't talk about their problems got to pretend they didn't have any. People who discussed what was wrong, on the other hand, fought and ached and felt miserable.

"Girls," I shouted. "Dinner!"

I heard the distant thunder of both your feet moving down the hallway upstairs. You were tentative — one foot on a step joined by another — whereas Amelia nearly skidded into the kitchen. "Oh, God," she moaned. "Spaghetti *again?*"

To be fair, it wasn't like I'd just opened a box of Prince. I'd made the dough, rolled it, cut it into strands. "No, this time it's fettuccine," I said, unfazed. "You can set the table."

Amelia stuck her head in the fridge. "News flash, we don't have any juice."

"We're drinking water this week. It's better for us."

"And conveniently cheaper. Tell you what. Take twenty bucks out of my college fund and splurge on chicken cutlets."

"Hmm, what is that sound?" I said, looking around with my brow furrowed. "Oh, right. The sound of me *not* laughing."

At that, Amelia cracked a smile. "Tomorrow, we'd better get some protein."

"Remind me to buy a little tofu."

"Gross." She set a stack of dishes on the table. "Remind me to kill myself before dinner then."

You came into the kitchen and scooted into your high chair. We didn't call it a high chair — you were nearly six, and you were quick to point out that you were a big girl — but you couldn't reach the table without some sort of booster; you were just too tiny. "To cook a billion pounds of pasta, you'd need enough water to fill up seventy-five thousand swimming pools," you said.

Amelia slouched into the chair beside you. "To eat a billion pounds of pasta, you only have to be born into the O'Keefe family."

"Maybe if you all keep complaining, I'll make something gourmet tomorrow night . . . like squid. Or haggis. Or calves' brains. That's protein, Amelia —"

"A long time ago there was this guy, Sawney Beane, in Scotland, who ate *people*," you said. "Like, a thousand of them."

"Well, luckily, we're not that desperate."

"But if we were," you said, your eyes lighting up, "I'd be *boneless*."

"Okay, enough." I dumped a serving of steaming pasta on your plate. "Bon appétit."

I glanced up at the clock; it was 6:10. "What about Dad?" Amelia said, reading my thoughts.

"We'll wait for him. I'm sure he'll be here any minute."

But five minutes later, Sean had not arrived. You were fidgeting in your seat, and Amelia was picking at the congealed mass of pasta on her plate. "The only thing more disgusting than pasta is ice-cold pasta," she muttered.

"Eat," I said, and you and your sister dove into your dinners like hawks.

I stared down at my meal, not hungry anymore. After a few minutes, you girls carried your plates to the sink. The plumber came back downstairs to say he was finished and left me a bill on the kitchen counter. The phone rang twice and was picked up by one of you.

At seven-thirty, I called Sean's cell, and it immediately rolled over into the voice mail.

At eight, I scraped the cold contents of my plate into the trash.

At eight-thirty, I tucked you into bed.

At eight-forty-five, I called the non-emergency line for dispatch. "This is Charlotte O'Keefe," I said. "Do you know if Sean took on another shift tonight?"

"He left around five forty-five," the dispatcher said.

"Oh, right, of course," I replied lightly, as if I'd known that all along, because I didn't want her to think I was the kind of wife who had no idea where her husband might be.

At 11:06, I was sitting in the dark on a couch in the family room, wondering if it could still arguably be called a family room if one's family was splintering apart, when the front door of the house opened gingerly. Sean tiptoed into the hallway, and I switched on the lamp beside me. "Wow," I said. "Traffic must have been a bitch."

He froze. "You're up."

"We waited for you for dinner. Your plate's still on the table, if you're in the mood for fossilized fettuccine."

"I went to O'Boys after my shift with some of the guys. I was going to call . . ."

I finished his sentence for him. "But you didn't want to talk to me."

He came closer, then, so that I could smell his aftershave. Licorice, and the faintest bit of smoke. You could blindfold me and I would be able to pick Sean out from a crowd with my other senses. But identification is not the same as knowing someone through and through — the man you fell in love with years ago might look the same and speak the same and smell the same yet be completely different.

I supposed Sean could say that about me, too.

He sat down on a chair across from me. "What do you want me to tell you, Charlotte? You want me to lie and say I look forward to coming home at night?"

"No." I swallowed. "I want . . . I just want things to go back to the way they were."

"Then stop," he said quietly. "Just walk away from what you've started."

Choices are funny things — ask a native tribe that's eaten grubs and roots forever if they're unhappy, and they'll shrug. But give them filet mignon and truffle sauce and then ask them to go back to living off the land, and they will always be thinking of that gourmet

290

meal. If you don't know there's an alternative, you can't miss it. Marin Gates had offered me a brass ring that I never, in my wildest dreams, would have considered — but now that she had, how could I not try to grab it? With every future break, with every dollar we moved further into debt, I would be thinking about how I should have reached out.

Sean shook his head. "That's what I thought."

"I'm thinking of Willow's future . . ."

"Well, I'm thinking about here and now. She doesn't give a shit about money. She cares about whether her parents love her. But that's not the message she's going to hear when you get up in that damn courtroom."

"Then you tell me, Sean, what's the answer? Are we just supposed to sit around and hope Willow stops breaking? Or that you —" I broke off abruptly.

"That I what? Get a better job? Win the fucking lottery? Why don't you just say it, Charlotte? You think I can't support all of you."

"I never said that —"

"You didn't have to. It came through loud and clear," he said. "You know, you used to say that you felt like I'd rescued you and Amelia. But I guess in the long run, I let you down."

"This isn't about you. It's about our family."

"Which you're ripping apart. My God, Charlotte, what do you think people see when they look at you now?"

"A mother," I said.

"A *martyr*," Sean corrected. "No one's ever as good as you when it comes to taking care of Willow. You don't trust anyone else to get it right. Don't you see how fucked up that is?"

I felt a tightening at the back of my throat. "Well, excuse me for not being perfect."

"No," Sean said. "You just expect that of the rest of us." With a sigh, he walked to the fireplace hearth, where a pillow and a quilt were neatly stacked. "If you don't mind, you're sitting on my bed."

I managed to hold in my sob until I was upstairs. I lay down on Sean's side of the mattress, trying to find the spot where he used to sleep. I turned my face in to the pillow, which still smelled of his shampoo. Although I had changed the sheets since he'd moved to the couch, I hadn't washed his pillowcase, on purpose — and now I wondered why. So I could pretend he was still here? So that I'd have something of him if he never came back?

On our wedding day, Sean told me that he'd step in front of a bullet to save me. I knew he'd wanted me to confess the same thing, but I couldn't. Amelia needed me to take care of her. On the other hand, if that bullet had been heading straight for Amelia, I wouldn't have thought twice before diving forward.

Did that make me a very good mother, or a very bad wife?

But this wasn't a bullet, and it hadn't been fired at us. It was an oncoming train, and the cost of saving my daughter was throwing myself onto the tracks. There was only one catch: my best friend was tied to me.

It was one thing to sacrifice your own life for someone else's. It was another thing entirely to bring into the mix a third party — a third party who knew you, who trusted you implicitly.

It had seemed so simple: a lawsuit that acknowledged how hard it was for us, and that would make things so much better. But in my haste to see the silver lining, I missed the storm clouds: the fact that accusing Piper and convincing Sean would sever those relationships. And now, it was too late. Even if I called Marin and told her to stop everything, it wouldn't make Piper forgive me. It wouldn't keep Sean from judging me.

You can tell yourself that you would be willing to lose everything you have in order to get something you want. But it's a catch-22: all of those things you're willing to lose are what make you recognizable. Lose them, and you've lost yourself.

For a moment I imagined tiptoeing down the stairs and kneeling in front of Sean and telling him I was sorry. I imagined asking him to start over. Then I looked up to find that the door had opened a crack, and your little white triangle of a face was poking through. "Mommy," you said, coming closer with your awkward gait and climbing onto the bed, "did you have a nightmare?"

Your body tucked into mine, back to front. "Yeah, Wills. I did."

"Do you need me to stay here with you?"

I wrapped my arms around you, a parenthesis. "Forever," I said.

Christmas had been too warm this year, green instead of white, Mother Nature's confirmation that life wasn't as it should have been. After two weeks of temperatures in the forties, winter returned with a vengeance. That night, snow fell. We woke up with our throats dry and the heat humming from the radiators. Outside, the air smelled of chimney smoke.

Sean was already gone by the time I came downstairs at seven. He'd left behind a neatly folded stack of bedding in the laundry room and an empty coffee mug in the sink. You came downstairs rubbing your eyes. "My feet are cold," you said.

"Then put on slippers. Where's Amelia?"

"Still asleep."

It was Saturday; there was no reason to wake her up early. I watched you rubbing your hip, probably not even aware of what you were doing. You needed exercise to strengthen the muscles around your pelvis, although it still hurt you to do it after your femur fractures. "Tell you what. If you go get the paper, we can make waffles for breakfast."

I watched your mind work through the calculations — the mailbox was a quarter of a mile down the driveway; it was freezing out. "With ice cream?"

"Strawberries," I bargained.

"Okay."

You went into the mudroom to pull your coat over your pajamas, and I helped you strap on your braces before stuffing your feet into low boots that could accommodate them. "Be careful on the driveway." You zipped up your jacket. "Willow? Did you hear me?"

"Yes, be careful," you parroted, and you opened up the front door and headed outside.

294

I stood at the doorway and watched for a few moments, until you turned around on the driveway, planted your hands on your hips, and said, "I'm *not* going to fall! Stop watching!"

So I stepped back and closed the door — but through the window, I tracked you for a few more moments anyway. In the kitchen, I began to pull ingredients from the fridge and I plugged in the waffle iron. I took out the plastic batter bowl you liked so much, because it was light enough for you to lift and pour.

I headed to the front porch again, to wait for you. But when I stepped outside, you were gone. I had a clear view from the driveway to the mailbox, and you were nowhere in it. Frantic, I stuffed my feet into a pair of boots and ran down the driveway. About halfway, I saw footsteps pressed into the snow that still blanketed the stiff grass, heading toward the skating pond.

"Willow!" I yelled. "Willow!"

Goddamn Sean, for not backing a load of fill into the pond like I'd asked him to.

Suddenly, there you were, at the edge of the reeds that fringed the thin ice.

You had one foot balanced on the surface. "Willow," I said softly, so that I didn't startle you, but when you turned around, your boot slipped and you pitched forward with your hands outstretched to break your fall.

I had seen it coming. I had seen it, and so I was already moving as you turned to face me. I stepped onto ice, which was still too new and thin to support any weight, and felt the lettuce edge shatter underneath my foot. My boot filled with frigid water, but I was able to wrap my arms around you, to keep you from falling.

I was soaked to midthigh, and your body was slung over my forearm like a sack of cake flour, the breath knocked out of you. I staggered backward, pulling my foot from the muck and the weeds that lined the bottom of the pond, and sat down hard to cushion your fall. "Are you all right?" I gasped. "Is anything broken?"

You did a quick internal assessment and shook your head.

"What were you *thinking*? You know better —"

"*Amelia* gets to walk on the ice," you said, your voice small.

"First, you're not Amelia. And second, this ice isn't strong enough."

You twisted around. "Like me."

I turned you gently, so that you were sitting on my lap, with your legs on either side of mine. A spider, that's what kids called it when they did it on swing sets, although you'd never been allowed. Too easily, a leg could snag on a chain, or get twisted with a friend's limbs.

"It's not like you," I said firmly. "Willow, you are the strongest person I know."

"But you still wish I didn't have to use a wheelchair. Or go to the hospital all the time."

Sean had insisted that you were well aware of what was going on around you; I had naïvely assumed that, after the talk we'd had months ago, if you did have doubts about my words, they'd be assuaged by my actions. But I had been worried about the things you'd hear me say — not the messages you might still read between the lines. "Remember how I told you that I'd have to say things that I don't mean? That's all it is, Willow." I hesitated. "Imagine you're at school and your friend asks you if you like her sneakers, and you don't — you think they're incredibly ugly. You wouldn't tell her you hate them, would you? Because it would make her sad."

"That's lying."

"I know. And it's wrong, most of the time, unless you're trying not to hurt someone's feelings."

You stared at me. "But you're hurting *my* feelings."

The knife in my stomach twisted. "I don't mean to."

"So," you said, thinking hard, "it's like when Amelia plays Opposite Day?"

Amelia had invented that when she was about your age. Confrontational even then, she'd refuse to do her homework and then burst out laughing when we yelled at her, saying it was Opposite Day and she'd already finished it all. Or she'd terrorize you, calling you Glass Ass, and when you came to us in tears, Amelia would insist that on Opposite Day, this meant you were a princess. I'd never been able to tell if Amelia had invented Opposite Day because she was imaginative or because she was subversive.

But maybe this was a way to unravel the tangled thicket that was wrongful birth, to spin a lie, like Rumpelstiltskin, into something golden. "Exactly," I said. "Just like Opposite Day."

You smiled at me so sweetly that I could feel the frost melting around us. "Okay then," you said. "I wish *you'd* never been born, too."

When Sean and I were first dating, I would leave treats in his mailbox. Sugar cookies cut in the shapes of his initials, a roll of babka, sticky buns with candied pecans, almond roca. I took literally the term *sweet heart*. I imagined him reaching in for his bills and catalogs and coming up instead with a jelly roll, a honey cake, a building block of fudge. "Will you still love me when I put on thirty pounds?" Sean would ask, and I'd laugh at him. "What makes you think I love you?" I'd say.

I did, of course. But it was always easier for me to show love than to say it. The word reminded me of pralines: small, precious, almost unbearably sweet. I would light up in his presence; I felt like a sun in the constellation of his embrace. But trying to put what I felt for him into words diminished it somehow, like pinning a butterfly under glass, or videotaping a comet. Each night he'd wrap his arms around me and tip into my ear that sentence, bubbles that burst on contact: *I love you*. And then he'd wait. He'd wait, and even though I knew he did not want to pressure me before I was ready to make my confession, I would feel in that silence his disappointment.

One day, when I came out of work still dusting flour off my hands so that I could rush to pick up Amelia from school, I found a small index card wedged under my windshield wiper. I LOVE YOU, it read.

I tucked it into my glove compartment, and that afternoon, I made truffles and left them in Sean's mailbox.

The next day, when I left work, there was an eight-and-a-half-by-eleven-inch piece of paper taped on my windshield: I LOVE YOU.

I called Sean. "I'm going to win," I said.

"I think we both are," he replied.

I'd baked a lavender panna cotta and left it on top of his MasterCard bill.

He countered with poster board. You could read the message all the way from the front window of the restaurant, which made me the object of plenty of ribbing from the maître d' and the head chef.

"What's your problem?" Piper said to me. "Just tell him how you feel, already." But Piper didn't understand, and I couldn't explain to her. When you showed someone how you felt, it was fresh and honest. When you told someone how you felt, there might be nothing behind the words but habit or expectation. Those three words were what everyone used; simple syllables couldn't contain something as rare as what I felt for Sean. I wanted him to feel what I felt when I was with him: that incredible combination of comfort, decadence, and wonder; the knowledge that, with just a single taste of him, I was addicted. So I cooked tiramisu and left it wedged between a package from Amazon.com and a flyer for a painting company.

This time, Sean phoned me. "Opening someone else's mailbox is a felony, you know," he said.

"So arrest me," I answered.

That day, I left work — trailed by the rest of the staff, who had come to view our courtship as a spectator sport — and found my car completely wrapped in butcher paper. Painted in letters as tall as me was Sean's message: I'M ON A DIET.

Sure enough, I baked him poppy scones, and they were still in the mailbox the next day when I went to leave off ginger cookies. And the next day, with those two items untouched, I couldn't even fit the strawberry tart. I carried it up to his house instead, and rang the doorbell. His blond hair was backlit; his white tee stretched across his chest. "How come you're not eating what I made for you?" I asked.

He gave me a lazy smile. "How come you won't say it back?"

"Can't you *tell?*"

Sean crossed his arms. "Tell what?"

"That I love you?"

He opened the screen door, grabbed me, and kissed me hard. "It's about time," he said, with a grin. "I'm freaking starving."

You and I didn't just cook waffles that morning. We made cinnamon bread and oatmeal cookies and blondies. I let you lick the spoon, the spatula, the bowl. Around eleven, Amelia loped into the kitchen, freshly showered. "What army's coming for lunch?" she asked, but then she took a corn muffin, broke it open, and breathed in the steam. "Can I help?"

We made a raspberry velvet cake and a plum tarte Tatin, apple turnovers and pinwheel cookies and

300

macaroons. We baked until there was hardly anything left in my pantry, until I had forgotten what you'd said to me at the pond, until we had run out of brown sugar, until we did not notice your father being gone the whole day, until we could not eat another bite.

"Now what?" Amelia asked, when every inch of counter space was covered with something we'd made.

It had been so long that, once I started, I hadn't been able to stop. And I suppose a part of me still functioned cooking for a restaurant crowd and not an individual family — much less one that was absent one member. "We could give it to our neighbors," you suggested.

"No way," Amelia said. "Let them buy it."

"We're not running a bakery," I pointed out.

"Why not? It could be like a vegetable stand, at the end of the driveway. Willow and me, we can make a big sign that says Sweets by Charlotte, and you can wrap everything in Saran Wrap . . ."

"We could cover up a shoe box," you said, "and put a slit in the top for the money, and charge ten dollars each."

"Ten dollars?" Amelia said. "Try a buck, peabrain."

"Mom! She called me peabrain . . ."

I was imagining whitewashed walls, a glass display case, wrought-iron tables with marble tops. I was picturing rows of pistachio muffins in an industrial stove, meringues that melted in your mouth, the angel-wing ring of the cash register. "Syllabub," I interrupted, and both you girls turned to me. "That's what the name on the sign should be."

That night, by the time Sean came home, I was fast asleep, and he was gone by the time I woke up, too. The only way I even knew he'd stopped in was a used mug sitting lonely in the bowl of the sink.

My stomach knotted; I pretended it was hunger, not regret. In the kitchen I made a piece of toast and took out a crisp white coffee filter for the machine.

When Sean and I were first married, he would make coffee for me every morning. He didn't drink coffee himself, but he was up early for his shift and would program the Krups machine so that a fresh pot would be waiting by the time I got out of the shower. I would come downstairs to find a mug waiting, with two spoonfuls of sugar already inside. Sometimes, it would be sitting on a note: SEE YOU LATER or I MISS YOU ALREADY.

This morning the kitchen was cold, the coffeemaker silent and empty.

I measured out the water and the coffee grounds, pushed a button so that the liquid would stream into the carafe. I reached for a mug in the cabinet and then, on second thought, took the one Sean had used out of the sink. I rinsed it clean and poured myself a cup of coffee. It tasted too strong, bitter. I wondered if Sean's lips had touched the mug in the same place as mine.

I had always been suspicious of women who described the dissolution of their marriages as something that happened overnight. *How could you not know?* I'd thought. *How could you miss all those signs?* Well, let me tell you how: you were so busy putting out a fire directly in front of you that you were

302

completely oblivious to the inferno raging at your back. I could not remember the last time Sean and I had laughed about something together. I could not remember the last time I'd gone and kissed him, just because. I had been so focused on protecting you that I'd left myself completely vulnerable.

Sometimes you and Amelia played board games, and when you rolled the dice, they got stuck in a crease of the couch or rolled onto the floor. *Do-over*, you'd say, and it was that easy to get a second chance. That's what I wanted now: a do-over. Except, if I was being honest with myself, I wouldn't know where to start.

I dumped the coffee into the sink and watched it swirl down the drain.

I didn't need caffeine. And I didn't need someone to make me coffee in the morning, either. Leaving the kitchen, I grabbed a jacket (Sean's, it smelled like him) and headed outside to get the newspaper.

The green box that held the local paper was empty; Sean must have taken it on the way out to wherever he'd gone. Frustrated, I turned and noticed the wheelbarrow full of baked goods that we had set out yesterday at the end of the driveway.

The wheelbarrow was empty, except for the shoe box Amelia had fashioned into an honor-system cash register, and the cardboard sign you'd painted with glitter to read SYLLABUB.

I grabbed the shoe box and ran back to the house, into your bedroom. "Girls," I said, "look!"

You both rolled over, still cocooned in sleep. "God," Amelia groaned, glancing at the clock.

I sat down on your bed and opened the shoe box. "Where did you get all the money?" you asked, and that was enough to make Amelia sit up in bed.

"What money?" she asked.

"From the stuff we baked," I said.

"Give me that." Amelia grabbed the box and started organizing the money into piles. There were bills and coins, in all denominations. "There's like a hundred dollars here!"

You crawled out of your bed and onto Amelia's. "We're rich," you said, and you took a fistful of dollars and tossed them overhead.

"What are we going to do with it?" Amelia asked.

"I think we should buy a monkey," you said.

"Monkeys cost way more than a hundred dollars," Amelia scoffed. "I think we should get a TV for our bedroom."

And I thought we should pay down the debt on our MasterCard, but I doubted you girls would agree.

"We already have a TV downstairs," you said.

"Well, we don't need a stupid monkey!"

"Girls," I interrupted. "There's only one way to get what we all want. We bake enough to make more money." I looked at each of you in turn. "Well? What are you waiting for?"

You and Amelia rushed to the adjacent bathroom, and then I heard running water and the methodic scrub of your toothbrushes. I pulled up the sheets on your bed and tucked in the blankets. On Amelia's bed, I did the same thing, but this time when I smoothed the quilt under the mattress, my fingers swept free dozens of candy wrappers, the plastic bag from a loaf of bread, crumbling packets of graham crackers. *Teenagers*, I thought, sweeping them all into the trash can.

In the bathroom, I could hear you two arguing about who had left the cap off the toothpaste. I reached into the shoe box and tossed another handful of cash into the air, listening instead to the hail of silver coins, the song of possibility.

Sean

I probably shouldn't have taken the newspaper. That's what I thought to myself as I sat in a booth at a diner two towns over from Bankton, nursing my glass of orange juice and waiting for the short-order cook to fry up my eggs. After all, it was the first thing Charlotte did every morning: sip a cup of coffee as she perused the headlines. Sometimes she'd even read the letters to the editor out loud, especially the ones that sounded as if they'd been written by nutcases one step away from a Ruby Ridge standoff. When I sneaked out at 6a.m., pausing before I grabbed the paper, I realized that this was going to piss her off. And, okay, maybe that was enough incentive for me to drive off with it. But now that I'd unfolded it and scanned the front page, I categorically knew I should have left it where it was, in its box.

Because right there, above the fold, was a story about me and my family.

LOCAL COP FILES WRONGFUL BIRTH SUIT

Willow O'Keefe is — in many ways — a normal five-year-old girl. She goes to full-day kindergarten at Bankton Elementary School, where she studies reading and math and music. She plays with her peers during recess. She buys lunch in the school cafeteria. But in one respect, Willow is not like other five-year-olds. Sometimes Willow uses a wheelchair, sometimes a walker, and sometimes, leg braces. That's because, during the course of her short life, she's suffered over sixty-two broken bones, due to a disease called osteogenesis imperfecta, a condition that Willow's had since birth and that — her parents allege — should have been diagnosed by the obstetrician early enough to allow for an abortion. Although the O'Keefes love their daughter dearly, her medical bills have spiraled past routine insurance coverage, and now her parents — Lieutenant Sean O'Keefe of the Bankton Police Department and Charlotte O'Keefe — are among a growing number of patients suing their obstetrician-gynecologists for not providing them with information about fetal abnormalities that, they say, would have led them to terminate the pregnancies.

More than half of the states in America recognize wrongful birth lawsuits, and many of these cases settle out of court for less money than a jury might award because medical malpractice insurance companies don't want a child like Willow presented to a jury. But lawsuits like this often open a can of worms in terms of ethical complications: what do such lawsuits suggest about the value society places on disabled people?

Who can judge parents, who see their disabled children suffering daily? Who — if anyone — has the right to choose what sorts of disabilities should determine abortion? And what is the effect on a child like Willow, who is old enough to hear her parents' testimony?

Lou St. Pierre, the president of the New Hampshire chapter of the American Association of People with Disabilities, says he understands why parents like the O'Keefes choose to file a lawsuit. "It can help with the incredible financial burden that a severely disabled child puts on a family," says St. Pierre, who was born with spina bifida and is wheelchair-bound. "But the caveat is the message that's being sent to that child: that disabled people can't live rich, full lives; that if you aren't perfect, you shouldn't be here."

Most recently, in 2006, a $3.2 million settlement in a 2004 wrongful birth case was overturned by the New Hampshire Supreme Court.

There was even a picture of the four of us — one that had been taken for a Meet Your Friendly Neighborhood Cop circular put out by the Bankton PD two years ago. Amelia didn't have her braces yet.

Your arm was in a cast.

I threw the paper across the booth so that it landed in the far seat. Fucking journalists. What did they do, wait at the courthouse to see what was coming up on the docket? Anyone who read this article — and who wouldn't? It was the local paper — would think I was in this for the cash.

I wasn't, and just to prove it, I took out my wallet and left twenty bucks on the table for a two-dollar meal I hadn't even been served.

Fifteen minutes later, after a quick stop at the precinct to look up Marin Gates's address, I showed up at her house. It wasn't at all what I was expecting. There were gnome garden statues, and the mailbox was a pig whose snout opened. The clapboards were painted purple. It looked like the kind of place Hansel and Gretel would live, not a no-nonsense attorney.

When I rang the bell, Marin answered the door. She was wearing a Beatles *Revolver* T-shirt and sweatpants that said UNH down the leg. "What are you doing here?"

"I need to talk to you."

"You should have called." She looked around, trying to find Charlotte.

"I'm here alone," I said.

Marin folded her arms across her chest. "I'm unlisted. How did you find out where I live?"

I shrugged. "I'm a cop."

"That's an invasion of privacy —"

"Good. You can sue me when you finish suing Piper Reece." I held up the morning paper. "Did you read this crap?"

"Yes. There's very little we can do about the press, except keep saying 'No comment.'"

"I'm out," I said.

"Sorry?"

"I quit. I want out of this lawsuit." Simply saying those words made me feel like I'd passed the weight of the world to some other sucker. "I'll sign anything you want me to, I just want to make it official."

Marin hesitated. "Come inside so we can talk," she said.

If I'd been surprised by the outside of her house, I was stunned by the interior. There was one entire wall covered with Hummel figurines on shelves, and the other walls were spotted with needle-point. Doilies bloomed like algae on the surface of the sofa. "Nice place," I lied.

She just stared at me, impassive. "I rent it fully furnished," she explained. "The woman who owns the house lives in Fort Lauderdale."

On the dining room table was a stack of files, and a legal pad. All around the floor were crumpled pieces of paper; whatever it was she was writing wasn't coming smoothly.

"Look, Lieutenant O'Keefe, I know you and I haven't gotten off to the best start, and I know the deposition was . . . challenging for you. But we'll take another stab at that, and things are going to be different once we're in court. I really do feel confident that the damages the jury will be willing to award —"

"I don't want your blood money," I said. "She can have it all."

"I think I see the problem here," Marin answered. "But this isn't about you and your wife. This is about Willow. And if you really want to give her the kind of life she deserves, you need to win a lawsuit like this. If

310

you pull out now, it just gives the defense one more hook to hang their hat on —"

Too late, she realized that this might actually be something I'd want.

"My daughter," I said tightly, "reads at a sixth-grade level. She's going to see that newspaper article, and a dozen others like it, I'm guessing. She's going to hear her mother tell the whole wide world she wasn't wanted. You tell me, Ms. Gates. Is it better that I sit in that courtroom actively undermining your chance of winning your case or that I step aside so there's somewhere for Willow to turn when she needs to know that someone loves her, no matter what she's like?"

"Are you so sure you'll be doing the right thing for your daughter?"

"Are *you*?" I asked. "I'm not leaving here until you give me paperwork to sign."

"You can't expect me to draft something on a Sunday morning when I'm not at the office —"

"Twenty minutes. I'll meet you there." I had just opened the door to walk outside when I was stopped by Marin's voice.

"Your wife," she asked. "What does she think about you doing this?"

I turned slowly. "She *doesn't* think about me," I said.

I didn't see Charlotte that night, or the next morning. I assumed it would take that long for Marin to tell my wife that I'd dropped out of the lawsuit. However, even a guy who's strong in his convictions understands self-preservation; there was no way I was headed home to talk to your mother until I had a few fortifying drinks under my belt — and, being a cop, had left enough time to let the alcohol pass safely through my system before I drove.

Maybe then I'd be lucky enough to find her asleep.

"Tommy," I said, motioning to the bartender, and I pushed my empty beer glass toward him. I had come to O'Boys with some of the patrol officers after our shift, but they'd all left to go home to their wives and kids for supper by now. It was too late for a pre-dinner drink and too early for the nighttime party crowd; other than Tommy and me, the only person in the bar was an old man who started drinking at three and stopped when his daughter came to pick him up at last call.

The bell over the door jingled, and a woman walked in. She peeled off a tight leopard-print coat only to reveal an even tighter hot pink dress. It was outfits like this that always fucked up rape cases for the prosecution.

"Cold out there," she said, sliding onto a stool beside me. I stared resolutely down at my empty beer glass. *Try wearing some clothes*, I thought.

Tommy passed me a fresh beer and turned to the woman. "What can I get you?"

"A dirty martini," she said, and then she turned to me and smiled. "You ever have one of those?"

I took a sip of beer. "I don't like olives."

"I like to suck the pimientos out," she admitted. She unclipped her hair — blond, curly — so that it fell like a river to the middle of her back. "Beer tastes like Kitty Litter, if you ask me."

I laughed at that. "When was the last time you tasted Kitty Litter?"

She arched her brows. "Haven't you ever just looked at something and *known* how it's going to taste?"

She did say *something*, didn't she? Not *someone*?

I've never cheated on Charlotte. I've never even thought about cheating on Charlotte. God knows, I come across enough young women in my career to have the opportunity, if I wanted to take advantage. To be honest, Charlotte was all I'd ever wanted — even after eight years. But the woman I'd married — the one who had promised to buy vanilla ice cream for me in her wedding vows, even though it was a poor substitute for chocolate — was not the same one I saw these days in our house. That woman was single-minded and distant, so focused on what she might get that she couldn't even see what she had.

"My name's Sean," I said, facing the woman.

"Taffy Lloyd," she said, and she took a sip of her martini. "Like the candy. The Taffy part, not the Lloyd."

"Yeah, I got that."

She narrowed her eyes. "Don't I know you?"

"I'm pretty sure I'd remember meeting you before —"

"No, I know it. I never forget a face —" She broke off, snapping her fingers. "You were in the newspaper," she said. "You've got a little girl who's really sick, right? How's she doing?"

I lifted my beer, wondering if she could hear my heart pounding as loud as I could. She recognized me from that article? If this woman did, how many others would? "She's doing all right," I said tersely, finishing my beer in another long swallow. "In fact, I've got to get home to her." The hell with driving; I'd walk.

I started to get up from my stool but was stopped by her voice. "I heard you're not suing anymore."

Slowly, I turned. "That wasn't in the newspaper."

Suddenly, she didn't look ditzy at all. Her eyes were a piercing blue, and they were fixed on mine. "Why did you want out?"

Was she a reporter? Was this a trap? I felt my guard rising, too late. "I'm just trying to do what's best for Willow," I muttered, shrugging into my jacket, cursing when my sleeve got tangled.

Taffy Lloyd set a business card down on the bar in front of me. "What's best for Willow," she said, "is for this lawsuit not to happen." With a nod, she swung her leopard coat over her shoulder and walked out the door, leaving behind most of her martini.

I picked up the card and traced my finger over the raised black lettering:

Taffy Lloyd, Legal Investigator
Booker, Hood & Coates

I drove. I drove routes I took in my police cruiser, great figure eights that looped closer and closer to the center of Bankton. I watched falling stars and drove where I thought they'd landed. I drove until I could barely keep my eyes open, until it was after midnight.

I let myself into the house on a whisper and, in the dark, fumbled my way into the laundry room to get the sheets and pillowcase for the couch. Suddenly, I was exhausted, so tired I couldn't even stand. I sank down on the sofa and buried my face in my hands.

What I couldn't understand was how this had gone so far, so fast. One minute I was storming out of the lawyer's office; the next, Charlotte had set up another appointment. I couldn't forbid her to do that — but to be honest, I had never figured she'd carry through with a lawsuit. Charlotte wasn't the type to take a risk. But that's where I'd messed up: This wasn't about Charlotte, in her mind. This was about you.

"Daddy?"

I looked up to find you standing in front of me, your bare feet white as a ghost's. "What are you doing up?" I said. "It's the middle of the night."

"I got thirsty."

I walked into the kitchen, with you padding along behind me. You were favoring your right leg — although another father might simply have wondered if his daughter was still half asleep, I was thinking of microfractures and hip displacements. I poured you a glass of water from the tap and leaned against the counter as you drank it. "Okay," I said, hoisting you into my arms, because I couldn't bear to watch you navigate the stairs. "It's way past your bedtime."

Your arms laced around my neck. "Daddy, how come you don't sleep in your bed anymore?"

I paused, halfway up the steps. "I like the couch. It's more comfortable."

I crept into your bedroom, careful not to disturb Amelia, who was softly snoring in the bed beside yours. I tucked you under the covers. "I bet if I wasn't like this," you said, "if my bones weren't all messed up — you'd still be sleeping upstairs."

In the dark, I could see the shine of your eyes, the apple curve of your cheek. I didn't answer. I didn't have an answer. "Go to sleep," I said. "It's too late to talk about this."

Suddenly, just like that, as if someone had spliced a future frame into a movie, I could see who you would become when you grew up. That stubborn resolve, the quiet acceptance of someone resigned to fighting an uphill battle — well, the person you resembled most at that moment was your mother.

Instead of going downstairs, I slipped into the master bedroom. Charlotte was sleeping on her right side, facing the empty side of the bed. I sat down gingerly on the edge of the mattress, trying not to move it as I stretched out on top of the covers. I rolled onto my side, so that I was mirroring Charlotte.

Being here, in my own bed, with my own wife, felt inevitable and uncomfortable at the same time — like getting to the end of a jigsaw puzzle and forcing the last piece into place, even though the edges don't match up the way they ought to. I stared at Charlotte's hand, curled into a fist against the covers, as if she was still ready to come up swinging even when she was unconscious. When I touched the edge of her wrist, her fingers opened like a rose. When I glanced up, I found her staring at me. "Am I dreaming?" she whispered.

316

"Yes," I said, and her hand closed around mine.

I watched Charlotte as she drifted back to sleep, trying to pinpoint the divide between when she was here with me and when she was spirited away, but it happened too quickly for me to measure. Gently I slipped my hand from hers. I hoped, for a moment when she woke up, she'd remember that I'd been here. I hoped that it would make up for what I was about to do.

There was a guy in the department whose wife had had breast cancer a few years ago. In solidarity, a bunch of us had shaved our heads when she went through chemo; we all did what we could to support George through his personal hell. And then his wife recovered, and everyone celebrated, and a week later, she told him she wanted a divorce. At the time, I thought it was the most callous thing a woman could possibly do: ditch the guy who's stood beside you through thick and thin. But now, I was starting to see that what looks like garbage from one angle might be art from another. Maybe it *did* take a crisis to get to know yourself; maybe you needed to get whacked hard by life before you understood what you wanted out of it.

I didn't like being here — it was like having a bad flashback. Reaching out for a napkin underneath a pitcher in the center of the massive polished table, I mopped at my forehead. What I really wanted to do was admit that this was a mistake and run. Jump out the window, maybe.

But before I could act on that sane thought, the door opened. In walked a man with prematurely silver hair — had I not noticed that the first time around? — followed by a blond woman wearing stylish glasses and a suit buttoned nearly to the throat. My jaw dropped; Taffy Lloyd cleaned up remarkably well. I nodded silently at her, and then at Guy Booker — the lawyer who'd made a fool out of me in this very office months ago. "I came to ask you what I can do," I said.

Booker looked at his investigator. "I'm not sure I understand what that means, Lieutenant O'Keefe . . ."

"It means," I said, "I'm on your side now."

Marin

What do you say to the mother you've never met?

Since Maisie had contacted me saying she had a valid address for my birth mother, I had drafted hundreds of letters. That was the way it worked: even though Maisie apparently had located my birth mother, I wasn't allowed to contact her directly. Instead, I was supposed to write a letter to my mother and mail it to *Maisie*, who would play middleman. She'd contact my mother and say she had a very important personal matter to discuss and would leave a phone number. Presumably, when my birth mother heard this, she would know what the personal matter was and would call in. Once Maisie verified that the woman was indeed my birth mother, she'd either read aloud or mail the letter I'd written.

Maisie had sent me a list of guidelines, which were supposed to help me write the letter:

This is your introduction to the birth parent for whom you have been searching. This person is virtually a stranger to you, so your letter will serve as a first impression. In order to not overwhelm your birth parent, it is recommended that your letter be no more than two pages. As long as your handwriting is legible, it is more appreciated to receive a handwritten letter, since that gives a sense of your personality to the recipient.

You should decide whether you want this first contact to be non-identifying. If you want to use your name, please understand this makes it possible for the other party to locate you. You may want to wait until you get to know the other party before releasing your address or phone number.

The letter should contain general information about you — age, education, occupation, talents or hobbies, marital status, and whether or not you have children. Including photographs of yourself and your family is much preferred. You may wish to explain why you are searching for your birth parent at this time.

If your background includes any difficult information, this is not the time to share it. Negative adoption information — such as having been placed with an abusive family — is not appropriate. It's better to share this information later, once a relationship has developed. Many birth parents report feelings of guilt over the decision to give a child up for adoption and fear that their decision, which was made for your benefit, might not have turned out as well as they'd wished. If negative information is shared at the outset, that information may overshadow all positive aspects of developing a rapport with you in the future.

If you feel grateful to your birth parent for the decision she made, you may briefly share this. If you desire information about family medical history, you may mention this. You may want to consider waiting to ask about the birth father. This may be a painful subject at first.

To reassure the birth parent that you want a mutually beneficial relationship, you may include a statement that you'd like to phone or meet but will respect her need for time to determine her comfort level regarding this.

I had read Maisie's guidelines so often I could practically recite them verbatim. It seemed to me that the really instructive information was missing. How much do you share to illustrate what you're really like but not to turn someone off? If I told her I was a Democrat, for instance, and she turned out to be a Republican, would she throw my letter in the trash? Should I mention how I'd marched to raise funds for AIDS research and that I advocated same-sex marriage? And this didn't even take into account the decision I had to make when it came to putting my letter down in black and white. I wanted to send a card — it felt like I was trying harder, as opposed to just a scribbled missive on a legal pad. But the cards I had spotlighted images as different as Picasso, Mary Engelbreit, and Mapplethorpe. The Picasso seemed too common; the Engelbreit, too Mary Sunshine; but

Mapplethorpe — well, what if she hated him on principle? *Get over it, Marin, I told myself. There aren't any naked bodies on the card; it's a damn flower.*

Now all I had to do was come up with the content to go inside.

Briony pushed open the door to my office, and I hastily stuffed my notes into a folder. Maybe it wasn't entirely PC to use my work time to feed my personal obsession, but the more involved I became with the O'Keefe case, the harder it was to put my birth mother out of my mind. Silly as it sounded, approaching her made me feel like I was saving my soul. If I *had* to represent a woman who wished she'd gotten rid of her child, then the least I could do was find my own mother and praise her for thinking differently.

The secretary tossed a manila envelope onto my desk. "Delivery from the devil," she said, and I glanced down to see the return address: Booker, Hood & Coates.

I ripped it open and read the amended list of interrogatories.

"You've got to be kidding," I murmured, and stood up to get my coat. It was time to make a house call to Charlotte O'Keefe.

A girl with blue hair answered the door, and I stared at her for a full five seconds before I recognized Charlotte's older daughter, Amelia. "Whatever you're selling," she said, "we don't need it."

"Amelia, right?" I forced a smile. "I'm Marin Gates. Your mom's lawyer."

She scrutinized me. "Whatever. She's not here right now. She left me to babysit."

From inside the house: "I'm *not* a baby!"

Amelia flicked her eyes toward me again. "What I meant to say is that she left me to *invalid*sit."

Suddenly your face poked around the doorframe. "Hi," you said, and you smiled. You were missing a tooth in front.

I thought: *The jury will love you.*

Then I hated myself for thinking that.

"Did you want to leave a message?" Amelia asked.

Well, I couldn't very well tell her that her father had become a defense witness. "I was hoping to talk to your mother in person."

Amelia shrugged. "We're not supposed to let in strangers."

"She's not a stranger," you said, and you reached out and pulled me over the threshold.

I didn't have a lot of experience with kids, and at the rate I was going, I might never, but there was something about your hand in mine, soft as a rabbit's foot and maybe just as lucky. I let myself be led to the couch in the living room and looked around at the machine-made Oriental rug, the dusty face of the television, the battered cardboard boxes of games stacked high on the fireplace hearth. Monopoly was in full swing from the looks of it; there was a board in play set on the coffee table in front of the couch. "You can take over for me," Amelia said, her arms folded. "I'm more of a communist than a capitalist anyway."

She vanished up the stairs, leaving me staring down at the game board. "Did you know which street gets landed on the most?" you asked.

"Um." I sat down. "Shouldn't they all be equal?"

"Not when you figure in the Get Out of Jail cards and stuff like that. It's Illinois."

I glanced down. You had built three hotels on Illinois Avenue.

And Amelia had left me with sixty dollars.

"How did you know that?" I asked.

"I read. And I like to know things no one else does."

I bet there was a great deal you knew that none of us did, or ever would. It was a little disconcerting to be sitting with an almost-six-year-old whose vocabulary probably rivaled mine. "So tell me something I don't know," I said.

"Dr Seuss invented the word *nerd*."

I laughed out loud. "Really?"

You nodded. "In *If I Ran the Zoo*. Which isn't as good as *Green Eggs and Ham*. Which is for babies, anyway," you said. "I like Harper Lee better."

"Harper Lee?" I repeated.

"Yeah. Haven't you ever read *To Kill a Mockingbird*?"

"Sure. I just can't believe *you* have." This was the first conversation I'd really had with the little girl who was the eye in the storm of this lawsuit, and I realized something remarkable: I liked you. I liked you a lot. You were genuine and funny and smart, and maybe your bones broke every now and then. I liked you for dismissing your condition as the least important part of

324

you — nearly as much as I disliked your mother for highlighting it.

"So, anyway, it was Amelia's turn. Which means you get to roll," you said.

I glanced down at the board. "You know what? I hate Monopoly." I did, truly. I had bad flashbacks from my childhood of a cousin who embezzled when he was the banker, of games that lasted four nights in a row.

"You want to play something else?"

Turning to the hearth again, and its toy detritus, I spied a dollhouse. It was a miniature of your home, with its black shutters and bright red door; there were even flowering shrubs for landscaping and long woven tongues of carpet. "Wow," I said, touching the shingles reverently. "This is amazing."

"My dad made it."

I lifted the house up on its platform and settled it on top of the Monopoly board. "I used to have a dollhouse."

It had been my favorite toy. I remembered tufted red velvet chairs in the miniature living room, and an old-time piano that played music when I turned its crank. A claw-footed tub, and candy-striped wallpaper. It looked completely Victorian, nothing like the modern house where I had grown up; yet I used to pretend, as I organized the beds and sofas and kitchen furniture, that this was an alternate universe, the home where I might have lived if I hadn't been given away.

"Look at this," you said, and you showed me how the little porcelain toilet seat lifted up. I wondered if dollhouse men forgot to put it back down, too.

In the refrigerator were little wooden steaks and milk bottles, and a tiny carton of eggs lined up like seed pearls. I raised the hinge of a woven basket to find two splinters of knitting needles and a ball of yarn.

"This is where the sisters live," you said, and you set mattresses onto the twin brass bed frames in one upstairs room. "And this is where their mom sleeps." Next door, on the big bed, you placed two pillows and a crazy quilt the size of my palm. Then you took another blanket and pillow, and made up a bed on the pink satin couch in the parlor. "And this," you said, "is for the daddy."

Oh my God, I thought. *How they've screwed you up.*

Suddenly the front door opened and Charlotte entered, a winter chill caught in the folds of her coat. She was carrying groceries in recyclable green bags draped over her arms. "Oh, that's *your* car," she said, dumping the food onto the floor. "Amelia!" she called upstairs. "I'm home!"

"Yay," Amelia's voice drifted down, devoid of enthusiasm.

Maybe it wasn't just you they were destroying.

Charlotte leaned down and kissed your forehead. "How you doing, sweet pea? You're playing with the dollhouse. I haven't seen you take that out in ages . . ."

"We have to talk," I said, getting to my feet.

"Okay." Charlotte bent to gather some of the grocery bags; I did the same and followed her into the kitchen. She began to unpack: orange juice, milk, broccoli.

326

Macaroni and cheese, dishwashing detergent, Ziploc bags.

Bounty. Joy. Life: brands that were a recipe for existence.

"Guy Booker's added a witness for the defense," I said. "Your husband."

Charlotte was holding a jar of pickles one moment, and the next, it had shattered all over the floor. "*What did you say?*"

"Sean's testifying against you," I said flatly.

"He can't do that, can he?"

"Well, once he asked to be released from the lawsuit —"

"He did *what?*"

The smell of vinegar rose; brine pooled on the tile floor. "Charlotte," I said, stunned. "He told me he talked to you first."

"He hasn't talked to me in weeks. How *could* he? How could he do this to us?"

You came into the kitchen then. "Did something break?"

Charlotte got down on her hands and knees and began to gather the pieces of glass. "Stay out of the kitchen, Willow." I reached for the new roll of paper toweling just as Charlotte let out a sharp cry; a shard of glass had pierced her finger.

It was bleeding. Your eyes went wide, and I hustled you toward the living room again. "Go get your mom a Band-Aid," I said.

By the time I got back to the kitchen, Charlotte was clutching her bloody hand against her shirt. "Marin," she said, staring up at me. "What am I supposed to do?"

It was probably a new experience for you, going to the hospital when you weren't the one who was hurt. But it became clear very quickly that your mother's cut had gone too deep, that a Band-Aid alone wasn't going to be the answer. I drove her to the ER, with you and Amelia sitting in the back of the car, your feet propped up on cardboard boxes full of legal folders. I waited while a doctor sewed two stitches into the tip of Charlotte's ring finger, as you sat beside her and held her good hand tight. I offered to stop at the pharmacy to fill the prescription for Tylenol plus codeine, but Charlotte said they still had plenty of painkillers at home left from your last break.

"I'm fine," she told me. "Really." I almost believed her, too, and then I remembered the way she'd clutched your hand during the stitches, and what she still planned to say to a jury in a matter of weeks about you.

I went back to the office, although the day was shot to hell. I took Maisie's guidelines for writing a letter to one's birth mother out of my top desk drawer and read through them one last time.

Families were never what you wanted them to be. We all wanted what we couldn't have: the perfect child, the doting husband, the mother who'd let us go. We lived in our grown-up dollhouses completely unaware that, at any moment, a hand might come in and change around everything we'd become accustomed to.

Hello, I scrawled.

I've probably written this letter a thousand times in my head, always reworking it to make sure it's just right. It took me thirty-one years to start my search, although I've always wondered where I came from. I think I had to figure out first why I wanted to search — and I finally know the answer. I owe my birth parents a very big thank-you. And almost equally important, I feel like you're owed the right to know that I'm alive, well, and happy.

I work for a law firm in Nashua. I attended college at UNH and then went to law school at the University of Maine. I volunteer monthly to give legal advice to those who can't afford it. I'm not married, but I hope that one day I will be. I like to kayak, read, and eat anything that's chocolate.

For many years I was reluctant to search for you, because I didn't want to intrude or ruin anyone's life. Then I had a health scare and realized I did not know enough about where I'd come from. To that end, I'd like to meet you and say thank-you in person — for giving me the opportunity to become the woman I am now — but I will also respect your wishes if you aren't ready to meet me now, or never will be.

I've written and rewritten this, read and reread it. It's not perfect, and neither am I. But I'm finally brave, and I'd like to think that maybe I inherited that from you.

Sincerely, Marin Gates

Sean

The guys who were repaving this stretch of Route 4 had spent the last forty minutes debating who was hotter, Jessica Alba or Pamela Anderson. "Jessica's one hundred percent real," said one guy, who was wearing fingerless gloves and missing two-thirds of the teeth in his mouth. "No implants."

"Like you know," said the foreman of the road crew.

From down near the line of traffic, another worker held a Slow sign that might have been a warning for the cars and might equally have been a self-description. "Pam's a thirty-six triple D — twenty-two — thirty-four," he said. "You know who else got measurements like that? A freakin' Barbie doll."

I leaned against the hood of my cruiser, bundled up in my winter gear, trying to pretend I was stone-deaf. Construction details were my least favorite part of being a cop, and a necessary evil. Without my blues flashing, the odds of some idiot striking one of the workers increased dramatically. Another guy approached, his breath punctuating the air in white balloons. "Wouldn't toss either of them out of bed," he said. "Would be even better if they were both there at once."

Here's the funny thing: ask any of these guys, and they'd tell you I was a tough guy. That my badge and my Glock were enough to raise me a notch in their esteem. They'd do what I told them to do, and they expected drivers to do what I told them to do, too. What they didn't know was that I was the worst kind of coward. At work, maybe, I could bark orders or collar criminals or throw my weight around; at home, I had taken to stealing out before anyone woke up; I had defected from Charlotte's lawsuit without even having the guts to tell her I was going to do it.

I'd spent enough time lying awake at night attempting to convince myself that this was courageous — that I was trying to find a middle ground where you would know you were loved and wanted — but the truth was, I got something out of this, too. I became a hero again, instead of a guy who couldn't manage to take care of his own family.

"Want to cast your vote, Sean?" the foreman asked.

"Wouldn't want to steal any of your fun," I said diplomatically.

"Oh, that's right. You're married. Not allowed to let that eye wander, not even onto Google . . ."

Ignoring him, I took a few steps forward as a car sped up through the intersection instead of slowing down. All I'd have to do was point at the driver and he'd take his foot off the gas. It was that simple: the fear that I'd actually write him a ticket would be enough to make him think twice about what he was doing. But this driver didn't slow down, and as the car screamed to a stop in the center of the intersection, I realized two

331

things simultaneously: (1) it was a woman driving, not a man; and (2) it was my wife's car.

Charlotte got out of the van and slammed the door shut behind her. "You son of a bitch," she said, striding over until she was close enough to start hitting me.

I grabbed her arms, acutely aware that she had stopped not only traffic but the work of the construction detail. I could feel their eyes on me. "I'm sorry," I muttered. "I had to do it."

"Did you think it could stay a secret until the trial?" Charlotte cried. "Maybe then everyone could have watched me when I found out my husband was a liar."

"*Which* one of us is the liar?" I said, incredulous. "Excuse me if I'm not willing to whore myself for money."

A bright flush rose on Charlotte's cheeks. "Excuse *me* if I'm not willing to let my daughter suffer because we're broke."

In that instant, I noticed a few things: that the right taillight on Charlotte's van had burned out. That she had a bandage wrapped around one finger on her left hand. That it had started to snow again. "Where are the girls?" I asked, trying to peer into the dark windows of the van.

"You have no right to ask that," she said. "You gave up that right when you went to the lawyer's office."

"Where are the girls, Charlotte?" I demanded.

"Home." She stepped away from me, her eyes bright with tears. "Somewhere I don't ever want to see you again."

332

Wheeling around, she walked back to the car. Before she could open the door, though, I blocked her. "How can't you see it?" I whispered. "Until you started all this, there was nothing wrong with our family. Nothing. We had a decent house —"

"With a roof that leaks —"

"I have a steady job —"

"That pays nothing —"

"And our children had a great life," I finished.

"What would you know about that?" Charlotte said. "You're not the one who's with Willow when we walk past the playground at her school and she watches kids doing things she's never going to do — easy things, like jumping off the swings or playing kickball. She threw out the DVD of *The Wizard of Oz*, did you know that? It was in the kitchen trash because some horrible little kid at school called her a Munchkin."

Just like that, I wanted to punch the little shit's lights out — never mind that he was six years old. "She didn't tell me."

"Because she didn't want you to fight her battles for her," Charlotte said.

"Then why," I asked, "are *you* doing it?"

Charlotte hesitated, and I realized I'd struck a nerve. "You can fool yourself, Sean, but you can't fool me. Go ahead and make me out to be the bitch, the villain. Pretend you're some white knight, if it works for you. It looks good on the surface, and you can tell yourself that you know her favorite color and the name of her favorite stuffed animal and what kind of jelly she likes on her peanut butter sandwiches. But that's not what makes her who she is. Do you know what she talks about on the way home from school? Or what she's most proud of? What she worries about? Do you know why she burst into tears last night and why, a week ago, she hid under her bed for an hour? Face it, Sean. You think you're her conquering hero, but you don't really know anything about Willow's life."

I flinched. "I know it's worth living."

She shoved me out of the way and got into the car, slamming the door and peeling away. I heard the furious honks of cars that had been stockpiled behind Charlotte's van and turned around to find the construction foreman still staring at me. "Tell you what," he said, "you can have Jessica *and* Pam."

That night I drove to Massachusetts. I didn't have any destination in mind, but I pulled off at random exits and swung through neighborhoods that were buttoned up tight for the night. I turned off my headlights and trolled the streets like a shark in the deep of the ocean. There is so much you can tell about a family from the place they live: plastic toys give you the ages of their kids; a string of Christmas lights flag their religious affiliation; the kinds of cars in the driveway call out soccer mom or teenage driver or NASCAR fan. But even at the houses that were nondescript, I had no problem imagining the people inside. I would close my eyes and picture a father at the dinner table, making his daughters laugh. A mother who cleared the plates, but not before she touched the man's shoulder in passing. I'd see a bookshelf full of bedtime stories, a stone paperweight crudely painted to look like a ladybug pinning down the day's mail, a fresh stack of clean laundry. I'd hear the Patriots game on a Sunday afternoon, and Amelia's iTunes playing through a speaker shaped like a donut, and your bare feet shuffling down the hallway.

I must have gone to fifty different houses like this. Occasionally, I'd find a light on — usually upstairs, usually a teenager's head silhouetted against the blue cast of a computer screen. Or a couple that had fallen asleep with the television still crackling. A bathroom light, to keep monsters away from a child. It didn't matter if I was in a white neighborhood or a black one, if the community was wealthy or dirt-poor — houses are cellular walls; they keep our problems from bleeding into everyone else's.

The last neighborhood I visited that night was the one that drew my truck magnetically, my heart's polar north. I parked at the base of my own driveway, headlights switched off, so that I would not give my presence away.

The truth was, Charlotte was right. The more times I picked up shifts to pay for your incidentals, the less time I spent with you. Once, I'd held you in my arms while you slept, and I'd watched dreams screening across your face; now, I loved you in theory if not in practice. I was too busy protecting and serving the rest of Bankton to focus on protecting and serving you; that had fallen to Charlotte instead. It was a treadmill, and I'd been knocked off it by this lawsuit, only to find that you were impossibly, undeniably, growing up.

That would change, I vowed. Carrying through with the step I'd taken when I went to Booker, Hood & Coates meant that I would actively spend more time with you. I'd get to fall for you all over again.

Just then, the wind whipped through the open window of the truck, wrinkling the wrappers of the baked goods and reminding me why I'd come back here tonight. Stacked in a wheelbarrow were the cookies and cakes and pastries that you and Amelia and Charlotte had been baking for the past few days.

I'd loaded them all — easily thirty wrapped packets, each one tagged with a green string and a construction paper heart — into my truck. You'd cut those out yourself; I could tell. *Sweets from Syllabub*, they read. I'd imagined your mother's hands stroking pastry dough, the look on your face as you carefully cracked an egg, Amelia frustrating her way through an apron's knot. I came here a couple times a week. I'd eat the first three or four; the rest I'd leave on the steps at the nearest homeless shelter.

I reached into my wallet and took out all my money, the cashed sum of the extra shifts I'd taken on at work to keep from having to go home. This I stuffed, bill by bill, into the shoe box, payment in kind for Charlotte. Before I could stop myself, I tore the paper heart off one packet of cookies. With a pencil, I wrote a customer's message across the blank back: *I love them.*

Tomorrow, you'd read it. All three of you would be giddy, would assume the anonymous writer had been talking about the food, and not the bakers.

336

Amelia

On the way home from Boston one weekend, my mother reinvented herself as the new Martha Freaking Stewart. To that end, we had to detour totally out of the way to Norwich, Vermont, to King Arthur Flour, so that we could buy a crapload of industrial baking pans and specialty flours. You were already cranky about spending the morning at Children's Hospital having new braces fitted — they were hot and stiff and left marks and bruises where the plastic rubbed into your skin, which the brace specialists tried to fix with a heat gun, but it never seemed to work. You wanted to go home and take them off, but instead, my mother bribed us with a trip to a restaurant — a reward neither one of us could turn down.

This may not seem like such a big deal, but it was, to us. We didn't eat out very much. My mom always said that she could cook better than most chefs anyway, which was true, but that really just made us sound less like losers than the truth: we couldn't afford it. It was the same reason that I didn't tell my parents when my jeans were becoming highwaters, why I never bought lunch although the French fries in the caf looked so incredibly delicious; it was the same reason why that Disney World Trip to Hell was so much of a disappointment. I was too embarrassed to hear my parents tell me that we were too broke to afford what I needed or wanted; if I didn't ask for anything, I didn't have to hear them say no.

There was a part of me that was angry my mother was using the baking money to buy all those pans and tins when she could have been buying me a Juicy Couture cashmere hoodie that would make other girls in school look at me with envy, instead of like I was something stuck to the bottoms of their shoes. But no, it was critical that we have Mexican vanilla extract and dried Bing cherries from Michigan. We had to have silicone muffin pans and a shortbread form and edgeless cookie sheets. You were totally oblivious to the fact that every penny we spent on turbinado sugar and cake flour was one less cent spent on us, but then again, what did I expect: you still believed there was a Santa Claus, too.

So I have to admit it surprised me a little when you let me choose the restaurant where we'd eat lunch. "Amelia never gets to pick," you said, and even though I hated myself for this, I felt like I was going to cry.

To make up for that, and because everyone expected me to be a jerk and why disappoint, I said, "McDonald's."

"Eww," you said. "They make four hundred Quarter Pounders out of one cow."

"Get back to me when you're a vegetarian, hypocrite," I answered.

"Amelia, stop. We're not going to McDonald's."

So instead of picking a nice Italian place we probably all would have enjoyed, I made her stop at a totally skanky diner instead.

It looked like the kind of place that had bugs in the kitchen. "Well," my mother said, looking around. "This is an interesting choice."

"It's nostalgic," I said, and I glared at her. "What's wrong with that?"

"Nothing, as long as botulism isn't one of your long-lost memories." After glancing at a Seat Yourself sign, she walked toward an empty booth.

"I want to sit at the counter," you said.

My mother and I both looked at the rickety stools, the long drop down. "No," we said simultaneously.

I dragged a high chair over to the table so that you could reach it. A harried waitress tossed menus at us, with a pack of crayons for you. "Be back in a minute for your order."

My mother guided your legs through the high chair, which was an ordeal, because with braces your legs didn't move that easily. Right away you flipped over your place mat and began to draw on the blank side. "So," my mother said. "What should we bake when we get home?"

"Donuts," you suggested. You were pretty psyched about the pan we'd bought, which looked like sixteen alien eyes.

"Amelia, what about you?"

I buried my face in my arms. "Hash brownies."

The waitress reappeared with a pad in hand. "Well, aren't you just cute enough to spread on a cracker and eat," she said, grinning down at you. "And a mighty fine artist, too!"

I caught your gaze and rolled my eyes. You poked two crayons up your nose and stuck out your tongue. "I'll have coffee," Mom said. "And the turkey club."

"There's more than one hundred chemicals in a cup of coffee," you announced, and the waitress nearly fell over.

Because we didn't go out much, I'd forgotten how strangers reacted to you. You were only as tall as a three-year-old, but you spoke and read and drew like someone much older than your real age — almost six. It was sort of freaky, until people got to know you. "Isn't she just a talkative little thing!" the waitress said, recovering.

"I'll have the grilled cheese, please," you replied. "And a Coke."

"Yeah, that sounds good. Make it two," I said, when what I really wanted was one of everything on the menu. The waitress was staring at you as you drew a picture that was about normal for a six-year-old but practically Renoir for the toddler she assumed you to be. She looked like she was going to say something to you, so I turned to my mother. "Are you sure you want turkey? That's, like, food poisoning waiting to happen . . ."

"Amelia!"

She was mad, but it got the waitress to stop ogling you and leave.

"She's an idiot," I said as soon as the waitress was gone.

"She doesn't know that —" My mother broke off abruptly.

"What?" you accused. "That there's something wrong with me?"

"I would *never* say that."

"Yeah, right," I muttered. "Not unless the jury's present."

"So help me, Amelia, if your attitude doesn't —"

I was saved by the waitress, who reappeared holding our drinks, in glasses that probably were see-through plastic in a former life but now just looked filmy. Your Coke was in a sippy cup.

Automatically, my mother reached out and began to unscrew the top. You took a drink, then picked up your crayon and began writing across the top of your picture: Me, Amelia, Mommy, Daddy.

"Oh, my *God*," the waitress said. "I have a three-year-old at home, and let me tell you, I can barely get her potty trained. But your daughter's already writing? And drinking out of a regular cup. Honey, I don't know what you're doing right, but I want to get me some of that."

"I'm not three," you said.

"Oh." The waitress winked. "Three and a half, right? Those months count when they're babies —"

"I'm *not* a baby!"

"Willow." Mom put a hand on your arm, but you threw it off, knocking over the cup and sending Coke all over the place.

"I'm *not!*"

Mom grabbed a stack of napkins and started mopping. "I'm sorry," she said to the waitress.

"Now *that*" — the waitress nodded — "looks more like three."

A bell rang, and she left to go back in the kitchen.

"Willow, you know better," my mother said. "You can't get angry at someone because she didn't know you have OI."

"Why not?" I asked. "*You* are."

My mother's jaw dropped. Recovering, she grabbed her purse and jacket and stood up. "We're leaving," she announced, and she yanked you out of your chair. At the last minute she remembered the drinks and slapped a ten-dollar bill on the table. Then she carried you out to the car, with me trailing behind.

We went to McDonald's on the way home after all, but instead of making me feel satisfied, it made me want to disappear underneath the tires, the pavement, all of it.

I had braces, too, but not the kind that kept my legs from bowing. Mine were the ordinary kind, the ones that had changed the whole shape of my head during the progression from palate expander to bands to wires. This much I had in common with you: the very second I got my braces, I began counting the days until they would be taken off. For those who've never had the displeasure, this is what braces feel like: you know those fake white vampire teeth you stick in your mouth at Halloween? Well, imagine that, and then imagine that they stay there for the next three years, with you drooling and cutting your gums on the uneven plastic bits, and that would be braces.

Which is why, one particular Monday in late January, I had the biggest, soppiest smile on my face. I didn't care when Emma and her posse wrote the word WHORE on the blackboard behind me in math class, with an arrow that pointed down at my head. I didn't care when you ate all the Cocoa Puffs so that I had to have Frosted Mini-Wheats as a snack after school. All that mattered was that at 4:30p.m. I was getting my braces off, after thirty-four months, two weeks, and six days.

My mother was playing it incredibly cool — apparently she didn't realize what a big deal this was. I'd checked; it was right on her calendar, like it had been for the past five months. I started to panic, though, when it was four o'clock and she set a cheesecake into the oven. I mean, how could she drive me into town to the orthodontist and not have to worry if her knife slipped out clean in an hour when she tested it?

My father, that had to be the answer. He hadn't been around much, but then again, that wasn't radical. Cops worked when they had to, not when they wanted to — or so he used to tell me. The difference was that, when he *was* home, you could cut the air between him and my mother with that same knife she was using to test her cheesecake.

Maybe this was all part of a calculated plan to throw me off. My father was going to show up in time to take me to the orthodontist; my mother would finish baking the cheesecake (which was my favorite anyway) and it would be part of a big ol' dinner that included things like corn on the cob, caramel apples, and bubble gum — all forbidden foods that were written on the reminder magnet on our fridge with a fat X across it, and for once, I'd be the one everybody could not take their eyes off.

I sat at the kitchen table, scuffing my sneaker on the floor. "Amelia," my mother sighed.

Squeak.

"Amelia. For God's sake. You're giving me a headache."

It was 4:04. "Aren't you forgetting something?"

She wiped her hands on a dish towel. "Not that I know of . . ."

"Well, when's Dad going to get here?"

She stared at me. "Honey," she said, the word that's a sweet, so that you know whatever's coming next has to be awful. "I don't know where your father is. He and I . . . we haven't . . ."

"My appointment," I burst out, before she could say anything else. "Who's taking me to the orthodontist?"

For a moment, she was speechless. "You must be joking."

"After three years? I don't think so." I stood up, poking my finger at the calendar on the wall. "I'm getting my braces off today."

"You are *not* going to Rob Reece's office," my mother said.

344

Okay, that's the detail I left out: the only orthodontist in Bankton — the one I'd been seeing all this time — happened to be married to the woman she was suing. Granted, due to all the drama, I'd missed a couple of appointments since September, but I had no intention of skipping *this* one. "Just because you're on some crusade to ruin Piper's life, I have to leave my braces on till I'm forty?"

My mother held her hand up to her head. "Not till you're forty. Just until I find you another orthodontist. For God's sake, Amelia, it slipped my mind. I've obviously had a lot going on lately."

"Yeah, you and every other human on this planet, Mom," I yelled. "Guess what? It's *not* all about you and what you want and what makes everyone feel sorry for your miserable life with some miserable —"

She slapped me across the face.

My mother had never, ever hit me. Not even when I ran into traffic when I was two, not even when I poured nail polish remover on the dining room table and destroyed the finish. My cheek hurt, but not as much as my chest. My heart had turned into a ball of rubber bands, and they were snapping, one by one.

I wanted her to hurt as much as she'd hurt me, so I spat out the words that burned like acid in my throat. "Bet you wish *I'd* never been born, too," I said, and I took off running.

By the time I got to Rob's office (I'd never called him Dr Reece), I was sweaty and red-faced. I don't think I'd ever run five whole miles in my life, but that's what I had just done. Guilt is a better fuel than you can imagine. I was practically the Energizer Bunny, and it had a lot less to do with getting closer to the orthodontist than it did with getting away from my mother. Panting, I walked up to the receptionist's desk, where there was a nifty computer kiosk to sign in. But I had only just settled my fingers on the keyboard when I noticed the receptionist staring at me. And the dental hygienist. And in fact, every single person in the office.

"Amelia," the receptionist said. "What are you doing here?"

"I have an appointment."

"I think we all just assumed —"

"Assumed what?" I interrupted. "That just because my mother's a jerk, I'm one, too?"

Suddenly Rob stepped into the reception area, snapping a pair of rubber gloves off his hands. He used to blow them up for Emma and me, and draw little faces on them. The fingers looked like the comb of a rooster and felt as soft as a baby's skin.

"Amelia," he said quietly. He wasn't smiling, not one iota. "I guess you're here about your braces."

It felt like I had been walking in a forest for the past few months, a place where even the trees might reach out to grab you and nobody spoke English — and Rob had said the first rational, normal sentence I'd heard in a long time. He knew what I wanted. If it was so easy for him, why did nobody else seem to get it?

I followed him into the examination room, past the snarky receptionist and the dental hygienist whose eyes

346

went so wide I thought they might pop out of her head. *Ha*, I thought, walking beside him proudly. *Take that.*

I expected Rob to say something like *Look, let's just get this over with and keep it strictly business*, but instead, as he settled the paper bib over my shoulders, he said, "Are things okay for you, Amelia?"

God, why couldn't Rob have been my father? Why couldn't I have lived in the Reece household, and Emma could have been in mine, so I could hate her instead of the other way around?

"Compared to what? Armageddon?"

He was wearing a mask, but I pretended that, behind it, he cracked a smile. I'd always liked Rob. He was geeky and small, not at all like my father. At sleepovers Emma would tell me my father was movie-star handsome and I'd tell her it was gross that she even *thought* about him like that; and she'd say if her dad was ever in a movie, it would be *Revenge of the Nerds.* And maybe that was true, but he also didn't mind taking us to movies that starred Amanda Bynes or Hilary Duff, and he let us play with brace wax and fashion it into little bears and ponies when we were bored.

"I'd forgotten how funny you can be," Rob said. "Okay, open up . . . You may feel a little pressure." He picked up a pair of pliers and began to break the bonds between the brackets and my teeth. It felt weird, like I was bionic. "Does that hurt?"

I shook my head.

"Emma doesn't talk much about you these days."

I couldn't speak, because his hands were in my wide-open mouth. But here's what I would have said: *That's because she's become an überbitch, and she hates my guts.*

"It's obviously a very uncomfortable situation," Rob said. "I have to admit I never thought your mother would let you come back to me for orthodontic care."

She didn't.

"You know, orthodontics is really just physics," Rob said. "If you had brackets or bands on crooked teeth alone, it wouldn't do anything. But when you apply force in different ways, things change." He looked down at me, and I knew that he wasn't talking about my teeth anymore. "Every action has an equal and opposite reaction."

Rob was cleaning the composite and cement off my teeth. I lifted my hand and put it to his wrist, so that he'd remove the electric toothbrush. My spit tasted tinny. "She's ruined my life, too," I said, and because of the saliva, it sounded like I was drowning.

Rob looked away. "You'll have to wear a retainer, or else there could be some shifting. Let's get some X-rays and impressions, so that we can make one up for you —" Then he frowned, touching a tool to the backs of my two front teeth. "The enamel's worn down a lot here."

Well, of course it was; I was making myself puke three times a day, not that you'd know it. I was just as fat as ever, because when I wasn't puking, I was stuffing my disgusting face. I held my breath, wondering if this would be the moment someone realized what I'd been

348

doing. I wondered if I'd actually been waiting for that all along.

"Have you been drinking a lot of soda?"

The excuse made me feel weak. I nodded quickly.

"Don't," Rob said. "They use Coke to clean up blood spills on highways, you know. Do you really want that in your body?"

It sounded like something you would have told me, from one of your trivia books. And that made my eyes fill with tears.

"Sorry," Rob said, lifting his hands. "I didn't mean to hurt you."

Me neither, I thought.

He finished polishing my teeth with the toothpaste that felt like sand and let me rinse. "That is one gorgeous occlusion," he said, and he held up a mirror. "Smile, Amelia."

I ran my tongue over my teeth, something I hadn't been able to do in nearly three years. The teeth felt huge, slick, like they belonged in someone else's mouth. I bared them — not a smile but more of a wolf's grimace. The girl in the mirror had neat rows of teeth, like the string of pearls in my mother's jewelry box that I'd stolen and hidden in one of my shoe boxes. I never wore them, but I liked the way they felt, so smooth and uniform, like a little army marching around your neck. The girl in the mirror could almost be pretty.

Which meant she couldn't be me.

"Here's something we give out to kids who've completed treatment," Rob said, handing me a little plastic bag with his name printed on it.

"Thanks," I muttered, and I leapt out of the chair, yanking the bib off.

"Amelia — wait. Your retainer —" Rob said, but by then, I had already fled into the reception area and out the front door. Instead of heading downstairs and out of the building, though, I ran upstairs, where they wouldn't think to come after me (Not that they would. I wasn't really that important, was I?), and locked myself in the bathroom. I opened the goody bag. There were Twizzlers and gummy bears and popcorn, all foods I hadn't eaten in so long I couldn't even remember how they tasted. There was a T-shirt that read SHIFT HAPPENS, SO WEAR YOUR RETAINER.

The toilet bowl had a black seat. With one hand I held my hair back, with the other, I stuck my index finger down my throat. Here's what Rob *hadn't* noticed: the little scab on that finger, which came from digging into my front teeth every time I did this.

Afterward, my teeth felt fuzzy and dirty and familiar again. I rinsed my mouth out with water from the sink and then looked in the mirror. My cheeks were flushed, my eyes bright.

I did not look like someone whose life was falling apart. I did not look like a girl who had to make herself vomit to feel like she could do something right. I did not look like the kind of daughter who was hated by her mother, ignored by her father.

To be honest, I didn't know who the hell I was anymore at all.

Piper

In four months, I had been reborn. Once, I'd used a paper tape ruler to determine fundal height, now I knew how to figure out a rough opening for windows using a measuring tape. Once, I had used a Doppler stethoscope to hear fetal heart tones; now I used a stud finder to locate the sweet spots behind a plaster wall. Once, I'd done quadruple screens, now I installed screen porches. I had applied myself to the task of learning as much about remodeling as I had about medicine, and as a result, I could have been board-certified as a contractor by now.

I had first remodeled the bathroom, then the dining room. I pulled up the carpets in the upstairs bedrooms to install parquet floors instead. I was planning to start faux-painting the kitchen this week. After a room was finished, it went back on my list to be renovated again, eventually.

There was, of course, a method to my madness. Part of it was feeling proficient at something again — something I hadn't known how to do *before* so I couldn't possibly mess up. And part of it was thinking that, if I changed every bit of my surroundings, I might be able to find a spot where I felt comfortable again.

My refuge of choice had become Aubuchon Hardware. No one I knew shopped at Aubuchon Hardware. Whereas I might run into former patients at the grocery store or the pharmacy, at Aubuchon I blissfully wandered the aisles in a state of complete anonymity. I went three or four times a week and gazed at the laser levels and the drill bits, the soldier rows of two-by-fours, the bloated tubes of PVC and their delicate cousins, copper piping. I sat on the floor with paint chips, whispering the names of the colors: Mulberry Wine, Riviera Azure, Cool Lava. They sounded like vacation photographs of places I'd always wanted to go.

Newburyport Blue was from Benjamin Moore's Historical Colors collection. It was a dark, grayish blue, like the ocean when it rains. I'd actually been to Newburyport. One summer, Charlotte and I had rented a house on Plum Island for our families. You were still small enough to be toted, with all the gear, through the tall grass to the beach. In theory, it had seemed like the perfect vacation: the sand was soft enough to break your fall; Emma and Amelia could pretend to be mermaids, with seaweed hair that had washed up on the shore; and it was close enough for Sean and Rob to commute down on their days off. There was only one caveat we hadn't anticipated: the water was so cold that even standing up to your ankles made you ache to the core of your privates. You kids spent your days splashing in tide pools, which were shallow enough to be heated by the sun, but Charlotte and I were too big for those.

Which is why one Sunday, when the guys had taken you kids to Mad Martha's for breakfast, Charlotte and I decided to try boogie boarding, even if it resulted in severe hypothermia. We shimmied into our wet suits ("They're supposed to be tight," I told Charlotte when she moaned about the size of her hips) and carried the boards down to the water's edge. I dipped my foot into the line of surf and gasped. "There's no way," I said, jumping backward.

Charlotte smirked at me. "Getting cold feet?"

"Very funny," I said, but to my shock, she'd already begun high-stepping over the waves, frigid as they were, and swimming out to a point where she could ride one in.

"How bad is it?" I yelled.

"Like an epidural — I don't have feeling below my waist," she shouted back, and then suddenly the ocean heaved, flexing one long muscle that lifted Charlotte on her board and sent her screaming through the surf to land at my feet on the sand.

She stood up, pushing her hair out of her face. "Chicken," she accused, and to prove her wrong, I held my breath and started wading into the water.

My God, it was cold. I paddled out on my board, bobbing beside Charlotte. "We're going to die," I said. "We're going to die out here and someone's going to find our bodies on the shore, like Emma found that tennis shoe yesterday —"

"Here we go," Charlotte shouted, and I looked over my shoulder to see an enormous wall of water looming down on us. "Paddle," Charlotte yelled, and I did what she told me to do.

But I hadn't caught the wave. Instead, it crashed over me, knocking the breath from my lungs and tumbling me end over end underwater. My boogie board, roped to my wrist, smacked me on the head twice, and then I felt sand being ground into my hair and my face, my fingers clawing at broken shells, as the ocean floor rose at an angle beneath me. Suddenly, a hand grabbed the back of my wet suit and dragged me forward. "Stand up," Charlotte said, using all her weight to move me far enough onto the sand to keep from getting pulled back by the tide.

I had swallowed a quart of salt water; my eyes were burning, and there was blood on my cheek and my palms. "Jesus Christ," I said, coughing and wiping my nose.

Charlotte pounded me on the back. "Just breathe."

"Harder . . . than it sounds."

Slowly feeling returned to my fingers and my feet, and that was worse, because I'd been beaten up badly by the wave. "Thanks . . . for being my lifeguard."

"The heck with that," Charlotte said. "I didn't want to have to pay for the second half of the rental house."

I laughed out loud. Charlotte helped me to my feet, and we began to trudge up the beach, dragging the boards behind us like puppies on leashes. "What should we tell the guys?" I asked.

"That Kelly Slater signed us for the world championships."

"Yeah, that'll explain why my cheek is bleeding."

"He was overcome by the beauty of my butt in this wet suit, and when he made a pass at me you had to beat him off," Charlotte suggested.

The reeds were whispering secrets. To the left was a swath of sand where Amelia and Emma had been playing yesterday, writing their names with sticks. They wanted to see if the writing would still be there today, or if the tide would have washed it away.

Amelia and Emma, it read.

BFFAA. Best friends forever and always.

I linked my arm with Charlotte's, and together we started the long climb to the house.

It struck me, now, as I sat on the floor of Aubuchon Hardware, with a flamenco fan of color chips in my hand, that I had never been back to Newburyport since then. Charlotte and I had talked about it, but she hadn't wanted to commit to renting a house not knowing if you'd be in a cast that following summer. Maybe Emma and Rob and I would go down there next summer.

But *I* wouldn't go, I knew that. I really didn't want to, without Charlotte.

I took a quart of paint off the shelf and walked to the mixing station at the end of the aisle. "Newburyport Blue, please," I said, although I did not have a particular wall in mind to paint it on yet. I'd keep it in the basement, just in case.

It was dark by the time I left Aubuchon Hardware, and when I got back home, Rob was washing plates and putting them into the dishwasher. He didn't even look at me when I walked into the kitchen, which is why I knew he was furious. "Just say it," I said.

He turned off the faucet and slammed the door of the dishwasher into place. "Where the hell have you been?"

"I . . . I lost track of time. I was at the hardware store."

"Again? What could you possibly need there?"

I sank down into a chair. "I don't know, Rob. It's just the place that makes me feel good right now."

"You know what would make me feel good?" he said. "A wife."

"Wow, Rob, I didn't think you'd ever go all Ricky Ricardo on me —"

"Did you forget something today?"

I stared at him. "Not that I know of."

"Emma was waiting for you to drive her to the rink."

I closed my eyes. Skating. The new session had started; I was supposed to sign her up for private lessons so that she could compete this spring — something her last coach finally felt she was ready for. It was first come, first served; this might have blown her chance for the season. "I'll make it up to her —"

"You don't have to, because she called, hysterical, and I left the office to get her down there in time." He sat down across from me, tilting his head. "What do you *do* all day, Piper?"

I wanted to point out to him the new tile floor in the mudroom, the fixture I'd rewired over this very table. But instead I looked down at my hands. "I don't know," I whispered. "I really don't know."

"You have to get your life back. If you don't, she's already won."

"You don't know what this is like —"

"I don't? I'm not a doctor, too? I don't carry malpractice insurance?"

"That's not what I mean and you —"

"I saw Amelia today."

I stared at him. "Amelia?"

"She came to the office to get her braces off."

"There's no way Charlotte would have —"

"Hell hath no fury like a teenager who wants her orthodontia removed," Rob said. "I'm ninety-nine percent sure Charlotte had no idea she was there."

I felt heat rise to my face. "Don't you think people might wonder why you're treating the daughter of the woman who's suing us?"

"You," he corrected. "She's suing *you*."

I reeled backward. "I can't believe you just said that."

"And I can't believe you'd expect me to throw Amelia out of the office."

"Well, you know what, Rob? You *should* have. You're my *husband*."

Rob got to his feet. "And she's a patient. And that's my job. Something, unlike you, that I give a damn about."

He stalked out of the kitchen, and I rubbed my temples. I felt like a plane in a holding pattern, making the turns with the airport in view and no clearance to land. In that moment, I resented Charlotte so much that it felt like a river stone in my belly, solid and cold. Rob was right — everything I was, everything I'd *been*

— had been put on a shelf because of what Charlotte had done to me.

And in that instant I realized that Charlotte and I still had something in common: she felt exactly the same way about what I'd done to *her*.

The next morning, I was determined to change. I set my alarm, and instead of sleeping past the school bus pickup, I made Emma French toast and bacon for breakfast. I told a wary Rob to have a nice day. Instead of renovating the house, I cleaned it. I went grocery shopping — although I drove to a town thirty miles away, where I wouldn't run into anyone familiar. I met Emma at school with her skating bag. "*You're* taking me to the rink?" she said when she saw me.

"Is that a problem?"

"I guess not," Emma said, and after a moment's hesitation, she launched into a diatribe about how unfair it was for the teacher to give an algebra test when he knew he was going to be absent that day and couldn't answer last-minute questions.

I've missed this, I thought. *I've missed Emma.* I reached across the seat and smoothed my hand over her hair.

"What's up with that?"

"I just really love you. That's all."

Emma raised a brow. "Okay, now you're skeeving me out. You aren't going to tell me you have cancer or something, are you?"

"No, I just know I haven't exactly been . . . present . . . lately. And I'm sorry."

We were at a red light, and she faced me. "Charlotte's a bitch," she said, and I didn't even tell her to watch her language. "Everybody knows the whole Willow thing isn't your fault."

"Everybody?"

"Well," she said. "Me."

That's good enough, I realized.

A few minutes later, we arrived at the skating rink. Red-cheeked boys dribbled out of the main glass doors, their enormous hockey bags turtled onto their backs. It always had seemed so funny to me, the dichotomy between the coltish figure skaters and the lupine hockey players.

The minute I walked inside I realized what I'd forgotten — no, not forgotten, just blocked entirely from my mind: Amelia would be here, too.

She looked so different from the last time I'd seen her — dressed in black, with fingerless gloves and tattered jeans and combat boots — and that blue hair. And she was arguing heatedly with Charlotte. "I don't care who hears," she said. "I told you I don't want to skate anymore."

Emma grabbed my arm. "Just go," she said under her breath.

But it was too late. We were a small town and this was a big story; the entire room, girls and their mothers, was waiting to see what would happen. And you, sitting on the bench beside Amelia's bag, noticed me, too.

You had a cast on your right arm. How had you broken it this time? Four months ago, I would have known all the details.

Well, unlike Charlotte, I had no intention of airing my dirty laundry in public. I drew in my breath and pulled Emma closer, dragging her into the locker room. "Okay," I said, pushing my hair out of my eyes. "So, you do this private lesson thing for how long? An hour?"

"Mom."

"I may just run out and pick up the dry cleaning, instead of hanging around to watch —"

"Mom." Emma reached for my hand, as if she were still little. "You weren't the one who started this."

I nodded, not trusting myself to say anything else. Here is what I had expected from my best friend: honesty. If she had spent the past six years of your life harboring the belief that I'd done something grievously wrong during her pregnancy, why didn't she ever bring it up? Why didn't she ever say, *Hey, how come you didn't . . .?* Maybe I was naïve to think that silence was implicit complacence, instead of a festering question. Maybe I was silly to believe that friends owed each other anything. But I did. Like, for starters, an explanation.

Emma finished lacing up her skates and hurried onto the ice. I waited a moment, then pushed out the locker room door and stood in front of the curved Plexiglas barrier. At one end of the rink was a tangle of beginners — a centipede of children in their snow pants and bicycle helmets, their legs widening triangles. When one went down, so did the others: dominoes. It wasn't so long ago that this had been Emma, and yet here she was on the other end of the rink, executing a sit-spin as her teacher skated around her, calling out corrections.

I couldn't see Amelia — or you or Charlotte for that matter — anywhere.

My pulse was almost back to normal by the time I reached my car. I slid into the driver's seat, turned on the engine. When I heard a sharp rap on the window, I nearly jumped out of my skin.

Charlotte stood there, a scarf wrapped around her nose and mouth, her eyes watering in the bite of the wind. I hesitated, then unrolled the window partway.

She looked as miserable as I felt. "I . . . I just had to tell you something," she said, halting. "This was never about you and me."

The effort of not speaking hurt; I was grinding my back teeth together.

"I was offered a chance to give Willow everything she'll ever need." Her breath formed a wreath around her face in the cold air. "I don't blame you for hating me. But you can't judge me, Piper. Because if Willow had been *your* child . . . I know you would have done the same thing."

I let the words hang between us, caught on the guillotine of the window's edge. "You don't know me as well as you think you do, Charlotte," I said coldly, and I pulled out of the parking spot and away from the rink without looking back.

Ten minutes later I burst into Rob's office during a consultation. "Piper," he said evenly, glancing down at the parents and pre-teen daughter, who were staring at my wild hair, my runny nose, the tears still streaking my face. "I'm in the middle of something."

"Um," the mother said quickly. "Maybe we should just let you two talk."

"Mrs Spifield —"

"No, really," she said, getting up and summoning the rest of the family. "We can give you a minute."

They hurried out of the office, expecting me to self-destruct at any moment, and maybe they weren't that far off the mark. "Are you happy?" Rob exploded. "You probably just cost me a new patient."

"How about *Piper, what happened? Tell me what I can do to help you?*"

"Well, pardon me if the sympathy card's been played so often that the face has worn straight off. Jesus, I'm trying to run a practice here."

"I just ran into Charlotte at the skating rink."

Rob blinked at me. "So?"

"Are you joking?"

"You live in the same town. A small town. It's a miracle you haven't crossed paths before. What did she do? Come after you with a sword? Call you out on the playground? Grow up, Piper."

I felt like the bull must when he is let out of his pen. Freedom, relief . . . and then comes the picador, lancing him. "I'm going to leave," I said softly. "I'm going to pick up Emma, and before you come home tonight, I hope you'll think about the way you treated me."

"The way *I* treated *you*?" Rob said. "I have been nothing but supportive. I have not said a word, even though you've abandoned your whole OB practice and turned into some female Ty Pennington. We get a lumber bill for two thousand dollars? No problem. You forget Emma's chorus recital because you're talking plumbing at Aubuchon Hardware? Forgiven. I mean, how ironic is it that you've become the do-it-yourself queen? Because you don't want our help. You want to wallow in self-pity instead."

"It's not self-pity." My cheeks were burning. Could the Spifields hear us arguing in the waiting room? Could the hygienists?

"I know what you want from me, Piper. I'm just not sure I can do it anymore." Rob walked to the window, looking out onto the parking lot. "I've been thinking a lot about Steven," he said after a moment.

When Rob was twelve, his older brother had committed suicide. Rob had been the one to find him, hanging from the rod in his closet. I knew all this; I'd known it since before we were married. It had taken me a while to convince Rob to have children, because he worried that his brother's mental illness was printed in his genes. What I hadn't known was that, these past few months, being with me had dragged Rob back to that time in his childhood.

"Back then no one knew the name for bipolar disorder, or how to take care of it. So for seventeen years my parents went through hell. My whole

363

childhood was colored by how Steven was feeling: if it was a good day or a bad day. And," he said, "it's how I got so good at taking care of a person who is completely self-absorbed."

I felt a splinter of guilt wedge into my heart. Charlotte had hurt me; in return, I'd hurt Rob. Maybe that's what we do to the people we love: take shots in the dark and realize too late we've wounded the people we are trying to protect. "Ever since you got served, I've been thinking about it. What if my parents had known in advance?" Rob said. "What if they had been told, before Steven was born, that he was going to kill himself before his eighteenth birthday?"

I felt myself go very still.

"Would they have taken those seventeen years to get to know him? To have those good times that came between the crises? Or would they have spared themselves — and me — that emotional roller coaster?"

I imagined Rob, coming into his brother's room to get him for dinner, and finding the older boy slumped to the side of the closet. The whole time I'd known my mother-in-law, I'd never seen a smile rise all the way to her eyes. Was this why?

"That's not a fair comparison," I said stiffly.

"Why not?"

"Bipolar illness can't be diagnosed in utero. You're missing the point."

Rob raised his gaze to meet mine. "Am I?" he said.

Marin

February 2008

"Just be yourselves," I coached. "We don't want you to do anything special because of the camera. Pretend we're not here."

I gave a nervous little smile and glanced at the twenty-two moon faces staring up at me: Ms. Watkins's kindergarten class. "Does anyone have any questions?"

A little boy raised his hand. "Do you know Simon Cowell?"

"No," I said, grinning. "Anyone else?"

"Is Willow a movie star?"

I glanced at Charlotte, who was standing just behind me, with the videographer I'd hired to film *A Day in the Life of Willow*, to be aired for the jury. "No," I said. "She's still just your friend."

"Ooh! Ooh! Me!" A classically pretty destined-to-be-cheerleader girl pumped her hand like a piston until I pointed to her. "If I pretend to be Willow's friend today, will I be on *Entertainment Tonight*?"

The teacher stepped forward. "No, Sapphire. And you shouldn't have to pretend to be anyone's friend in here. We're *all* friends, right?"

"Yes, Ms. Watkins," the class intoned.

Sapphire? That girl's name was really Sapphire? I'd looked at the masking tape above the wooden cubbies when we first came in — names like Flint and Frisco and Cassidy. Did no one name their kids Tommy or Elizabeth anymore?

I wondered, not for the first time, if my birth mother had picked out names for me. If she'd called me Sarah or Abigail, a secret between the two of us that was overturned, like fresh earth, when my adoptive parents came and started my life over.

You were using your wheelchair today, which meant kids had to move out of the way to accommodate you if you approached with your aide to work at the art table or use Cuisenaire rods. "This is so strange," Charlotte said softly. "I never get to watch her during school. I feel like I've been admitted to the inner sanctum."

I had hired the camera crew to film one entire day with you. Although you were verbal enough to hold your own as a witness during this trial, putting you on the stand would not have been humane. I couldn't bring myself to have you in the courtroom when your mother was testifying out loud about wanting to terminate her pregnancy.

We'd shown up on your doorstep at 6a.m., in time to watch Charlotte come into your room to rouse you and Amelia. "Oh, my God, this sucks," Amelia had groaned when she opened her eyes and saw the videographer. "The whole world's going to see my bed hair."

She had jumped up and run to the bathroom, but with you, it took more time. Every transition was careful — from the bed to the walker, from the walker to the bathroom, from the bathroom back to the bedroom to get dressed. Because mornings were the most painful for you — the curse of sleeping on a healing fracture — Charlotte had given you pain medication thirty minutes before we arrived, then let it start working to ease the soreness in your arm while you dozed for a while before she helped you get out of bed. Charlotte picked out a sweatshirt that zippered up the front so that you wouldn't have to raise your arms to slip it over your head — your latest cast had been removed only a week ago and your upper arm was still stiff. "Besides your arm, what hurts today?" Charlotte asked.

You seemed to do a mental inventory. "My hip," you said.

"Like yesterday, or worse?"

"The same."

"Do you want to walk?" Charlotte asked, but you shook your head.

"The walker makes my arm ache," you said.

"Then I'll get the chair."

"No! I don't want to use the chair —"

"Willow, you don't have a choice. I'm not going to carry you around all day."

"But I hate the chair —"

"Then you'll just have to work hard so you get out of it faster, right?"

Charlotte explained, on camera, that you were caught between a rock and a hard place — the arm injury, an old wound, was still healing, but the hip pain was new. The adaptive equipment — a walker to help you stand with support — meant putting pressure on your arm, which you could do for only short periods of time, and which left instead only the dreaded folding manual wheelchair. You hadn't been fitted for a new one since you were two; at age six, you were nearly twice that size and complained of back and muscle pain after a full day's use — but insurance wouldn't upgrade your chair until you were seven.

I had expected a flurry of morning activity, made even more overwhelming by all of your needs, but Charlotte moved methodically — letting Amelia run around trying to find lost homework while she brushed your hair and fixed it in two braids, cooked scrambled eggs and toast for breakfast, and loaded you into the car along with the walker, the thirty-pound wheelchair, a standing table, and the braces — to use during physical therapy. You couldn't take the bus — jarring over bumps could cause microfractures — so Charlotte drove you instead, dropping Amelia off at the middle school on the way.

I followed you in my own van. "What's the big deal?" the cameraman asked when we were alone in the car. "She's just small and disabled, so what?"

"She also can snap a bone if you hit the brakes," I said. But there was a part of me that knew the cameraman was right. A jury watching Charlotte tie her daughter's shoes and strap her into a car seat like an infant would think your life was no worse than any baby's. What we needed was something more dramatic — a fall or, better yet, a fracture.

My God, what kind of person was I, wishing a six-year-old would get hurt?

At the school, Charlotte lugged the equipment out of the van and set it in a corner of the classroom. There was a quick powwow with the teacher and your aide, Charlotte explaining which injuries were bothering you today. Meanwhile, you sat in your chair near the cubbies as children funneled around your to hang up their jackets and take off their boots. Your shoelace had come untied, and although you tried to lean over to fix it, your foreshortened arms couldn't quite span the distance. A little girl bent down to help you. "I just learned how to tie them," she said, matter-of-fact, and she looped the laces and knotted them. As she bounced off, you watched her. "I know how to tie my own shoes," you said, but your voice had an edge to it.

When it was time for snack, your aide had to lift you up to wash your hands, because the sink was too tall to accommodate your wheelchair. Five children jockeyed to sit next to you. But you got only about three minutes to eat because you were scheduled for physical therapy. That day alone, I'd learned, we'd be filming you at PT, OT, speech therapy, and visiting a prosthetic specialist. It made me wonder when or if you ever got to just be a kindergartner.

"How do you think it's going so far?" Charlotte asked as we walked down the hall to the physical therapy room, trailing you and your wheelchair and your aide. "Do you think it will be enough for a jury?"

"Don't worry," I said. "That's my job."

The physical therapy room was adjacent to the gymnasium. Inside, on the gleaming floor, a teacher was setting a line of kickballs down. There was a wall of glass, through which you could watch what was going on in the gym. It seemed cruel to me. Was it supposed to inspire a kid like you to work harder? Or just depress the hell out of you?

Twice a week, you had PT with Molly in school. Once a week, you were taken to her office. She was a skinny redhead with a surprisingly low voice. "How's the hip?"

"It still hurts," you told her.

"Like *I'd rather die than walk, Molly,* hurts? Or just *ouch,* it hurts?"

You laughed. "Ouch."

"Good. Then show me your stuff."

She lifted you out of your chair and set you upright on the floor. I held my breath — I hadn't seen you moving without a walker — and you began to shuffle your feet in tiny hiccups. Your right foot lifted off the floor, your left one dragged, until you paused at the edge of a red mat. It was only an inch thick, but it took you ten whole seconds to lift your left leg enough to gain the clearance.

She bounced a large red ball to the middle of the mat. "You want to start with this today?"

"Yes," you said, and your face lit up.

"Your wish is my command," Molly said, and she sat you down on the ball. "Show me how far you can reach with your left hand."

You reached across your body, putting an S curve into your spine. Even giving it all your effort, you could barely keep your shoulders from facing squarely forward. This put your eyes in line with the window, where your classmates were engaged in a raucous game of dodgeball. "I wish I could do that," you said.

"Keep stretching, Wonder Woman, and you just might," Molly replied.

But this wasn't really true — even if you learned enough flexibility to dodge and weave, your bones wouldn't withstand a firm hit.

"You're not missing anything," I said. "I hated dodgeball. I was always the one picked last."

"I'm the one picked *never*," you said.

That, I thought, *will be a great sound bite*.

Apparently, I wasn't the only one. Charlotte glanced at the camera and then turned to the physical therapist, who had your belly bent over the ball and was rocking you back and forth. "Molly? How about using the ring?"

"I was going to hold off another week or two before I did any weight-bearing exercises —"

"Maybe we can work on the soft tissue? To improve her range?"

She settled you on the floor. The soles of your feet touched together, a yoga pose I could manage only on a good day. Reaching onto the wall, Molly untied what looked like a gymnastics ring, which was dangling from the ceiling. She adjusted the height until it hovered just over your head. "Right arm this time," she said.

You shook your head. "I don't want to."

"Just give it a try. If it hurts too much, we'll stop."

You inched your arm higher, until your fingertips brushed the rubber ring. "Can we stop now?"

"Come on, Willow, I know you're tougher than that," Molly said. "Wrap your fingers around and give it a squeeze . . ."

To do that, you had to lift your arm even higher. Tears glazed your eyes, which made your sclera look electric. The cameraman zoomed in on your face, a close-up.

"Ow," you said, starting to cry in earnest as your hand clutched the ring. "Please, Molly . . . can I stop?"

Suddenly Charlotte wasn't sitting beside me anymore. She'd run to you, prised your fingers free. Tucking your arm close to your side, she cradled you. "It's okay, baby," she crooned. "I'm sorry. I'm sorry Molly made you try."

At that, Molly's head snapped around — but she kept her mouth shut when she saw the camera rolling.

Charlotte's eyes were closed; she might have been crying, too. I felt like I was violating something private. So I reached over and put my hand on the long nose of the camera, gently forced it toward the floor.

The videographer cut the power.

Charlotte sat cross-legged with you curled in the bowl of her body. You looked embryonic, spent. I watched her stroke your hair and whisper to you as she stood, lifting you in her arms. Charlotte turned, so that she was facing us and you weren't. "Did you get that on film?" she asked.

Once, I watched a news story about two couples whose newborns had been switched by accident at the hospital. They learned only years later, when one baby was found to have some god-awful hereditary disease that the parents didn't have in their genetic makeup. The other family was tracked down and the mothers had to trade their sons. One mother — the one who was getting a healthy child back, as a matter of fact — was absolutely inconsolable. "He doesn't feel right in my arms," she kept sobbing. "He doesn't smell like my boy."

I wondered how long it took for a baby to become yours, for familiarity to set in. Maybe as long as it took a new car to lose that scent, or a brand-new house to gather dust. Maybe that was the process more commonly described as bonding: the act of learning your child as well as you know yourself.

But what if the child never knew the parent quite as well?

Like me, and my birth mother. Or you. Did you wonder why your mother had hired me? Why you were being followed around by a camera crew? Did you wonder, as we walked back to the classroom, whether your mother had brought you to tears on purpose, so that the jury would squirm?

Charlotte's words kept ringing in my ears: *I'm sorry Molly made you try.* But Molly hadn't. Charlotte had insisted on it. Had she been doing it because she truly cared about the range of motion in your right arm after your latest break? Or because she knew it would bring you to tears for the camera?

I was not a mother; I might never be. But I'd certainly had my share of friends who couldn't stand their own mothers — either they were too absent or too smothering; they complained too much or they noticed too little. Part of growing up was distancing yourself from your mother.

It was different for me. I'd grown up with a tiny buffer of space between my adoptive mother and myself. Once, in chemistry, I'd learned that objects never really touch — because of ions repelling, there's always an infinitesimal space, so that even when it feels like you're holding hands or rubbing up against something on the atomic level, you're not. That was how I felt these days about my adoptive family: to the naked eye, we looked like a seamless, happy group. But I knew that, no matter how hard I tried, I'd never close that microscopic gap.

Maybe this was normal. Maybe mothers — consciously or subconsciously — repelled their daughters in different ways. Some knew what they were doing — like my birth mother, handing me over to another family. And some, like Charlotte, didn't. Her exploiting you on film for what she believed to be the greater good made me hate her, hate this case. I wanted to finish filming; I wanted to get as far away from her as possible before I did something that was forbidden in my line of work: tell her how I really felt about her and her lawsuit.

But just as I was trying to figure out a way to wrap this up early, I got what I'd been wishing for — a crisis. Not in the form of you falling down but, instead, equipment failure: while Charlotte was packing up your equipment after school, she saw that your wheelchair tire had gone dead flat.

"Willow," she said, exasperated. "Didn't you *notice*?"

"Do you have a spare?" I asked, wondering if there was a closet in the O'Keefe house that had extra parts for wheelchairs and braces, just as there was one full of splints, Ace bandages, slings, and doll plaster. "No," Charlotte said. "But the bike store might." She pulled out her cell phone and called Amelia. "I'm going to be a little late . . . No, she didn't break. But her wheelchair did."

The bike store didn't have a size 22 wheel in stock, but they thought they might be able to order one in by the end of the week. "Which means," Charlotte explained, "that either I can spend twice as much at a medical supply store in Boston or else Willow's minus her chair for the rest of the week."

An hour late, we pulled up to the middle school. Amelia was sitting on top of her backpack, glowering. "Just so you know," she said, "I have three tests tomorrow."

"Why didn't you study while you were waiting for us?" you asked.

"Did I ask you for your opinion?"

By four o'clock I was exhausted. Charlotte was on the computer, trying to find discount wheelchair manufacturers online. Amelia was writing flash cards with French vocabulary on them. You were upstairs in your room, sitting on the floor with a pink ceramic pig on your lap.

"Sorry about your chair," I said.

You shrugged. "Stuff like that happens a lot. Last time, the bike store had to get hair out from the front wheels because they stopped turning."

"That's pretty disgusting," I said.

"Yeah . . . I guess it is."

I settled down beside you as the videographer moved inconspicuously to a corner of the room. "You seem to have a lot of friends at school."

"Not really. Most of the kids, they say stupid things like how lucky I am to get to ride in a wheelchair when they have to walk all the way down to the gym or around the playground or whatever."

"But you don't think it's lucky."

"No, because it's only fun at first. It's not so fun if you do it your whole life." She looked up at me. "Those kids today? They're not my friends."

"They all wanted to sit next to you at snack —"

"What they wanted was to be in the movie." You shook the ceramic pig in your lap. It jingled. "Did you know real pigs think, like we do? And they can learn tricks like dogs, only faster."

"That's impressive. Are you saving up to buy one?"

"No," you said. "I'm giving my allowance money to my mother, so she can buy the tire for my wheelchair and not have to worry about how much it costs." You pulled the black plug from between the pig's legs, and a trickle of dimes and nickels, with the occasional wadded dollar, tumbled out. "Last time I counted I had seven dollars and sixteen cents."

376

"Willow," I said slowly. "Your mother didn't ask you to pay for that wheel."

"No, but if it doesn't cost her any extra, she won't have to get rid of me."

I was struck silent. "Willow," I said, "you know your mother loves you."

You looked up at me.

"Sometimes, mothers say and do things that seem like they don't want their kids . . . but when you look more closely, you realize that they're doing those kids a favor. They're just trying to give them a better life. Do you understand?"

"I guess." You tipped over the piggy bank again. It sounded as if it were full of broken glass.

"Can I talk to you?" I said as I walked into the study where Charlotte was poring over the results of a search engine.

She jumped up. "I'm sorry. I know. You didn't come here to film me surfing the Net for wheelchair tire patch kits."

I closed the door behind me. "Forget about the camera, Charlotte. I was just upstairs with Willow, counting her piggy bank savings. She wants to give it to you. She's trying to buy her way into your good graces."

"That's ridiculous," Charlotte said.

"Why? What great leap of logic would you make if you were six years old and you knew that your mother had filed a lawsuit because something was wrong when you were born?"

"Aren't you my lawyer?" Charlotte said. "Aren't you supposed to be helping me instead of telling me I'm a rotten mother?"

"I *am* trying to help you. I don't know how the hell I'm going to cobble together a video for the jury from this footage, to be honest. Because right now, if they saw it, they might feel sorry for Willow — but they'd *hate* you."

Suddenly all of the fight went out of Charlotte. She sank back into the chair she'd been sitting on when I came into the room. "When you first mentioned wrongful birth, I felt like Sean did. Like it was the most disgusting term I'd ever heard in my life. All these years I've just gone along doing what needed to be done. I knew people watched me with Willow and thought, *That poor girl. That poor mother.* But you know, I never really pictured it that way. She was my baby and I was going to take care of her, and that was that." Charlotte looked up at me. "Then, you and Robert Ramirez started talking, asking me questions. And I thought, *Someone gets it.* It felt like I'd been living underground, and for a moment, I'd been given this glimpse of the sky. Once you've seen that, how can you go back where you came from?"

I felt my cheeks burn. I knew exactly what Charlotte was talking about, and I did not like thinking I had anything in common with her. But I remembered the day when I'd been told I was adopted, when I realized there was another mother, another father out there somewhere I had never met. For years, even when it wasn't in the forefront of my mind, it was still present, an itch just beneath the skin.

Lawyers were notorious for finding cases in the most unlikely places, especially ones with huge potential damages awards. But was the dissolution of this family really my fault? Had Bob and I created a monster?

"My mother's in a nursing home now," Charlotte said. "She can't remember who I am, so I've become the keeper of the memories. I'm the one who tells her about the time she baked brownies for the entire senior class when I ran for student council, and how I won by a landslide. Or how she used to collect sea glass with me during the summer and put it in a jar next to my bed. I wonder what memories Willow will have to tell me, if it comes to that. I wonder if there's a difference between being a dutiful mother and being a good mother."

"There is," I said, and Charlotte looked up at me, expectant.

Even if I couldn't articulate the difference as an adult, as a child, I had felt it. I thought for a moment. "A dutiful mother is someone who follows every step her child makes," I said.

"And a good mother?"

I lifted my gaze to Charlotte's. "Is someone whose child wants to follow *her*."

Interfering Agents: A substance added to sugar syrup in order to prevent it from crystallizing.

We've all had a crystallizing moment, when suddenly everything begins to come together . . . whether we want it to or not. The same thing happens in the production of candy — there's a time when the mixture starts to turn into something it wasn't moments before. A single unincorporated sugar crystal can change the texture from smooth to grainy, and eventually, if you don't prevent it, you get rock candy. But ingredients added to sugar syrup before boiling can keep that moment of crystallization from occurring. Common interfering agents are corn syrup, glucose, and honey; cream of tartar, lemon juice, or vinegar.

If it's not candy you're trying to prevent from becoming crystal clear — but, instead, your life — well, the best interfering agent is always a lie well told.

CRÈME CARAMEL

CARAMEL

1 cup sugar
⅓ cup water
2 tablespoons light corn syrup
¼ teaspoon lemon juice

380

CUSTARD

1½ cups whole milk
1½ cups light whipping cream
3 large eggs
2 large egg yolks
⅔ cup sugar
1½ teaspoons vanilla extract
Pinch of salt

You can make one large crème caramel, but I like to make individual ones in ramekins. To make the caramel, mix the sugar, water, corn syrup, and lemon juice in a medium non-reactive saucepan (a light-colored one, so you can see the color of the syrup). Simmer over medium-high heat, wiping the sides of the pan with a wet cloth to make sure there are no sugar crystals lurking that might cause crystallization. Cook for about 8 minutes, until the syrup turns from clear to gold, swirling the pan to make sure browning occurs evenly. Continue to cook for another 4 to 5 minutes, swirling the pan constantly, until large bubbles on the mixture's surface turn honey-colored. Remove the pan immediately from the heat and pour a portion of the caramel into each of eight ungreased 5- or 6-ounce ovenproof ramekins. Allow the caramel to cool and harden, about 15 minutes. (Ramekins can be covered with plastic wrap and refrigerated for up to two days, but return them to room temperature before you move on to the next step.)

To make the custard, heat the milk and cream in a medium saucepan over medium heat, stirring occasionally until a thermometer in the liquid reads 160 degrees F. Remove the mixture from the heat. Meanwhile, whisk the eggs, yolks, and sugar in a large bowl until just combined. Whisk the warm milk mixture, vanilla, and salt into the egg mixture until just mixed but not foamy. Strain the mixture through a mesh sieve into a large measuring cup and set it aside.

Bring 2 quarts of water to a boil. Meanwhile, fold a dish towel to fit the bottom of a large roasting pan. Divide the reserved custard mixture among the ramekins and place the filled ramekins in the pan, making sure they do not touch. Set the pan on the center rack of a preheated 350 degree F oven. Fill the pan with boiling water to reach halfway up the ramekins and cover the entire pan loosely with aluminum foil, so that steam can escape. Bake 35 to 40 minutes, until a paring knife inserted halfway between the center and edge of the custard comes out clean.

Transfer the custards to a wire rack and cool to room temperature. To unmold, slide a paring knife around the outer edge of each custard, hold a serving plate over the top of the ramekin, invert, and shake gently to release the custard. Serve immediately.

Charlotte

August 2008

The 2008 Biennial Osteogenesis Imperfecta Convention was being held in Omaha, at a huge Hilton with a conference center, a big pool, and over 570 people who looked like you. As we walked into the registration area, I suddenly felt like a giant, and you turned to me from your wheelchair with the biggest smile on your face. "Mom," you said, "I'm normal here."

We'd never been to a conference before. We'd never been able to find the money to come to one. But Sean had not slept at our house in months — and although you hadn't asked why, it had less to do with you not noticing than with you not wanting to hear the answer. Frankly, neither did I. Sean and I had not used the word *separation*, but just because you didn't put a name to something did not mean it wasn't there. Sometimes, I caught myself wondering what Sean would like for dinner, or picking up the phone to call his cell before I remembered not to. Your face lit up when he came to visit you; I wanted to give you something else to look forward to. So when the flyer for this conference came via email from the OI Foundation, I knew that I'd found the perfect prize.

Now, as I watched you eyeing a phalanx of girls your age roll by in their own wheelchairs, I realized we should have done this earlier. Even Amelia wasn't making any sarcastic remarks — just taking in the small groups of people in wheelchairs, walkers, or on their own two feet, greeting each other like long-lost relatives. There were pre-teen girls — some who looked like Amelia, others who were short of stature, like you — taking pictures of each other with disposable cameras. Boys the same age were terrorizing the escalators, teaching each other how to ride their wheelchairs up and down them.

A little girl with black ringlets walked up to you, her braces jingling. "You're new," she said. "What's your name?"

"Willow."

"I'm Niamh. It's a weird name because there's no *v* but it sounds like there is. You've got a weird name, too." She looked up at Amelia. "Is this your sister? Does she have OI?"

"No."

"Huh," Niamh said. "Well, that's too bad for her. The coolest programs are for kids like us."

There were forty information sessions over a three-day weekend — everything from "Financial Planning for Your Special-Needs Child" to "Writing the IEP" and "Ask a Doctor." You had your own Kids' Club events — arts and crafts, scavenger hunts, swimming, video game competitions, how to be more

384

independent, how to improve your self-esteem. I hadn't been too keen on giving you up for a day's activities, but they were staffed by nurses. Pre-teens with OI had Game Night, and The Adventures of Bone Boy and Milk Maid. Even Amelia could attend special talks for non-OI siblings.

"Niamh, there you are!" A teenage girl who looked about Amelia's age came closer with a pack of kids trailing behind her. "You can't just run off," she said, grasping Niamh's hand. "Who's your friend?"

"Willow."

The older girl crouched down so that she was eye level with you in your chair. "Nice to meet you, Willow. We're just across the lobby over there playing Spit if you want to join us."

"Can I?" you asked.

"If you're careful. Amelia, can you push her —"

"I've got it." A boy stepped forward and took the handles of your chair. He had dirty blond hair that swept into his eyes and a smile that could have melted a glacier — or Amelia, at whom he kept staring. "Unless you're coming?"

Amelia, to my disbelief, blushed.

"Maybe later," she said.

Although there had been handicapped-accessible rooms blocked out at the hotel, we didn't book one. Amelia and I didn't particularly want a roll-in shower, and the idea of using a loaner shower seat for you made my skin crawl. You could easily clean up in the bathtub and wash your hair under the faucet. We'd attended the keynote speech, which was about current research on OI, and gone to a sprawling buffet dinner — one that included low tables so that wheelchair users or very small people could see and reach the food.

"Lights out," I said, and Amelia buried herself under the covers, the iPod buds still in her ears. The screen glowed beneath the sheets. You rolled onto your side, your face already wreathed in dreams. "I love it here," you said. "I want to stay here forever."

I smiled. "Well, it won't be much fun when all your OI friends go back home."

"Can we come again?"

"I hope so, Wills."

"Next time, can Dad come with us?"

I stared at the digital alarm clock as one number bled into the next. "I hope so," I repeated.

This is how we wound up coming to the convention:

One morning, when you and Amelia were at school, I was baking. It was what I did when you were gone now; there was a Zen rhythm to beating together the sugar and the shortening, to folding in the egg whites, to scalding the milk. My kitchen steamed with the smells of vanilla and caramel, cinnamon and anise. I'd whisk royal icing; I'd roll out perfect pie crusts; I'd punch down dough. The more my hands moved, the less likely I was to let my mind wander.

Back then, it had been March — two months since Sean opted out of the lawsuit. For a few weeks after our row in the middle of the highway, I'd left the pillows and bedding on the fireplace hearth, a just-in-case, as close as I could come to an apology. He came to the house every now and then to see you girls, but when he did, I felt like I was intruding. I would balance my checkbook, I would clean the bathroom, while listening to your laughter downstairs.

This is what I wish I'd had the guts to say to him: I made a mistake, but so did you. Aren't we even now?

Sometimes I missed Sean viscerally. Sometimes I was angry at him. Sometimes I just wanted to turn back time, to go back to the moment he had asked, *What do you think about a vacation to Disney World?* But mostly I wondered why the head could move so swiftly while the heart dragged its feet. Even when I felt sure of myself and confident, even when I started to think that you girls and I would be fine on our own, I still loved him. It felt like anything else permanent that has gone missing: a lost tooth, a severed leg. You might know better, but that doesn't keep your tongue from poking at the hole in your gum, or your phantom limb from aching.

So every morning I baked to forget, until the windows steamed and just breathing felt like sitting down at the finest table. I baked until my hands were red and raw and my nails were caked with flour. I baked until I stopped wondering why a lawsuit could move so exceedingly slowly. I baked until I didn't wonder where next month's mortgage payment would come from. I baked until it grew so hot in the kitchen that I wore only a tank top and jogging shorts under my apron, until I imagined myself under the golden dome of a flaky crust of my own making, wondering if Sean would break through before I suffocated.

Which is why I was stunned when the doorbell rang in the middle of a fleet of beignets. I was not expecting anyone — I had nothing to expect anymore, period. On the porch stood a stranger, making me even more aware of the fact that I was only half dressed and my hair was grayed with confectioners' sugar.

"Are you Ms. Syllabub?" the man asked.

He was short and round, with a double chin and a matching curve to his receding hairline. He was holding a plastic bag full of my shortbread, tied with a green ribbon.

"That's just a name," I said. "But it's not mine."

"But —" He glanced at my attire. "You're the baker?"

"Yes," I said. "I'm the baker." Not the gold digger, not the bitch, not even the mother. Something separate and apart, an identity as bright and clear as stainless steel. I held out my hand. "Charlotte O'Keefe."

He planted his feet squarely on the doormat. "I'd like to buy your pastries."

"Oh, you didn't need to come up here for that," I said. "You can just leave a couple of dollars in the honesty box."

"No, you don't understand. I want to buy all of them." He handed me a card, the kind with raised lettering. "My name's Henry DeVille. I run a chain of Gas-n-Get convenience stores in New Hampshire, and I'd like to feature your baked goods." He flushed. "Mostly because I can't stop eating them."

388

"Really?" I said, a slow smile breaking over my face.

"I was visiting my sister one day last month — she lives two roads up from here, but I had gotten lost, and I was starving. And since then I've made eight two-hour treks just to get whatever it is you're selling on a particular day. I may not be the best judge of business, but I'm pretty much a Ph.D. when it comes to good desserts."

It had taken me a week to agree. I didn't have the time or the inclination to drive all over New Hampshire delivering muffins in the morning; I didn't know how much I could promise to produce. For every caveat I raised, Henry had a solution, and within a week I had run a draft contract past Marin that was sweet enough to get me to agree. To celebrate, I baked Henry an almond-blueberry coffee cake. He sat at my kitchen table, drinking coffee, eating cake with a newly minted businesswoman. "I've tried to pinpoint it," he mused, watching me sign the contract. "There's a certain something in your cooking that's like nothing I've ever tasted. It's addictive, really."

I smiled at him as best I could and pushed the paper across the table before he could change his mind. Because Henry DeVille was correct — there was an ingredient in my baking more concentrated than any extract, more pungent than any spice; an ingredient that everyone would recognize and no one was able to name: it was regret, and it rose when one least expected.

The next morning, as part of the Be Fit! campaign that headed this year's festival, you and I headed down to the exercise course, where participants could wheel or walk a quarter or a half mile. When you finished, clutching a certificate close to your chest, we had a quick breakfast before the day's small group sessions. Amelia was sleeping in, but I was planning to attend a workshop on body image for young girls with OI.

As soon as you were welcomed back to the Kids' Zone — the nurse who gave you a high five, I noticed, had gotten you to lift your right arm higher than any physical therapist in the past four months — I headed to the ladies' room to wash my hands before the session began. Like everything else at the hotel, the restrooms were OI-friendly: the outer door was propped open for easy access; a low table held extra soap and towels.

As I ran the faucet, another woman entered, carrying a glass of milk — it was being served as part of the overall theme of keeping healthy; the problem with OI is a deficiency in collagen, not calcium. "I love this," she said, grinning. "It's got to be the only conference that serves milk between the sessions instead of coffee and juice."

"It was probably cheaper than shots of pamidronate," I said, and she laughed.

"I don't think we've met yet. I'm Kelly Clough, mother of David, Type V."

"Willow, Type III. I'm Charlotte O'Keefe."

"Is Willow having fun?"

"Willow's in heaven," I said. "She can barely wait to go to the zoo tonight." The Henry Doorly Zoo was opening their facility after hours for the convention

390

participants tonight; during breakfast, you had made a list of what animals you wanted to see.

"For David it's all about swimming." She glanced at me in the mirror. "There's something about you that's really familiar."

"Well, I've never been to a convention before," I said.

"No, your name . . ."

There was a flush, and a moment later, a woman our age came out of a room stall. She positioned her walker in front of the handicap-accessible sink and turned on the water. "Do you read Tiny Tim's blog?" she asked.

"Sure," Kelly said. "Who doesn't?"

Well. Me, for one.

"She's the one who's suing for wrongful birth." The woman turned, wiping her hands on a towel before facing me. "I think it's disgusting, frankly. And I think it's even more disgusting that you're here. You can't play both sides. You can't sue because a life with OI isn't worth living and then come here and talk about how excited your daughter is to be with other kids like her and how great it is that she can go to the zoo."

Kelly had taken a step backward. "That's *you*?"

"I didn't mean —"

"I can't believe any parent would think that way," Kelly said. "We all have to scrape the bottoms of our bank accounts to make things work. But I never, ever would wish I hadn't had my son."

I felt myself shaking uncontrollably. I wanted to be a mother, like Kelly, who took her son's disability in stride. I wanted you to grow up like this other woman, forthright and confident. I just also wanted the resources for you to be able to do it.

"Do you know what I've spent the past six months doing?" the woman with OI said. "Training for the Paralympics. I'm on the swim team. If your daughter came home with a gold medal one day, would that convince you her life wasn't a waste?"

"You don't understand —"

"Actually," Kelly said, "*you* don't."

She turned on her heel, walking out of the restroom with the other woman trailing behind. I turned the water on full blast and splashed some onto my face, which felt as if it had gone up in flames. Then, with my heart still hammering, I stepped into the hallway.

The nine o'clock sessions were filling. My cover had been blown; I could feel the needles of a hundred eyes on me, and every whisper held my name. I kept my gaze trained on the patterned carpet as I pushed past a knot of wrestling boys and a toddler being carried by a girl with OI not much bigger than himself. A hundred steps to the elevators . . . fifty . . . twenty.

The elevator doors opened, and I slipped inside and punched a button. Just as the doors were closing, a crutch jammed between them. The man who had signed us in yesterday was standing on the threshold, but instead of smiling at me in welcome, like he had twelve hours earlier, his eyes were dark as pitch. "Just so you know — it's not my disability that makes my life a constant struggle," he said. "It's people like you." Then, with a rasping of metal, he stepped back and let the elevator doors close.

I made it to the room and slid the key card inside, only to remember that Amelia was probably still sleeping. But — thank God — she was gone, downstairs eating breakfast or AWOL, and right now I didn't care which. I lay down on the bed and pulled the covers over my head. Then, finally, I let myself burst into tears.

This was worse than being judged by a jury of my peers. This was being judged by a jury of *your* peers.

I was, pure and simple, a failure. My husband had left me; my mothering skills had been warped to include the American legal system. I cried until my eyes had swollen and my cheeks hurt. I cried until there was nothing left inside me. Then I sat up and walked to the small desk near the window.

It held a phone, a blotter, and a binder listing the services offered by the hotel. Inside this were two postcards and two blank fax cover sheets. I took them out and reached for the pen beside the telephone.

Sean, I wrote. *I miss you.*

Until he moved out, Sean and I had never spent any time apart from each other, unless you counted the week before our wedding. Although he'd moved into the house where Amelia and I lived, I had wanted to create at least the semblance of excitement, so he'd bunked on the couch of another police officer in the days leading up to the ceremony. He'd hated it. I'd find him driving by in his cruiser while I was at work at the restaurant, and we'd sneak into the cold room in the kitchen and kiss intensely. Or he'd stop by to tuck Amelia in at night and then pretend to fall asleep on the couch watching TV. *I'm onto you*, I told him. *And this isn't going to work.* At the ceremony, Sean surprised me with vows he'd written himself: *I'll give you my heart and my soul,* he said. *I'll protect you and serve you. I'll give you a home, and I won't let you kick me out of it ever again.* Everyone laughed, including me — imagine, mousy little Charlotte being the kind of sultry seductress who'd have that much control over a man! But Sean made me feel like I could fell a giant with a single word or a gentle touch. It was powerful, and it was a me I had never imagined.

Somewhere, in the deep creases of my mind — the folds where hope gets caught — I believed that whatever was wrong between Sean and me was reparable. It had to be, because when you love someone — when you create a child with him — you don't just suddenly lose that bond. Like any other energy, it can't be destroyed, just channeled into something else. And maybe right now I'd turned the full spotlight of my attention on you. But that was normal; the levels of love within a family shifted and flowed all the time. Next week, it could be Amelia; next month, Sean. Once this lawsuit was over, he'd move back home. We'd go back to the way we used to be.

We *had* to, because I couldn't really swallow the alternative: that I would be forced to choose between your future and my own.

The second letter I had to write was harder. *Dear Willow,* I wrote.

I don't know when you'll be reading this, or what will have happened by then. But I have to write it, because I owe you an explanation more than anyone else. You are the most beautiful thing that's ever happened to me, and the most painful. Not because of your illness, but because I can't fix it, and I hate seeing those moments when you realize that you might not be able to do what other kids do.

I love you, and I always will. Maybe more than I should. That's the only reason I can give for all this. I thought that if I loved you hard enough, I could move mountains for you; I could make you fly. It didn't matter to me how that happened — just as long as it did. I wasn't thinking of who I might hurt, only who I could rescue.

The first time you broke in my arms, I couldn't stop crying. I think I've spent all these years trying to make up for that moment. That's why I can't stop now, even though there are times I want to. I can't stop, but there isn't a moment I don't worry about what you'll remember in the long run. Will it be the arguments I had with your father? The way your sister turned into someone we didn't recognize? Or will you remember the way you and I once spent an hour watching a snail cross our porch? Or how I cut your lunchbox sandwiches into your initials? Will you remember how, when I wrapped you in a towel after your bath, I held you a moment longer than it took to dry you?

I have always had a dream of you living on your own. I see you as a doctor, and I wonder if that's because I've seen you with so many. I imagine a man who will love you like crazy, maybe even a baby. I bet you'll fight for her as fiercely as I tried to fight for you.

What I could never puzzle out, however, was how you'd get from where you are to where you might one day be — until I was given the materials to make a bridge. Too late I learned that that bridge was made of thorns, that it might not be strong enough to hold us all.

When it comes to memories, the good and the bad never balance. I am not sure how I came to measure your life by the moments when it's fallen apart — surgeries, breaks, emergencies — instead of the moments in between. Maybe that makes me a pessimist, maybe it makes me a realist. Or maybe it just makes me a mother.

You will hear people saying things about me. Some are lies, some are truth. There's only one fact that matters: I don't want you to ever suffer another break.

Especially one between you and me, because that might never set properly.

Sean

I was hemorrhaging money.

Not only was my paycheck being stretched to cover the mortgage and the car payment and the credit card finance charges but now any cash I might have been able to sock away was being poured, forty-nine dollars per night, into the Sleep Inn motel, where I'd been living since the day Charlotte came to ream me out at the highway construction detail.

This is why, when Charlotte told me she was leaving one Friday to take the girls to an OI convention for the weekend, I checked out of the Sleep Inn and let myself into my own house.

It's a weird thing, coming back home as a stranger. You know how, when you go into someone else's house, it smells — sometimes like fresh laundry, sometimes like pine needles, but distinct from any other? You don't notice it where you live until you haven't been there for a while. The first night, I'd walked around soaking in the familiar: the newel post on the banister that still popped off because I'd never gotten around to fixing it; the herd of stuffed animals on your bed; the baseball I'd caught while on a trip to Fenway with a bunch of other cops back in '90, a Tom Brunansky homer to center field in a game that put the Sox in first place over Toronto for the season.

I went into my bedroom, too, and sat down on Charlotte's side of the bed. That night, I slept on her pillow.

The next morning, as I packed up my toiletries, I wondered if Charlotte would go to wash her face and be able to smell the scent of me on the towels. If she'd notice that I'd finished off the loaf of bread and the roast beef. If she'd care.

It was my day off, and I knew what I had to do.

The church was quiet at this time on a Saturday morning. I sat down in a pew, looking up at a stained-glass window that reached long, blue fingers down the aisle.

Forgive me, Charlotte, for I have sinned.

Father Grady, who was close to the altar, noticed me. "Sean," he said. "Is Willow all right?"

He probably thought the only time I'd willingly set foot in a church was if I had to pray hard for my daughter's failing health. "She's doing okay, Father. I actually was hoping I could talk to you for a minute."

"Sure." He sank down into the pew in front of me, turning sideways.

"It's about Charlotte," I said slowly. "We're having some problems seeing eye to eye."

"I'm happy to talk to both of you," the priest said.

"It's been months. I think we're past that point."

"I hope you're not talking about divorce, Sean. There is no divorce in the Catholic Church. It's a mortal sin. God made your marriage, not some piece of paper." He smiled at me. "Things that look impossible suddenly seem a lot better, once you get God onboard."

"God's got to make exceptions every now and then."

"No way. If He did, people would go into marriage thinking there was a way out when the going got tough."

"My wife," I said flatly, "plans to swear on a Bible in court and then say she wishes she'd aborted Willow. Do you think God would want me married to someone like that?"

"Yes," the priest said immediately. "The biggest purpose of marriage, after having children, is to support and help your spouse. You might be the one who manages to make Charlotte see she's wrong."

"I tried. I can't."

"A sacrament — like marriage — means living a life better than your natural instincts, so that you're modeling God. And God never gives up."

That, I thought to myself, wasn't entirely true. There were plenty of places in the Bible where God backed Himself into a corner and, instead of toughing it out, simply started over. Look at the great flood, at Sodom and Gomorrah.

"Jesus didn't get to drop that Cross," Father Grady said. "He carried it all the way uphill."

Well, in one respect the priest was right. If I stayed in this marriage, either Charlotte or I was going to wind up being crucified.

"How about you and Charlotte come see me together sometime next week?" Father Grady said. "We'll figure this out."

I nodded, and he patted my hand and headed toward the altar again.

Lying to a priest was a sin, too, but that was the least of my worries.

Adina Nettle's office was nothing like Guy Booker's, although they apparently had gone to law school together. Adina, Guy said, was the one you wanted if you were getting a divorce. He'd used her twice now himself.

She had overstuffed couches with those lacy things that look like they belong on valentines draped over the backs. She served tea but not coffee. And she looked like everybody's grandmother.

Maybe that's why she got what she wanted in settlements.

"You're not too cold, Sean? I can turn down the air-conditioning . . ."

"I'm fine," I said. For the past half hour, I'd drunk three cups of Earl Grey and told Adina about our family. "We go back and forth to different hospitals, depending on what the problem is," I said. "Omaha, for orthopedics. Boston, for pamidronate. Local hospitals for most breaks."

"It must be very difficult, not knowing what's going to happen."

"No one knows what's going to happen," I said soberly. "We just have emergencies more often than most folks."

"Your wife must not be able to work, then," Adina said.

"No. We've been trying to make ends meet ever since Willow was born." I hesitated. "And I can't say it's any easier with me living in a motel."

Adina made a note on her legal pad. "Sean, divorce is financially devastating to most people, and it's going to be even more so for you, because you and Charlotte are living from paycheck to paycheck — plus you've got the added stressor of your daughter's illness. And there's a strange catch-22 here, too — if you want custody, that means you're going to be working less, making even less money. When you're not working, your children are with you. You won't have any free time anymore."

"That doesn't matter," I said.

Adina nodded. "Does Charlotte have job skills?"

"She used to be a pastry chef," I said. "She hasn't worked since Willow was born, but last winter she started a little stand at the end of the driveway."

"A stand?"

"Like a vegetable stand. But with cupcakes."

"If you cut back on your hours to be with the children, will you be able to afford to keep the house? Or will it have to be sold so that you can have two smaller households?"

"I . . . I don't know." Our savings were shot to hell, that much was clear.

"Based on what you've told me, with all of Willow's adaptive equipment and her schedule, it seems that keeping her in one location would be easier for

everyone involved . . . even when it comes to visita-
tion . . ." Adina glanced up at me. "There is one other
option. You could live at the house until the divorce is
finalized."

"Wouldn't that be — a little uncomfortable?"

"Yes. It's also cheaper, which is why a majority of
couples who are in the process of divorcing choose to
do it. *And* it's easier on the children."

"I don't get it —"

"It's very simple. We draw up a negotiated plan, so
that you're in the house when your wife isn't and vice
versa. That way you each have time with the girls while
the divorce is pending, and the household expenses are
no greater than they are right now."

I looked down at the floor. I didn't know if I could
be that generous. I didn't know if I could stand to see
Charlotte in the thick of this lawsuit and not want to
kill her for the things she said. But then again, I would
be right there, a call away, if you needed someone to
hold you in the middle of the night. If you needed
reinforcement to believe that the world would not be
anywhere near as bright without you in it.

"There's only one catch," Adina said. "It's not
ordinary in New Hampshire for a father to get physical
possession of a child, especially in a case where the
child has special needs and the mother has been a
stay-at-home caretaker the child's whole life. So how
are you going to convince a judge that you're the better
parent?"

I met the lawyer's eye. "I'm not the one who started
a wrongful birth lawsuit," I said.

After I walked out of the attorney's office, the world seemed different. The road looked too clear, the colors too jarring. It was like getting a pair of glasses that were overcorrected, and I felt myself moving more carefully.

At a stoplight, I looked out the window and saw a young woman crossing the street with a cup of coffee in her hand. She caught my eye and smiled. In the past, I would have looked away, embarrassed — but now? Were you allowed to smile back, to look, to acknowledge other women, if you'd taken the first steps to ending your marriage?

I had two hours before my shift started, and I headed toward Aubuchon Hardware. The irony didn't escape me — I was shopping at a home improvement mecca, although I didn't currently *have* a home. But while staying in the house this weekend, I'd noticed that the ramp I'd built for your wheelchair three years ago was rotting out in one spot where we had some standing water this spring. My plan was to build you a new one today, so you'd see it when you returned from your conference.

The way I figured it, I'd need three or four sheets of three-quarter-inch pressure-treated plywood, plus a stretch of indoor-outdoor carpeting to give traction under the wheels of your chair. I headed for the service desk to try to estimate the cost. "You're talking about $34.10 a sheet," the employee said, and I found myself backpedaling through the math. If the wood alone cost over a hundred bucks, I'd have to work more overtime, and that wasn't even counting the cost of the carpet material. The more hours I spent at work, the less I would have with you girls. The more money I spent on the ramp, the less I'd have for another night's motel room.

"Sean?"

Piper Reece was standing three feet away.

"What are you doing here?" she asked, but before I could answer, she held up her hands, revealing a packet of wire connectors and a GFCI receptacle. "I'm replacing one. I've been pretty handy lately, but this is the first time I've fooled around with electricity." She laughed nervously. "I keep seeing the headline: 'Woman Found Electrocuted in Her Own Kitchen. Counter was *not* clean at the time of death.' It's supposed to be easy, right? Like, the chances of being zapped during a do-it-yourself project can't be nearly as high as the chances of getting into a car accident on your way to the hardware store, right?" She shook her head and blushed. "I'm babbling."

I've got to go. The words were in my mouth, smooth and round like cherry pits, but what came out was this: "I could help you."

Stupid, stupid, stupid ass. That's what I kept telling myself I was, once the back of my truck was loaded with three sheets of pressure-treated plywood and carpeting and I was headed to Piper Reece's house. There was no real explanation for why I hadn't simply turned my back and walked away from her except for this: in all the years I'd known Piper, I'd never seen her as anything but confident and self-assured — to the

404

point where she was too sharp, too arrogant. Today, though, she'd been completely flustered.

I liked her better this way.

I knew the way to her house, of course. When I pulled onto her street, I experienced the slightest panic — would Rob be home? I didn't think I could handle both of them at once. But his car was gone, and as I turned off the engine, I took a deep breath. Five minutes, I told myself. Install the freaking GFCI and get out of there.

Piper was waiting at the front door. "This is really so nice of you," she said as I stepped inside.

The hallway hadn't always been this color. And when I walked into it, I saw that the kitchen had been remodeled. "You've had some work done in here."

"Actually, I did it myself," Piper admitted. "I've had a lot more time lately."

An uncomfortable silence settled over us like a shroud. "Well. Everything looks completely different."

She stared at me. "Everything *is* completely different."

I jammed my hands into the pockets of my jeans. "So the first thing you have to do is cut off the power at the circuit box," I said. "I'm guessing that's in the basement?"

She led me downstairs, and I switched off the breaker. Then I walked into the kitchen. "Which one is it?" I asked, and Piper pointed.

"Sean? How are you doing?"

I deliberately pretended to hear her incorrectly. "Just taking out the busted one," I said. "Look, it's that easy, once you unscrew it. And then you have to take all the white wires and pigtail them together into one of these little caps. After that, you take the new GFCI and use your screwdriver to connect the pigtail over here — see where it says 'white line'?"

Piper leaned closer. Her breath smelled of coffee and remorse. "Yes."

"Do the same thing with the black wires, and connect them to the terminal that says 'hot line.' And last of all, you connect the grounding wire to the green screw and stuff it all back into the box." With the screwdriver, I reattached the cover plate and turned to her. "Simple."

"Nothing's simple," she said, and she stared at me. "But you know that. Like, for example, crossing over to the dark side."

I put the screwdriver down gently. "It's *all* the dark side, Piper."

"Well, still. I feel like I owe you a thank-you."

I shrugged, looking away. "I'm really sorry this all happened to you."

"I'm really sorry it happened to *you*," Piper answered.

I cleared my throat, took a step backward. "You probably want to go down and throw the breaker, so you can test the outlet."

"That's all right," Piper said, and she offered me a shy smile. "I think it's going to work."

Amelia

Okay, let me just tell you that it's not easy to keep a secret in close quarters. My house was bad enough, but have you ever noticed how thin the walls of a hotel bathroom are? I mean, you can hear *everything* — which meant that when I needed to make myself sick, I had to do it in the big public restrooms in the lobby, which required sitting in a stall until I could peek left and right and not see any other pairs of shoes.

After I'd gotten up this morning and found a note from Mom, I'd gone downstairs to eat and then found you in the kids' area. "Amelia," you said when you saw me. "Aren't those cool?" You were pointing to little colored rods that some of the kids had affixed to the wheels of their chairs. They made an annoying clicking sound when you pushed, which to be honest would get awfully old awfully quick, but — to be fair — they *were* pretty awesome when they glowed in the dark.

I could practically see you taking mental notes as you sized up the other kids with OI. Who had which color wheelchair, who put stickers on their walkers, which girls could walk and which ones had to use a chair, which kids could eat by themselves and which needed

407

help being fed. You were placing yourself in the mix, figuring out where you fit in and how independent you were by comparison. "So what's on the docket for this morning?" I asked. "And where's Mom?"

"I don't know — I guess at one of the other meetings," you said, and then you beamed at me. "We're going swimming. I've already got on my bathing suit."

"That sounds kind of fun —"

"You can't come, Amelia. It's for people like *me*."

I knew you didn't mean to sound like such a snot, but it still hurt to be cut out. I mean, who else was left to ignore me? First Mom, then Emma, now even my little disabled sister was dissing me. "Well, I wasn't inviting myself," I said, stung. "I have somewhere to go anyway." But I watched you wheel yourself into the pack as one of the nurses called the first group of kids to head toward the pool. You were giggling, whispering with a girl who had a bumper sticker on the back of her chair: HOGWARTS DROPOUT.

I wandered out of the kiddie zone and into the main hallway of conference rooms. I had no idea what presentation my mother was planning to attend, but before I could even think about that, one of the signs outside the doors caught my attention: TEENS ONLY. I poked my head inside and saw a collection of kids my age with OI — some in wheelchairs, some just standing — batting around balloons.

Except they weren't balloons. They were condoms.

"We're going to get started," the woman in the front of the room said. "Hon, can you close the door?"

She was, I realized, talking to me. I didn't belong here — there were special programs for siblings like me who didn't have OI. But then again, looking around the room, I could see there were plenty of kids who weren't as bad off as you were — maybe no one would know my bones were perfectly fine.

Then I noticed the boy from yesterday — the one who'd come over to get that little girl Niamh when we were still registering. He looked like the kind of guy who would play the guitar and make up songs about the girl he loved. I'd always thought it would be amazing to have a guy sing to me; although what on earth could he find interesting enough about me to write a song about? *Amelia, Amelia . . . take off your shirt and let me feel ya?*

I stepped into the room and closed the door behind me. The boy grinned, and I lost all sensation in my legs.

I sat down on a stool beside him and pretended I was far too cool to notice the fact that he was close enough for me to feel his body heat. "Welcome," the woman at the front of the room said. "I'm Sarah, and if you're not here for Birds and Bees and Breaks, you're in the wrong place. Ladies and gentlemen, today we're going to talk about sex, sex, and nothing but sex."

There was some edgy laughter; the tips of my ears started to burn.

"Nothing like beating around the bush," the boy beside me said, and then he smiled. "Oops. Bad metaphor."

I looked around, but he was very clearly speaking to me. "*Very* bad," I whispered.

"I'm Adam," he said, and I froze. "You've got a name, don't you?"

Well, yeah, but if I told it to him, he might know I wasn't supposed to be here. "Willow."

God, that smile again. "That's a really pretty name," he said. "It suits you."

I stared down at the table and blushed furiously. This was a *talk* about sex, not a lab where we got to do it. And yet, no one had ever said anything to me even remotely resembling a come-on, unless *Hey, dork, do you have an extra pencil?* counted. Was I subliminally irresistible to Adam because my bones were strong?

"Who can guess what your number one risk is if you have OI and you have sex?" Sarah asked.

A girl's hand inched up. "Breaking your pelvis?"

The boys behind me snickered. "Actually," Sarah said, "I have talked to hundreds of people with OI who are sexually active. And the only person I've ever known to break a bone during sex did it by falling off the bed."

This time, everyone laughed out loud.

"If you have OI, the biggest risk in sexual activity is acquiring a sexually transmitted disease, which means" — she looked around the room — "you're no different from someone *without* OI who has sex."

Adam pushed a piece of paper across the table to me. I unfolded it: *R U Type I?*

I knew enough about your illness to understand why he'd think that. There were people who had Type I OI who went through their whole lives not even knowing it — just breaking a few more bones than ordinary folks.

410

Then again, there were other Type Is who broke as many bones as you did. Often, Type Is were taller, and they didn't always have those heart-shaped faces that you saw on Type IIIs, like you. I was normal height; I wasn't in a wheelchair, I didn't have any scoliosis — and I was in a session for kids with OI. Of course he thought I had Type I.

I scribbled on the other side of the paper and passed it back: *Actually, I'm a Gemini.*

He had really nice teeth. Yours were kind of messed up — that happened a lot with OI kids, along with hearing loss — but his looked all Hollywood white and perfectly even, like he could have starred in a Disney Channel movie.

"What about getting pregnant?" a girl asked.

"Anyone with OI — any type — can get pregnant," Sarah explained. "Your risks would vary, though, depending on your individual situation."

"Would the baby have OI, too?"

"Not necessarily."

I thought of that picture I'd seen in the magazine, of the lady with Type III who'd had a baby in her arms nearly the same size as she was. The problem wasn't with the plumbing, though. It was with the partner. Every day wasn't an OI convention; each of these kids was probably the only one with OI in his or her school. I tried to fast-forward you to my age. If I couldn't even get a guy to notice my existence, how would *you* — tiny, freakishly smart, in your wheelchair or walker? I felt my hand rising, as if a balloon were attached to the wrist. "There's just one problem with that," I said. "What if nobody ever wants to have sex with you?"

Instead of the laughter I expected, there was dead silence. I looked around, stunned. Was I *not* the only person my age absolutely positively sure I was going to die a virgin?

"That," Sarah said, "is a really good question. How many of you had a boyfriend or girlfriend when you were in fifth or sixth grade?" A smattering of hands rose. "How many of you have had a boyfriend or girlfriend after that?"

Two hands, out of twenty.

"A lot of kids who don't have OI will be put off by a wheelchair, or by the fact that you don't look the same way they do. And it's totally clichèd, but believe me, those are the kids you don't want to be with anyway. You want someone who cares about *who* you are, not *what* you are. And even if you have to wait for that, it's going to be worth it. All you have to do is look around you at this convention to see that people with OI fall in love, get married, have sex, get pregnant — not necessarily in that order." As the room broke up laughing again, she began to walk among us, handing out condoms and bananas.

Maybe this *was* a lab after all.

I had seen couples here who clearly both had OI; I'd seen couples where one partner did and one didn't. If someone able-bodied fell in love with you, maybe it would take some of the stress off Mom, eventually. Would you come back to a convention like this and flirt with a kid like Adam? Or one of the wild boys who rode his wheelchair up and down the escalator? I couldn't imagine that was easy on any account — not practically, on a daily basis, and not emotionally, either. Having another person with OI in your life meant you had to worry about yourself *and* about someone else.

Then again, maybe that had nothing to do with OI, and everything to do with love.

"I think we're supposed to be partners," Adam said, and just like that, I couldn't breathe. Then I realized he was talking about the stupid banana and condom. "You want to go first?"

I tore open the foil packet. Can you see someone's pulse? Because mine was certainly banging hard enough under my skin.

I started to unroll the condom along the length of the banana. It got all bunched up on top. "I don't think that's right," Adam said.

"Then you do it."

He peeled off the condom and tore open a second foil packet. I watched him balance the little disk at the top of the banana and smooth it down the length in one easy motion. "Oh, my God," I said. "You are way too good at that."

"That's because my sex life consists entirely of fruit right now."

I smirked. "I find that hard to believe."

Adam met my gaze. "Well, I find it hard to believe you have a hard time finding someone who wants to have sex with you."

I grabbed the banana out of his hand. "Did you know a banana is a reproductive organ of the plant it grows on?"

God, I sounded like an idiot. I sounded like *you*, spouting off your trivia.

"Did you know grapes explode if you put them in the microwave?" Adam said.

"Really?"

"Totally." He paused. "A reproductive organ?"

I nodded. "An ovary."

"So where are you from?"

"New Hampshire," I said. "How about you?"

I held my breath, thinking maybe he was from Bankton, too, and in the high school, which was why I hadn't met him yet. "Anchorage," Adam answered.

It figured.

"So you and your sister both have OI?"

He'd seen me with you in the wheelchair. "Yeah," I said.

"That must be kind of nice. To have someone in the house who gets it, you know?" He grinned. "I'm an only child. My parents took one look at me and broke the mold."

"Or the mold broke." I laughed.

Sarah passed by our table and pointed to the banana. "Wonderful," she said.

We were. Except for the fact that he thought my name was Willow and I had OI.

A makeshift game of condomball had broken out, as groups of kids batted the inflated condoms around the

414

room. "Hey, isn't Willow the name of that girl whose mom is suing because of her OI?" Adam asked.

"How did you know that?" I said, stunned.

"It's all over the blogs. Don't you read them?"

"I've . . . been busy."

"I thought the girl was way younger —"

"Well, you thought wrong," I interrupted.

Adam tilted his head. "You mean, it's *you*?"

"Could you just kind of keep it quiet?" I asked. "I mean, it's not something I feel like talking about."

"I bet," Adam said. "It must suck."

I imagined how you must be feeling. You'd said a few things in our room, in those gray minutes before we fell asleep, but I think you kept a lot to yourself. I considered what it would be like to be noticed for only one trait — like being left-handed, or brunette, or double-jointed — instead of for the whole of you. Here was Sarah talking about finding someone who loved you for who you were, not what you appeared to be — and your own mother couldn't even seem to manage it. "It's like tug-of-war," I said quietly, "and I'm the rope."

Underneath the table, I felt Adam squeeze my hand. He threaded our fingers together, his knuckles locking against mine. "Adam," I whispered, as Sarah started to speak about STDs and hymens and premature ejaculation, and we continued to hold hands under the table. I felt as if I had a star in my throat, as if all I had to do was open my mouth for light to pour out of me. "What if someone sees us?"

He turned his head; I felt his breath on the curve of my ear. "Then they'll think I'm the luckiest guy in this room."

With those words, my body became electric, with all the power generating from the place our palms touched. I didn't hear another word Sarah said for the next thirty minutes. I couldn't think of anything but how different Adam's skin was from mine and how close he was and how he wasn't letting go.

It wasn't a date, but it wasn't not a date, either. We were both planning on going to the zoo for that evening's family activity, so Adam made me promise to meet him at the orangutans at six o'clock.

Okay, he asked *Willow* to meet him there.

You were so excited about going to the zoo that you could barely sit still the whole minibus ride over there. We didn't have a zoo in New Hampshire, and the one near Boston was nothing to write home about. We'd been planning to go to Disney's Animal Kingdom during our vacation at Disney World, but you remember how *that* turned out. Unlike you, my mother was practically a china statue. She stared straight ahead on the minibus and didn't try to talk to anyone, as opposed to yesterday, when she was Miss Chatty. She looked like she might shatter if the driver hit a speed bump too fast.

Then again, she wouldn't be the only one.

I kept checking my watch so often that I felt like Cinderella. Actually, I felt like Cinderella for a lot of reasons. Except instead of wearing a glittery blue dress,

I was borrowing your identity and your illness, and my prince happened to be someone who'd broken forty-two bones.

"Apes," you announced as soon as we crossed through the gates of the zoo. They'd opened the place for the OI convention after normal business hours, which was cool because it felt like we'd been trapped here after the gates had been locked for the night, and practical because I'm sure it was — well — a zoo during the day, and most people with OI would have been bobbing and weaving to avoid being knocked by the crowds. I grabbed your chair and started to push you up a slight incline, which was when I realized there was something really wrong with my mother.

She normally would have looked at me as if I'd grown a second head and asked why I was volunteering to push your chair when usually I whined bloody murder if she even asked me to unlatch your stupid car seat.

Instead, she just marched along like a zombie. If I'd asked her what animals we passed, I bet she would have just turned to me and said *Huh?*

I pushed you up close to the wall to see the orangutans, but you had to stand to see over it. You balanced yourself against the low concrete barrier, your eyes lighting when you saw the mother and her baby. The mother orangutan was cradling the teeniest little ape I'd ever seen, and another baby that was probably a few years old kept pestering her, pulling at her leg and swinging a foot in front of them and being a total pain in the butt. "It's us," you said, delighted. "Look, Amelia!"

But I was busy glancing all around for Adam. It was six o'clock on the dot. What if he was blowing me off? What if I couldn't even keep a guy interested in me when I was pretending to be someone else?

Suddenly he was there, a fine sweat shining on his forehead. "Sorry," he said. "The hill was killer." He glanced at my mother and you, facing the orangutans. "Hey, that's your family, right?"

I should have introduced him. I should have told my mother what I was doing. But what if you said my name — my real name — and Adam realized I was a total liar? So instead I grabbed Adam's hand and pulled him off to a side path that wound past a flock of red parrots and a cage where there was supposed to be a mongoose, but apparently it was an invisible one. "Let's just go," I said, and we ran down to the aquarium.

Because of where it was tucked in the zoo, it wasn't crowded. There was one family in there with a toddler in a spica cast — poor kid — looking at the penguins in their fake formal wear. "Do you think they know they've got a raw deal?" I asked. "That they've got wings, and can't fly?"

"As opposed to a skeleton that keeps falling apart?" Adam said. He tugged me into another room, a glass tunnel. The light was blue, eerie; all around us, sharks were swimming. I looked up at the soft white belly of a shark, the ridged diamond rows of its teeth. At the hammerheads, wriggling like Star Wars creatures as they passed us by.

418

Adam leaned against the glass wall, staring up at the transparent ceiling. "I wouldn't do that," I said. "What if it breaks?"

"Then the Omaha zoo has a huge problem." Adam laughed.

"Let's see what else there is," I said.

"What's your rush?"

"I don't like sharks," I admitted. "They freak me out."

"I think they're awesome," Adam said. "Not a single bone in their body."

I stared at him, his face blue in the aquarium light. His eyes were the same color as the water, a deep, pure cobalt.

"Did you know that they hardly ever find shark fossils, because they're made of cartilage, and they decompose really fast? I've always kind of wondered if that's true of people like us, too."

Because I am a moron, and destined to live alone my whole life with a dozen cats, at that very moment I burst into tears.

"Hey," Adam said, pulling me into his arms, which felt like home and totally strange all at once. "I'm sorry. That was a really stupid thing to say." One of his hands was on my back, rubbing down each pearl of my spine. One was tangled in my hair. "Willow?" he said, tugging on my ponytail so that I'd look up at him. "Talk to me?"

"I'm not Willow," I burst out. "That's my sister's name. I don't even have OI. I lied, because I wanted to sit in on that class. I wanted to sit next to you."

His fingers curled around the back of my neck. "I know."

"You . . . what?"

"I googled your family, during the break after the sex class. I read all about your mom and the lawsuit and your sister, who's just as young as they said she was on the OI blogs."

"I'm a horrible person," I admitted. "I'm sorry. I'm really sorry I'm not the person you wanted me to be."

Adam stared at me soberly. "No, you're not. You're better. You're *healthy*. Who wouldn't want that for someone you really, really like?"

And then, suddenly, his mouth was touching mine, and his tongue was touching mine, and even though I'd never done this and had only read about it in *Seventeen*, it wasn't wet or gross or confusing. Somehow, I knew which way to turn and when to open and close my lips and how to breathe. His hands splayed on my shoulder blades, on the spot you'd once broken, on the place where I'd have wings if I had been born an angel.

The room was closing in around us, just blue water and those boneless sharks. And I realized that Sarah had gotten part of her sex talk wrong: it wasn't fractures you had to worry about, it was dissolving — losing yourself willingly, blissfully, in someone else. Adam's fingers were warm on my waist, skirting the bottom of my shirt, but I was afraid to touch him, afraid that I would hold him too tightly and hurt him.

"Don't be scared," he whispered, and he put my hand over his heart so that I could feel it beating.

420

I leaned forward and kissed him. And again. As if I were passing him all those silent words I could not say, the ones that explained my biggest secret: that I might not have OI but I knew how he felt. That I was breaking apart, too, all the time.

Charlotte

On the flight home from the convention, I formulated a plan. When I landed, I would call Sean and ask him if he could come over to talk. I would tell him that I wanted to fight for what we had between us, just as hard as I wanted to fight for your future. I would say that I needed to finish what I had started but that I didn't think I could do it without his understanding, if not his support.

I'd tell him I loved him.

It was a strange trip. You were exhausted after three days of interaction with other OI kids, and you fell asleep immediately, still clutching the piece of paper that listed the email addresses of your new friends. Amelia had been brooding ever since we had gone to the zoo — although I assumed it was a residual effect of my frantic reprimand there after she disappeared for two full hours. Once we had landed and collected our luggage, I told you girls to use the restroom, since it was a long ride back from Logan Airport to Bankton. I instructed Amelia to help you if you needed it, and I stood guard over our luggage cart outside. I watched a few families pass by, little kids wearing Mickey Mouse ears, mothers and daughters with matching cornrows and deep tans, fathers dragging car seats. Everyone in an airport is either excited to be going somewhere or relieved to be back home.

I was neither.

I took out my cell phone and dialed Sean. He didn't pick up, but then again, he rarely did when he was at work. "Hi," I said. "It's me. I just wanted to tell you we landed. And . . . I've been doing some thinking. Do you think you might be able to come over tonight? To talk?" I hesitated, as if I expected an answer then and there, but this was a one-way conversation — not unlike all the others we'd had recently. "Well, anyway. I hope the answer's yes. Bye," I said, and I hung up the phone as you girls came out of the restroom, waiting for me to take the lead.

Mailboxes made the best breeding grounds: I was certain, sometimes, that in that dark, cozy tunnel bills multiplied exponentially. As soon as we got home, I sent you and Amelia up to your rooms to unpack your suitcases while I sorted through the mail.

It had not been in the box but, instead, left neatly in a pile on the counter for me. There was fresh milk and juice and eggs in the fridge, and the ramp you used to wheel yourself up to the front door had been rebuilt. Sean had been here while we were gone, and that made me think that maybe he was trying to wave a white flag, too.

There was a bill from the credit card company, with its astronomical finance charge. Another one from the hospital — co-payments for a visit six months ago. There was an invoice for our insurance premium. A mortgage payment. A phone bill. A cable bill. I began to sort the stack into bills and non-bills, and you could probably guess which stack was taller.

In the non-bill pile were a few catalogs, some junk mail, a belated birthday card for Amelia from an ancient aunt who lived in Seattle, and a letter from the Rockingham County Family Court. I wondered if this had something to do with the trial, although Marin had told me that would take place in superior court.

I opened the letter and started to read.

In the Matter of Sean P. O'Keefe and Charlotte A. O'Keefe; Case Number 2008-R-0056

Dear Ms. Charlotte A. O'Keefe,
Please be advised that we have received in this office a Petition for Divorce in the above named matter. If you wish, you or your attorney may come to Rockingham County Family Court within ten days and accept service.

Until further order of the court, each party is restrained from selling, transferring, encumbering, hypothecating, concealing, or in any manner whatsoever disposing of any property, real or personal, belonging to either or both parties except (1) by written agreement of both parties or (2) for reasonable and necessary living expenses or (3) in the ordinary and usual course of business.

If you do not accept service within the ten days, the Petitioner may elect to have you served by alternate means.

Very truly yours,
Micah Healey, Coordinator

I did not realize I'd cried out until Amelia skidded into the kitchen. "What's the matter?"

I shook my head. I couldn't breathe, couldn't speak.

Amelia snatched the letter out of my hand before I could recover. "Dad wants a *divorce?*"

"I'm sure this is some kind of mistake," I said, getting to my feet and retrieving the letter. Of course I had known it was coming, hadn't I? When your husband moves out of the house for months, you cannot fool yourself into thinking all is normal. But still . . . I folded the letter in half, then folded it again. *A magic trick,* I thought desperately. *And when I unfold it, all the writing will have disappeared.*

"Where's the mistake?" Amelia snapped. "Wake up, Mom. That's a pretty clear way of saying he doesn't feel like having you in his life anymore." She hugged her arms tight across her middle. "Come to think of it, there's a lot of that going around lately."

She whirled around to storm upstairs, but I grabbed her arm. "Don't tell Willow," I begged.

"She's not nearly as dumb as you think. She can tell what's going on, even when you try to hide it."

425

"That's exactly why I don't want her to know. Please, Amelia."

Amelia yanked free. "I don't owe you anything," she muttered, and she fled.

I sank into a kitchen chair. Huge patches of my body seemed to have gone numb. Was that what Sean had felt? That I'd lost all sense — both literally and figuratively?

Oh, God. He'd get my voice message on his cell phone, which — in light of this document — turned me into the world's biggest fool.

I had no idea how divorces worked. Could he get one if I said I didn't want to? Once the complaint was filed with the court, could you change your mind? Could I change Sean's?

With shaking hands, I reached for the telephone and called Marin Gates's private line. "Charlotte," she said. "How was the convention?"

"Sean's suing for divorce."

The line went silent.

"I'm sorry," Marin finally said, and I think she really was. But a moment later, she was all business. "You need a lawyer."

"You *are* a lawyer."

"Not the kind who can help you with this. Call Sutton Roarke — she's listed in the yellow pages. She's the best divorce attorney I know."

I drew in my breath. "I feel . . . like such a loser. Like a statistic."

"Well," Marin said quietly. "No one likes to hear they're not wanted."

426

Her words made me think of Amelia's, and felt like the snap of a whip. And they made me think of my testimony in court, which Marin and I had been practicing. But before I could respond, she spoke again. "I truly wish it hadn't come to this, Charlotte."

I had so many questions: How did I tell you without hurting you? How could I possibly keep forging ahead with this lawsuit, knowing another one was pending? When I heard my voice, though, I was asking something entirely different. "What happens next?" I said, but Marin had already hung up the phone.

I made an appointment with Sutton Roarke, and then went through the motions of cooking and feeding you girls dinner. "Can I call Daddy?" you asked as soon as we sat down. "I want to tell him about this weekend."

My head was throbbing, my throat felt like it had been beaten from the inside with fists. Amelia looked at me and then down at her peas. "I'm not hungry," she said. Moments later, she asked to be excused, and I didn't even try to keep her at the table. What was the point, when I didn't feel like being there, either?

I set the dirty dishes into the dishwasher. I wiped down the table. I put up a load of laundry, all with the motions of an automaton. I kept thinking that, if I did these ordinary things, maybe my life would bounce back into normal.

As I sat on the lip of the tub, helping you with your bath, you talked enough for both of us. "Niamh and me, we've both got Gmail accounts," you chattered. "And every morning at six forty-five, when we wake up before school, we're going to get online and talk to each other." You twisted around to look at me. "Can we invite her over sometime?"

"Hmm?"

"Mom, you're not even listening. I asked about Niamh —"

"What about her?"

You rolled your eyes. "Just forget it."

We dressed you in your pajamas, and I tucked you in, kissed you good night. An hour later, when I went to check on Amelia, she was already under the covers, but then I heard her whispering and pulled back the sheets to find her on the telephone. "What!" she said, as if I'd accused her of something, and she curled the receiver into her chest like a second heart. I backed out of the room, too emotionally wrecked to wonder what she was hiding, distantly aware that she'd most likely learned that skill from me.

When I went downstairs, a shadow moved in the living room, nearly scaring me to death. Sean stepped forward. "Charlotte —"

"Don't. Just . . . don't, okay?" I said, my hand still covering my hammering heart. "The girls are already in bed, if you've come to see them."

"Do they know?"

"Do you even care?"

"Of course I do. Why do you think I'm doing this?"

A small, desperate sound rose in my throat. "I honestly don't know, Sean," I said. "I realize things haven't been great between us —"

"That's the understatement of the century —"

"But this is like having a hangnail and getting your arm amputated as treatment, isn't it?"

He followed me into the kitchen, where I poured powder into the dishwasher and stabbed at the buttons. "It's more than a hangnail. We've been bleeding out. You can tell yourself what you want to about our marriage, but that doesn't mean it's the truth."

"So the only answer is a divorce?" I said, shocked.

"I really didn't see any other way."

"Did you even *try*? I know it's been hard. I know you're not used to me sticking up for something I want instead of what you want. But, my God, Sean. You accuse *me* of being litigious, and then you go file for divorce? You don't even *talk* about it with me? You don't try marriage counseling or going to Father Grady?"

"What good would that have done, Charlotte? You haven't listened to anyone but yourself for a long time. This isn't overnight, like you think. This has been a year. A year of me waiting for you to wake up and see what you've done to this family. A year of wishing you'd put as much effort into our marriage as you do into taking care of Willow."

I stared at him. "You did this because I've been too busy to have sex?"

"No, see, that's exactly what I mean. You take everything I say, and you twist it. I'm not the bad guy here, Charlotte. I'm just the one who never wanted anything to change."

"Right. So instead we're just supposed to sit in a rut, trying to keep afloat for how many more years? At what point do we face foreclosure on the house or declare bankruptcy —"

"Stop making this about money —"

"It *is* about money," I cried. "I just spent a weekend with hundreds of people who have rich, happy, productive lives, and who also have OI. Is it a crime to want the same opportunities for Willow?"

"How many of *their* parents sued for wrongful birth?" Sean accused.

I saw, for a blink of an eye, the faces of the women in the restroom who'd judged me just as harshly. But I wasn't about to tell Sean about them. "Catholics don't get divorced," I said.

"They don't think about aborting babies, either," Sean said. "You're conveniently Catholic, when it suits you. That's not fair."

"And you've always seen the world in black and white, when what I'm trying to prove — what I'm *certain* of — is that it's really just a thousand shades of gray."

"That," Sean said softly, "is why I went to a lawyer. That's why I didn't ask you to go to counseling, or to the priest. That world of yours, it's so gray you can't see the landmarks anymore. You don't know where you're headed. If you want to get lost in there, go ahead. But I'm not letting you take the girls down with you."

I could feel tears streaking down my face; I wiped them away with my sleeve. "So that's it? Just like that? You don't love me anymore?"

"I love the woman I married," he said. "And she's gone."

That was when I broke down. After a moment of hesitation, I felt Sean's arms come around me. "Just leave me alone," I cried, but my hands clenched his shirt even more tightly.

I hated him, and at the same time, he was the one I had turned to for comfort for the past eight years. Old habits, they died hard.

How long until I forgot the temperature of his hands on my skin? Until I didn't remember the smell of his shampoo? How long until I could not hear the sound of his voice, even when he wasn't speaking? I tried to store up every sensation, like grain for the winter.

The moment cooled, until I stood uncomfortably in the circle of his embrace, awkwardly aware that he didn't want me there. Bravely, I took a step backward, putting inches between us. "So what do we do now?"

"I think," Sean said, "we have to be adults. No fighting in front of the girls. And maybe — if you're okay with it — I could move back in. Not into the bedroom," he added quickly. "Just the couch. Neither of us can afford to take care of two places, *and* the girls. The lawyer told me most people who are in the middle of a divorce stay in the same house. We just, you know, figure out a way so that if you're here, I'm not. And vice versa. But we both get to be with the kids."

"Amelia knows. She read the letter from the court," I said. "But not Willow."

Sean rubbed his chin. "I'll tell her we're working some things out between us."

"That's a lie," I said. "That suggests there's still a chance."

Sean was quiet. He didn't say there was a chance. But he didn't say there wasn't, either.

"I'll get you an extra blanket," I said.

That night in bed I lay awake, trying to list what I really knew about divorce.

1. It took a long time.
2. Very few couples did it gracefully.
3. You were required to divide everything that belonged to both of you, which included cars and houses and DVDs and children and friends.
4. It was expensive to surgically excise someone you loved from your life. The losses were not just financial but emotional.

Naturally, I knew people who had been divorced. For some reason, it always seemed to happen when their kids were in fourth grade — all of a sudden, that year in the school phone directory, the parents would be listed individually instead of linked with ampersands. I wondered what it was about fourth grade that was so stressful on a marriage, or maybe it was just hitting that ten- to fifteen-year mark. If that was the case, Sean and I were precocious for our marital age.

I had been a single mother for five years before I met and married Sean. Although I truly considered Amelia the one good element of a disastrous relationship, and never would have married her father, I also knew what it was like to have other women scan your left hand for an absent ring, or never to have another adult in the house to talk to after the kids were asleep. Part of what I loved about being married to Sean was the ease of it — letting him see me when my hair was Medusa-wild in the mornings and kiss me when my teeth weren't brushed yet, knowing which television show to click on when we sat down with a mutual sigh on the couch, instinctively recognizing which drawer housed his underwear or T-shirts or jeans. So much of marriage was implicit and non-verbal. Had I gotten so complacent I'd forgotten to communicate?

Divorced. I whispered the word out loud. It sounded like a snake's hiss. Divorced mothers seemed to have evolved into their own breed. Some went to the gym incessantly, hell-bent on getting remarried as soon as possible. Others just looked exhausted all the time. I remembered Piper once having a dinner party and not knowing whether to invite a woman who had recently been divorced because she didn't know whether it would be uncomfortable to be the only single in a room full of doubles. "Thank God that's not us. Can you imagine having to *date* again?" Piper had shuddered. "It's like being a teenager twice."

I knew there were couples who mutually decided that relationships were past repair, but it was still always one partner who brought up the solution of divorce. And even if the other spouse went along with it, she'd secretly be stunned at how quickly someone who claimed to care about you could imagine a life that didn't include you.

My God.

What Sean had done to me was exactly what I'd done to Piper.

I reached for the telephone receiver on my nightstand and, although it was 2:46 in the morning, dialed Piper's number. The phone was next to her side of the bed, too, although she slept on the left and I slept on the right. "Hello?" Piper said, her voice thick and unfamiliar.

I covered the base of the receiver. "Sean wants a divorce," I whispered.

"Hello?" Piper repeated. "Hello!" There was an angry, muffled sigh, and the sound of something being knocked over. "Whoever the hell this is, you shouldn't be calling this late."

Piper used to be accustomed to waking up in the middle of the night; as an OB, she was on call most of the time. Much in her life must have changed if this was her reaction, instead of the assumption that someone was in labor.

Much in *everyone's* life had changed, and I had been the catalyst.

The canned voice of the operator filled my ear. *If you want to make a call, please hang up and try again.*

I pretended instead it was Piper. *Oh, God, Charlotte*, she would say. *Are you all right? Tell me everything. Tell me every last little thing.*

The next morning I woke up with the panic of someone who knows she's overslept because the sun is too high and bright in the sky. "Willow?" I called, leaping out of bed and running to your room. Every morning, you'd

434

sing out to me, so that I could help you transition from bed to the bathroom and then back into your room to dress. Had I slept through it? Or had you?

But your bedroom was empty, the sheets and comforters pulled tidy. Near Amelia's bed were your unpacked suitcases, zipped up and ready to be carried to the attic.

As I went downstairs, I heard you laughing. Sean was standing at the stove with a dish towel wrapped around his head, flipping pancakes. "It's supposed to be a *penguin*," you said. "Penguins don't have ears."

"Why couldn't you have just asked for something normal, like your sister did?" Sean said. "She's got a perfect bear over there."

"Which would be cool," Amelia said, "if I hadn't asked for a lizard." But she was smiling. When was the last time I'd seen Amelia smile before noon?

"One penguin-slash-donkey, coming right up," Sean said, sliding a pancake onto your plate.

You both noticed me standing in the kitchen. "Mom, look who woke me up today!" you said.

"I think maybe you've got that backward, Wills," Sean said. His smile did not quite reach his eyes as he met my gaze. "I figured you could probably use a few extra hours of sleep."

I nodded and wrapped my robe tighter. *Like origami,* I thought. *I could fold myself in half and then in half again, and so on, until I was someone else entirely.* "Thank you."

"Daddy!" you cried. "The pancake's on fire!"

435

Not on fire, exactly, but charred and smoking. "Oh, shoot," Sean said, whirling around to scrape it off the pan.

"And here I thought you'd gone and learned how to cook."

Sean looked up over the open trash can. "It's amazing what desperation — and a box of Bisquick — can do for a guy," he admitted. "I thought, since I've got the day off, I'd hang out with the girls. Finish up the wheelchair ramp for Willow."

What he was telling me, I realized, was that this was the first step in our informal shared custody — shared household — split marriage situation. "Oh," I said, trying to sound nonchalant. "I guess I'll just run some errands then."

"You should go out and have fun," he suggested. "See a movie. Visit a friend."

I didn't have any friends, anymore.

"Right," I said, forcing a smile. "Sounds great."

There was a fine line, I thought an hour later as I pulled out of the driveway, between being kicked out of your house and not being welcome there, but from my vantage point, they looked pretty much the same. I drove to the gas station and filled up, and then just . . . well . . . began to aimlessly tool around in the car. For all of your life, I'd either been with you or been waiting for a phone call to tell me you had broken; this freedom was almost overwhelming. I didn't feel relieved, just untethered.

Before I realized it, I had driven to Marin's office. This would have made me laugh if it wasn't so blatantly depressing. Grabbing my purse, I went inside and took the elevator upstairs. Briony, the receptionist, was on the phone when I entered, but she waved me back down the hallway.

I knocked on Marin's door. "Hi," I said, peeking around the corner.

She looked up. "Charlotte! Come on in." As I sat down in one of the leather chairs, she stood up and came around to lean against the desk. "Did you talk to Sutton?"

"Yes, it's . . . overwhelming."

"I can imagine."

"Sean's at my house now," I blurted out. "We're trying to work out a schedule, so that we're both taking care of the girls."

"That sounds awfully mature."

I glanced up at her. "How can I miss him more when he's two feet away from me than when he's not around?"

"You're not really missing him. You're missing the idea of what she could have been."

"*He*," I corrected, and Marin blinked.

"Right," she said. "Of course."

I hesitated. "I know it's office hours and everything, but would you want to go grab a cup of coffee? I mean, we could pretend that it's an attorney-client thing . . ."

"It *is* an attorney-client thing, Charlotte," Marin said stiffly. "I'm not your friend . . . I'm your lawyer, and to be perfectly honest, that's already required putting aside some of my personal feelings."

I felt a flush rise up my neck. "Why? What did I ever do to you?"

"Not you," Marin said. She looked uncomfortable, too. "I just — This is not the kind of case I would personally endorse."

My own lawyer thought I shouldn't sue for wrongful birth?

Marin stood up. "I'm not saying you don't have a good chance of winning," she clarified, as if she'd heard me out loud. "I'm just saying that morally — philosophically — well, I understand where your husband is coming from, that's all."

I stood up, reeling. "I can't believe I'm arguing with my own attorney about justice and accountability," I said, grabbing my purse. "Maybe I should be hiring another firm." I was halfway down the hallway when I heard Marin call after me. She was standing in the doorway, her fists clenched at her sides.

"I'm trying to find my birth mother," she said. "That's why I'm not thrilled about your case. It's why I won't be having coffee with you or hoping that we'll have a sleepover and do each other's hair. If this world existed the way you want, Charlotte, with babies being disposable if they aren't exactly what a woman wants or needs or dreams of, you wouldn't even *have* a lawyer right now."

"I love Willow," I said, swallowing hard. "I'm doing what I think is best for her. And you're judging me for that?"

"Yes," Marin admitted. "The same way I judge my mother for doing what she thought was best for me."

For a few moments after she went back into her office, I stood in the hallway, leaning against the wall for support. The problem with this lawsuit was that it didn't exist in a vacuum. You could look at it theoretically and think, *Hm, yes, that makes perfect sense.* But no real thought occurred in such sterile conditions. When you read a news article about me suing Piper, when you saw *A Day in the Life of Willow* on video, you brought with you preconceived notions, opinions, a history.

It was why Marin had to swallow her anger while she worked on my case.

It was why Sean couldn't understand my reasoning.

And it was why I was so afraid to admit that one day, looking back on this, you might hate me.

Wal-Mart became my playground.

I wandered up and down the aisles, trying on hats and shoes, looking at myself in mirrors, stacking Rubbermaid bins one inside the other. I pedaled an exercise bike and pushed buttons on talking dolls and listened to sample tracks from CDs. I couldn't afford to buy anything, but I could spend hours looking.

I didn't know how I would support you kids by myself. I knew that alimony and child support figured into that somehow, but no one had ever explained the math to me. Presumably, though, I would have to be able to provide for you if any court was going to find me a fit parent.

I could bake.

The thought snaked into my mind before I could dismiss it. No one made a living with cupcakes, with pastries. True, I had been selling for a few months now; I'd made enough money to fly to the Omaha OI convention and to attract the attention of a string of service stations. But I couldn't work for a restaurant or expand my market past the Gas-n-Get. At any moment, you might fall and need me.

"Pretty sweet, huh?"

I turned to find a Wal-Mart employee standing beside me, staring up at a trampoline that had been half erected to show actual size. He looked to be about twenty, and he had such severe acne that his face looked like a swollen tomato. "When I was a kid, I wanted a trampoline more than anything else in the world."

When he was a kid? He was *still* a kid. He had a lifetime of mistakes left to make.

"So, you got children who like to jump?" he asked.

I tried to picture you on this trampoline. Your hair would fly out behind you; you'd somersault and not break. I glanced at the price tag, as if this item was actually something I would consider. "It's expensive. I think I may have to browse a little more before I decide."

"No prob," he said, and he sauntered off, leaving me to trail my hands over shelves full of tennis racquets and stubbled skateboards, to smell the acrid wheels of the bicycles, strung overhead like haunches in a butcher's shop, to envision you bouncing and healthy, a girl you would never be.

★   ★   ★

440

The church I went to later that day was not my own. It was thirty miles north, in a town I knew only from the highway road sign. It smelled overpoweringly of beeswax, and the morning Mass had recently let out, so a number of parishioners were praying quietly in the pews. I slipped into one and said an Our Father under my breath and stared up at the Cross on the altar. All my life I'd been told that if I fell off a cliff, God was there to catch me. Why wasn't that true, physically, for my daughter?

There was a memory I'd been having lately: a nurse on the birthing ward looked at you in your foam-lined bassinet, with tiny bandages wrapped around your limbs. "You're young," she said, patting my arm. "You can have another one."

I could not recall whether you had just been born or if this was several days later. If anyone else was there to hear her, or if she'd even been real or just a trick of the drugs I was taking for pain. Did I make her up, so that she could say aloud what I had been thinking silently? *This is not my baby; I want the one I've dreamed of.*

I heard a curtain open, and I stepped up to the empty confessional. I slid open the grate between me and the priest. "Forgive me, Father, for I have sinned," I said. "It has been three weeks since my last confession." I took a deep breath. "My daughter is sick," I said. "Very sick. And I've started a lawsuit against the doctor who treated me when I was pregnant. I'm doing it for the money," I admitted. "But to get it, I have to say that I'd have had an abortion, if I'd known about my baby's illness earlier."

441

There was a viscous silence. "It's a sin to lie," the priest said.

"I know . . . that's not what brought me to Confession today."

"Then what did?"

"When I say those things," I whispered, "I'm afraid I might be telling the truth."

Marin

September 2008

Jury selection was an art, combined with pure luck. Everyone had theories about how best to select juries for different kinds of cases, but you never really knew if your hypothesis was right until after the verdict. And it was important to note that you didn't really get to pick who was *on* your jury — just who was *off* it. A subtle difference — and a critical one.

There was a pool of twenty jurors for voir dire. Charlotte was fidgeting beside me in the courtroom. Her living arrangement with Sean, ironically, made it possible for her to be here today; otherwise, she would have been stressing over child-care arrangements for you — which was going to be challenging enough during the trial.

Usually when I tried a case, I hoped for a certain judge — but this time around it had been hard to know what to wish for. A female judge who had children might have sympathy with Charlotte — or might find her plea absolutely revolting. A conservative judge might oppose abortion on moral grounds — but also might agree with the defense's position that a doctor shouldn't be the one to determine which children were too impaired to be born. In the end, we had drawn Judge Gellar, the justice who'd sat the longest on the superior court in the state of New Hampshire and who, if he were to have it his way, would die on the bench.

The judge had already called the potential jurors to order and explained the nuts and bolts of the case to them — the terminology of wrongful birth, the plaintiff and the defendant, the witnesses. He'd asked if anyone knew the witnesses or parties in the case, had heard about the case, or had personal or logistical problems with sitting on the case — like child-care issues or sciatica that made it impossible to sit for hours at a time. Various people raised their hands and told their stories: they'd read all the news articles about the lawsuit; they'd been pulled over for a traffic ticket by Sean O'Keefe; they were scheduled to be out of town for their mother's ninety-fifth birthday celebration. The judge gave a little canned speech about how, if we chose to dismiss them, they shouldn't take it personally and how we all truly appreciated their service — when, I bet, most of those jurors were hoping they would be allowed to leave and go back to their real lives. Finally, the judge called us up to the bench to conference about whether anyone should be dismissed. In the end, he struck two jurors for cause: a man who was deaf and a woman whose twins had been delivered by Piper Reece.

That left a pool of thirty-eight individuals, who had been given questionnaires that Guy Booker and I had slaved over for weeks. Used to get a sense of the people

444

in the pool — and to either strike jurors based on their answers or formulate further questions during the individual interviews — the survey we'd created had involved a complicated tango. I'd asked:

Do you have small children? If so, did you have a positive birthing experience?

Do you do any volunteer work? (Someone who volunteered at Planned Parenthood would be great for us. Someone who volunteered at the church home for unwed mothers — not so much.)

Have you or any family member ever filed a lawsuit?

Have you or any family member ever been a defendant in a lawsuit?

Guy had added:

Do you believe physicians should make medical decisions in the best interests of their patients or leave the decisions up to them?

Do you have any personal experience with disability or with people who have disabilities?

However, those were the easy ones. We both knew that this case hinged on jurors who could be open-minded enough to understand a woman's right to terminate a pregnancy; to that end, I wanted to rule out pro-lifers, while Guy's defense would be greatly enhanced if there were no pro-choice folks on the jury. We had both wanted to submit the question *Are you pro-life or pro-choice?* but the judge had not allowed it. After three weeks of arguing, Guy and I had finessed the question to this instead: *Do you have any real-life experience with abortion, either personal or professional?*

An affirmative answer meant I could try to have the person stricken. A negative answer would allow us to pussyfoot more tenderly around the issue when it came to individual voir dire.

Which was, finally, where we stood right now. After reviewing the questionnaires, I had separated them into piles of the people I thought I liked for this jury and the people I thought I didn't. Judge Gellar would put each juror on the stand for questioning, and Guy and I had to either get the witness stricken for cause, accept him or her for the jury, or use one of our three precious peremptory strikes — a Get Off This Jury Now card that allowed us to remove a juror for no reason at all. The catch was knowing when to use these peremptory strikes and when to save them in case a more odious person came along.

What I wanted for Charlotte's jury were housewives who gave everything and thought nothing of it. Parents whose lives revolved around their kids. Soccer moms, PTA moms, stay-at-home dads. Victims of domestic violence who tolerated the intolerable. In short, I wanted twelve martyrs.

So far, Guy and I had interviewed three people: a graduate student at UNH, a used car salesman, and a lunch lady at a high school cafeteria. I had used the first of my peremptory challenges to strike the grad student when I learned that he was the head of the Young Republicans on campus. Now, we were on our fourth potential juror, a woman named Juliet Cooper. She was in her early fifties, a good age for a juror, someone with maturity and not just hotheaded opinions. She had two teenage children and worked as a switchboard operator at a hospital. When she sat down in the witness stand, I tried to make her feel comfortable by offering up a wide smile. "Thanks for being here today, Mrs Cooper," I said. "Now, you work outside the home, is that correct?"

"Yes."

"How have you been able to balance that with child rearing?"

"I didn't work when they were little. I thought it was important to be at home with them. It's really only when they reached high school that I got a job again."

So far, so good — a woman whose children came first. I scanned her questionnaire again. "You said here that you filed a lawsuit?"

I had done nothing more than state a fact she herself had written down, but Juliet Cooper looked like I'd just slapped her. "Yes."

The difference between witness examinations and jury selection interviews was that, in the former, you only asked questions to which you knew the answers. In the latter, though, you asked completely open-ended questions — because finding out something you didn't know might help you remove the potential juror. What if, for example, Juliet Cooper had filed her own medical malpractice suit and it had turned out badly for her?

"Can you elaborate?" I pressed.

"It never went to trial," she murmured. "I withdrew the complaint."

"Would you have a problem being fair and impartial toward someone who carried through with a lawsuit?"

"No," Juliet Cooper said. "I'd just think she was braver than me."

Well, that seemed to bode well for Charlotte. I sat down to let Guy begin his questioning. "Mrs Cooper, you mention a nephew who's wheelchair-bound?"

"He served in Iraq and lost both his legs when a car bomb went off. He's only twenty-three; it's been devastating to him." She looked at Charlotte. "I think there are some tragedies that you just can't get past. Your whole life will never be quite the same, no matter what."

I loved this juror. I wanted to clone her.

I wondered if Guy would strike this juror. But chances were, he was just as touchy about how disabilities would play for him as I was. Whereas I'd thought at first that mothers of disabled children would be locks for Charlotte, I had reconsidered. Wrongful birth — a term with which Guy was going to slather the courtroom — could be horribly offensive to them. It seemed that the better juror, from my point of view, would be either someone who had sympathy but no first-hand experience with disabilities or, like Juliet Cooper, someone who knew so much about disability that she understood how challenging your life had been.

"Mrs Cooper," Guy said, "on the question that asked about religious or personal beliefs about abortion, you wrote something and then crossed it out, and I can't quite read it."

"I know," she replied. "I didn't know what to say."

"It's a very tough question," Guy admitted. "Do you understand that the decision to abort a fetus is central to making a judgment in this case?"

"Yes."

"Have you ever had an abortion?"

"Objection!" I cried out. "That's a HIPAA violation, Your Honor!"

"Mr Booker," the judge said. "What on earth do you think you're doing?"

"My job, Judge. The juror's personal beliefs are critical, given the nature of this case."

I knew exactly what Guy was doing — taking the risk of upsetting the juror, which he'd weighed to be less important than the risk of losing the trial because of her. There had been every chance I'd have had to ask an equally contentious question. I was just glad that it had been Guy instead, because it allowed me to play good cop. "What Mrs Cooper did or didn't do in her past is not at all integral to this lawsuit," I declared, turning to the jury pool. "Let me apologize for my colleague's invasion of your privacy. What Mr Booker is conveniently forgetting is that the salient issue here isn't abortion rights in America but a single case of medical malpractice."

Guy Booker, as the defendant's attorney, would be using a combination of smoke and mirrors to suggest that Piper Reece had not made an error in judgment: that OI couldn't be conclusively diagnosed in utero, that you can't be blamed for not seeing something you can't see, that no one has the right to say life's not worth living if you're disabled. But no matter how much smoke Guy blew in the jury's direction, I would redirect them, remind them that this was a medical malpractice suit and someone had to pay for making a mistake.

I was vaguely aware of the irony that I was championing the juror's right to medical privacy when — on a personal level — it had made my life a nightmare. If not for the sealing of medical records, I would have known my birth mother's name months ago; as it was, I was still in the great black void of chance, awaiting news from the Hillsborough Family Court and Maisie.

"You can stop grandstanding, Ms. Gates," the judge said. "And as for you, Mr Booker, if you ask a follow-up question like this again, I'll hold you in contempt."

Guy shrugged. He finished up his questioning, and then we both approached the bench again. "The plaintiff has no objection to Mrs Cooper sitting on this panel," I said. Guy agreed, and the judge called up the next potential juror.

Her name was Mary Paul. She had gray hair pulled into a low ponytail and wore a shapeless blue dress and crepe-soled shoes. She looked like someone's grandmother, and smiled kindly at Charlotte as she took the stand. *This*, I thought, *could be promising*.

"Ms. Paul, you say here that you're retired?"

"I don't know if *retired* is really the word for it . . ."

"What kind of work were you doing previously?" I asked.

"Oh," she said. "I was a Sister of Mercy."

It was going to be a very long day.

Sean

When Charlotte finally came home from jury selection, you were soundly kicking my ass in Scrabble. "How did it go?" I asked, but I could tell before she even said a word; she looked like she'd been run over by a truck.

"They all kept staring at me," she said. "Like I was something they'd never seen before."

I nodded. I didn't know what to say, really. What did she expect?

"Where's Amelia?"

"Upstairs, becoming one with her iPod."

"Mom," you said, "do you want to play? You can just join in, it doesn't matter if you missed the beginning."

In the eight hours I'd been with you today, I hadn't managed to bring up the divorce. We'd taken a field trip to the pet store and had gotten to watch a snake eat a dead mouse; we had watched a Disney movie; we had gone food shopping and bought SpaghettiOs — Chef Boyardee, which your mother called Chef MSG. We'd had, in short, the perfect day. I didn't want to be the one who took the light out of your eyes. Maybe Charlotte had known this, which was why she'd suggested that I be the one to tell you. And maybe for that reason, too, she looked at me now and sighed. "You've got to be kidding," she said. "Sean, it's been three weeks."

"It hasn't been the right time . . ."

You stuck your hand into the bag of letters. "We're down to two-letter words," you said. "Daddy tried to do Oz, but that's a place and it's not allowed."

"There's never going to be a right time. Honey," she said, turning to you, "I'm really wiped out. Can I take a Scrabble rain check?" She walked into the kitchen.

"I'll be right back," I told you, and I followed her. "I know I have no right to ask you this, but — I'd like you to be there when I tell her. I think it's important."

"Sean, I've had an awful day —"

"And I am about to make it more awful. I know." I looked down at her. "Please."

Wordlessly, she walked back into the family room with me and sat down at the table. You turned, delighted. "So you *do* want to play?"

"Willow, your mom and I have some news for you."

"You're going to move back home for good? I knew it. At school Sapphire said that once her father moved out he fell in love with a dirty whore and now her parents aren't together anymore, but I said that you'd never do that."

"I told you so," Charlotte said to me.

"Wills, your mother and I . . . we're getting divorced."

She looked at each of us. "Because of me?"

"No," Charlotte and I said in unison.

"We both love you, and Amelia," I said. "But your mom and I can't be a couple anymore."

452

Charlotte walked toward the window, her back to me.

"You're still going to see both of us. And live with both of us. We're going to do everything we can to make things easy for you, so not much has to change —"

Your face was pinching up tighter and tighter as I spoke, becoming a flushed and angry pink. "My goldfish," you said. "He can't live in two houses."

You had a betta that we'd gotten you last Christmas, the cheapest concession to a pet we could provide. To everyone's shock, it had lived longer than a week. "We'll get you a second one," I suggested.

"But I don't *want* two goldfish!"

"Willow —"

"I hate you," you shouted, starting to cry. "I hate *both* of you!"

You were out of your chair like a shot, running faster than I thought you could to the front door. "Willow!" Charlotte called out. "Be —"

Careful.

I heard the cry before I could reach the doorway. In your hurry to get away from me, from this news, you had not been cautious, and you were lying on the porch where you'd slipped. Your left femur was bent at a ninety-degree angle, breaking through the bloody surface of your thigh; the sclera of your eyes was an unholy blue. "Mommy?" you said, and then your eyes rolled back in your head.

"Willow!" Charlotte screamed, and she knelt down beside you. "Call an ambulance," she ordered, and then she bent closer to you and began to whisper.

For a fraction of a second, as I looked at the two of you, I believed she *was* the better parent.

Do not, if you can help it, break a bone on a Friday night. Even more important, do not break a femur the weekend of the annual convention of American orthopedic surgeons. Leaving Amelia home alone, Charlotte rode in the ambulance with you, and I followed in my truck. Although most of your serious breaks were handled by the orthopods in Omaha, this one was too severe to simply immobilize until they could assess it; we were headed to the local hospital, only to learn in the emergency room that the orthopedic surgeon called to consult was a resident.

"A resident?" Charlotte had said. "Look, no offense, but I'm not letting a resident rod my daughter's femur."

"I've done this kind of surgery before, Mrs O'Keefe," the doctor said.

"Not on a girl with OI," Charlotte countered. "And not on Willow."

He wanted to put a Fassier-Duval rod — one that would telescope as you grew — into your femur. It was the newest rod available, and it threaded into the epiphysis, whatever that was, which kept it from migrating, like the older rods used to. Most important, you wouldn't be in a spica cast, which was the postoperative care for femur rodding in the past — instead, you'd be in a functional brace, a long leg splint, for three weeks. Uncomfortable, especially during the summertime, but nowhere near as debilitating.

454

I was stroking your forehead while this battle raged. You had regained consciousness, but you didn't speak, only stared straight ahead. It scared the crap out of me, but Charlotte said this happened a lot when it was a bad break; it had something to do with endorphins released by the body to self-medicate. And yet, you had started to shiver, as if you were in shock. I'd taken off my jacket to cover you when the thin hospital blanket didn't seem to work.

Charlotte had badgered and argued; she had dropped names — and finally she got the guy to call his attending at the convention center in San Diego. It was mesmerizing to watch, like an orchestrated battle: the push, the retreat, the turn toward you before the next round. And it was, I realized, something your mother was very, very good at.

The resident reappeared a few minutes later. "Dr Yaeger can get on a red-eye and be here for a ten o'clock surgery tomorrow morning," he said. "That's the best we can do."

"She can't stay like this overnight," I said.

"We can give her morphine to sedate her."

They moved you onto a pediatric floor, where the murals of balloons and circus animals stood completely at odds with the shrieks of crying babies and the faces of shell-shocked parents wandering the halls. Charlotte watched over you while the orderlies slipped you from the stretcher to the bed — one sharp, hollow cry as your leg was moved — and gave instructions to the nurse (IV on your right side, because you were a lefty) when your morphine drip was set up.

It was killing me, to watch you in pain. "You were right," I said to Charlotte. "You wanted to put a rod in her leg and I said no."

Charlotte shook her head. "*You* were right. She needed time to get up and run around to strengthen her muscles and bones, or this might have happened even sooner."

At that, you whimpered, and then you started to scratch. You raked at your arms, at your belly.

"What's wrong?" Charlotte asked.

"The bugs," you said. "They're all over me."

"Baby, there aren't any bugs," I said, watching as she scraped her arms raw.

"But it itches . . ."

"How about we play a game?" Charlotte suggested. "Poodle?" She reached up for your wrist and pulled it down to your side. "Do you want to pick the word?"

She was trying to distract you, and it worked. You nodded.

"Can you poodle underwater?" Charlotte asked, and you shook your head. "Can you poodle while you're asleep?"

"No," you said.

She looked at me, nodding. "Um, can you poodle with a friend?" I asked.

You almost smiled. "Absolutely not," you said as your eyes started to drift shut.

"Thank God," I said. "Maybe she'll sleep through now."

But, as if I'd cursed your chances, you suddenly jumped — an exaggerated full-body tremor that made

456

you come right off the bed, and dislodged your leg. Immediately, you screamed.

We had just managed to calm you down again when the same thing happened: as soon as you began to fall asleep, you startled as if you were falling off a cliff. Charlotte pushed the nurse's call button.

"She's jumping," Charlotte explained. "It keeps happening."

"Morphine does that to some people," the nurse said. "The best thing you can do is try to keep her still."

"Can't we take her off it?"

"If you do, she's going to be thrashing around a lot more than she already is," the nurse replied.

When she left the room, you jerked again, and a low, long moan rose from your throat. "Help me," Charlotte said, and she crawled onto the hospital bed, pinning down your upper body.

"You're crushing me, Mom . . ."

"I'm just going to help you stay good and still," Charlotte said calmly.

I followed her lead, gently laying myself across your lower body. You whimpered when I touched your left leg, which had the break. Charlotte and I both waited, counting the seconds until your body tensed, your muscles twitched. I had once watched a blast at a building site that was covered with netting made of old tires and rubber so that the explosion stayed contained, manageable: this time, when your body leapt beneath ours, you didn't cry.

How had Charlotte known to do this? Was it because she'd been with you more times than I could count when a break happened? Was it because she'd learned to be proactive, instead of reactive, in a hospital? Or was it because she knew you better than I ever would?

"Amelia," I said, remembering that we'd left her behind, that it had been hours.

"We have to call her."

"Maybe I should go get her —"

Charlotte turned her head so that her cheek was pillowed on your belly. "Tell her to call Mrs Monroe next door if there's an emergency. You have to stay. It'll take both of us to keep Willow quiet all night."

"Both of us," I repeated, and before I could censor myself, I touched Charlotte's hair.

She froze. "I'm sorry," I murmured, pulling away.

Beneath me, you moved, a tiny earthquake, and I tried to be a blanket, a carpet, a comfort. Charlotte and I rode out the tremors, absorbing your pain. She wove her fingers through mine, so that our hands rested like a beating heart between us. "I'm not," she said.

Amelia

Once upon a time there was a girl who wanted to put her fist through a mirror. She would tell everyone it was so that she could see what was on the other side, but really, it was so that she wouldn't have to look at herself. That, and because she thought she might be able to steal a piece of glass when no one was looking, and use it to carve her heart out of her chest.

So when no one was watching, she went to the mirror and forced herself to be brave enough to open her eyes just this one last time. But to her surprise, she didn't see her reflection. She didn't see anything at all. Confused, she stretched her hand up to touch the mirror and realized that the glass was missing, that she could fall through to the other side.

That's exactly what happened.

Things got even stranger, though, when she walked through this other world and found people staring at her — not because she was so disgusting but because they all wanted to look like her. At school, kids at different lunch tables fought to have her sit with them. She always got the answers right when she was picked by a teacher in class. Her email inbox was overflowing with love letters from boys who could not live without her.

At first, it felt incredible, like a rocket was taking off under her skin every time she was out in public. But then, it got a little old. She didn't *want* to give out her autograph when she bought a pack of gum at the gas station. She would wear a pink shirt, and by lunchtime, the rest of the school was wearing pink shirts, too. She got tired of smiling all the time in public.

She realized that things weren't all that different on this side of the mirror. Nobody really cared about her here. The reason people copied her and fawned over her had very little to do with who she was, and far more to do with who they needed her to be, to make up for some gaping hole in their own lives.

She decided she wanted to go back to the other side. But she had to do it when no one was watching, or they'd follow her there. The only problem was, there was never no one watching. She had nightmares about the people who trailed after her, who would cut themselves to pieces on the broken glass as they crawled through the mirror after her; how they'd lie bleeding on the floor and how the look in their eyes would change when they saw her on this side, unpopular and ordinary.

When she couldn't stand another minute, she started to run. She knew there were people following, but she couldn't stop to think about them. She was going to fly through the space in the mirror, no matter what it took. But when she got there, she smacked her head against the glass — it had been repaired. It was whole and thick and impossible to break through. She flattened her palms against it. *Where are you going?* everyone asked. *Can we come, too?* She didn't answer. She just stood there, looking at her old life, without her in it.

I was really careful when I sat down on your bed. "Hey," I whispered, because you were still pretty much out of it and might have been asleep.

Your eyes slitted open. "Hey."

You looked really tiny, even with the big splint on your leg. Apparently, with the new rod in your femur, a future break wouldn't be as bad as this one had been. On a TV show once I'd seen an orthopedic surgeon with drills, saws, metal plates, you name it — it was like she was a construction worker, not a doctor, and the thought of all that hammering and banging going on inside you made me feel like I was going to pass out.

I couldn't tell you why, too, this break had scared me the most. I guess maybe I was getting it confused with the other things that brushed up against it that were equally as terrifying: the letter about divorce, the phone call from Dad at the hospital telling me I'd have to stay home alone overnight. I hadn't told anyone, because obviously Mom and Dad were completely wrapped up in what was happening to you, but I never actually slept. I stayed awake at the kitchen table holding the biggest knife we had, just in case someone broke into the house. I'd kept myself awake on pure adrenaline, wondering what would happen if the rest of my family never actually made it home.

But instead, the opposite happened. Not only were you back but so were Mom and Dad — and they weren't just putting on a good show for you, they were really *together*. They took turns watching over you; they finished each other's sentences. It was as if I'd smashed through that fairy-tale mirror and wound up in the alternate universe of my past. There was a part of me that believed your latest break had linked them again, and if that was true, it was worth whatever pain you'd gone through. But there was another part of me that thought I was only hallucinating, that this happy family unit was just a mirage.

I didn't really believe in God, but I wasn't above hedging my bets, so I had prayed a silent bargain: if we can be a family again, I won't complain. I won't be mean to my sister. I won't throw up anymore. I won't cut.

I won't I won't I won't.

You, apparently, weren't feeling quite as optimistic. Mom said that since you'd come through the surgery, you kept crying and you didn't want to eat anything. It was supposed to be the anesthesia in your system that was making you weepy, but I decided to make it my personal mission to cheer you up. "Hey, Wiki," I said, "you want some M&M's? They're from my Easter candy stash."

You shook your head.

"Want to use my iPod?"

"I don't want to listen to music," you murmured. "You don't have to be nice to me just because I won't be around here much longer."

462

That sent a chill down my spine. Had someone not told me something about your surgery? Were you, like, *dying*? "What are you talking about?"

"Mom wants to get rid of me because things like this keep happening." You swiped the tears from your eyes with your hands. "I'm not the kind of kid anyone wants."

"What are you talking about? It's not like you're a serial killer. You don't torture chipmunks or do anything revolting, except try to burp 'God Bless America' at the dinner table —"

"I only did that once," you said. "But think about it, Amelia. Nobody keeps things that get broken. Sooner or later, they get thrown away."

"Willow, you are not being sent off, believe me. And if you are, I'll run away with you first."

You hiccuped. "Pinkie promise?"

I hooked your pinkie with mine and tugged. "Promise."

"I can't go on a plane," you said seriously, as if we needed to plot our itinerary now. "The doctor said I'll set off metal detectors at the airport. He gave Mom a note."

One that I would probably forget, like I forgot the other doctor's note on our last vacation.

"Amelia," you asked, "where would we go?"

Back, I thought immediately. But I couldn't begin to tell you how to get there.

Maybe Budapest. I didn't really know where Budapest was, but I liked the way the word exploded on my tongue. Or Shanghai. Or the Galápagos, or the isle of Skye. You and I could travel the globe together, our own little sisterly freak show: the girl who breaks, and the girl who can't hold herself together.

"Willow," my mother said. "I think we need to have a talk." She'd been standing at the threshold of the bedroom, watching us, I wondered for how long. "Amelia, can you give us a minute?"

"Okay," I said, and I slunk outside. But instead of going downstairs, which was what she meant, I hovered in the hallway, where I could hear everything.

"Wills," I heard my mother say, "no one's throwing you away."

"I'm sorry about my leg," you said, teary. "I thought if I didn't break anything for a long time, you'd think I was just like any other kid —"

"Accidents happen, Willow." I heard the bed creak as my mother sat down on it. "Nobody is blaming you."

"You do. You wish you'd never had me. I *heard* you say it."

What happened after that — well, it felt like a tornado in my head. I was thinking about this lawsuit, and how it had ruined our lives. I was thinking of my father, who was downstairs for maybe only seconds or minutes longer. I was thinking of a year ago, when my arms were scar-free, when I still had a best friend and wasn't fat and could eat food without it feeling like lead in my stomach. I was thinking of the words my mother said in response to you, and how I must have heard them wrong.

Charlotte

"Charlotte?"

I had come to the laundry room to hide, figuring that the load of clothes spinning in the dryer would mask any sound I made while I was crying, but Sean was standing behind me. Quickly I wiped my eyes on my sleeves. "Sorry," I said. "The girls?"

"They're both fast asleep." He took a step forward. "What's wrong?"

What *wasn't* wrong? I'd just had to persuade you that I loved you, breaks and all — something you'd never questioned until I undertook this lawsuit.

Didn't everyone lie? And wasn't there a difference between, for example, killing a person and telling the police you hadn't and smiling down at a particularly ugly baby and telling her mother how cute she was? There were lies we told to save ourselves, and then there were lies we told to rescue others. What counted more, the mistruth, or the greater good?

"Nothing's wrong," I said. There I went, fibbing again. I couldn't tell Sean what you'd said to me; I couldn't bear to hear his *I told you so*. But, my God, was everything that came out of my mouth a lie? "It's just been a really hard few days." I folded my arms tightly across my waist. "Did you, um, did you need me for something?"

He pointed to the top of the dryer. "I just came to get my bedding."

I knew I should be practicing, but I didn't understand formerly married couples who remained congenial. Yes, it was in the best interests of the children. Yes, it was less stressful. But how could you forget that this particular "friend" had seen you naked? Had carried your dreams when you were too tired to? You could paint your history over any way you liked, but you'd always see those first few brushstrokes. "Sean? I'm glad you were here," I said, honest at last. "It made everything . . . easier."

"Well," he said simply, "she's my daughter, too." He took a step toward me to reach the bedding, and I instinctively backed away. "Good night," Sean said.

"Good night."

He started to take the pillows and quilt into his arms and then turned. "If I were like Willow, and I needed someone to fight hard for me when I couldn't? I'd pick you."

"I'm not sure Willow would agree," I whispered, blinking back tears.

"Hey," he said, and I felt his arms come around me. His breath was warm on the crown of my hair. "What's this?"

I tilted my face up to his. I wanted to tell him everything — what you had said to me, how tired I was, how much I was wavering — but instead we stared at

466

each other, telegraphing messages that neither one of us was brave enough to speak out loud. And then, slowly, so that we both knew the mistake we were making, we kissed.

I could not tell you the last time I had kissed Sean, not like this, not beyond a see-you-later-honey peck over the kitchen sink. This was deep and rough and consuming, as if we both meant to be left in ashes when we were through. His beard stubble scraped my chin raw, his teeth bit down, his breath filled my lungs. The room glittered at the edge of my vision, and I broke away for air. "What are we doing?" I gasped.

Sean buried his face against my throat. "Who gives a damn, as long as we keep doing it."

Then his hands were slipping underneath my shirt, branding me; my back was touching the humming metal-and-glass fishbowl of the dryer as Sean pushed me against it. I heard the clink of his belt buckle striking the floor and only then realized I had been the one to throw it aside. Wrapping myself around him, I became a vine, thriving, tangled. I threw back my head and burst into bloom.

It was over as quickly as it had started, and suddenly we were what we had been going into this: two middle-aged people who were lonely enough to be desperate. Sean's jeans were puddled at his ankles; his hands were supporting my thighs. The handle of the dryer was cutting into my back. I let one leg fall to the floor and wrapped a sheet from his pile of bedding around my waist.

He was blushing, a deep, rootless red. "I'm sorry."

"Are you?" I heard myself say.

"Maybe not," he admitted.

I tried to finger-comb my hair back from the tangle on my face. "So what do we do now?"

"Well," Sean said. "There's no rewind button."

"No."

"And you're wearing my top sheet around your . . . you know."

I glanced down.

"And the couch is wicked uncomfortable," he added.

"Sean," I said, smiling. "Come to bed."

I thought that, on the day of the trial, I'd wake up with butterflies in my stomach or a raging headache, but as my eyes slowly adjusted to the sunlight, all I could think was *It's going to be okay*. It did not hurt that there were muscles in my body that were deliciously sore, that left me rolling over and stretching to hear the music of the shower running, and Sean in it.

"Mom?"

I slipped on a robe and ran into your bedroom. "Wills, how do you feel?"

"Itchy," you said. "And I have to pee."

I positioned myself to carry you. You were heavy, but this was a blessing compared with a spica cast, which was the alternative. I helped you lift up your nightgown and settled you on the toilet seat, then waited for you to call me back in so that I could help you wash your hands. I decided that I would buy you a big bottle of Purell on the way home from court today. Which reminded me — you weren't going to be happy about the arrangements I'd made for you. After much debate with Marin about leaving you home while I was in the courtroom, she had let me interview and choose a private pediatric nurse to be with you for the duration of the trial. The astronomical cost, she said, would be deducted from whatever damages we won. It was not ideal, but at least I wouldn't have to worry about your safety. "Remember Paulette?" I said. "The nurse?"

"I don't want her to come . . ."

"I know, baby, but we don't have a choice. I have to go somewhere important today, and you can't be by yourself."

"What about Daddy?"

"What about me?" Sean said, and he plucked you out of my arms and carried you downstairs as if you didn't weigh anything.

He was dressed in a coat and tie instead of his uniform. *He's coming to court with me,* I thought, beginning to smile from the inside out.

"Amelia's in the shower," Sean said over his shoulder as he settled you on the couch. "I told her she has to take the bus in today. Willow —"

"A nurse is coming to stay with her."

He looked down at you. "Well, that'll be fun."

You grimaced. "Yeah, right."

"How about pancakes for breakfast, then, to make it up to you?"

"Is that all you can cook?" you asked. "Even *I* know how to make ramen noodles."

"Do you want ramen noodles for breakfast?"

"No —"

"Then stop complaining about the pancakes," Sean said, and then he looked up at me soberly. "Big day."

I nodded and pulled the tie of my robe tighter. "I can be ready to go in fifteen minutes."

Sean stilled in the process of covering you with a blanket. "I figured we'd take separate cars." He hesitated. "I have to meet with Guy Booker beforehand."

If he was meeting with Guy Booker, it meant that he was still planning to testify for Piper's defense.

If he was meeting with Guy Booker, it meant nothing had changed.

I had been lying to myself, because it was easier than facing the truth: sex wasn't love, and one single, stopgap Band-Aid of a night couldn't fix a broken marriage.

"Charlotte?" Sean said, and I realized he'd asked me a question. "Do you want some pancakes?"

I was sure he did not know that pancakes were among the oldest types of baked goods in America; that in the 1700s, when there had been no baking powder or baking soda, they'd been leavened by beating air into the eggs. I was sure he did not know that pancakes went as far back as the Middle Ages, when they were served on Fat Tuesday, before Lent. That if the griddle was too hot, pancakes would get tough and chewy; if it was too cool, they'd turn out dry and tough.

I was also sure he did not remember that pancakes were the very first breakfast I ever cooked for him as his wife, when we returned from our honeymoon. I had

470

made the batter and spooned it into a Baggie, cut off a bottom corner, and used it to shape the pancakes. I'd served Sean a stack of hearts.

"I'm not hungry," I said.

Amelia

So let me tell you why I didn't take the bus that morning: no one had bothered to check outside the front door, and it wasn't until Paulette the nurse arrived and totally freaked out when she had to beat off an army of photographers and reporters that we realized how many people had gathered to snap the coveted picture of my parents leaving for court.

"Amelia," my father said tightly, "in the car. Now!"

For once, I just did what he said.

That would have been bad enough, but some of them followed us to my school. I kept an eye on them in the passenger mirror. "Isn't this how Princess Diana died?"

My father hadn't spoken a word, but his jaw was set so tight I thought he might crack a tooth. At a red light, he faced me. "I know it's going to be hard, but you have to pretend this is any other normal day."

I know what you're thinking: this is the point where Amelia inserts a really snarky, inappropriate comment, like *That's what they said about 9/11, too,* but I just didn't have one in me. Instead, I found myself shaking so hard I had to slip my hands underneath my thighs.

472

"I don't know what normal is anymore," I heard myself say, in the tiniest voice ever.

My father reached out and brushed my hair off my face. "When this is all over," he said, "do you think you might like to live with me?"

Those words, they made my heart pump triple time. Someone *wanted* me; someone was *choosing* me. But I also sort of felt like throwing up. It was a nice fantasy, but if we were being totally realistic, what court would grant custody to a man who wasn't even related to me by blood? That meant I'd be stuck with my mother, who would know by then that she was my second choice. And besides, what about you? If I lived alone with Dad, maybe I'd finally get some attention, but I'd also be leaving you behind. Would you hate me for it?

When I didn't answer and the light turned green, my father started driving again. "You can think about it," he said, but I could tell he was a little bit hurt.

Five minutes later, we were at the circular driveway of my school. "Are the reporters going to follow me in?"

"They're not allowed," my father said.

"Well." I pulled my backpack onto my lap. It weighed thirty-three pounds, which was a third of my body weight. I knew this for a fact because last week the school nurse had a scale set up where you could weigh your bag and yourself, since kids my age weren't supposed to be hauling around bags that were too heavy. If you divided your backpack weight by your body weight and got more than 15 percent, you were going to wind up with scoliosis or rickets or hives or

God knew what. Everyone's pack had been too heavy, but that didn't keep teachers from assigning the same amount of homework.

"Um, good luck today," I said.

"Do you want me to come in and talk to the guidance counselor or the principal? Tell them you might need extra attention today . . .?"

That was the *last* thing I needed — to stand out like even more of a sore thumb. "I'm fine," I said, and I opened the truck door.

The cars peeled off after my dad's truck, which made it a little easier for me to breathe. At least that's what I thought, until I heard someone call my name. "Amelia," a woman said, "how do you feel about this lawsuit?"

Behind her was a man with a TV camera on his shoulder. Some other kids walking into the school threw their arms around me, as if I were their friend. "Dude!" one of them said. "Can you do this on TV?" He held up his middle finger.

Another journalist materialized from behind the bushes on my left. "Does your sister talk to you about how she feels, knowing her mother's suing for wrongful birth?"

Was this a family decision?

Are you going to testify?

Until I heard that, I'd forgotten: my name was on some stupid list, just in case. My mother and Marin had said that I'd probably never testify, that it was just a precaution, but I didn't like being on lists. It made me feel like someone was counting on me, and what if I let them down?

Why weren't they following Emma? She went to this school, too. But I already knew the answer: in their eyes, in everyone's eyes, Piper was the victim. I was the one related to the vampire who'd decided to suck her best friend dry.

"Amelia?"

Over here, Amelia . . .

Amelia!

"Leave me alone!" I shouted. I covered my ears with my hands and shoved my way into the school, blindly pushing past kids kneeling at their lockers and teachers navigating with their mugs of coffee and couples making out as if they wouldn't see each other for years, instead of just the next forty-five minutes of class. I turned in to the first doorway I could find — a teachers' bathroom — and locked myself inside. I stared at the clean porcelain rim of the toilet.

I knew the word for what I was doing. They showed us movies about it in health class; they called it an eating *disorder*. But that was completely wrong: when I did it, everything fell into place.

For example, when I did it, hating myself made perfect sense. Who wouldn't hate someone who ate like Jabba the Hutt and then vomited it all up again? Someone who went to all the trouble to get rid of the food inside her but was still just as chubby as ever? And I understood that whatever I was doing wasn't nearly as bad as the girl in my school who was anorexic. Her limbs looked like toothpick and sinew; no one in their right mind would ever confuse me with her. I wasn't doing this because I looked in the mirror and saw a fat girl even though I was skinny — I *was* fat. I couldn't even starve myself the right way, apparently.

But I had sworn that I'd stop. I had sworn that I'd stop making myself sick, in return for a family that stayed together.

You promised, I told myself.

Less than twelve hours ago.

But suddenly there I was, sticking my finger down my throat, throwing up, waiting for the relief that always came.

Except this time, it didn't.

Piper

I learned from Charlotte that baking is all about chemistry. Leavening happens biologically, chemically, or mechanically, and creates steam or gases that make the mixture rise. The key to great baked goods is to pick the right leavening agent for the batter or dough, so that bread has a smooth texture, popovers pop, meringue foams, and soufflés rise.

This, Charlotte said to me one day, while I was helping her bake a birthday cake for Amelia, *is why baking works.* She wrote on a napkin:

$$KC_4H_5O_6 + NaHCO_3 \rightarrow CO_2 \uparrow + KNaC_4H_4O_6 + H_2O$$

I got a B− in Orgo, I told her.

Cream of tartar plus sodium bicarbonate gives you carbon dioxide gas and potassium sodium tartrate and water, she said.

Show-off, I replied.

I'm only saying it's not as simple as beating eggs and flour together, Charlotte said. *I'm trying to make this a teachable moment here.*

Pass me the damn vanilla extract, I said. *Do they really teach that in culinary school?*

They don't just hand over scalpels to med students, do they? You have to learn why you're doing what you're doing first.

I shrugged. *I bet Betty Crocker wouldn't know a scientific equation if it flew out of her oven.*

Charlotte began to mix the batter. *She knew it in principle: one ingredient in a bowl is a start. But two ingredients in a bowl, well, that's a whole story.*

Here's what Charlotte didn't mention: that sometimes even the most careful baker can make a mistake. That the balance between the acid and the soda might be off, the ingredients not mixed, the salts trapped behind.

That you'd be left with a bitter taste in your mouth.

On the morning of the trial, I stayed in the shower for a very long time, letting the water strike my back like a punishment. Here it was: the moment I would face Charlotte in court.

I had forgotten the sound of her voice.

Besides the obvious difference, there was not much distinction between losing a best friend and losing a lover: it was all about intimacy. One moment, you had someone to share your biggest triumphs and fatal flaws with; the next minute, you had to keep them bottled inside. One moment, you'd start to call her to tell her a snippet of news or to vent about your awful day before realizing you did not have that right anymore; the next, you could not remember the digits of her phone number.

Once the shock had worn off when I was served, I had gotten furious. Who the hell did Charlotte think she was, ruining my life in order to bolster her own? Anger, though, is too fierce a flame to last for long, and when it burned out, I was left numb and wondering. Would she get what she wanted from this? And what *did* she want? Revenge? Money? Peace of mind?

Sometimes I woke up with words weighing down my tongue like stones, left over from a recurring nightmare where Charlotte and I met face-to-face. I had a thousand things to say to her, and not one of them ever came out. When I looked at her, to see why she wasn't speaking, either, I noticed that her mouth had been sewn shut.

I had not gone back to work. The one time I'd tried, I had been shaking so hard when I got to the front door that I never went inside. I knew of other doctors who had been sued for malpractice and went back to their routines, but this lawsuit went beyond the question of whether or not I could have diagnosed osteogenesis imperfecta in utero. It wasn't skeletal breaks I had not seen in advance but rather the wishes of a best friend whose mind I'd thought I knew inside out. If I had not been able to read Charlotte correctly, how could I trust myself to understand the needs of patients who were virtual strangers?

I had wondered for the first time about the terminology of running your own office as a doctor. It was called a *practice*. But shouldn't we have gotten it right by the time we opened one?

We were, of course, taking a huge financial hit. I had promised Rob that I would go back to work by the end of the month, whether or not the trial was over. I had not specified, however, what sort of work I'd go back to. I still could not imagine myself shepherding a routine pregnancy. What about pregnancy was routine?

In the course of preparing with Guy Booker, I had gone back over my notes and my memories a thousand times. I almost believed him when he said that no physician would be blamed for not diagnosing OI at the eighteen-week ultrasound; that even if I had an inkling about it, the recommended course of action would have been to wait several weeks to see if the fetus was Type II or Type III. I had behaved responsibly as a doctor.

I just hadn't behaved responsibly as a friend.

I should have been looking more closely. I should have pored over Charlotte's records with the same thoroughness with which I would have pored over my own, had I been the patient. Even if I was in the right in a courtroom, I had failed her as a friend. And in a roundabout way, that was how I'd failed her as a doctor, too — I should have declined when she asked me to treat her in my practice. I should have known that somehow, some way, the relationship we had outside the examination room would color the relationship we had inside it.

The water in the shower was running cold now; I turned it off and wrapped a towel around myself. Guy Booker had given me very specific instructions on what I should wear today: no business suits, nothing black, hair loose around my face. I'd bought a twinset at T.J. Maxx because I never wore them but Guy said that it would be perfect. The idea was to look like an ordinary

480

mom, a person any woman on the jury might identify with.

When I came downstairs, I heard music in the kitchen. Emma had left for the bus stop before I'd even gotten into the shower, and Rob — well, Rob had been at work by seven-thirty every morning for the past three weeks. It was less of a burgeoning work ethic, I believed, than a burning desire to be out of the house by the time I awakened, just in case we'd have to have a civil conversation without Emma there to serve as a buffer.

"It's about time," Rob said as I walked into the kitchen. He reached over to the radio and turned down the volume, then pointed to a plate on the table that was piled high with bagels. "The store only had one pumpernickel," he said. "But there's also jalapeño-cheddar, and cinnamon-raisin —"

"But I heard you leave," I said.

Rob nodded. "And I came back. Veggie cream cheese, or regular?"

I didn't answer, just stood very still, watching him.

"I don't know if I ever got around to telling you," Rob said, "but the kitchen? It's so much brighter, now that you painted it. You'd be a hell of an interior designer. I mean, don't get me wrong, I think you're better suited to be an obstetrician, but still . . ."

My head was starting to pound. "Look, I don't want to sound ungrateful, but what are you doing here?"

"Toasting a bagel?"

"You know what I mean."

The toaster popped, Rob ignored it. "There's a reason we have to say 'for better or for worse.' I've been a total asshole, Piper. I'm sorry." He looked down at the space between us. "You didn't ask for this lawsuit; it was lobbed at you. I have to admit, it made me think about things I thought I'd never have to think about again. But regardless of all that, you didn't do anything wrong. You didn't provide any less than the standard of care for Charlotte and Sean. If anything, you went above and beyond."

I felt a sob rise in my throat. "Your brother," I managed.

"I don't know how different my life would have been if he'd never been born," Rob said quietly. "But I *do* know this: I loved him, while he was here." He glanced up at me. "I can't take back what I said to you, and I can't erase my behavior these past few months. But I was hoping, all the same, that you might not mind me coming to court."

I didn't know how he'd cleared his schedule, or for how long. But I looked up at Rob and saw behind him the new cabinets I'd installed, the track of blue lighting, the warm copper paint on the walls, and for the first time I did not see a room that needed perfecting; I saw a home. "On one condition," I hedged.

Rob nodded. "Fair enough."

"I get the pumpernickel bagel," I said, and I walked right into his open arms.

Marin

An hour before the trial was supposed to start, I really didn't know whether or not my client was planning to show up. I'd tried to call her all weekend, and had not been able to reach her landline or her cell. When I reached the courthouse and saw the news crews lining the steps, I tried to phone her again.

You've reached the O'Keefes, the message machine sang.

That wasn't exactly true, if Sean was proceeding with a divorce. But then, if I had learned anything about Charlotte, it was that the sound bite offered to the public might not be what was true behind the scenes, and to be honest, I didn't particularly care, as long as she didn't confuse her rhetoric when I had her on the witness stand.

I knew when she arrived. The roar on the steps was audible, and when she finally breached the door of the courthouse, the press poured in after her. I immediately hooked my arm through hers, muttering "No comment" as I dragged Charlotte down a hallway and into a private room, locking the door behind me.

"My God," she said, still stunned. "There are so many of them."

"Slow news day in New Hampshire," I reasoned. "I would have been happy to wait for you out in the parking lot and take you through the back way, but that would actually have meant you'd *returned* my seven thousand messages this weekend, so that we could arrange a time to meet."

Charlotte stared blankly out the window at the white vans and their satellite dishes. "I didn't know you called. I wasn't home. Willow broke her femur. We spent the weekend at the hospital, having a rod surgically implanted."

I felt my cheeks burn with embarrassment. Charlotte hadn't been ignoring my calls; she'd been putting out a fire. "Is she all right?"

"She broke it running away from us. Sean told her about the divorce."

"I don't think any kid wants to hear something like that." I hesitated. "I know you've got a lot on your mind, but I wanted to have a few minutes to talk to you about what's going to happen today —"

"Marin," Charlotte said. "I can't do this."

"Come again?"

"I can't do this." She looked up at me. "I really don't think I can go through with it."

"If this is about the media —"

"It's about my daughter. It's about my husband. I don't care how the rest of the world sees me, Marin. But I do care what *they* think."

484

I considered the countless hours I'd spent preparing for this trial, all the expert witnesses I'd interviewed and all the motions I'd filed. Somehow, in my mind, it was tangled up with the fruitless search for my mother, who had finally responded to Maisie the court clerk's phone call, asking her to send along my letter. "Now's a little late to break this news to me, don't you think?"

Charlotte faced me. "My daughter thinks I don't want her, because she's broken."

"Well, what did you think she'd believe?"

"Me," Charlotte said softly. "I thought she'd believe me."

"Then *make* her. Get up on that witness stand and say that you love her."

"That's sort of at odds with saying I'd have terminated the pregnancy, isn't it?"

"I don't think they're mutually exclusive," I said. "You don't want to lie on the stand. *I* don't want you to lie on the stand. But I certainly don't want you judging yourself before a jury does."

"How *can't* they? You even did it, Marin. You as much as admitted that, if your mother had been like me, you wouldn't be here today."

"My mother *was* like you," I confessed. "She didn't have a choice." I sat down on a desk across from Charlotte. "Just a few weeks after she gave birth to me, abortion became legal. I don't know if she would have made the same decision if I'd been conceived nine months later. I don't know if her life would have been any better. But I do know it would have been different."

"Different," Charlotte repeated.

"You told me a year and a half ago that you wanted Willow to have opportunities to do things she might not otherwise be able to do," I said. "Didn't you deserve the same?"

I held my breath until Charlotte lifted her face to mine. "How long before we start?" she asked.

The jury, which had looked so disparate on Friday, seemed to be a unified body already first thing Monday morning. Judge Gellar had dyed his hair over the weekend, a deep black Grecian Formula that drew my eyes like a magnet and made him look like an Elvis impersonator — never a good image to associate with a judge you are desperate to impress. When he instructed the four cameras that had been allowed in to report on the trial, I almost expected him to break out in a resounding chorus of "Burning Love."

The courtroom was full — of media, of disability-rights advocates, of people who just liked to see a good show. Charlotte was trembling beside me, staring down at her lap. "Ms. Gates," Judge Gellar said. "Whenever you're ready."

I squeezed Charlotte's hand, then stood up to face the jury. "Good morning, ladies and gentlemen," I said. "I'd like to tell you about a little girl named Willow O'Keefe."

I walked toward them. "Willow's six and a half years old," I said, "and she's broken sixty-eight bones in her lifetime. The most recent one was Friday night, when her mom got home from jury selection. Willow was running and slipped. She broke her femur and had to have surgery to put a rod inside it. But Willow's also broken bones when she's sneezed. When she's bumped into a table. When she's rolled over in her sleep. That's because Willow has osteogenesis imperfecta, an illness you might know as brittle bone syndrome. It means she has been and always will be susceptible to broken bones."

I held up my right hand. "I broke my arm once in second grade. A girl named Lulu, who was the class bully, thought it would be funny to push me off the jungle gym to see if I could fly. I don't remember much about that break, except that it hurt like crazy. Every time Willow breaks a bone, it hurts just as much as it would if you or I broke a bone. The difference is that hers break more rapidly, and more easily. Because of this, from her birth, osteogenesis imperfecta has meant a lifetime of setbacks, rehabilitation, therapy, and surgeries for Willow, a lifetime of pain. And what osteogenesis imperfecta has meant for her mother, Charlotte, is a life interrupted."

I walked back toward our table. "Charlotte O'Keefe was a successful pastry chef whose strength was an asset. She was used to hauling around fifty-pound bags of flour and punching dough — and now every movement of hers is done with finesse, since even lifting her daughter the wrong way can cause a break. If you ask Charlotte, she'll tell you how much she loves Willow. She'll tell you her daughter never lets her down. But she can't say the same about her obstetrician, Piper Reece — her friend, ladies and gentlemen — who knew that there was a problem with the fetus and failed to disclose it to Charlotte so that she could make decisions every prospective mother has the right to make."

Facing the jury again, I spread my palms wide. "Make no mistake, ladies and gentlemen, this case is not about feelings. It's not about whether Charlotte O'Keefe adores her daughter. That's a given. This case is about facts — facts that Piper Reece knew and dismissed. Facts that weren't given to a patient by a physician she trusted. No one is blaming Dr Reece for Willow's condition; no one is saying she caused the illness. However, Dr Reece *is* to blame for not giving the O'Keefes all the information she had. You see, at Charlotte's eighteen-week ultrasound, there were already signs that the fetus suffered from osteogenesis imperfecta — signs that Dr Reece ignored," I said.

"Imagine if you, the jury, came into this courtroom expecting me to give you details about this case, and I did — but I held back one critical piece of information. Now imagine that, weeks after you'd rendered your verdict, you learned about this information. How would that make you feel? Angry? Troubled? Cheated? Maybe you'd even find yourself losing sleep at night, wondering if this information, presented earlier, might have changed your vote," I said. "If I withheld information during a trial, that would be grounds for appeal. But when a physician withholds information from a patient, that's malpractice."

I surveyed the jury. "Now imagine that the information I withheld might affect not just the outcome of the jury trial you sat on . . . but your whole future." I walked back to my seat. "That, ladies and gentlemen, is exactly what brings Charlotte O'Keefe here today."

Charlotte

I could feel Piper staring.

As soon as Marin stood and started talking, she had a direct view of me from across the room, where she sat at a table with her attorney. Her gaze was blazing a hole in my skin; I had to turn away to stop it from burning.

Somewhere behind her was Rob. His eyes were on me, too, like pinpricks, like lasers. I was the vertex, and they were the rays of the angle. Acute, somewhat less than the whole.

Piper didn't look like Piper anymore. She was thinner, older. She was wearing something we would have made fun of while we were shopping, an outfit we would have consigned to the Skating Moms crowd.

I wonder if I looked different, too — or if that was even possible, given that, the very moment I'd sued her, I'd become someone she never thought I could be.

Marin slipped into her seat beside me with a sigh. "Off and running," she whispered as Guy Booker rose and buttoned his suit jacket.

"I wouldn't doubt that Willow O'Keefe's had — what was it Ms. Gates said? — sixty-eight broken bones. But Willow also had a mad scientist birthday party in February. She's got a poster of Hannah Montana hanging over her bed, and she got the highest grade on a district-wide reading test last year. She hates the color orange and the smell of cooked cabbage and asked Santa for a monkey last Christmas. In other words, ladies and gentlemen, in many ways Willow O'Keefe is no different from any other six-and-a-half-year-old girl."

He walked toward the jury box. "Yes, she is disabled. And yes, she has special needs. But does that mean she doesn't have a right to be alive? That her birth was a wrongful one? Because that's what this case is really about. The tort is called wrongful birth for a reason, and believe me, it's a tough one to wrap your heads around. But yes indeed, this mother, Charlotte O'Keefe, is saying that she wishes her own child had never been born."

I felt a shock go through me, as sure as lightning.

"You're going to hear from Willow's mother about how much her daughter suffers. But you'll also hear from her father about how much Willow *loves* life. And you'll hear him say how much joy that child's brought into *his* life, and just what he thinks about this so-called wrongful birth. That's right. You're not misunderstanding me. Charlotte O'Keefe's own husband disagreed with the lawsuit his wife started and refused to be part of a scheme to milk the deep pockets of a medical insurance company."

Guy Booker walked toward Piper. "When a couple first find out that they're pregnant, they immediately hope the child will be healthy. No one wants a child to be born less than perfect. But the truth is, there are no guarantees. The truth is, ladies and gentlemen, that Charlotte O'Keefe is in this for two reasons, and two reasons only: to get some money, and to point the finger at someone other than herself."

There were times when I was baking that I opened the oven at eye level and was hit by a wave of heat so strong and severe that it temporarily blinded me. Guy Booker's words had the same effect at that moment. I realized that Marin was right. I could say that I loved you and that I wanted to sue for wrongful birth and not contradict myself. It was a little like telling someone, after she'd seen the color green, to completely forget its existence. I could never erase the mark of your hand holding mine, or your voice in my ear. I couldn't imagine life without you. If I'd never known you, the tale would be different; it would not be the story of you and me.

I had never allowed myself to think that someone might have been responsible for your illness. We had been told that your disease was a spontaneous mutation, that Sean and I weren't carriers. We had been told that nothing I might have done differently during my pregnancy would have saved you from breaking in utero. But I was your mother, and I had carried you under the umbrella of my heart. I was the one who had summoned your soul to this world; I was the reason you'd wound up in this broken body. If I hadn't worked so hard to have a baby, you wouldn't have been born. There were countless reasons, as far as I could see, that I was to blame.

Unless it was Piper's fault. If that was the case, then I was off the hook.

Which meant that Guy Booker was *also* right.

This lawsuit, which I'd filed because of you, which I'd sworn was all about you, was actually all about me.

IV

Do you remember still the falling stars
that like swift horses through the heavens raced
and suddenly leaped across the hurdles
of our wishes — do you recall? And we
did make so many! For there were countless
  numbers
of stars: each time we looked above we were
astounded by the swiftness of their daring play,
while in our hearts we felt safe and secure
watching these brilliant bodies disintegrate,
knowing somehow we had survived their fall.

— Rainer Maria Rilke, *Falling Stars*

Proof: the part of a recipe where dough is allowed to rise.

Twice, during the baking of bread, proof is required. Yeast is proofed in water and a small bit of sugar to make sure it's still active before going any further in the recipe. But proofing also describes a step where the dough doubles in size, the moment when it suddenly grows in dynamic proportion to what you started out with.

What makes the dough rise? The yeast, which converts glucose and other carbohydrates into carbon dioxide gas. Different breads proof differently. Some require only a single proofing; others need many. Between these stages, the baker is told to punch down the dough.

It's no surprise to me that — in baking, and in life — the cost of growth is always a small act of violence.

SUNDAY MORNING STICKY ROLLS

DOUGH

3¾ cups flour
⅓ cup sugar
1 teaspoon salt
2 packages active dry yeast
1 cup heated milk

1 egg
⅓ cup butter, softened

CARAMEL

¾ cup dark brown sugar
½ cup unsalted butter
¼ cup light corn syrup
¾ cup pecan halves
2 tablespoons butter, softened

FILLING

½ cup pecans, chopped
2 tablespoons sugar
2 tablespoons brown sugar
1 teaspoon cinnamon

You once told me that the best part of a lazy Sunday is to wake up and smell something so delicious you follow your nose downstairs. This is one of those recipes that, like most breads, requires you to be thinking ahead — but then again, when wasn't I thinking ahead for you?

To make the dough, mix together 2 cups of the flour, ⅓ cup sugar, salt, and yeast in a large bowl. Add the heated milk, egg, and ⅓ cup butter, and beat at low speed for a minute. Add flour if necessary to make the dough easier to shape.

On a lightly floured surface, knead dough for 5 minutes. This, I will add, was your favorite part — you

498

would stand on a chair and throw your weight into it. When finished, put the dough into a greased bowl and flip it over once, so the greased side faces up. Cover and let it proof until it doubles in size, about 1½ hours. It's ready if you poke it and the mark of your finger is left behind.

Caramel comes next: Stirring constantly, heat ¾ cup brown sugar and ½ cup butter to boiling. Remove from the heat and add the corn syrup. Pour the mixture into a 13 by 9 by 2-inch ungreased pan. Sprinkle pecan halves over the mixture.

For the filling, mix together the chopped pecans, 2 tablespoons sugar, 2 tablespoons brown sugar, and cinnamon. Set aside.

Punch down the dough with your fist. Then, on a lightly floured surface, flatten it into a rectangle, about 15 by 10 inches. Spread it with 2 tablespoons of butter, then dust it evenly with the chopped pecan mixture. Beginning at the 10-inch side of the rectangle, roll the dough up tightly and pinch the edge closed. Roll it, stretch it, and mold it until it is cylindrical.

Cut into eight even slices and place them in a pan, not quite touching. Wrap the pan tightly with foil and refrigerate for at least 12 hours. Dream of them rising, that proof again, evidence that some things grow bigger than we ever expect.

Heat the oven to 350 degrees F and bake 35 minutes. When golden, remove from the oven. Immediately invert on a platter, and serve warm.

Marin

Minutes later

I've always sort of wondered about the term *bearing witness*. Is it that testifying is such a hardship? Or is it childbirth lingo, the idea that a witness brings forth something new to the trial? That's certainly true, but not in the way you'd imagine. Witness testimony is always flawed. It's better than circumstantial evidence, sure, but people aren't camcorders; they don't record every action and reaction, and the very act of remembering involves choosing words and phrases and images. In other words, every witness who's supposed to be giving a court facts is really just giving them a version of fiction.

Charlotte O'Keefe, who was on the witness stand now, was not even really capable of bearing witness to her own life, in spite of the fact that she'd lived it. By her own admission, she was biased; by her own admission, she remembered her history only when it was entwined with Willow's.

I would make a lousy witness, of course. I didn't know where my story started.

Charlotte had knotted her hands in her lap and sailed through the first three questions:

What's your name?

Where do you live?

How many children do you have?

She'd stumbled on the fourth question, though:

Are you married?

Technically, the answer to that was yes. But practically, it had to be spelled out — or Guy Booker would use Charlotte and Sean's separation to his own legal advantage. I had coached Charlotte through the right response, and we had not managed to practice it yet without her bursting into tears. As I waited for her to answer, I found myself holding my breath.

"Right now I am," Charlotte said evenly. "But having a child with so many special needs — it's caused a lot of problems in my marriage. My husband and I are separated right now." She exhaled, a slow whistle.

Good girl, I thought.

"Charlotte, can you tell us about how Willow was conceived?" At the gasp of an elderly juror, I added, "Not the nuts and bolts . . . more like the decision you made to become a parent."

"I was already a parent," Charlotte said. "I'd been a single mother for five years. When I met Sean, we both knew we wanted more children — but that didn't seem to be in the cards. We tried to get pregnant for almost two years, and we were just about to start fertility treatments when, well, it just happened."

"How did that feel?"

"We were ecstatic," Charlotte replied. "You know how sometimes, your life is so perfect you're afraid for the next moment, because it couldn't possibly be quite as good? That's what it felt like."

"How old were you when you became pregnant?"

"Thirty-eight." Charlotte smiled a little. "A geriatric pregnancy, they call it."

"Were you concerned about that?"

"I knew that the odds of having a Down syndrome child were higher once you were over thirty-five."

I approached the stand. "Did you speak to your obstetrician about that?"

"Yes."

"Can you tell the court who your obstetrician was at the time?"

"Piper Reece," Charlotte said. "The defendant."

"How did you select the defendant as your ob-gyn?"

Charlotte looked down at her lap. "She was my best friend. I trusted her."

"What did the defendant do to address your concerns about having a baby with Down syndrome?"

"She recommended that I do some blood tests — a quad screen, it was called — to see if I had an even greater chance than the norm to have a baby with neural defects, or Down syndrome. Instead of my risk being one in two hundred and seventy, it was one in one hundred and fifty."

"What did she recommend?" I asked.

"Amniocentesis," Charlotte replied, "but I knew that carried a risk, too. Since I was scheduled to have a routine ultrasound anyway at eighteen weeks, she said we could read the results of that first, then make a decision about the amnio based on what we saw. It wasn't as accurate as amnio, but there were supposedly certain things that might turn up that would suggest Down syndrome, or rule it out as less likely."

"Do you remember that ultrasound?" I asked.

Charlotte nodded. "We were so excited to see our baby. And at the same time, I was nervous — because I knew the technician was going to be looking for those Down syndrome markers. I kept watching her, for clues. And at one point she tipped her head and said, 'Hmm.' But when I asked her what she'd seen, she told me that Dr Reece would read the results."

"What did the defendant tell you?"

"Piper came into the room, and I knew, just from her face, that the baby didn't have Down syndrome. I asked her if she was sure, and she said yes — that the technician had even remarked on how clear the images were. I made her look me in the eye and tell me that everything looked all right — and she said that there was only one measurement that was the slightest bit off, a femur that was in the sixth percentile. Piper said that wasn't something to worry about, since I was short, that by the next ultrasound, that same measurement could be up in the fiftieth percentile."

"Were you concerned about the sonogram images being clear?"

"Why would I be?" Charlotte said. "Piper didn't seem to be, and I assumed that was the whole point of an ultrasound — to get a good picture."

"Did Dr Reece advise having a more detailed follow-up ultrasound?"

"No."

"Did you have any other ultrasounds during your pregnancy?"

"Yes, when I was twenty-seven weeks pregnant. It wasn't a test as much as a lark — we did it after-hours in her office, to find out the sex of the baby."

I faced the jury. "Do you remember that ultrasound, Charlotte?"

"Yes," she said softly. "I'll never forget it. I was lying on the table, and Piper had the wand on my belly. She was staring at the computer screen. I asked her when I'd get a chance to look, but she didn't answer. I asked her if she was okay."

"What was her response?"

Charlotte's eyes looked across the room and locked with Piper's. "That she was okay. But that my daughter wasn't."

Charlotte

"What are you talking about? What's the matter?" I'd sat up on my elbows, looking at the screen, trying to make sense of the images as they jostled with my movements.

Piper pointed to a black line that looked to me like all the other black lines on the screen. "She's got broken bones, Charlotte. A bunch of them."

I shook my head. How could that be? I had not fallen.

"I'll call Gianna Del Sol. She's the head of maternal-fetal medicine at the hospital; she can explain it in more detail —"

"Explain *what?*" I cried, riding the high wire of panic.

Piper pulled the transducer away from my belly, so that the screen went clear. "If it's what I think it is — osteogenesis imperfecta — it's really rare. I've only read about it, during medical school. I've never seen a patient who has it," she said. "It affects collagen levels, so that bones break easily."

"But the baby," I said. "It's going to be okay, right?"

This was the part where my best friend embraced me and said, *Yes, of course, don't be silly.* This was the part where Piper told me it was the kind of problem that, ten years from now, we'd laugh about at your birthday party. Except Piper didn't say any of that. "I don't know," she admitted. "I honestly don't know."

We left my car at Piper's office and drove back to the house to tell Sean. The whole way, I ran a loop of memory in my mind, trying to think back to when these breaks might have happened — at the restaurant, when I'd dropped that stick of butter and bent down to retrieve it? In Amelia's room, when I stumbled over a tangled pair of pajama pants? On the highway when I stopped short, so the seat belt tightened against my belly?

I sat at the kitchen table while Piper told Sean what she knew — and what she didn't. From time to time, I could feel you inside me, rolling a slow tango. I was afraid to touch my hands to my abdomen, and acknowledge you. For seven months we had been a unit — integrated and inseparable — but right now, you felt alien to me. Sometimes in the shower when I did a self-breast exam I had wondered what I would do if I were diagnosed — chemo, radiation, surgery? — and I had decided that I would want the tumor cut out of me right away, that I couldn't bear sleeping at night and knowing it was growing beneath my skin. You — who had been so precious to me hours ago — suddenly felt that way: unfamiliar, upsetting, *other*.

After Piper left, Sean became a man of action. "We'll find the best doctors," he vowed. "We'll do whatever it takes."

But what if there was nothing that could be done?

506

I watched Sean in his feverish zeal. Me, I was swimming through syrup, viscous and pendulous. I could barely move, much less take charge. You, who had once brought Sean and me so close together, were now the spotlight that illuminated how different we were.

That night, I couldn't fall asleep. I stared at the ceiling until the red flush from the LED numbers on the clock radio spread like wildfire; I counted backward, from this moment to the one where you were conceived. When Sean got out of bed quietly, I pretended that I was asleep, but that was only because I knew where he was headed: to look up osteogenesis imperfecta on the Internet. I'd thought about doing that, too, but I wasn't as brave as he was. Or maybe I was less naïve: unlike him, I believed what we learned could actually be worse than what we already knew.

Eventually, I did drift off. I dreamed that my water had broken, that I was having contractions. I tried to roll over to tell Sean, but I couldn't. I couldn't move at all. My arms, my legs, my jaw; somehow I knew that I was broken beyond repair. And somehow I knew that whatever had been inside me all these months had liquefied, was soaking into the sheets beneath me, was no longer a baby at all.

The next day was a whirlwind: from a high-level ultrasound, at which even I could see the breaks, to a meeting with Gianna Del Sol to discuss the findings. She threw out terms that meant nothing at the time: Type II, Type III. Rodding. Macrocephaly. She told us that one other child with OI had been born at this hospital, years earlier, who'd had ten breaks — and who had died within an hour.

Then she sent us to a geneticist, Dr Bowles. "So," he said, getting right down to business — no *I'm so sorry you had to hear this news.* "The best-case scenario here," he said, "would be a baby that survives the birth, but even if that's the case, a Type III might have cerebral hemorrhage caused by birth trauma or an increased circumference of the head compared to the rest of the body. She will most likely develop severe scoliosis, have surgeries for multiple broken bones, need rodding in her spine, or vertebrae fused together. The shape of her rib cage won't allow her lungs to grow, which can lead to repeated respiratory infections, or even death."

Amazingly, this was a whole different run of symptoms from the ones Dr Del Sol had given us already.

"And of course, we're talking hundreds of broken bones, and realistically a very good chance she'll never walk. Basically," the geneticist said, "what you're looking at is a lifetime, however short, of pain."

I could feel Sean next to me, coiled like a cobra, ready to take out his own anger and grief on this man, who was talking to us as if it were not you, our daughter, who was the subject but a car whose oil we needed to change.

Dr Bowles looked at his watch. "Any questions?"

"Yes," I said. "Why didn't anyone tell us before?"

I thought of all the blood tests I'd taken, the earlier ultrasound. Surely if my baby was going to be this sick — this hurt for her whole life — something would have shown up earlier?

"Well," said the geneticist, "neither you nor your husband is a genetic carrier of OI, so it wouldn't have been routinely tested for prior to conception, or flagged by the obstetrician as something to keep an eye on. It's good news, actually, that the disease was a spontaneous mutation."

My baby is a mutant, I thought. *Six eyes. Antennae. Take me to your leader.*

"If you have another child, there's no reason to believe this will happen again," he said.

Sean came out of his seat, but I put a hand on his arm to restrain him.

"How do we know whether the baby will . . ." I couldn't say it. I lowered my eyes, so that he knew what I meant. ". . . at birth, or live longer?"

"It's very difficult to tell at this point," Dr Bowles said. "We'll schedule repeated ultrasounds, of course, but sometimes a parent whose child has a lethal prognosis will end up with a baby that survives, or vice versa." He hesitated. "There is another option — several places in this country will terminate a pregnancy for maternal or fetal medical reasons, even this far along."

I watched Sean fit his teeth around the word he did not want to say out loud. "We don't want an abortion."

The geneticist nodded.

"How?" I asked.

Sean stared at me, horrified. "Charlotte, do you know about those things? I've seen pictures —"

"There are many different methods," Bowles answered, looking directly at me. "Intact D and E is one, but so is induction after stopping the fetus's heart."

"Fetus?" Sean said, exploding. "That's not a fetus. That's my daughter we're talking about."

"If termination isn't an option —"

"Option? Fuck that. It should never even have been on the table," Sean said. He reached for me, pulling me to my feet. "Do you think Stephen Hawking's mother had to listen to this load of bullshit?"

My heart was hammering and I could not catch my breath. I didn't know where Sean was taking me, and I didn't particularly care. I just knew that I couldn't listen to that doctor for one more moment, talking about your life or lack thereof as if it were a textbook he was reading on the Holocaust, the Inquisition, Darfur: truths that were so awful and graphic that you instead skipped over them, conceding their horror without suffering the details.

Sean dragged me down the hallway and into an elevator that was just closing. "I'm sorry," he said, leaning against the wall. "I just . . . I *couldn't*."

We were not alone inside. To my right was a woman about ten years older than I was, pushing one of those state-of-the-art wheelchairs with a child sprawled across it. This one was a boy in his teens, thin and angular, his head supported by a brace on the back of the chair. His elbows twisted, so that his arms were flailed outward; his glasses were askew on the bridge of his nose. His mouth was open, and his tongue — thick and jellied — filled the bowl of his mouth. "Aaaaah," the boy sang. "Aaaaah!"

His mother touched her hand to his cheek. "Yes, that's right."

I wondered if she really understood what he was trying to say. Was there a language of loss? Did everyone who suffered speak a different dialect?

I found myself staring at the woman's fingers, stroking her son's hair. Did this boy know his mother's touch? Did he smile at her? Would he ever say her name?

Would you?

Sean reached for my hand and squeezed it tightly. "We can do this," he whispered. "We can do it together."

I didn't speak until the elevator stopped at floor three and the woman pushed her son's wheelchair off into the hallway. The doors sealed shut again, isolating Sean and me in a vacuum. "Okay," I said.

"Tell us about Willow's birth," Marin said, pulling me back to the present.

"She was early. Dr Del Sol had scheduled a C-section, but instead, I went into labor and everything happened very quickly. When she was born, she was screaming, and they took her away from me to X-ray her, to do tests. It was hours before I saw Willow, and when I did, she was lying on a foam pad in a bassinet, with bandages wrapped around her arms and legs. She

511

had seven healing fractures and four new breaks caused by the birth."

"Did anything else happen in the hospital?"

"Yes, Willow broke a rib, and it pierced her lung. It was . . . it was the most frightening thing I've ever seen in my life. She went blue, and suddenly there were dozens of doctors in the room and they started doing CPR and stuck a needle in between her ribs. They told me her chest cavity had filled with air, which made her heart and trachea shift to the wrong side of her body, and then her heart had stopped beating. They did chest compressions — breaking even more of her ribs — and put in a chest tube to make the organs go back where they belonged. They cut her," I said. "While I watched."

"Did you talk to the defendant afterward?" Marin asked.

I nodded. "Another doctor told me that Willow had been without oxygen for a while, and that we wouldn't know if there would be brain damage. He suggested that I sign a DNR form."

"What's that?"

"It means do not resuscitate. If anything like this happened to Willow again, the doctors wouldn't intervene. They'd let Willow die." I looked into my lap. "I asked Piper for advice."

"Because she was your physician?"

"No," I said. "Because she was my friend."

Piper

I had failed.

That's what I thought, when I looked down at you, battered and buttressed, a fountain of a chest tube blooming out from beneath your fifth rib on the left side. I had been asked by my best friend to help her conceive, and this was the outcome. After the wrenching question about whether or not you belonged in this world, it seemed that you were giving Charlotte your own answer. Without saying a word, I walked up to Charlotte, who was staring down at you as you slept, as if glancing away for even a moment might give you incentive to code again.

I had read your chart. The fractured rib had caused an expanding pneumothorax, a mediastinal shift, and cardiopulmonary arrest. The resultant intervention had caused nine further fractures. The chest tube had been inserted through the fascia and into the pleural space of your chest, sutured into place. You looked like a battle-field; the war had been fought on the broken ground of your tiny body.

Without saying a word, I walked up to Charlotte and reached for her hand. "Are you okay?" I asked.

"I'm not the one you need to worry about," she replied. Her eyes were red-rimmed; her hospital robe askew. "They asked if we wanted to sign a DNR."

"*Who* asked that?" I had never heard of anything so stupid. Not even Terri Schiavo had been made DNR until tests indicated severe, irreversible brain damage. It was hard enough to get a pediatrician to be hands off when dealing with a severely preterm fetus with a high probability of death or lifetime morbidity — to suggest a DNR for a neonate on whom they'd just done the full-court press in terms of a code seemed improbable *and* impossible.

"Dr Rhodes —"

"He's a resident," I said, because that explained everything. Rhodes barely knew how to tie his shoes, much less talk to a parent who'd been through an intense trauma with a child. Rhodes should never have brought up the DNR to Charlotte and Sean — particularly since Willow hadn't yet been tested to see if she was mens sana. In fact, while he was ordering that test, he might have wanted to get one for himself.

"They cut her open in front of me. I heard her ribs break when they . . . when they . . ." Charlotte's face was white, haunted. "Would you sign one?" she whispered.

She had asked me the same question, in not so many words, before you were even born. It was the day after her twenty-seven-week ultrasound, when I had sent her to Gianna Del Sol and the healthcare team for high-risk pregnancies at the hospital. I was a good obstetrician, but I knew my limits — and I couldn't provide her with the care she now needed. However, Charlotte had been traumatized by a stupid geneticist whose bedside manner was better suited to patients already in the morgue, and now I was doing damage control while she sobbed on my couch.

"I don't want her to suffer," Charlotte said.

I did not know how to tiptoe around the topic of a late-term abortion. Even someone who wasn't Catholic, like Charlotte, would have a hard time swallowing that option — and yet, it was never chosen lightly. Intact D & Es were performed only by a handful of physicians in the country, physicians who were highly skilled and committed to ending pregnancies where there was a great maternal or fetal health risk. For certain conditions that weren't apparent before the twelve-week cutoff for abortions, these doctors provided an alternative to giving birth to a baby with no chance of survival. You could argue that either outcome would leave a scar on the parent, but then again, as Charlotte had pointed out, there were no happy endings here.

"I don't want *you* to suffer," I replied.

"Sean doesn't want to do it."

"Sean isn't pregnant."

Charlotte turned away. "How do you fly across the country with a baby inside you, knowing you'll be coming back without one?"

"If it's what you want, I'll go with you."

"I don't know," she sobbed. "I don't know what I want." She looked up at me. "What would you do?"

515

Two months later, we stood on opposite sides of your hospital NICU bassinet. The room, filled with so many machines to keep their tiny charges alive and functional, was bathed in a rich blue light, as if we were all swimming underwater. "Would you sign one?" Charlotte asked me again, when I didn't answer the first time.

You could argue that it was less traumatizing to terminate a pregnancy than it was to sign a DNR for a child who was already in this world. Had Charlotte made the decision to terminate at twenty-seven weeks, her loss would have been devastating but theoretical — she would not have met you yet. Now, she was forced to question your existence again — but this time, she could see the pain and suffering in front of her eyes.

Charlotte had come to me for advice multiple times: about conceiving, about whether or not to have a late-term abortion, and now, about a do not resuscitate order.

What would I do?

I would go back to the moment Charlotte had asked me to help her have a baby, and I'd refer her to someone else.

I'd go back to when we were more likely to laugh together than to cry.

I'd go back to the time before you had come between us.

I'd do whatever I had to, to keep you from feeling like everything was breaking apart.

516

If you chose to stop a loved one's suffering — either before it began or during the process — was that murder, or mercy?

"Yes," I whispered. "I would."

Marin

"The learning curve was huge," Charlotte said. "From figuring out how to hold Willow, or how to change her diaper without breaking a bone, to knowing that we might simply be carrying her in our arms and hear that little pop that meant she'd broken something. We found out where to order car beds and adapted infant carriers, so that the straps wouldn't snap her collarbones. We started to understand when we had to go to the emergency room and when we could splint the break ourselves. We stocked our own waterproof casts in the garage. We traveled to Nebraska, because they had orthopedic surgeons who specialized in OI, and we started Willow on a course of pamidronate infusions at Children's Hospital in Boston."

"Do you ever — well, for lack of a better term — get a break?"

Charlotte smiled a little. "Not really. We don't make plans. We don't bother, because we never know what's going to happen. There's always a new trauma we have to learn to deal with. Breaking a rib, for example, isn't like breaking your back." She hesitated. "Willow did that last year."

Someone in the jury sucked in their breath, a whistling sound that made Guy Booker roll his eyes and that absolutely delighted me. "Can you tell the court how you've managed to pay for all this?"

"That's a huge problem," Charlotte said. "I used to work, but after Willow was born, I couldn't. Even when she was in preschool, I had to be ready to run if she had a break, and you can't do that when you're the head pastry chef at a restaurant. We tried to hire a nurse that we trusted to take care of her, but it cost more than my salary, and sometimes the agency would send along women who knew nothing about OI, who didn't speak English, who couldn't understand what I told them about taking care of Willow. I had to be her advocate, and I had to be there all the time." She shrugged. "We don't give big birthday or Christmas gifts. We don't have IRAs or a college fund for the kids. We don't take vacations. All of our money goes to pay for what the insurance doesn't."

"Like?"

"Willow's in a clinical study for her pamidronate, which means it's free, but once she's a certain age she can't be part of the study anymore, and each infusion is over a thousand dollars. Leg braces cost five thousand dollars each, rodding surgeries are a hundred thousand. A spinal fusion, which Willow will have to have as a teen, can be several times that, and that's not counting the flight to Omaha to have it done. Even if insurance pays for part of these things, the rest is left to us. And there are plenty of smaller items that add up: wheelchair maintenance, sheepskin to line casts, ice packs, clothes that can accommodate casts, different pillows to make Willow more comfortable, ramps for handicapped access into the house. She'll need more equipment as she gets older — reachers and mirrors and other adaptations for short stature. Even a car with pedals that are easier to press down on, so they don't cause microfractures in her feet, costs tens of thousands of dollars to get rigged correctly, and Vocational Rehabilitation will pay for only one vehicle — the rest are your responsibility, for life. She can go to college, but even that will cost more than usual, because of the adaptations necessary — and the best schools for kids like Willow aren't nearby either, which means more travel expenses. We cashed out my husband's 401(k) and took out a second mortgage. I've maxed out two credit cards." Charlotte looked over at the jury. "I know what I look like to all of you. I know you think I'm in this for a big payday, that this is why I started this lawsuit."

I stilled, not sure what she was doing; this was not what we had practiced. "Charlotte, have you —"

"Please," she said. "Let me finish. It *is* about cost. But not the financial kind." She blinked back tears. "I don't sleep at night. I feel guilty when I laugh at a joke on TV. I watch little girls the same age as Willow at the playground, and I hate them sometimes — that's how bitterly jealous I can get when I see how easy it is for them. But the day I signed that DNR in the hospital, I made a promise to my daughter. I said, *If you fight, I will, too. If you live, I will make sure your life is the best it can possibly be.* That's what a good mother does, right?" She shook her head. "The way it usually works, the parent takes care of the child, until years later, when the roles are reversed. But with Willow and me, I'll always be the one taking care of her. That's why I'm here today. That's what I want you to tell me. How am I supposed to take care of my daughter after I'm gone?"

You could have heard a pin drop, a heart beat. "Your Honor," I said. "Nothing further."

Sean

The sea was a monster, black and angry. You were equally terrified and fascinated by it; you'd beg to go watch the waves crash against the retaining wall, but every time they did, you shivered in my arms.

I had taken the day off work because Guy Booker had said that all witnesses had to come to the trial on the first day. But as it turned out, I couldn't be in the courtroom anyway, until my testimony. I stayed for ten minutes — just long enough for the judge to tell me to leave.

This morning, I'd realized that Charlotte thought I was coming to court to support her. I could see why, after the night before, she would expect that. In her arms, I had been explosive, enraged, and tender by turns — as if we were playing out our feelings in a pantomime beneath the sheets. I knew she was upset when I told her I was meeting Guy Booker, but she should have understood better than anyone why I still needed to testify against her in this lawsuit: you did what you had to do to protect your child.

After leaving the courthouse, I'd driven home and told the hired nurse to take the afternoon off. Amelia would need to be picked up at school at three, but in the meantime, I asked what you wanted to do. "I can't do anything," you said. "*Look* at me."

It was true, your entire left leg was splinted. But all the same, I didn't see why I couldn't get a little creative to boost your spirits. I carried you out to the car, wrapped in blankets, and tucked you sideways across the backseat so that your leg was stretched along it. You could still wear your seat belt this way, and as you began to spot the familiar landmarks that led to the ocean, you got more and more animated.

There was nobody at the beach in late September, so I could park sideways across the lot that butted up to the retaining wall, giving you a bird's-eye view. The truck's cab sat high enough for you to see the waves, creeping forward and slinking backward like great gray cats. "Daddy?" you asked. "How come you can't skate on the ocean?"

"I guess you can, way up in the Arctic, but for the most part, there's too much salt in the water for it to freeze."

"If it did freeze, wouldn't it be awesome if there were still waves? Like ice sculptures?"

"That would be cool," I agreed. I glanced over my headrest at you. "Wills? You okay?"

"My leg doesn't hurt."

"I wasn't talking about your leg. I was talking about what's going on today."

"There were a lot of TV cameras this morning."

"Yeah."

"Cameras make my stomach hurt."

I threaded my arm around the seat to reach your hand. "You know I'd never let any of those reporters bother you."

"Mom should bake for them. If they really loved her brownies or her toffee bars, they might just say thank you and leave."

"Maybe your mom could add arsenic to the batter," I mused.

"What?"

"Nothing." I shook my head. "Your mom loves you, too. You know that, right?"

Outside, the Atlantic reached a crescendo. "I think there are two different oceans — the one that plays with you in the summer, and the one that gets so mad in the winter," you said. "It's hard to remember what the other one's like."

I opened my mouth, thinking that you hadn't heard what I said about Charlotte. And then I realized that you had.

Charlotte

Guy Booker was just the sort of person that Piper and I would have laughed at if we'd come across him at Maxie's Pad — an attorney who had gotten so big in his own head that he had a personalized license plate which read HOTSHOT on his mint green T-Bird. "This is really about the money, isn't it?" he said.

"No. But the money means the difference between good care and lousy care for my daughter."

"Willow receives Katie Beckett monies through Healthy Kids Gold, doesn't she?"

"Yes, but even so, that doesn't cover all the medical expenses — and none of the out-of-pocket ones. For example, when a child's in a spica cast, she needs a different kind of car seat. And the dental problems that are part and parcel of OI might run thousands of dollars a year."

"If your daughter had been born a gifted pianist, would you be asking for money for a grand piano?" Booker said.

Marin had told me that he would try to get me angry, so that the jury would like me less. I took a deep breath and counted to five. "That's comparing apples and oranges, Mr Booker. This isn't an arts education we're talking about. It's my daughter's life."

Booker walked toward the jury; I had to suppress an urge to check if he left a trail of oil. "You and your husband don't see eye to eye about this lawsuit, Ms. O'Keefe, correct?"

"No, we do not."

"Would you agree that the cause of your pending divorce is that your husband, Sean, doesn't support this lawsuit?"

"Yes," I said softly.

"He doesn't believe Willow was a wrongful birth, does he?"

"Objection," Marin called out. "You can't ask her what his opinion is."

"Sustained."

Booker folded his arms. "Yet, you're going through with the lawsuit anyway, even though it will most likely split up your family, aren't you?"

I pictured Sean in his coat and tie this morning, that tiny lift of spirit I'd had when I thought he was coming to court with me instead of against me. "I still think it's the right thing to do."

"Have you had conversations with Willow about this lawsuit?" Booker asked.

"Yes," I said. "She knows I'm doing this because I love her."

"You think she understands that?"

I hesitated. "She's only six. I think a lot of the mechanics of the lawsuit have gone over her head."

526

"What about when she's older?" said Booker. "I bet Willow's pretty good when it comes to computer skills?"

"Sure."

"Have you ever thought about the moment years from now when your daughter gets on the Internet and googles herself? You? This case?"

"Well, God knows I'm not looking forward to that, but I hope that, if it happens, I'll be able to explain to her why it was necessary . . . and that the quality of her life that day is a direct result of the lawsuit."

"God knows," Booker repeated. "Interesting choice of words. You're a practicing Catholic, aren't you?"

"Yes."

"As a practicing Catholic, you're aware that it's a mortal sin to have an abortion?"

I swallowed. "Yes, I am."

"Yet the premise of this lawsuit is that, if you'd known about Willow's condition earlier, you would have terminated the pregnancy, right?"

I could feel the eyes of the jury on me. I had known that there was a point where I would be put on display — the sideshow oddity, the zoo animal — and this was it. "I know what you're doing," I said tightly. "But this case is about malpractice, not abortion."

"That's not an answer, Ms. O'Keefe. Let's try again: if you'd found out that you were carrying a child who was profoundly deaf and blind, would you have terminated the pregnancy?"

"Objection," Marin cried. "That's irrelevant. My client's child isn't deaf and blind."

527

"It goes to the mind-set of whether or not the child's mother could have done what she says she could," Booker argued.

"Sidebar," Marin said, and they both approached the bench, continuing to argue loudly in front of everyone. "Judge, this is prejudicial. He can ask what my client's decision was regarding actual medical facts that the defendant did not share with her —"

"Don't tell me how to try my case, sweetheart," Booker said.

"You arrogant pig —"

"I'm going to allow the question," the judge said slowly. "I think we all need to hear what Mrs O'Keefe has to say."

Marin gave me a measured look as she walked past the witness stand — a reminder that I had been called to the mat, and was expected to deliver. "Ms. O'Keefe," Booker repeated, "would you have aborted a profoundly deaf and blind child?"

"I . . . I don't know," I said.

"Are you aware that Helen Keller was profoundly blind and deaf?" he asked. "What if you found out that the baby you were carrying was missing a hand? Would you have terminated that pregnancy?"

I kept my lips pressed tight, silent.

"Are you aware that Jim Abbott, a one-handed pitcher, pitched a no-hitter in major league baseball and won an Olympic gold medal in 1988?" Booker said.

"I'm not Jim Abbott's mother. Or Helen Keller's. I don't know how difficult their childhoods were."

"Well, then, we're back to the original question: If you had known about Willow's condition at eighteen weeks, would you have aborted her?"

"I was never given that option," I said tightly.

"Actually, you were," Booker countered. "At twenty-seven weeks. And by your own testimony, it wasn't a decision you could make then. So why should a jury believe that you would have been able to make it several weeks earlier?"

Malpractice, Marin had drilled into my head, over and over. *That's why you instigated this lawsuit. No matter what else Guy Booker claims, it's about a standard of care and a choice you weren't offered.*

I was shaking so hard that I slipped my hands beneath my thighs. "This case isn't about what I might have done."

"Sure it is," Booker said. "Otherwise, it's a waste of our time."

"You're wrong. This case is about what my doctor *didn't* do —"

"Answer the question, Ms. O'Keefe —"

"Specifically," I said, "she didn't give me a choice about ending the pregnancy. She should have known something was wrong from that very first ultrasound, and she should have —"

"Ms. O'Keefe," the lawyer yelled, "*answer the question!*"

I wilted against the chair and pressed my fingers to my temples. "I can't," I whispered. I looked down at the grain of the wood on the railing before me. "I can't answer that question for you now, because now there *is*

529

a Willow. A girl who likes pigtails but not braids, and who broke her femur this weekend, and who sleeps with a stuffed pig. A girl who's kept me awake at night for the past six and a half years wondering how to get through the next day without an emergency, and planning, as a backup, how to go from crisis to crisis to crisis." I looked up at the lawyer. "At eighteen weeks of pregnancy, at twenty-seven weeks of pregnancy, I didn't know Willow like I do today. So I can't answer your question now, Mr Booker. But the reality is, nobody gave me a chance to answer it back *then*."

"Ms. O'Keefe," the lawyer said flatly. "I'm going to ask you one last time. Would you have aborted your daughter?"

I opened my mouth, and then I closed it.

"Nothing further," he said.

Amelia

That night, I ate dinner alone with my parents. You were sitting on the living room couch with a tray and *Jeopardy!* so that your leg could stay elevated. From the kitchen, I could hear the buzzer every now and then, and Alex Trebek's voice: *Ooh, I'm sorry, that's incorrect.* As if he really gave a damn.

I sat between my mother and father, a conduit between two separate circuits. *Amelia, can you pass the green beans to your mother? Amelia, pour your father a glass of lemonade.* They weren't talking to each other, and they weren't eating — none of us were, really. "So," I said cheerfully. "During fourth period, Jeff Congrew ordered a pizza into French class and the teacher didn't even notice."

"Are you going to tell me what happened today?" my father asked.

My mother lowered her eyes. "I really do *not* want to talk about it, Sean. It was bad enough getting *through* it."

The silence was a blanket so huge, it seemed to cover the entire table. "Domino's delivered," I said.

My father cut two precise squares of his chicken. "Well, if you won't tell me what happened, I guess I'll be able to read all about it tomorrow in the paper. Or maybe, hey, it'll be on the eleven o'clock news . . ."

My mother's fork clattered against her plate. "Do you think this is easy for me?"

"Do you think this is easy for any of us?"

"How could you?" my mother exploded. "How could you act like everything was getting better between us and then . . . then this?"

"The difference between you and me, Charlotte, is that I'm never *acting*."

"It was pepperoni," I announced.

They both turned to me. "What?" my father said.

"It's not important," I muttered. *Like me.*

You called out from the living room. "Mom, I'm done."

So was I. I got up and scraped the contents of my plate, which was everything, into the trash. "Amelia, aren't you forgetting to ask something?" my mother said.

I stared at her dully. There were a thousand questions, sure, but I didn't want to hear the answers to any of them.

"May I be excused?" my mother prompted.

"Shouldn't you be asking Willow that?" I said sarcastically.

As I passed you in the living room, you glanced up. "Did Mom hear me?"

"Not by a long shot," I said, and I ran up the stairs.

What was wrong with me? I had a decent life. I was healthy. I wasn't starving or maimed by a land mine or orphaned. Yet somehow, it wasn't enough. I had a hole in me, and everything I took for granted slipped through it like sand.

I felt like I had swallowed yeast, like whatever evil was festering inside me had doubled in size. In the bathroom, I tried to throw up, but I hadn't eaten enough at dinner. I wanted to run barefoot till my feet bled; I wanted to scream, but I'd been silent for so long that I'd forgotten how.

I wanted to cut.

But.

I had promised.

I took the telephone handset off its cradle beside my mother's bed and carried it into the bathroom for privacy, since any minute now, you would hobble upstairs to get ready for bed. I had programmed Adam's number in. We hadn't spoken in a few days, because he'd broken his leg and had surgery — he'd IMed me from the hospital — but I was hoping he was home now. I *needed* him to be home now.

He had given me his cell number — I was surely the only kid over age thirteen who didn't have one, but we couldn't afford it. It rang twice, and then I heard his voice, and I nearly burst into tears. "Hey," he said, "I was just going to call you."

It was proof that there was someone in this world who thought I mattered. I felt like I'd just been pulled back from a cliff. "Great minds think alike."

"Yeah," he said, but his voice sounded thin and distant.

I tried to remember how he had tasted. I hated that I had to pretend I knew, when in reality, it had already faded, like a rose you press into a dictionary under the Qs, hoping you can call back summer at any time, but then in December it's nothing more than crumbling, brown bits of dried flower. Sometimes at night I'd whisper to myself, pretending that the words came out in the low, soft curve of Adam's voice: *I love you, Amelia. You're the one for me.* And then I'd open my lips the tiniest bit and pretend that he was a ghost, and that I could feel him sinking into me, onto my tongue, down my throat, into my belly, the only meal that could fill me.

"How's the leg?"

"Hurts like hell," Adam said.

I curled the phone closer. "I really miss you. It's crazy here. The trial started, and there were reporters all over the front lawn. My parents are certifiable, I swear —"

"Amelia." The word sounded like a ball being dropped from the Empire State Building. "I wanted to talk to you because, um, this isn't working out. This long-distance thing —"

I felt a pang between my ribs. "Don't."

"Don't what?"

"Don't say it," I whispered.

"I just . . . I mean, we might never even see each other again."

I felt a hook snag at the bottom of my heart, drawing it down. "I could come visit," I said, my voice small.

"Yeah, and then what? Push me around in a wheelchair? Like I'm some kind of charity case?"

"I would never —"

534

"Just go get yourself some football player — that's what girls like you want, right? Not some guy who bumps into a fucking table and snaps his leg in half —"

By now I was crying. "That doesn't matter —"

"Yes it does, Amelia. But you don't understand. You'll *never* understand. Having a sister who's got OI doesn't make you an expert."

My face was flaming. I hung up the phone before Adam could say anything else and held my palms to my cheeks. "But I love you," I said, although I knew he couldn't hear me.

First the tears came. Then the fury: I picked up the phone and hurled it against the bathtub wall. I grabbed the shower curtain and pulled it down in one good yank.

But I wasn't mad at Adam; I was angry at myself.

It was one thing to make a mistake; it was another thing to keep making it. I knew what happened when you let yourself get close to someone, when you started to believe they loved you: you'd be disappointed. Depend on someone, and you might as well admit you're going to be crushed, because when you really needed them, they wouldn't be there. Either that, or you'd confide in them and you added to their problems. All you ever really had was yourself, and that sort of sucked if you were less than reliable.

I told myself that if I didn't care, this wouldn't have hurt so much — surely that proved I was alive and human and all those touchyfeely things, for once and for all. But that wasn't a relief, not when I felt like a skyscraper with dynamite on every floor.

That's why I reached into the tub and turned on the water: so that I would drown out my sobs, so that when I grabbed the razor blade I'd hidden in the box of tampons and drew it over my skin like a violin's bow, no one would hear the song of my shame.

This past summer, my mother ran out of sugar and drove to the local convenience store mid-recipe, leaving us alone for twenty minutes — which is not that long a period of time, you'd think. But it was long enough to start a fight with you about which TV show we should watch; it was long enough to yell *There's a reason Mom wishes you were dead;* it was long enough to watch your face crumple and feel my conscience kick in.

"Wiki," I'd said, "I didn't really mean it."

"Just shut up, Amelia —"

"Stop being such a baby —"

"Well, you stop being such a dickhead!"

That word, on your lips — it was enough to stop me in my tracks. "Where did you hear *that*?"

"From you, you stupid jerk," you said.

Just then, a bird smacked into the window so loudly that we both jumped.

"What was that?" you asked, standing on the couch cushions to get a better look.

I climbed up next to you, careful, because I always had to be. The bird was little and brown, a swallow or a sparrow, I could never tell the difference. It was sprawled on the grass.

"Is it dead?" you asked.

"Well, how would I know that?"

"Don't you think we ought to check?"

So we went outside and trudged halfway around the house. Big surprise, the bird was still exactly where it had been moments before. I squatted down and tried to see if its chest was moving at all.

Nada.

"We need to bury it," you said soberly. "We can't just leave it out here."

"Why? Things die all the time in nature —"

"But this one was our fault. The bird probably heard us yelling and that's why it flew into the window."

I highly doubted that the bird heard us at all, but I wasn't going to argue with you.

"Where's the shovel?" you asked.

"I don't know." I thought for a moment. "Hang on," I said, and I ran into the house. I took the big metal mixing spoon Mom had in her bowl and carried it outside. There was still batter on it, but maybe that would be okay, like sending Egyptian mummies off to the afterlife with food and gold and their pets.

I dug a small hole in the ground about six inches away from where the bird was. I didn't want to touch it — that totally creeped me out — so I sort of flicked it into the hole with the edge of the spoon. "Now what?" I asked, looking up at you.

"Now we have to say a prayer," you said.

537

"Like a Hail Mary? What makes you think the bird was Catholic?"

"We could sing a Christmas carol," you suggested. "That's not really religious. It's just pretty."

"How about instead we say something nice about birds?"

You agreed to that. "They come in rainbow colors," you said.

"They fly well," I added. Until about ten minutes ago, anyway. "And they make nice music."

"And birds remind me of chicken and chicken tastes really great," you said.

"Okay, that's good enough." I shoveled the soil on top of the dead bird, and then you crouched down and made a pattern on the top with bits of grass, like sprinkles on a cake. We walked side by side into the house again.

"Amelia? You can watch whatever you want on TV."

I turned to you. "I don't wish you were dead," I admitted.

When we sat down on the couch again, you curled up against my side, like you used to when you were a toddler.

What I wanted to say to you, but didn't, was this: *Don't use me as your model. I'm the last person you should look up to.*

For weeks after we buried that dumb bird, every time it rained, I would not sit near that window. Even now, I wouldn't walk near that part of the yard. I was afraid that I'd hear something crunch and I'd look down and find the broken bones of the skeleton, the brittle wings, the chiseled beak. I was smart enough to look away, so that I'd never have to see what might surface.

People always want to know what it feels like, so I'll tell you: there's a sting when you first slice, and then your heart speeds up when you see the blood, because you know you've done something you shouldn't have, and yet you've gotten away with it. Then you sort of go into a trance, because it's truly dazzling — that bright red line, like a highway route on a map that you want to follow to see where it leads. And — God — the sweet release, that's the best way I can describe it, kind of like a balloon that's tied to a little kid's hand, which somehow breaks free and floats into the sky. You just know that balloon is thinking, *Ha, I don't belong to you after all*; and at the same time, *Do they have any idea how beautiful the view is from up here?* And then the balloon remembers, after the fact, that it has a wicked fear of heights.

When reality kicks in, you grab some toilet paper or a paper towel (better than a washcloth, because the stains don't ever come out 100 percent) and you press hard against the cut. You can feel your embarrassment; it's a backbeat underneath your pulse. Whatever relief there was a minute ago congeals, like cold gravy, into a fist in the pit of your stomach. You literally make yourself sick, because you promised yourself last time would be the last time, and once again, you've let yourself down. So you hide the evidence of your weakness under layers of clothes long enough to cover the cuts, even if it's summertime and no one is wearing jeans or long sleeves. You throw the bloody tissues into the toilet and watch the water go pink before you flush them into oblivion, and you wish it was really that easy.

I once saw a movie where a girl got her throat slashed, and instead of a scream, there was this low sigh — like it didn't hurt, like it was just a chance to finally let go. I knew that feeling was coming, so I waited a moment between my second and third cuts. I watched the blood welling on my thigh and I tried to hold off as long as I could before I drew the razor across the skin again.

"Amelia?"

Your voice. I looked up, panicked. "What are you doing in here?" I said, folding my legs up, so that you couldn't get a better glimpse of what you'd probably already seen. "Haven't you ever heard of privacy?"

You were teetering on your crutches. "I just wanted to get my toothbrush, and the door wasn't locked."

"Yes it was," I argued. But maybe I was wrong? I had been so focused on calling Adam, maybe I had forgotten. I fixed my meanest stare on you. "Get *out!*" I yelled.

You hobbled back to our room, leaving the door open. I quickly lowered my legs and pressed a wad of toilet paper against the cuts I'd made. Usually I waited until they stopped bleeding before I left the bathroom, but I just pulled up my jeans with that strategically placed padding and went into our bedroom. I stared at you, practically daring you to say something to me about what you'd seen, so that I could scream at you again, but you were sitting on the bed, reading. You didn't say anything to me at all.

I always hated when my scars started to fade, because as long as I could still see them, I knew why I was hurting. I wondered if you felt the same way, once your bones healed.

I lay back on my pillows. My thigh throbbed.

"Amelia?" you said. "Will you tuck me in?"

"Where's Mom and Dad?" You didn't really have to answer that — even if they were physically downstairs, they were so far removed from us that they might as well have been on the moon.

I could still remember the first night I hadn't needed my parents to tuck me in. I might have been about your age, in fact. Before that night, there had been a routine — lamps off, sheets cozied tight, kiss on the forehead — and monsters in the drawers of my desk and hiding behind books on the shelf. And then one day, I just put down the book I'd been reading and closed my eyes. Had my parents been proud of this newly self-sufficient kid? Or had they felt like they'd lost something they couldn't even name?

"Well, did you brush your teeth?" I asked, but then I remembered you had been trying to do just that when I was busy cutting. "Oh, forget your teeth. One night won't make a difference." I got out of bed and awkwardly leaned over yours. "Good night," I said, and then I bobbed down like a pelican, fishing, and pecked your forehead.

"Mom tells me a story."

"Then get Mom to tuck you in," I said, throwing myself back on my own mattress. "I don't have any stories."

You were quiet for a second. "We could make one up together."

"Whatever floats your boat," I sighed.

"Once upon a time there were two sisters. One of them was really, really strong, and one of them wasn't." You looked at me. "Your turn."

I rolled my eyes. "The strong sister went outside into the rain and realized the reason she was strong was because she was made out of iron, but it was raining and she rusted. The end."

"No, because the sister who wasn't strong went outside when it was raining, and hugged her really tight until the sun came out again."

When we were little, we'd sometimes sleep in the same bed. It never started out that way, but in the middle of the night I'd wake up and find you vined around me. You gravitated toward warmth; me, I liked to seek out the cold spots in my sheets. I'd spend hours trying to move away from you in the little twin bed, but I never even thought of moving you back into your own. Polar north can't get away from a magnet; the magnet finds it, no matter what.

"Then what happened?" I whispered, but you had already drifted off to sleep, and I was left to dream my own ending.

Sean

By unspoken arrangement, I slept on the couch that night. Except "sleep" was too optimistic an outcome. I basically tossed and turned. The one time I did nod off, I had a nightmare that I was on the witness stand and looked at Charlotte, and when I started to respond to Guy Booker's question, black gnats poured out of my mouth.

Whatever wall Charlotte and I had broken down last night had been reconstructed twice as high and twice as thick. It was a strange thing, to still be in love with your wife and to not know if you liked her. What would happen when this was all over? Could you forgive someone if she hurt you and the people you love, if she truly believed she was only trying to help?

I had filed for divorce, but that wasn't what I really wanted. What I really wanted was for all of us to go back two years, and start over.

Had I ever really told her that?

I threw off the blanket and sat up, rubbing my hands down my face. Wearing just my boxers and a police department tee, I padded upstairs and slipped into our bedroom. I sat down on the bed. "Charlotte," I whispered, but there was no response.

I touched the bundle of quilts, only to realize it was a pillow trapped under the sheets. "Charlotte?" I said out loud. The bathroom door was wide open; I turned on the light, but she wasn't inside. Starting to worry — Was she just as upset as I was about the trial? Had she been sleepwalking? — I walked down the hallway, checking your bathroom, the guest room, the narrow staircase that led to the attic.

The last door was your room. I stepped inside and immediately saw her. Charlotte was curled on your bed, her arm wrapped tight around you. Even in her sleep, she wasn't willing to let you go.

I touched your hair, and then your mother's. I brushed Amelia's cheek. And then I lay down on the throw rug on the floor and pillowed my head on my arm. Go figure: with all of us together again, I fell asleep in a matter of minutes.

Marin

"Do you know what this is about?" I asked, as I hurried along the courthouse hallway beside Guy Booker.

"Your guess is as good as mine," he said.

We had been called to chambers before the start of the second day of the trial. Being called to chambers, this early on, was not usually a good thing — particularly not if it was something Guy Booker didn't know about, either. Whatever pressing issue Judge Gellar had to address most likely was not one I wanted to hear.

We were led in to find the judge sitting at his desk, his too-black hair a helmet. It reminded me of those old Superman action figures — you just knew that Superman's coif never blew around in the wind when he flew, some marvel of physics and styling gel — and it was distracting enough for me not even to notice the second person in the room, who was sitting with her back to us.

"Counselors," Judge Gellar said. "You both know Juliet Cooper, juror number six."

The woman turned around. She was the one who — during voir dire — had been the target of Guy's intrusive questions about abortion. Maybe the defense attorney's hammering of Charlotte yesterday about the same issue had triggered a complaint. I stood up a little straighter, convinced that the reason the judge had convened us had little to do with me and much to do with Guy Booker's questionable practice of the law.

"Ms. Cooper will be excused from the jury. Beginning immediately, the alternate juror will be rotated into the pool."

No lawyer likes to have the jury change in the middle of a trial, but neither do judges. If this woman was being excused, it must have been for a very good reason.

She was looking at Guy Booker, and very deliberately *not* looking at me. "I'm sorry," she murmured. "I didn't know I had a conflict of interest."

Conflict of interest? I had assumed it was a health issue, some emergency that required her to fly to the bedside of a dying relative or go immediately for chemo. A conflict of interest meant that she knew something about my client or Guy's — but surely she would have realized this during jury selection.

Apparently, Guy Booker felt the same way. "Is it possible to hear what the conflict is, exactly?"

"Ms. Cooper is related to one of the parties in this case," Judge Gellar said, and he met my gaze. "You, Ms. Gates."

I used to imagine that I saw my birth mother everywhere and just didn't know it. I'd smile an extra moment longer at the lady who handed me my ticket at the movie theater; I'd make conversation about the weather with my bank teller. I'd hear the cultured voice of a receptionist at a rival firm and imagine that it was her; I'd bump into a lady in a cashmere coat in the lobby downstairs and stare at her face as I apologized. There were any number of people I could cross paths with who might be my mother; I could run into her dozens of times each day without ever knowing.

And now she was sitting across from me, in Judge Gellar's chambers.

He and Guy Booker had left us alone for a few minutes. And to my surprise, even with almost thirty-six years' worth of questions, the dam didn't break down easily. I found myself staring at her hair — which was a frizzy red. All my life. I'd looked different from the other people in my family, and I had always assumed that I was a carbon copy of my birth mother. But I didn't resemble her, not at all.

She was holding on to her purse with a death grip. "A month ago I got a phone call from the courthouse," Juliet Cooper said. "Saying that they had some information for me. I thought something like this might happen one day."

"So," I said, but my voice was wheezy, dry. "How long have you known?"

"Only since yesterday. The clerk mailed me your card a week ago, but I couldn't make myself open it. I wasn't ready." She looked up at me. Her eyes were brown. Did that mean my father's had been blue, like mine? "It was what happened in court yesterday — all those questions about the mother wanting to get rid of her baby — that made me finally get up the nerve to do it."

I felt as if I'd been pumped full of helium: surely, then, this meant that she hadn't *really* wanted to give me up, just like Charlotte hadn't *really* wanted to give up Willow.

"When I got to the end of the card, I saw your name, and realized I knew it already, from the trial." She hesitated. "It's a pretty unique name."

"Yes." *What had you wanted to call me instead? Suzy, Margaret, Theresa?*

"You're very good," Juliet Cooper said, shyly. "In court, I mean."

There was three feet of space between us. Why wasn't either of us crossing it? I had imagined this moment so many times, and it always ended with my mother holding me tight, as if she needed to make up for ever having let me go.

"Thank you," I said. Here's what I hadn't realized: the mother you haven't seen for almost thirty-six years isn't your mother, she's a stranger. Sharing DNA does not make you fast friends. This wasn't a joyous reunion. It was just awkward.

Well, maybe she was as uncomfortable as I was; maybe she was afraid to overstep her bounds or assumed I held a grudge against her for giving me up in the first place. It was my job, then, to break the ice, wasn't it? "I can't believe that I spent all this time looking for you and you turned up on my jury," I said, smiling. "It's a small world."

"Very," she agreed, and went dead silent again.

548

"I knew I liked you during voir dire," I said, trying to make a joke, but it fell flat. And then I remembered something else Juliet Cooper had said during jury selection: She used to be a stay-at-home mother. She'd only gone back to work when her children went to high school. "You have kids. Other kids."

She nodded. "Two girls."

For an only child, that was remarkable: Not only had I found my birth mother but I had gained siblings. "I have sisters," I said out loud.

At that, something shuttered in Juliet Cooper's eyes. "They are not your sisters."

"I'm sorry. I didn't mean —"

"I was going to write you a letter. I was going to send it to the Hillsborough court and ask them to forward it to you," she said. "Listening to Charlotte O'Keefe brought it all back for me: there are just some babies who are better off not being born." Juliet stood up abruptly. "I was going to write you a letter," she repeated, "and ask you not to contact me again."

And just like that, my birth mother abandoned me for the second time in my life.

When you're adopted, you may have the happiest life in the world, but there's always a part of you that wonders if you'd been cuter, quieter, an easy delivery — well, maybe then your birth mom wouldn't have given you up. It's silly, of course — the decision to give a child up for adoption is made months in advance — but that doesn't keep you from thinking it all the same.

I had gotten straight As in college. I'd graduated at the top of my law school class. I did this, of course, to make my family proud of me — but I didn't specify which family I was talking about. My adoptive parents, sure. But also my birth parents. I think there was always a hidden belief that if my birth mother stumbled across me and saw how smart I was, how successful, she couldn't help but love me.

When in fact, she couldn't help but leave me.

The door of the conference room opened, and Charlotte slipped inside. "There was a reporter in the ladies' room. She came after me with a microphone while I was going into a — Marin? Have you been crying?"

I shook my head, although it was clear that I was. "Something in my eye."

"*Both* of them?"

I stood up. "Let's go," I said brusquely, and I left her to follow in my wake.

Dr Mark Rosenblad, who treated you at Children's Hospital in Boston, was my next witness. I decided to shake myself off autopilot and give the performance of a lifetime for the juror who'd taken Juliet Cooper's place, who happened to be a fortyish man with thick glasses and an overbite. He smiled at me as I directed all my questions about Rosenblad's qualifications in his general direction.

With my luck, I'd lose the trial and have this guy ask me out on a date.

"You're familiar with Willow, Dr Rosenblad?" I said.

"I've treated her since she was six months old. She's a great kid."

"What type of OI does she have?"

"Type III — or progressively deforming OI."

"What does that mean?"

"It's the most severe form of OI that isn't lethal. Children who have Type III will have hundreds of broken bones over the course of a lifetime — not just from contact but sometimes caused by rolling over in their sleep or reaching for something on a shelf. They often develop severe respiratory infections and complications because of the barrel shape of their rib cages. Often Type III kids have hearing loss or loose joints and poor muscle development. They'll get severe scoliosis that requires spinal rodding or even having the vertebrae fused together — although that's a tricky decision, because from that moment on, the child won't grow any taller, and these kids have short stature to begin with. Other complications can include macrocephaly — fluid on the brain — cerebral hemorrhage caused by birth trauma, brittle teeth, and for some Type IIIs, basilar invagination — the second vertebra moves upward and cuts off the opening in the skull where the spinal cord passes through to the brain, causing dizziness, headache, periods of confusion, numbness, or even death."

"Can you tell us what the next ten years will be like for Willow?" I asked.

"Like many kids her age with Type III OI, she's been on pamidronate since she was a baby. It's improved the quality of her life significantly — prior to bisphosphonates,

Type III kids would rarely walk and would have been wheelchair-bound. Instead of having several hundred breaks in her life, thanks to the pamidronate, she may have only a hundred — we're not sure. Some of the research that's coming back now through teenagers who began getting infusions as babies, like Willow, shows that the bones — when they *do* break — aren't breaking along normal fracture patterns, and that makes them more difficult to treat. The bone's getting denser because of the infusions, but it's still imperfect bone. There's also some evidence of jawbone abnormalities, but it's unclear whether that's related to the pamidronate or just part of the dentinogenesis that goes with OI. So some of these complications might occur," Dr Rosenblad said. "In addition, she'll still have breaks, and surgeries to repair them. She was recently rodded in one thigh; I imagine the other will follow suit. Eventually she'll have spinal surgery. She's had pneumonia annually. Virtually all Type IIIs develop some sort of chest wall abnormalities, vertical collapse, and kyphoscoliosis, all of which lead to lung disease and cardiopulmonary distress. A number of individuals with Type III die due to respiratory or neurological complications, but with any luck, Willow will be one of our success stories — and will go into adulthood and live a fully functional and important life."

For a moment, I just stared at Dr Rosenblad. Having met you, and talked to you, and even seen you struggling to wheel yourself up an incline or reach for something on a counter that was too tall, I found it hard to conceive that all these medical nightmares awaited you. It was, of course, the hook Bob Ramirez and I had planned to hang this lawsuit on from the get-go, but even *I* had come to take your life for granted.

"If Willow does survive into adulthood, will she be able to take care of herself?"

I couldn't look at Charlotte while I asked this; I didn't think I could stand to see her face at the use of *if* instead of *when*.

"She's going to need someone to take care of her, to some extent, no matter how independent she becomes. There are always going to be breaks and hospitalizations and physical therapy. Holding down a job will be difficult."

"Beyond the physical challenges," I asked, "will there be emotional challenges as well?"

"Yes," Dr Rosenblad said. "Kids with OI often have anxiety issues, because of the worry and avoidance behavior they exhibit to keep from suffering a break. They sometimes develop post-traumatic stress disorder after particularly severe fractures. In addition, Willow's already started to notice she's different from other kids and limited because of her OI. As kids with OI grow up, they want to be independent — but they can't be as functionally independent as able-bodied teens. The struggle can cause kids with OI to become introverted, depressed, perhaps even suicidal."

When I turned around, I saw Charlotte. Her face was buried in her hands.

Maybe a mother wasn't what she seemed to be on the surface. Maybe Charlotte had sued Piper Reece because she loved Willow too much to let her go. Maybe my birth mother let me go because she knew she couldn't love me.

"In the six years you've treated Willow, have you gotten to know Charlotte O'Keefe?"

"Yes," the doctor replied. "Charlotte's incredibly attuned to her daughter. She's almost got a sixth sense when it comes to Willow's level of discomfort, and for making sure steps are taken before it gets out of hand." He glanced at the jury. "Remember Shirley MacLaine in *Terms of Endearment?* That's Charlotte. Sometimes she's so stubborn I want to sock her — but that's because I'm the one she's standing up to."

I sat back down, opening the questioning to Guy Booker. "You've been treating this child since she was six months old, correct?"

"Yes. I was working at Shriners in Omaha at the time, and Willow was part of our pamidronate trials there. When I moved to Children's in Boston, it made more sense to treat her closer to home."

"Now how often do you see her, Dr Rosenblad?"

"Twice a year, unless there's a break in between. And let's just say I've never seen Willow only twice a year."

"How long have you been using pamidronate to treat children with OI?"

"Since the early nineties."

"And you said that, prior to the advent of pamidronate for OI, these children had a much more limited life in terms of mobility, correct?"

"Absolutely."

"So would you say that the medical technology in your field has increased Willow's health potential?"

"Dramatically," Dr Rosenblad said. "She's able to do things now that kids with OI couldn't do fifteen years ago."

"So if this trial were taking place fifteen years ago, the picture you'd be painting for us of Willow's life might be even more grim, wouldn't you agree?"

Dr Rosenblad nodded. "That's correct."

"Given that we live in America, where medical research is blooming in laboratories and hospitals like yours on a daily basis, isn't it likely that Willow might see even more medical advances in her lifetime?"

"Objection," I said. "Speculative."

"He's an expert in his field, Judge," Booker countered.

"He can give his opinion," Judge Gellar said, "based on his knowledge as to what medical research is currently being done."

"It's possible," Dr Rosenblad replied. "But like I also pointed out, the wonder drugs that we thought bisphosphonates were might, over the long term, reveal some other problems we hadn't counted on for OI patients. We just don't know yet."

"Conceivably, however, Willow could grow to adulthood?" Booker asked.

"Absolutely."

"Could she fall in love?"

"Of course."

"Could she have a baby?"

"Possibly."

"Could she work outside the home?"

"Yes."

"Could she live independently of her parents?"

"Maybe," Dr Rosenblad said.

Guy Booker spread his hands across the railing of the jury box. "Doctor, you treat illness, don't you?"

"Sure."

"Would you ever treat a broken finger by amputating the arm?"

"That would be a bit extreme."

"Isn't it extreme to treat OI then by preventing the patient from being born?"

"Objection," I called out.

"Sustained." The judge glared at Guy Booker. "I won't have my courtroom turned into a pro-life rally, Counselor."

"I'll rephrase. Have you ever encountered a parent whose child is diagnosed with OI in utero who chooses to terminate the pregnancy?"

Rosenblad nodded. "Yes, often in cases where you're talking about the lethal form of OI, Type II."

"What about the severe form?"

"Objection," I said. "What does this have to do with the plaintiff?"

"I want to hear this," Judge Gellar said. "You may answer the question, Doctor."

Rosenblad stepped through the minefield of his response. "Terminating a wanted pregnancy is no one's first choice," he said, "but when faced with a fetus who will become a severely disabled child, different families have different levels of tolerance. Some families know they'll be able to provide enough support for a child with disabilities, some are smart enough to know, in advance, they won't."

"Doctor," Booker said, "would you call Willow O'Keefe's birth a wrongful one?"

I felt something at my side and realized that Charlotte was trembling.

"I am not in a position to make that decision," Rosenblad said. "I'm just the physician."

"My point exactly," Booker answered.

Piper

I had not seen my ultrasound technician Janine Weissbach since she left my practice four years ago and went to work at a hospital in Chicago. Her hair, which had been blond, was now a sleek chestnut, and there were fine lines bracketing her mouth. I wondered if I looked the same to her, or if betrayal had aged me beyond recognition.

Janine had been allergic to nuts, and once there had been a minor war between her and a nurse on staff who'd brewed hazelnut coffee. Janine broke out in hives just from the smell that permeated our little lounge; the nurse swore she didn't realize that liquefied nuts counted when it came to allergy; Janine asked how she'd ever passed her nursing exam. In fact, the brouhaha had been the biggest upset in my practice . . . until, of course, this.

"How is it that you came to know the plaintiff in this case?" Charlotte's lawyer asked.

Janine leaned closer to the microphone on the witness stand. She used to sing karaoke, I remembered, at a local nightclub. She had referred to herself as pathologically single. Now, though, she wore a wedding band.

558

People changed. Even the people you thought you knew as well as you knew yourself.

"She was a patient at the office where I was working," Janine said. "Piper Reece's ob-gyn practice."

"You're employed by the defendant?"

"I was for three years, but now I work at Northwestern Memorial Hospital."

The lawyer was staring off at a wall, as if she wasn't even listening. "Ms. Gates," the judge prompted.

"Sorry," she said, snapping to attention. "You're employed by the defendant?"

"You just asked me that."

"Right. Um, can you tell us the circumstances under which you met Charlotte O'Keefe?"

"She came in for an eighteen-week ultrasound."

"Who else was there?"

"Her husband," Janine said.

"Was the defendant there?"

For the first time, Janine met my eye. "Not at first. The way we did it, I'd perform the ultrasound and discuss it with her; and she'd read the results and talk to the patient."

"What happened during Charlotte O'Keefe's ultrasound, Ms. Weissbach?"

"Piper had told me to be on the lookout for anything that might signify Down syndrome. The patient's quad screen had shown a slightly elevated risk. I was excited to be working with a new machine — it had only just arrived, and was state of the art. I got Mrs O'Keefe settled on the table, put some gel onto her abdomen,

559

and then moved the transducer around to get several clear views of the fetus."

"What did you see?" the lawyer asked.

"The femurs were measuring on the small side, which can sometimes be a flag for Down syndrome, but none of the other indicators were present."

"Anything else?"

"Yes," Janine said. "Some of the images were incredibly clear. Particularly the one of the fetal brain."

"Did you mention these findings to the defendant?"

"Yes. She said that the femur wasn't off the charts, that it could simply be because the mother was short," Janine answered.

"What about the clarity of the images? Did the defendant have anything to say about that?"

"No," Janine said. "She didn't."

The night I'd driven Charlotte home from her twenty-seven-week ultrasound, the one with all the broken bones visible, I'd stopped being her friend and started being a doctor. I sat at the kitchen table and used medical terminology, which almost acted like a sedative itself: the pain in Charlotte's and Sean's eyes dulled as I heaped them with information they could not understand. I talked to them about the physician I'd already called for a consultation.

At one point, Amelia had flitted into the kitchen. Charlotte hastily wiped her eyes. "Hey, sweetie," she said.

"I came to say good night to the baby," Amelia said, and she ran up to Charlotte where she sat and wrapped her arms as best as she could around her mother's belly.

Charlotte made a tiny sound, a mewling. "Not so tight," she managed, and I knew what she was thinking: had this eager love broken some of your bones?

"But I want her to come out," Amelia said. "I'm sick of waiting."

Charlotte stood up. "I think I might go lie down, too." She held out her hand for Amelia, and they walked out of the kitchen.

Sean sank into the seat she'd vacated. "It's me, right?" He looked up at me, haunted. "I'm the reason the baby's like this."

"No —"

"Charlotte had one kid who was perfectly fine," he said. "Do the math."

"This is probably a spontaneous mutation. There's nothing you could have done to prevent it." I couldn't have prevented it, either. But that didn't keep me from feeling guilty, just like Sean. "You have to take care of her, because she can't fall apart right now. Don't let her look this up on the Internet before you see the doctor tomorrow; don't tell her you're worried."

"I can't lie," Sean said.

"Well, you will, if you love her."

Now, all these years later, I wondered why I could not forgive Charlotte for following this very same advice.

I didn't like Guy Booker, but then again, when you choose malpractice insurance providers, you're not going for the folks you want to have over for Christmas dinner. He was good at making someone squirm on the witness stand, like an insect being pinned by a collector who wanted to scrutinize it more closely. "Ms. Weissbach," Booker said, standing up to do his cross-examination, "have you ever seen another fetus that had a similar finding in the measurement of the femur?"

"Of course."

"Do you happen to know the outcome?"

Charlotte's lawyer stood up. "Objection, Your Honor. The witness is just a technologist, not a physician."

"She sees this every day," Booker countered. "She's specially trained to read sonograms."

"Sustained."

"Well," Janine said, miffed. "For your information, it's not so easy to read the results of an ultrasound. I may just be a technologist, but I'm also supposed to point out things that might be problematic." She jerked her chin toward me. "Piper Reece was my boss. I was just doing my job."

She did not say anything more, but I could hear it all the same: *Unlike you.*

Charlotte

Something was wrong with my lawyer. She was fidgeting; she kept missing questions and forgetting answers. It got me wondering: Was doubt contagious? Had Marin sat next to me all day while I fought the urge to stand up and put an end to all this, and then awakened this morning with the same gut instincts?

She had called in a witness I did not know — Dr Thurber, who was British but had become the head of radiology at Lucile Packard Children's Hospital at Stanford before moving to Shriners in Omaha and applying his knowledge as a radiologist to OI kids. According to the endless list of credentials Marin had led him through, Dr Thurber had read thousands of ultrasounds during his career, had lectured throughout the world, and donated two weeks of his vacation every year to provide care to expectant mothers in impoverished countries.

Basically, he was a saint. A really smart one.

"Dr Thurber," Marin said, "for those of us who aren't familiar with ultrasounds, can you explain the technology?"

"It's a diagnostic tool, in terms of obstetrics," the radiologist said. "The equipment is a real-time scanner. Sound waves get emitted from a transducer, which is placed against the mother's abdomen and moved around to reflect the contents of the uterus. The image gets projected onto a monitor — a sonogram."

"What are ultrasounds used for?"

"To diagnose and confirm pregnancy, to assess fetal heartbeat and fetal malformations, to measure the fetus in order to assess the gestational age and growth, to see the location of the placenta, to determine the amount of amniotic fluid — among other things."

"When are ultrasounds traditionally performed during pregnancy?" Marin asked.

"There's no hard-and-fast rule, but sometimes scans can be done at about seven weeks to confirm pregnancy and rule out ectopic or molar pregnancies. Most women have at least one ultrasound performed between eighteen and twenty weeks."

"What happens during that ultrasound?"

"By then, the fetus is large enough to check out the anatomy and to look for congenital malformations," Dr Thurber said. "Certain bones will be measured, to make sure the baby is the right size based on the date of conception. They'll make sure organs are in the right place, and that the spine's intact. Basically, it's a confirmation that everything's where it's supposed to be. And of course, you get to go home with a picture that stays taped to your fridge for the next six months."

There were a few laughs on the jury. Had I had a picture of you, from your ultrasound? I couldn't remember. When I think back to that day, I only feel this great tidal wash of relief, from the moment Piper told me you were healthy.

"Dr Thurber," Marin asked, "did you have an opportunity to review the eighteen-week ultrasound that was performed on Charlotte O'Keefe?"

"I did."

"And what did you see?"

He glanced at the jury. "Based on the ultrasound, there was definite cause for concern. Normally when you do an ultrasound, you're looking at the brain through the skull, so it's usually a little fuzzy, a little bit muddy and gray, because of reverberation artifacts from the side of the skull that the ultrasound beam first hits. In Mrs O'Keefe's sonogram, however, the intracranial contents were crystal clear — even that near field of the cerebral hemisphere, which is normally obscured. This suggests a demineralized calvarium. There are several conditions in which the skull presents undermineralized, including skeletal dysplasia, and OI. One then has the obligation to look at the long bones, and in fact femur length is a part of every obstetric ultrasound. In Mrs O'Keefe's case, the femur was also measuring a bit short. The combination of the short femur and the demineralized skull is strongly suggestive of osteogenesis imperfecta." He let the words hang in the courtroom. "In fact, had the technologist pushed down on Mrs O'Keefe's belly as she was doing the ultrasound, she would have been able to watch the screen and see the skull of the fetus being squashed out of shape."

I folded my hands over my stomach, as if you were still inside.

"If Mrs O'Keefe had been your patient, Doctor, what would you have done?"

"I would have taken more images of the chest — looking for rib fractures. I would have measured all the other long bones to confirm that this was a generalized short-bone condition. And at the very least I'd have referred the case to a center with more experience."

Marin nodded. "What if I told you that Mrs O'Keefe's obstetrician did none of those things?"

"Then," Dr Thurber said, "I'd say that physician made a very big mistake."

"Nothing further," Marin said, and she slipped into the seat beside me. She immediately let out a heavy sigh.

"What's the matter?" I whispered. "He's very good."

"Did it ever occur to you that you're not the only one with problems?" Marin snapped.

Guy Booker got up to cross-examine the radiologist. "They say hindsight is twenty-twenty, don't they, Dr Thurber?"

"So I've heard."

"How long have you testified as an expert witness?"

"For ten years," the doctor said.

"I'm guessing you don't do this for free?"

"No, I'm paid, like all expert witnesses," Thurber replied.

Booker looked at the jury. "Right. There sure seems to be a lot of money flying around these days, isn't there?"

"Objection," Marin said. "Does he really expect the witness to answer his rhetorical questions?"

"Withdrawn. Doctor, isn't it true that osteogenesis imperfecta is very rare?"

"Yes."

"So a small-town OB, for example, might go through her entire professional life without ever seeing a case?"

"That's true," Thurber answered.

"Isn't it fair to say that only a specialist would have been looking for OI on an ultrasound?"

"There *is* the old medical saying about hearing hoofbeats and assuming it's a horse instead of a zebra," Thurber agreed, "but any trained obstetrician should be able to look at an ultrasound and spot red flags. She might not be able to identify what they signify, but she would know them for their abnormality, and would recognize that the patient's care needs to be taken to the next level."

"Is there any condition other than osteogenesis imperfecta that can give you such a clear image of the near field of the brain during an ultrasound?"

"The lethal form of congenital hypophosphatasia, but it's extremely rare and it still wouldn't have changed the need for the patient to be referred to a tertiary-care center."

"Dr Thurber," Booker said, "do you ever get a particularly clear image of intracranial contents of the skull . . . on a *healthy* baby?"

"Occasionally. If the plane of the ultrasound on a particular image happens by chance to go through one of the normal cranial sutures, instead of bone, the interior of the brain will be shown clearly. However, we take multiple pictures of the brain looking at different intracranial structures, and the sutures are very thin. It would be virtually impossible to see multiple pictures of the brain for multiple projections where the transducer manages to hit a suture every single time. If I saw one image that showed the near field of brain very clearly but the other images did not, I would assume that single image had been taken through a cranial suture. In this case, however, *all* of the images of the brain show the intracranial contents unusually well."

"How about that femur length? Have you ever measured a short femur during an eighteen-week ultrasound and then seen a perfectly healthy baby delivered?"

"Yes. Sometimes the technologists' measurement can be off by a hair because the fetus is moving around or in an odd position. They measure two or three times and take the longest axis, but even being a whisker off at eighteen weeks — we're talking millimeters — can drop the percentile significantly. Many times when we see a borderline-short femur length, it's just undermeasured."

Booker walked toward him. "As useful as ultrasound technology is, it's not an exact science, is it? Certain images might be clearer than others?"

"The clarity with which we see all structures in the fetus is variable, yes. It depends on many things — the size of the mother, the position of the fetus. There's a continuum, really. On any given day we might not be able to see them well, or conversely we might be able to see everything clearly."

"At an eighteen-week ultrasound, Doctor, can you definitively say that a child is going to have Type III OI?"

"You can tell that there's something wrong skeletally. You can see indicators — like the ones that were in Charlotte O'Keefe's file. As the gestational age increases, if you see broken bones, you can generally guess that the fetus has Type III OI."

"Doctor, if Charlotte O'Keefe had been your patient, and you'd seen the results of her eighteen-week ultrasound, and there were no broken bones, you would have recommended she have follow-up care?"

"Based on the short femur length and demineralized calvarium? Absolutely."

"And once you saw broken bones on a subsequent ultrasound, would you have done what Piper Reece did: immediately refer Mrs O'Keefe to a maternal-fetal-medicine practitioner at a tertiary-care center?"

"Yes."

"But would you have conclusively diagnosed Mrs O'Keefe's fetus with OI *at* eighteen weeks, based solely on that first ultrasound?"

He hesitated. "Well," Thurber said. "No."

Amelia

Sometimes I wonder what really constitutes an "emergency." I mean, every teacher in my school knew about the trial and the fact that both of my parents were not only in it but squaring off against each other. The whole state knew, and maybe even the whole country, thanks to the newspaper and television coverage. Surely even if they thought my mother was insane or moneygrubbing, they felt a smidgen of sympathy for me, being trapped in the middle? And yet, I still got yelled at in math for not paying attention. I had a huge English test tomorrow, vocabulary, on ninety words that I was most likely never going to use in my life.

To that end, I was making flash cards for myself. *Hypersensitive*, I wrote. *Too too too sensitive.* But wasn't that the point? If you were sensitive, weren't you bound to take things too seriously in the first place?

Trepidation: fear. Use it in a sentence: *I have trepidations about taking this stupid test.*

"Amelia!"

I heard you calling, but I also knew I didn't have to answer. After all, my mother — or maybe Marin — was paying that nurse who smelled like mothballs to watch over you. This was the second day she'd been here when I got off the bus, and to tell you the truth, I wasn't impressed. She was watching *General Hospital* when she should have been playing with you.

"Amelia!" you yelled, louder this time.

I screeched the chair back from my desk and thundered downstairs. "*What?*" I demanded. "I'm trying to study."

Then I saw it: Nurse Ratched had barfed all over the floor.

She was leaning against the wall, her face the color of Silly Putty. "I think I ought to go home . . ." she wheezed.

Well, duh. I didn't want to catch the bubonic plague.

"Do you think you can watch Willow till your mother gets back?" she asked.

As if I hadn't been doing just that my whole life. "Sure." I hesitated. "You are going to clean it up, first, right?"

"Amelia!" Willow hissed. "She's *sick*!"

"Well, I'm not going to do it," I whispered, but the nurse was already heading to the kitchen to mop up her mess.

"I still have to study," I said, after we were left alone. "Let me go up and get my notebook and flash cards."

"No, I'll go upstairs instead," you answered. "I kind of want to lie down."

So I carried you — you were that light — and settled you on the bed with your crutches next to you. You picked up your latest book to start reading.

Scrutinize: to observe carefully.

Stature: the full height of a human.

I glanced at you over my shoulder. You were the size of a three-year-old, even though you were six and a half now. I wondered how small you'd stay. I thought about how there are kinds of goldfish that get bigger when you put them in large ponds and wondered if that would help: what if, instead of sitting in this bed, in this stupid house, I showed you the whole wide world?

"I could quiz you," you said.

"Thanks, but I'm not ready yet. Maybe later."

"Did you know Kermit the Frog is left-handed?" you asked.

"No."

Dissipated: dissolved, faded away.

Elude: to escape from. I wish.

"Do you know how big a grave is when it's dug?"

"Willow," I said, "I'm trying to study here. Could you just shut up?"

"Seven feet, eight inches, by three feet, two inches, by six feet," you whispered.

"Willow!"

You sat up. "I'm going to the bathroom."

"Great. Don't get lost," I snapped. I watched you carefully lever your crutches so that you could hop your way off the bed. Usually Mom walked you to the bathroom — or, really, *hovered* — and then privacy kicked in and you booted her out and closed the door. "Do you need a hand?" I asked.

"Nope, just some collagen," you said, and I almost cracked a smile.

572

A moment later, I heard the bathroom door lock. *Scrupulous, devout, annihilate. Lethargic, lethal, subside.* The world would be a much easier place if, instead of handing over superstuffed syllables all the time, we just said what we really meant. Words got in the way. The things we felt the hardest — like what it was like to have a boy touch you as if you were made of light, or what it meant to be the only person in the room who wasn't noticed — weren't sentences; they were knots in the wood of our bodies, places where our blood flowed backward. If you asked me, not that anyone ever did, the only words worth saying were *I'm sorry.*

I made it through Lesson 13 and Lesson 14 — *devious, aghast, rustic* — and glanced down at my watch. It was only three o'clock. "Wiki," I said, "what time did Mom say she'd be home —" And then I remembered you weren't there.

You hadn't been, for a good fifteen or twenty minutes.

No one had to go to the bathroom that long.

My pulse started racing. Had I been so engrossed in learning the definition of *arbitration* that I hadn't heard a telltale fall? I ran to the bathroom door and rattled the knob. "Willow? Are you okay?"

There was no answer.

Sometimes I wonder what really constitutes an emergency.

I lifted up my leg and used my foot to break down the door.

Sean

The soup that came out of the vending machine at the courthouse looked — and tasted — just like the coffee. It was my third cup today, and I still wasn't quite sure what I was drinking.

I was sitting near the window of my hiding place — my biggest accomplishment on this, the second day of the trial. I had planned to sit in the lobby until Guy Booker needed me — but I hadn't counted on the press. The ones who hadn't squeezed into the courtroom figured out who I was quickly enough and swarmed, leaving me to back away muttering *No comment*.

I'd poked through the maze of the courthouse corridors, trying doorknobs until I found one that opened. I had no idea what this room was used for normally, but it was located almost directly above the courtroom where Charlotte was right now.

I didn't really believe in ESP or any of that crap, but I hoped she could feel me up here. Even more, I hoped that was a good thing.

Here was my secret: in spite of the fact that I had defected to the other side, in spite of the fact that my marriage had crashed on the rocks, there was a part of me that wondered what would happen if Charlotte won.

With enough money, we could send you to a camp this summer, so that you could meet other kids like you.

With enough money, we could buy a new van, instead of repairing the one that was seven years old with spit and glue.

With enough money, we could pay off our credit card debt and the second mortgage we'd taken out after the health insurance bills escalated.

With enough money, I could take Charlotte away for a night and fall in love with her again.

I truly believed that the cost of success for us shouldn't be the cost of failure for a good friend. But what if we hadn't known Piper personally, only professionally? Would I have endorsed a case like that against a different doctor? Was it Piper's involvement I objected to — or the whole lawsuit?

There were so many things we hadn't been told:

How it feels when a rib breaks, when I'm doing nothing more than cradling you.

How much it hurts to see the look on your face when you watch your older sister skating.

How even the people in a position to help have to cause pain first: the doctors who reset your bones, the folks who mold your leg braces by letting you play in them and get blisters, so that they know what to fix.

How your bones were not the only things that would break. There would be hairline cracks we would not see for years in my finances, my future, my marriage.

Suddenly I wanted to hear your voice. I took out my cell phone and started to dial, only to hear a loud beep as the battery died. I stared down at the receiver. I could go out to the car and get the charger, but that would mean running the gauntlet again. While I was weighing the costs and the benefits, the door to my sanctuary opened, and a slice of noise from the hallway slipped inside, followed by Piper Reece.

"You'll have to find your own hiding place," I said, and she jumped.

"You scared me to death," Piper said. "How did you know that's what I was doing?"

"Because it's why *I'm* here. Shouldn't you be in court?"

"We took a recess."

I hesitated, then figured I had nothing to lose. "How's it going in there?"

Piper opened her mouth, as if she were going to reply, and then shut it. "I'll let you get back to your phone call," she murmured, her hand on the doorknob.

"It's dead," I said, and she turned around. "My phone."

She folded her arms. "Remember when there were no cell phones? When we didn't have to listen to everyone's conversations?"

"Some things are better left private," I said.

Piper met my gaze. "It's awful in there," she admitted. "The last witness was an actuary who gave estimates on the out-of-pocket cost for Willow's care, and the grand total, based on her life expectancy."

"What did he say?"

"Thirty thousand annually."

"No," I said. "I meant, how long will she live?"

Piper hesitated. "I don't like thinking of Willow in terms of numbers. Like she's already a statistic."

"Piper."

"There's no reason she won't have a normal life expectancy," Piper said.

"But not a normal life," I finished.

Piper leaned against the wall. I had not turned the lights on — I didn't want anyone to know I was in here, after all — and in the shadows her face looked lined and tired. "Last night I dreamed about the first time we had you over for dinner — to meet Charlotte."

I could recall that night like it was yesterday. I had gotten lost on the way to Piper's house because I was so nervous. For obvious reasons, I'd never before been invited to someone's house after giving her a speeding ticket; and I wouldn't have gone at all, but the day before pulling Piper's car over for doing fifty in a thirty-mile-an-hour zone, I'd gone to the house of my best friend — another cop — and found my girlfriend in his bed. I had nothing to lose when Piper called the department a week later and asked; it was impulsive and stupid and desperate.

When I got to Piper's, and was introduced to Charlotte, she'd held out her hand for me to shake and a spark had caught between our palms, shocking us both. The two little girls had eaten in the living room while the adults sat at the table; Piper had just served me a slice of caramel-pecan torte that Charlotte had made. "What do you think?" Charlotte had asked.

The filling was still warm and sweet; crust dissolved on my tongue like a memory. "I think we should get married," I said, and everyone laughed, but I was not entirely kidding.

We had been talking about our first kisses. Piper told a story about a boy who'd enticed her into the woods behind the jungle gym on the pretext that there was a unicorn behind an ash tree; Rob talked about being paid five bucks by a seventh-grade girl for a practice run. Charlotte hadn't been kissed, it turned out, till she was eighteen. "I can't believe that," I said.

"What about you, Sean?" Rob asked.

"I can't remember." By then, I had lost sense of everything but Charlotte. I could have told you how many inches away from my leg hers was beneath the table. I could have told you how the curls of her hair caught the candlelight and held on to it. I could not remember my first kiss, but I could have told you Charlotte would be my last.

"Remember how we had Amelia and Emma in the living room," Piper said now. "We were having such a good time no one thought to check on them?"

Suddenly I could see it — all of us crowded into the tiny downstairs bathroom, Rob yelling at his daughter, who had commandeered Amelia into helping her dump dry dog food into the toilet bowl.

Piper started to laugh. "Emma kept saying it was only a cupful."

But it had soaked up the water and swollen to fill the bowl. It was amazing, in fact, how quickly it had gotten out of control.

578

Beside me, Piper's laughter had turned the corner, and in that way emotion has of hopping boundaries, she was suddenly crying. "God, Sean. How did we get here?"

I stood awkwardly, and then after a moment I slipped an arm around her. "It's okay."

"No, it's not," Piper sobbed, and she buried her face against my shoulder. "I have never, ever in my life been the bad guy. But every time I walk into that courtroom, that's exactly what I am."

I had hugged Piper Reece before. It was what married couples did — you went to someone's house and you handed over the obligatory bottle of wine and kissed the hostess on the cheek. Maybe distantly I was aware that Piper was taller than Charlotte, that she smelled of an unfamiliar perfume instead of Charlotte's pear soap and vanilla extract. At any rate, the embrace was triangular: you connected at the cheek, and then your bodies angled away from each other.

But right now Piper was pressed against me, her tears hot against my neck. I could feel the curve and weight of her body. And I could tell the exact moment she became aware of mine.

And then she was kissing me, or maybe I was kissing her, and she tasted of cherries, and my eyes closed, and the moment they did, all I could see was Charlotte.

We both pushed away from each other, our eyes averted. Piper pressed her hands to her cheeks. *I have never, ever in my life been the bad guy*, she had said.

There is a first time for everything.

"I'm sorry," I said, at the same time Piper began to speak.

"I shouldn't have —"

"It didn't happen," I interrupted. "Let's just say it didn't happen, all right?"

Piper looked up at me sadly. "Just because you don't want to see something, Sean, doesn't mean it wasn't there."

I didn't know if we were talking about this moment, or this lawsuit, or both. There were a thousand things I wanted to say to Piper, all of which began and ended with an apology, but what tumbled off my lips instead was this: "I love Charlotte," I said. "I love my wife."

"I know," Piper whispered. "I did, too."

Charlotte

The movie that had been filmed to show a day in your life was the last bit of evidence that Marin would offer to the jury. It was the emotional counterpart to the cold, hard facts the actuary had given, about what it costs in this country to have a disabled child. It felt like ages since the video crew had followed you around school, and to be honest, I had worried about the outcome. What if the jury looked at our daily routine and didn't find it remarkably different from anyone else's?

Marin had told me that it was her job to make sure the presentation came off in our favor, and as soon as the first images projected onto the courtroom screen, I realized I should not have worried. Editing is a marvelous thing.

It began with an image of your face, reflected in the windowpane you were peering through. You weren't speaking, but you didn't have to. There was a lifetime of longing in your eyes.

The view panned out the window, then, to watch your sister skating on the pond.

Then came the first few strains of a song as I knelt down to strap on your braces before school, because you could not reach them yourself. After a moment I recognized it: "I Hope You Dance."

In the pocket of my jacket, my cell phone began to vibrate.

We were not allowed to have cell phones on in court, but I'd told Marin that I had to be reachable, just in case — and we'd compromised with this. I slipped my hand into my pocket and looked at the screen to see who was calling.

HOME, it read.

On the projector screen, you were in class, and kids were funneling around you like a school of fish, doing some kind of spider dance at circle time, while you sat immobile in your wheelchair.

"Marin," I whispered.

"Not now."

"Marin, my phone's ringing —"

She leaned closer to me. "If you pick up that phone right now instead of watching this film, the jury will crucify you for being heartless."

So I sat on my hands, getting more and more agitated. Maybe the jury thought it was because I couldn't watch this. The phone would stop vibrating and then start a moment later. On the screen I watched you at physical therapy, walking forward toward the mat biting your lower lip. The phone vibrated again, and I made a small sound in the back of my throat.

What if you'd fallen? What if the nurse didn't know what to do? What if it was something even worse than a simple break?

582

I could hear snuffling sounds behind me, purses being opened and rummaged through for Kleenex. I could see the jury riveted by your words, your elfin face.

The phone buzzed again, an electrical shock to my system. This time I slipped it out of my pocket to see the text message icon. I hid the receiver under the table and flipped it open.

WILLOW HURT — HELP

"I have to get out of here," I whispered to Marin.

"In fifteen minutes . . . We absolutely cannot recess right now."

I looked up at the screen again, my heart hammering. Hurt, how? Why wasn't the nurse doing something?

You were sitting on the mat, your legs frogged. Above you a red ring dangled. You winced as you reached for it. *Can we stop now?*

Come on, Willow, I know you're tougher than that . . . wrap your fingers around and give it a squeeze.

You tried, for Molly. But tears were streaming from your eyes, and the sound that came from you was a sharp, staccato burst. *Please, Molly . . . can I stop?*

The phone was vibrating again. I wrapped my hand around it.

And then I was on the mat with you, holding you in my arms, rocking you, and telling you that I would make it better.

If I had been more aware of what was happening in the courtroom, I would have noticed that every woman on the jury was crying, and some of the men. I would

583

have seen the TV cameras in the back of the gallery that were recording for playback on that night's news. I would have seen Judge Gellar close his eyes and shake his head. But instead, the moment the screen went to black, I bolted.

I could feel everyone watching me as I ran up the aisle and out the double doors, and they probably thought I was overcome with emotion or too fragile to look at you in Technicolor. The moment I shoved past the bailiffs I hit the redial button on my phone. "Amelia? What's the matter?"

"She's bleeding," Amelia sobbed, hysterical. "There was blood all over the place and she wasn't moving and —"

Suddenly, an unfamiliar voice was on the phone. "Is this Mrs O'Keefe?"

"Yes?"

"I'm Hal Chen, one of the EMTs who —"

"What's wrong with my daughter!"

"She's lost a great deal of blood, that's all we know right now. Can you meet us at Portsmouth Regional?"

I don't know if I even said yes. I didn't try to tell Marin. I just ran — across the lobby, out the courthouse doors. I pushed past the reporters, who were caught unawares, who pulled themselves together just in time to focus their cameras and point their microphones at the woman who was sprinting away from this trial, headed toward you.

Amelia

When I had been really little and the wind blew like mad at night, I had trouble sleeping. My father would come in and tell me that the house wasn't made of straw or sticks, that it was brick, and like the little pigs knew, nothing could tear it down. Here's what the little pigs didn't realize: the big bad wolf was only the start of their problems. The biggest threat was already inside the house with them, and couldn't be seen. Not radon gas or carbon monoxide, but just the way three very different personalities fit inside one small space. Tell me that the slacker pig — the one who only mustered up straw — really could get along with the high-maintenance bricklayer pig. I think not. I'll bet you if that fairy tale went on another ten pages, all three of those pigs would have been at each other's throats, and that brick house would have exploded after all.

When I broke down the door of the bathroom with my ninja kick, it gave more easily than I expected, but then again, the house was old and the jamb just splintered. You were in plain sight, but I didn't see you. How could I, with all that blood everywhere?

I started to scream, and then I ran into the bathroom and grabbed your cheeks. "Willow, wake up. Wake *up*!"

It didn't work, but your arm jostled, and out of your hand fell my razor blade.

My heart started to race. You'd seen me cutting the other night; I'd been so angry, I couldn't remember if I'd hidden the blade back in its usual hiding place. What if you had been copying what you'd seen?

It meant this was all my fault.

There were cuts on your wrist. By now, I was hysterical crying. I didn't know if I should wrap a towel around you and try to stop the bleeding or call an ambulance or call my mother.

I did all three.

When the firemen came with the ambulance, they raced upstairs, their boots muddy on the carpet. "Be careful," I cried, hovering in the doorway of the bathroom. "She's got this brittle bone disease. She'll break if you move her."

"She'll bleed out if we don't," one of the firemen muttered.

One of the EMTs stood up, blocking my view. "Tell me what happened."

I was crying so hard that my eyes had nearly swollen shut. "I don't know. I was studying in my room. There was a nurse, but she went home. And Willow — And she —" My nose was streaming, my words curdled. "She was in the bathroom for a really long time."

"How long?" the fireman asked.

"Maybe ten minutes . . . five?"

"Which one?"

"I don't know," I sobbed. "I don't know."

"Where did she get the razor blade?" the fireman asked.

I swallowed hard and forced myself to meet his gaze. "I have no idea," I lied.

Buckle: a cake made in one layer with berries in the batter.

When you don't have what you want, you have to want what you have. It's one of the first lessons the colonists learned when they came to America and found that they couldn't make the trifles and steamed puddings they'd loved in England because the ingredients didn't exist here. That discovery led to a rash of innovation, in which settlers used seasonal fruits and berries to make quick dishes that were served for breakfast or even a main course. They came with names like buckle and grunt, crumble and cobbler and crisp, brown Betty, sonker, slump, and pandowdy. There have been whole books written on the origins of these names — grunt is the sound of the fruit cooking; Louisa May Alcott affectionately called her family home in Concord, Massachusetts, "Apple Slump" — but some of the strange titles have never been explained.

The buckle, for one.

Maybe it's because the top is like a streusel, which gives it a crumbled appearance. But then why not call it a crumble, which is actually more like a crisp?

I make buckles when nothing else is going right. I imagine some beleaguered Colonial woman bent over her hearth with a cast-iron pan, sobbing into the batter — and that's where I imagine the name came from. A buckle is the moment you break down, you give in, because when you cook one, you simply can't mess up. Unlike with pastries and pies, you don't have to worry about getting the ingredients just right or mixing the dough to a certain consistency. This is baking for the baking impaired; this is where you start, when everything else around you has gone to pieces.

BLUEBERRY PEACH BUCKLE

TOPPING

⅓ cup unsalted butter, cut into small pieces
½ cup light brown sugar
¼ cup all-purpose flour
I teaspoon cinnamon
I teaspoon fresh ginger, peeled and grated

BATTER

1½ cups flour
½ teaspoon baking powder
Pinch of salt
¾ cup unsalted butter, room temperature
¾ cup dark brown sugar
I teaspoon vanilla extract
3 large eggs
2–3 cups wild blueberries (can substitute frozen if fresh are not available)
  2 ripe peaches, peeled, pitted, and sliced[1]

---

[1] The best way to peel peaches is to cut a small cross at the base of each peach and drop the fruit into a pot of boiling water for 1 minute. Remove it with a slotted spoon and immediately place the peach in ice water. Peel the peach — the skin will come right off — and slice into thin wedges or small pieces for the buckle.

Butter and flour an 8 by 8-inch pan; preheat the oven to 350 degrees F.

First, make the topping: in a small bowl, combine the butter, brown sugar, flour, cinnamon, and ginger until it resembles coarse meal, and set aside.

Then, make the batter by sifting together the flour, baking powder, and salt. Set this mixture aside, too.

In the bowl of an electric mixer, using the paddle attachment, combine the butter and brown sugar until creamy and soft (3–4 minutes). Add the vanilla. Beat the eggs into the flour mixture one at a time until just combined. Fold in the berries and peaches. Spread the batter in the prepared pan and crumble the topping mixture on top. Bake for 45 minutes or until a tester comes out clean and the top of the buckle is golden.

Charlotte

I think you can love a person too much.

You put someone up on a pedestal, and all of a sudden, from that perspective, you notice what's wrong — a hair out of place, a run in a stocking, a broken bone. You spend all your time and energy making it right, and all the while, you are falling apart yourself. You don't even realize what you look like, how far you've deteriorated, because you only have eyes for someone else.

It is not an excuse, but it is the only answer I can give for why I would find myself here, by your bed; you with your wrist bandaged and broken from where the doctors had to press down to stop the bleeding; you with your broken ribs from the CPR they began when your heart stopped.

I had been used to hearing that you'd broken a bone, or needed surgery, or would be casted. But there were words that had come out of the doctors' mouths today that I never would have expected: *blood loss, self-harm, suicide*.

How could a six-year-old girl want to kill herself? Was this the only way I'd sit up and take notice? Because yes, you had my attention.

Not to mention my paralyzing regret.

All of this time, Willow, I'd just wanted you to see how important you were to me, how I would do anything within my power to give you the best life possible . . . and you didn't want that life at all.

"I don't believe it," I whispered fiercely, even though you were still sleeping, drugged to rest through the night. "I don't believe you wanted to die."

I ran my hand down your arm, until my fingers just brushed the gauze that had been wrapped around the deep cut on your wrist. "I love you," I said, my voice hollow with tears. "I love you so much that I don't know who I'd be without you. And even if it takes *my* whole life to do it, I'll make you see why *yours* made a difference."

I would win this lawsuit, and with the money, I'd take you to see the Paralympics. I'd buy you a sports wheelchair, a service dog. I'd fly you halfway around the world to introduce you to people who, like you, beat the odds to become someone bigger than anyone ever expected. I would prove to you that being different isn't a death sentence but a call to arms. Yes, you would continue to break: not bones but barriers.

Your fingers twitched against mine, and your eyes slowly blinked open. "Hi, Mommy," you murmured.

"Oh, Willow," I said, crying hard by now. "You scared us to death."

"I'm sorry."

I lifted your good hand and pressed a kiss into the palm for you to carry like a sweet, until it melted. "No," I whispered. "*I* am."

Sean stirred from the chair where he was sleeping, in the corner of your room. "Hey," he said, his whole face lighting up when he saw you were awake. He sat down on the side of the bed. "How's my girl?" He brushed your hair away from your face.

"Mom?" you asked.

"What, baby?"

You smiled then, the first real smile I'd seen on your face in ages. "You're both here," you said, as if that was what you'd wanted all along.

Leaving Sean with you, I went downstairs to the lobby and called Marin back; she had left multiple messages on my voice mail. "It's about time," she snapped. "Here's a news flash, Charlotte. You aren't allowed to leave a trial in the middle, especially without telling your lawyer where the hell you're going. Do you have any idea how foolish it looks when the judge asks me where my client is, and I can't answer?"

"I had to go to the hospital."

"For Willow? What did she break this time?" Marin asked.

"She cut herself. She lost a lot of blood, and some of the intervention the doctors had to do broke some bones, but she's going to be all right. She's here for observation overnight." I drew in my breath. "Marin, I can't come to court tomorrow. I have to stay with her."

"One day," Marin said. "I can get a continuance for one day. And . . . Charlotte? I'm glad Willow's okay."

My breath tumbled out in a gasp. "I don't know what I'd do without her."

Marin was quiet for a moment. "You'd better not let Guy Booker hear you say that," she said, and then she hung up.

I didn't want to go back home, because there, I'd have to see the blood. I imagined it was everywhere — on the shower curtain, the tiled floor, the drain of the bathtub. I pictured myself using a bleach solution and a damp cloth and having to wring it into the sink dozens of times, my hands burning and my eyes scalded. I imagined the water running pink, and even after a solid thirty minutes of cleaning I would still smell the fear of losing you.

Amelia was downstairs in the cafeteria, where I'd left her with a cup of hot chocolate and a cardboard boat of French fries. "Hey," I said.

She came halfway out of her chair. "Is Willow —"

"She's just waking up."

Amelia looked like she was going to faint, and I couldn't blame her — she was the one who'd walked in on you, who had called the ambulance. "Did she say anything?"

"Not a lot." I reached out and covered her hand with mine. "You saved Willow's life today. There is nothing I can say that would possibly make you understand how much I want to thank you."

"I wasn't going to just let her bleed to death," she said, but she was trembling.

"Do you want to see her?"

"I . . . I don't know if I can yet. I keep picturing her in that bathroom . . ." She curled into herself, the way teenage girls do, like fiddlehead ferns. "Mom? What would have happened if Willow had died?"

"Don't even think about that, Amelia."

"I didn't mean now . . . not today. I meant, like, years ago. When she was first born." She looked up at me, and I realized she wasn't trying to upset me, she was asking honestly what her life would have been like if it hadn't taken a backseat to a sibling who had a serious disability.

"I can't tell you, Amelia," I said honestly. "I'm just really, really glad she didn't. Not then, and thanks to you, not today. I need *both* of you too badly."

As I stood up, waiting for Amelia to dump out the rest of her fries, I wondered whether the psychiatrist we would take you to would tell me that I had irrevocably damaged you. I wondered if the reason you'd slit your wrist was that, in spite of all the vocabulary you knew, you didn't have the words to tell me to just stop already. I wondered how you even knew that slitting your wrist was one way to check out of this world.

As if she could read my mind, Amelia spoke. "Mom? I don't think Willow was trying to kill herself."

"What makes you say that?"

"Because she knows," Amelia said, falling into step beside me. "She's the only thing that's holding our family together."

Amelia

I wasn't left alone with you until three hours after you woke up, when Mom and Dad went out into the hall to talk to one of your doctors. You looked at me, because you knew that we wouldn't have very long before everyone else descended again. "Don't worry," you said. "I won't tell anyone it was yours."

My knees nearly gave way underneath me; I had to hold on to that weird plastic crib rail on the side of the hospital bed. "What were you *thinking?*" I said.

"I just wanted to see what it was like," you said. "When I saw you —"

"You shouldn't have."

"Well, I did. And you looked . . . I don't know . . . so *happy.*"

Once in a science class my teacher had told a story about a woman who went into the hospital because she couldn't eat anything, not one bite, and the doctors operated only to find a hair ball the whole size and shape of her stomach inside her. Later on, her husband mentioned that, yes, he'd seen her chewing on her hair every now and then, but he never imagined it had gotten so out of control. That's what I felt like now: sick to my stomach, full of a habit that had grown so solid I couldn't even swallow anymore.

"It's a stupid way to be happy. It's what I did because I couldn't be happy the normal way." I shook my head. "I look at you, Wiki, with so much shit raining down on you, and you never let it get you down. But me, I can't even be satisfied with all the good stuff in my life. I'm pathetic."

"I don't think you're pathetic."

"Oh yeah?" I laughed, but without any humor; it sounded flat as cardboard. "Then what am I?"

"My big sister," you said simply.

I could hear the door open a crack, Dad's voice thanking the doctor. Quickly I swiped a tear from my eye. "Don't try to be like me, Willow," I said. "Especially since I was only trying to be like *you*."

Then my father was in the room, and my mother. They glanced from your face to mine and back again. "What are you two talking about?" Dad asked.

We did not look at each other. "Nothing," we said, for once in unison.

Piper

"I don't have to go to court tomorrow," I said, still reeling, as I put the phone down and turned to face Rob.

His fork stayed suspended in midair over his plate. "You mean she's finally come to her senses and dropped this lawsuit?"

"No," I said, sitting down beside Emma, who was pushing her Chinese food around on her plate. I wondered how much to say with her present, then decided, if she was old enough to deal with this trial, she was old enough to hear the truth. "It's Willow. She cut herself with a razor blade, apparently, pretty badly."

Rob's silverware clattered to the table. "Jesus," he said softly. "She was trying to kill herself?"

Until he said that, it honestly hadn't crossed my mind. You were only six and a half, for God's sake. Girls your age were supposed to be dreaming of ponies and Zac Efron, not trying to commit suicide. But then again, all sorts of things happened that weren't theoretically supposed to: Bumblebees flew; salmon swam upstream. Babies were born without the bone structure to bear their weight. Best friends were pitted against each other.

"You don't really think — Oh, Rob. Oh, God."

"Is she going to be okay?" Emma asked.

"I don't know," I admitted. "I hope so."

"Well, if this isn't a giant cosmic hint for Charlotte to set some priorities," Rob said, "then I don't know what is. I don't even remember Willow ever *complaining*."

"A lot can change in a year," I pointed out.

"Especially when your mother is too busy wringing blood out of a stone to pay attention to her kids —"

"Enough," I murmured.

"Don't tell me you're going to defend that woman."

"That woman used to be my friend."

"*Used* to be, Piper," Rob repeated.

Emma threw her napkin on the table, a red flag. "I think I know why she did it," she whispered.

We both turned to her at once.

Emma was nearly white, her eyes bright with tears. "I know friends are supposed to save each other, but we're not really friends anymore —"

"You and Willow?"

She shook her head. "Me and Amelia. I saw her once, in the girls' bathroom. She was cutting her arm with a pop top from a soda can. She didn't see me, and I turned around and ran. I was going to tell someone — you, or the guidance counselor — but then I sort of wished she would die. I thought maybe her mother deserved it, you know, for suing us. But I didn't think — I never wanted Willow —" She broke down, crying. "Everyone does it — cuts. I figured it was just something she was going through, like the way she used to make herself throw up."

"She *what?*"

"She didn't think I knew, but I did. I could hear her, when I slept over at her house. She thought I was asleep, but she'd go into the bathroom and make herself sick —"

"But she stopped?"

Emma looked up at me. "I can't remember," she said, in a very tiny voice. "I thought so, but maybe I just stopped hanging around with her to see."

"Her teeth," Rob added. "When I took off her braces, the enamel was worn down. It's the kind of thing we attribute to either soda . . . or eating disorders."

When I was still practicing, I'd had a patient with bulimia who'd been pregnant. As soon as I managed to convince her to stop making herself vomit for the sake of her fetus, she started cutting. I'd consulted a psychiatrist and found out that the two often went hand in hand. Unlike anorexia, which was about being perfect all the time, bulimia was rooted in self-hatred. Cutting was a way of not committing suicide, ironically; it was a coping mechanism for someone who couldn't control herself any other way, and like bingeing and purging, it became a dirty little secret that added to the cycle of anger at herself for not being who she really wished she could be.

I could only begin to imagine what it was like to live in a house where the subliminal message was that daughters who did not measure up should not exist.

600

It could have been a coincidence; Emma might have happened upon the one and only time Amelia tried to hurt herself; Rob's armchair diagnosis might have been far off the mark. But all the same, if the warning signs were present and you noticed them, weren't you obligated to offer the information?

For God's sake — that was the crux of this whole lawsuit.

"If it were Emma," Rob said quietly, "wouldn't *you* want to know?"

I blinked at him. "You don't seriously think that Charlotte would listen to me if I told her her daughter was in trouble?"

Rob tilted his head. "Maybe that's exactly why you have to try."

As I drove through Bankton, I cataloged everything I knew about Amelia O'Keefe:

She wore size 7 shoes.

She didn't like black licorice.

She could skate like an angel, and make it look easier than it ever was.

She was tough. Once, during a skating show, she'd done an entire program with a hole in her stockings and a blister rubbing her heel bloody.

She knew all the words to the *Wicked* sound track.

She bused her own plate, when I had to remind Emma to do it.

She'd fitted seamlessly, easily, thoughtlessly into our own home life, so much so that, when they were smaller, Emma and Amelia had been called the Twins

601

by most of the teachers in the elementary school. They'd borrowed clothes from each other; they'd gotten their hair cut in tandem; they'd had sleepovers in the same narrow twin bed.

Maybe I was guilty of thinking of Amelia as an extension of Emma. Knowing ten concrete things about her did not make me an expert, but it was ten things more than her parents were paying attention to right now.

I did not realize where I was heading until I pulled into the hospital access drive. The guard at the booth waited for me to unroll my window. "I'm a doctor," I said, not quite a lie, and he waved me ahead to the parking lot.

Technically, I still had operating privileges here. I'd known the OB staff well enough to be invited to their Christmas parties. But right now the hospital was so unfamiliar that when I walked through the sliding glass doors I nearly buckled at the smells: industrial cleaner and lost hope. I might not feel ready to take on a real patient yet, but that didn't mean I couldn't pretend to treat a fictional one. So I put on my best harried physician face and walked up to the elderly volunteer in a pink smock. "I'm Dr Reece; I was called here on a consult . . . I need the room number for Willow O'Keefe?"

Because it was after visiting hours, and because I wasn't wearing a lab coat, I was stopped by the nurses at the pedi desk. None of them were familiar, which actually worked in my favor. I knew, of course, the name of Willow's OI doctor. "Dr Rosenblad at

Children's asked me to check in on Willow O'Keefe," I said, in the no-nonsense tone that usually keeps nurses from second-guessing. "Is the chart outside the door?"

"Yes," one nurse said. "Did you want us to page Dr Suraya?"

"Dr Suraya?"

"The treating physician?"

"Oh," I said. "No. I won't be more than a few minutes," and I hurried down the hall as if I had a thousand things to do.

The door to your room was ajar, and the lights were low. You were asleep on the bed, and Charlotte was asleep in a chair beside you. She was holding on to a book: *1,000,001 Things You Never Knew*.

Your arm was splinted, in addition to your left leg. Bandages wrapped your ribs tight. I could guess, even without reading your chart, what collateral damage had been done during the act of saving your life.

I leaned down very gently and kissed the crown of your head. Then I tugged the book out of Charlotte's hands and set it on the nightstand. I already knew she wouldn't wake up — she slept so heavily. Sean was always saying she snored like a longshoreman, although the few times we had bunked together during family trips, I'd only noticed her making a soft, soughing sound when she slept. I had always wondered if this was because she was more comfortable with Sean to really let go or because he didn't understand her the way I did.

She mumbled in her sleep, and shifted, and I froze like a deer in headlights. Now that I was here, I didn't know what I'd been expecting. Did I think that Charlotte wouldn't be sleeping by your side? That she would welcome me with open arms when I said I was worried about you? Maybe the reason I had driven all the way here was that I needed to see for myself, even for a moment, that you were all right. Maybe when Charlotte woke up, she would smell my perfume and wonder if she'd dreamed about me. Maybe she would remember that she'd fallen asleep holding the book, and wonder who'd moved it for her.

"You," I whispered, "are going to be just fine."

As I slipped away down the hospital corridor, I realized I was talking to all three of us.

Sean

To my surprise, Guy Booker showed up just after 9p.m. to tell me that the judge had agreed to a one-day continuance — so I wouldn't have to testify starting tomorrow morning.

"That's good, since she's still at the hospital," I told him. "Charlotte's there with her. I came home with Amelia."

"How's Willow doing?"

"She'll pull through okay. She's a fighter."

"Well, I know it was awful to get that call. But you do realize how great this is for our case?" he said. "It's too late to say the lawsuit's made her suicidal, but then again, if she'd died today —" He broke off abruptly, but not before I grabbed him by the collar and threw him against the wall.

"Finish your sentence," I growled.

The blood drained from Booker's face.

"You were going to say that, if she died, there wouldn't be any damages, weren't you, you son of a bitch?"

"If *you* thought it, then the jury will think it, too," Booker choked out. "That's all."

I let him drop and turned my back. "Get out of my house."

He was bright enough to slink out the door without another word, but less than a minute later, the doorbell rang again. "I told you to get lost," I said, but instead of Guy Booker, it was Piper on the front porch.

"I . . . I'll just go . . ."

I shook my head. "You weren't who I was expecting."

The memory of the kiss in the courthouse rose between us, pushing us each back a step. "I have to talk to you, Sean," Piper said.

"I told you, just forget —"

"This isn't about what happened this afternoon. This is about your daughter," Piper said. "I think she might be bulimic."

"No, she has OI."

"You have another daughter, Sean. I'm talking about Amelia."

We were having this conversation with the door wide open, both of us shivering. I stepped back to let Piper inside. She stood uncomfortably in the front hall. "There's nothing wrong with Amelia," I said.

"Bulimia's an eating disorder. Which, by definition, is kept under wraps by the person who's suffering from it. Emma's heard her throwing up late at night. And Rob noticed during her last orthodontic checkup that the enamel's been worn off the backs of her teeth — something that can be caused by repeated vomiting. Look, you can hate me for bringing this up, but especially given what we're in the middle of right now,

I would rather save Amelia's life than know I had the chance to and didn't."

I looked up at the stairs. Amelia was in the shower, or at least she was supposed to be. She wouldn't go into the bathroom you shared; instead she was using the one attached to the master bedroom. Although I'd cleaned up any evidence of what had happened to you, Amelia said it still freaked her out.

As a police officer, I sometimes had to consider the line between privacy and good parenting. I saw enough kids who appeared squeaky clean on the outside and were then busted for possession or theft or vandalism to know that people were never what you expected them to be — especially if they happened to be between the ages of thirteen and eighteen. I didn't tell Charlotte, but sometimes I went through Amelia's drawers just to see what she might be hiding. I'd never found anything. Then again, I had been looking for drugs, for alcohol — I had never thought to look for signs of an eating disorder. I wouldn't even know what to look *for*. "She's not skin and bones," I said. "Maybe Emma got it wrong."

"Bulimics don't starve themselves, they binge and then purge. You wouldn't see a weight loss. And there's one more thing, Sean. In school, in the girls' bathroom, Emma saw Amelia cutting herself."

"Cutting?" I repeated.

"Like with a razor blade," Piper replied, and suddenly, I understood. "Just go talk to her, Sean."

"What do I say?" I asked, but she had already slipped out the door.

As Amelia showered, I could hear the water running through the pipes. Pipes — the same pipes we'd had the plumber in to fix four times over the past year, because they kept leaking. He'd said it was acid, which hadn't made sense at the time.

Vomit was wicked acidic.

I walked upstairs and went into the bedroom you and your sister shared. If Amelia was bulimic, shouldn't we have noticed food disappearing? I sat down at the desk and rummaged through the drawers but didn't find anything except for packets of gum and a few old exams. Amelia brought home straight As. How could a kid who worked so hard, who did so many things right, have gone so far off track?

The bottom cabinet of Amelia's desk didn't close. I unhooked the drawer from its metal runners and pulled out a box of gallon-size Ziploc bags. I turned the box over in my hands as if I were examining a rare artifact. It didn't really make sense for Amelia to have these up here when they were readily available in the pantry; it made even less sense for her to go to the trouble of hiding them behind the drawer. Then I turned to the bed. I pulled down the sheets but found only the stuffed, molting moose Amelia had slept with since I'd met Charlotte. I knelt beside the bed and ran my hands beneath the mattress.

They came by the fistfuls: torn candy wrappers, bread loaf wrappers, empty packages of cookies and crackers. They fluttered over my feet like plastic butterflies. Closer to the head of the bed were satin bras with the price tags still attached — in sizes far too big for Amelia — make-up with CVS price stickers, pieces of costume jewelry still riveted to their plastic display squares.

I sank to the floor, sitting in the center of all the evidence I hadn't been willing to see.

Amelia

I was dripping wet and wrapped in a towel, and all I wanted to do was crawl into my pajamas and go to sleep and pretend today had never happened, but sitting on the floor in the middle of my room was my father. "Do you mind? I'm kind of not dressed . . ."

He turned around, and that's when I noticed everything piled on the floor in front of him. "What is all this?" he asked me.

"Okay, so I'm a total pig. I'll clean my room —"

"Did you steal these?" He lifted a handful of cosmetics and jewelry. They were horrible things — makeup I'd rather die than wear, earrings and necklaces for old ladies — but somehow sneaking them into my pockets had made me feel like a superhero.

"No," I said, looking him in the eye.

"Who's the bra for?" he asked. "Thirty-six D."

"A friend," I answered, and too soon realized I had screwed myself over: my father would know I didn't *have* any friends.

"I know what you're doing," he said, getting to his feet heavily.

610

"Well, maybe you could tell me, then. Because I don't really understand why we have to have an inquisition while I'm freezing and soaking wet —"

"Did you make yourself throw up before you took that shower?"

My cheeks burned with the truth. It was the perfect time, because the running water covered the sound of retching. I'd gotten it down to a science. But I tried for a laugh. "Oh, yeah, right. I do that before *every* shower. Which is clearly why I'm a size eleven when everyone else in my grade is a size zer— "

He took a step forward, and I wrapped the towel more tightly around myself. "Just stop the lying," he said. "Just . . . stop." My father reached for me and yanked my wrist toward him. I thought he was trying to pull away the towel, but that was nowhere near as humiliating as what he was actually trying to see: my forearms and my thighs, with their gray-scale ladders of scars.

"She saw me doing it," I said, and I didn't have to explain that I was talking about you.

"Jesus Christ," my father thundered. "What were you thinking, Amelia? If you were upset, why didn't you come to us?"

But I bet he knew the answer to that one.

I burst into tears. "I never meant to hurt her. I just wanted to hurt myself."

"Why?"

"I don't *know*. Because it's the only thing I can manage to do right."

He grabbed my chin, forcing me to look into his eyes. "The reason I'm angry isn't that I hate you," my father said tightly. "It's because I goddamn *love* you." And then his arms were tight around me, the towel the thinnest barrier between us, and it wasn't creepy or embarrassing; it was just what it was. "This stops right now, you hear me? There are treatment programs and things like that — and you're going to get yourself fixed. But until then, I'm going to watch you. I'm going to watch you like a hawk."

The more he yelled, the more tightly he held on to me. And here's the weirdest thing of all: now that the worst had happened — now that I'd been found out — it wasn't disastrous. It felt, well, inevitable. My father was furious, but me, I couldn't stop smiling. *You see me*, I thought, my eyes closing. *You see me.*

Charlotte

That night, I slept in the chair beside your hospital bed, and I dreamed of Piper. We were at Plum Island again and we were boogie-boarding, but the waves had gone red as blood and stained our hair and our skin. I rode in on a wave so majestic and forceful that it made the shore buckle. I looked behind me, but you were being thrashed underneath the cutting edge of the wave, rolling head over heels, your body raked over the sea glass and the porous stones. *Charlotte*, you cried, *help me!* I heard you, but I started walking away.

I was awakened by Sean, shaking my shoulder. "Hey," he whispered, looking at you. "She slept through the night?"

I nodded, stretched the muscles of my neck. And then I noticed Amelia standing behind him. "Shouldn't Amelia be in school?"

"The three of us have to talk," Sean said, in a tone that brooked no argument. He glanced down at you, asleep. "You think she'll be okay for a few minutes, while we grab some coffee?"

I left word at the nurses' desk and followed Sean into the elevator, with Amelia trailing meekly behind. What the hell had happened between them?

613

In the cafeteria, Sean poured coffee for both of us while Amelia lifted the tiny boxes of cereal and tried to decide between Cheerios and Cinnamon Toast Crunch. We sat at a table. At this hour of the morning, the large room was filled with residents cramming down bananas and lattes before making rounds. "I have to go to the bathroom," Amelia said.

"Well, you can't," Sean flatly replied.

"If you have something to say, Sean, we can wait till she gets back —"

"Amelia, why don't you tell your mother why you can't go to the bathroom?"

She looked down at her empty plastic bowl. "He's afraid . . . that I'll throw up again."

I stared at Sean quizzically. "Has she got a virus?"

"Try bulimia," Sean said.

I felt rooted to the chair. Surely I'd heard him wrong. "Amelia's not bulimic. Don't you think we'd *know* if Amelia was bulimic?"

"Yeah. Just like we knew that she's been cutting herself for a year or so now? Shoplifting all kinds of crazy shit — including razor blades — which is how Willow got her hands on one?"

My jaw dropped. "I don't understand."

"Nope," Sean said, leaning back in his chair. "Neither do I. I can't figure out why a kid who's got two parents that love her, and a roof over her head, and a pretty damn good life would hate herself enough to do any of that."

I faced Amelia. "Is it true?"

614

She nodded, and I felt a twinge in my heart. Had I been blind? Or had I just been so busy watching you break that I failed to notice my older daughter going to pieces?

"Piper stopped by last night to tell me that Amelia might be having a problem. Apparently, we didn't see it — but Emma has. Repeatedly."

Piper. At the name, I felt myself go as still as glass. "She came to the house? And you let her in?"

"For God's sake, Charlotte —"

"You can't believe anything Piper says. For all you know, this is part of some ploy to get us to drop the lawsuit." Distantly I realized that Amelia had confessed to the behavior, but that hardly seemed to matter. All I could see was Piper, standing in my house, pretending to be the perfect mother when I'd screwed up.

"You know, I'm starting to see why Amelia might have done this in the first place," Sean muttered. "You are completely out of control."

"Brilliant, there's your old MO," I said. "Blame Charlotte, because then none of this is your fault."

"Did you ever consider that you're not the only victim in the universe?" Sean said.

"*Stop it!*"

We both turned at the sound of Amelia's voice.

She had her hands pressed over her ears, and tears in her eyes. "Just stop it!"

"I'm sorry, baby," I said, reaching out to her, but she jerked away.

"No you're not. You're just glad it wasn't something else that happened to Willow. That's all you ever care

615

about," Amelia accused. "You want to know why I cut? Because it hurts less than all of *this*."

"Amelia —"

"Just stop pretending you care about me, okay?"

"I'm not pretending." Her sleeve had slipped, and I could see the scars tracking up to her elbow like some secret linear code. Last summer, Amelia had insisted on wearing long sleeves, even when it was ninety degrees outside. To be honest, I'd thought it was a sign of modesty. In a world where so many girls her age were hardly wearing anything, I thought it was refreshing that she wanted to be covered up. I hadn't even begun to think that she might be not shy but truly calculating.

And because I didn't have the words for this — because I knew at this point Amelia would not want to hear anything I'd want to say — I reached for her wrist again. This time, she let me take it. I thought of all the times, as a child, she had fallen off her bike and run crying into the house; of the times I'd lifted her onto the counter to clean gravel out of a scraped knee and to set it healing with a brush of my lips and a Band-Aid; of how once she stood by me as I wrapped your leg in a makeshift magazine splint, wringing her hands and urging me to kiss it and make it better. Now, I drew her arm closer, and pushed up the sleeve, and pressed my lips to the fine white lines that marched up her arm like the marks on a measuring cup, yet one more attempt to count the ways I'd failed.

Piper

The next day, Amelia came to the courthouse. I saw her walking with Sean down the corridor to the room that he'd hidden in before. I wondered if you were still in the hospital, if — given the situation — that might not be a blessing.

I knew I was the witness the jury had been waiting for — either to vilify or to vindicate. Guy Booker had begun his defense by putting the other two OBs who had bought into my practice on the stand as character references: Yes, I was an excellent physician. No, I'd never been sued before. In fact, I'd been named the New Hampshire Obstetrician of the Year by a regional magazine. Malpractice, they said, was a ridiculous charge.

Then it was my turn. Guy had been asking me questions for three-quarters of an hour: about my training, my role in the community, my family. But when he asked me the first question about Charlotte, I could feel the atmosphere in the room change. "The plaintiff testified that you two were friends," Guy said. "Is that true?"

"We were best friends," I said, and very slowly, she lifted her head. "I met her nine years ago. In fact, I was the one who introduced her to her husband."

"Were you aware of the fact that the O'Keefes were trying to conceive a child?"

"Yes. To be honest, I think I wanted them to get pregnant just as much as they wanted it. After Charlotte asked me to be her doctor, we spent months looking at her ovulation cycle and doing everything short of fertility treatments to enhance conception — which is why it was such a thrill when we found out she was going to have a baby."

Booker entered some papers into evidence and handed them to me. "Dr Reece, are you familiar with these pages?"

"Yes, they're notes I made in Charlotte O'Keefe's medical file."

"Do you remember them?"

"Not really. I've gone back and reviewed my notes, obviously, to prepare for this trial, but there wasn't something so extraordinary that I remembered it immediately."

"What do the notes say?" Booker asked.

I read from the pages. "Femur length measuring short at sixth percentile, within the curve of normality. Near field of fetal brain particularly clear."

"Did that strike you as unusual?"

"Unusual," I said, "but not abnormal. It was a new machine, and everything else on the fetus looked great. At eighteen weeks, based on that ultrasound, I fully expected the baby to be born healthy."

"Were you disturbed by the fact that you could see the intracranial contents so well?"

"No," I said. "We're trained to see something that looks wrong, not something that looks too *right*."

"Did you ever see something that looked wrong on Charlotte O'Keefe's sonogram?"

"Yes, when we did one at twenty-seven weeks." I glanced at Charlotte and remembered that moment when I first looked at the screen and tried to make the image into something it wasn't, the sinking feeling in my stomach when I realized that I would have to be the one to tell her. "There were healing fractures of the femur and tibia, as well as several beaded ribs."

"What did you do?"

"I told her that she needed to see another doctor, someone in maternal-fetal medicine who was better equipped to deal with a high-risk pregnancy."

"Was that twenty-seven-week ultrasound the first indication you had that there might be something wrong with the plaintiff's baby?"

"Yes."

"Dr Reece, have you had other patients who were diagnosed with abnormal fetuses in utero?"

"Several," I said.

"Have you ever advised a couple to terminate the pregnancy?"

"I've presented that option to numerous families when malformations are diagnosed that aren't compatible with life."

Once, I had a case where a thirty-two-week fetus had hydrocephaly — so much fluid on the brain that I knew the baby couldn't be born vaginally, much less survive. The only way to deliver would have been C-section, but

619

the fetal head was so large that the incision would have destroyed the mother's uterus. She was young, it was her first pregnancy. I offered her the options, and eventually we drained the fluid from the head by piercing it with a needle, causing a cranial hemorrhage. The baby was then delivered vaginally, and died within minutes. I remembered showing up at Charlotte's house that night with a bottle of wine, and telling her I had to drink the day away. I'd slept on her couch afterward, and had awakened to find her standing over me with a steaming mug of coffee and two Tylenol for my throbbing head. "Poor Piper," she had said. "You can't save them all."

Two years later, that same couple came back to me when they were having another baby — who was born, thank goodness, perfectly healthy.

"Why didn't you counsel termination for the O'Keefes?" Guy Booker asked.

"There was no definitive reason to believe the baby would be born impaired," I said, "but even beyond that, I never thought termination would be an option for Charlotte."

"Why not?"

I looked up at Charlotte. *Forgive me*, I thought.

"For the same reason she didn't agree to amniocentesis when we thought there was a risk of Down syndrome," I said. "She'd already told me she wanted this baby, no matter what."

Charlotte

It was hard to sit here and listen to Piper giving a chronicle of our friendship. I imagine it had been just as hard for her when I had been the witness. "Were you close to the plaintiff after she gave birth?" Guy Booker asked.

"Yes. We'd see each other once or twice a week, and we talked every day. Our kids would play together."

"What sorts of things did you do together?"

God, what *had* we done? It didn't really matter. Piper had been the kind of friend with whom I didn't have to fill in the spaces with random conversation. It was okay to just *be* with her. She knew that sometimes I needed that — to not have to take care of anyone or anything, to simply exist in my own space, adjacent to hers. Once, I remembered, we told Sean and Rob that Piper had a conference in Boston at the Westin Copley Place, and that I was going along to talk about having a baby with OI. In reality, there had been no conference. We checked in to the Westin and ordered room service and watched three sappy movies in a row, until we could not keep our eyes open.

Piper had paid. She always paid — treating me to lunch out, or coffee, or drinks at Maxie's Pad. When I tried to go dutch, she'd make me put my wallet away. *I'm lucky enough to be able to afford it*, she said, and we both knew that I wasn't.

"Did the plaintiff ever have a conversation with you where she blamed you for her daughter's birth?"

"No," Piper said. "In fact, the week before I was served, we went shopping together."

Piper and I had tried on the same red blouse in between Emma's and Amelia's buying fits, and to my shock, it had looked fantastic on both of us. *Let's both get one*, Piper had said. *We can wear them home and see if our husbands can tell us apart.*

"Dr Reece," Booker asked, "how has this lawsuit affected your life?"

She sat up a little straighter in the chair. It wasn't very comfortable; it hurt your back, made you wish you were somewhere else. "I've never been sued before," Piper said. "This was the first time. It's made me doubt myself, even though I know I didn't do anything wrong. I haven't practiced since. Every time I try to get back on that horse . . . well, it starts moving away from me. I suppose I understand that, even if you're a good physician, bad things sometimes happen. Bad things that nobody wishes for, and that nobody can explain." She looked directly at me, so intently that a shiver went down my spine. "I miss being a doctor," Piper said, "but nowhere near as much as I miss my best friend."

"Marin," I whispered suddenly, and my lawyer bent her head toward mine. "Don't."

"Don't what?"

"Don't . . . just don't make it worse for her."

Marin raised her eyebrow. "You have *got* to be kidding," she murmured.

"Your witness," Booker said, and she rose to her feet.

"Isn't it a violation of medical ethics to treat someone you know well on a personal level?" Marin asked.

"Not in a small town like Bankton," Piper said. "If that was the case, I wouldn't have any patients. As soon as I realized there was a complication, I stepped down."

"Because you knew you were going to be blamed?"

"No. Because it was the right thing to do."

Marin shrugged. "If it was the right thing to do, why didn't you call in a specialist as soon as you saw complications during the eighteen-week ultrasound?"

"There *weren't* complications during that ultrasound," Piper said.

"That's not what the experts have said. You heard Dr Thurber say that the standard of care, after an ultrasound reading like Charlotte's, would have been a follow-up ultrasound, at the very least."

"That's Dr Thurber's opinion. I respectfully disagree."

"Hm. I wonder whom a patient would rather listen to: a doctor who's established in his field, with numerous awards and citations . . . or a small-town OB who hasn't been near a patient in over a year."

"Objection, Your Honor," Guy Booker said. "Not only was that *not* a question but my witness doesn't need to be vilified."

"Withdrawn." Marin walked toward Piper, tapping a pen against her open palm. "You were best friends with Charlotte, right?"

"Yes."

"What did you talk about?"

Piper smiled a little. "Everything. Anything. Our kids, our pipe dreams. How we sometimes wanted to kill our husbands."

"But you never bothered to have a conversation about terminating this pregnancy, did you?"

During interrogatories I had told Marin that Piper had not discussed aborting the baby with me. And the way I had remembered it up to this point, that's exactly the way it was. But memory is like plaster: peel it back and you just might find a completely different picture.

"Actually," Piper said, "we did."

Although Piper and I were best friends, we didn't touch very often. A quick hug sometimes, a pat on the back. But we weren't like teenage girls, who walk with their arms twined around each other. Which was why it felt so strange to be sitting beside her on a couch, her arm wrapped around me while I cried against her shoulder. She was bony, bird-like, when I would have expected her to be strong and fierce.

I had held my hands over the bowl of my belly. "I don't want her to suffer."

Piper sighed. "I don't want *you* to suffer."

I thought of the conversation Sean and I had had after we left the geneticist's office the day before, after being told you had — at worst — lethal OI and — at best — severe OI. I had found him in the garage, sanding the rails of the cradle he'd been making in anticipation of your arrival. *It's like butter*, he said, holding out the narrow piece of wood. *Feel it.* But to me, it looked like a bone, and I couldn't bring myself to touch it. "Sean doesn't want to do it," I said.

"Sean isn't pregnant."

I asked you how an abortion was performed, and I asked you to be honest. I had pictured being on the plane, having flight attendants ask me when I was due, whether it was a boy or a girl, those same flight attendants not making eye contact on the flight home. "What would you do?" I asked her.

She hesitated. "I'd ask myself what scares me the most."

That's when I looked up at her, the one question on my lips that I had not been brave enough to ask Sean, or Dr Del Sol, or even myself. "What if I can't love her?" I whispered.

Piper smiled at me, then. "Oh, Charlotte," she said. "You already do."

Marin

The defense called Dr Gianna Del Sol to the stand, to establish that there was nothing she would have done differently if she'd been the primary physician to treat Charlotte instead of the referral. But when they called Dr R. Romulus Wyndham, an OB and bioethicist with a list of credentials that took a half hour to run through, I started to worry. Not only was Wyndham smart but he was movie-star pretty, and he had the jury eating out of his hand. "Some tests that flag abnormality early are false positives," he said. "In 2005, for example, a team from Reprogenetics kept growing fifty-five embryos that were diagnosed as abnormal during preimplantation genetic diagnosis. After a few days, they were shocked to find out that forty-eight percent of them — nearly half — were normal. Which means there's evidence that embryos with genetically flawed cells might heal themselves."

"Why might that be medically important to a physician like Piper Reece?" Booker asked.

"Because it's proof that termination decisions made too early might not be prudent."

As Booker took his seat, I rose in one smooth motion. "Dr Wyndham, that study you just cited — how many of those embryos had osteogenesis imperfecta?"

"I . . . I don't know that any of them did."

"What was the nature of the abnormality, then?"

"I can't say, precisely —"

"Were they major abnormalities?"

"Again, I'm not —"

"Isn't it true, Dr Wyndham, the study could have been showing embryos with very minor abnormalities that corrected themselves?"

"I suppose so."

"There's also a difference between waiting to see what happens to a days-old embryo and a weeks-old fetus, isn't there, in terms of the point when you can safely and legally terminate a pregnancy?"

"Objection," Guy Booker said. "If I can't run a pro-life rally in court, she can't run a pro-choice rally."

"Sustained," the judge said.

"Isn't it true that if doctors followed your wait-and-see approach and withheld information about fetal conditions, it might make it harder to terminate a pregnancy — logistically, physically, and emotionally?"

"Objection!" Guy Booker called out again.

I walked toward the bench. "Please, Your Honor, this isn't about abortion rights. It's about the standard of care that my client should have received."

The judge pursed his lips. "All right, Ms. Gates. But make your point fast."

Wyndham shrugged. "Any obstetrician knows how hard it is to counsel patients with fetal abnormalities to terminate pregnancies when, in one's medical opinion, the baby won't survive. But it's part of the job."

"It might be part of Piper Reece's job," I said. "But that doesn't mean she did it."

We had a two-hour recess for lunch, because Judge Gellar had to go to the DMV to apply for a motorcycle license. Apparently, according to the clerk of the court, he planned to take a Harley cross-country next summer during his month off the bench. I wondered if that was what had made him dye his hair: black went better with leather.

Charlotte left the minute court was recessed, so that she could visit you at the hospital. I hadn't seen Sean or Amelia since this morning, so I stepped out onto the janitor's loading dock, a door most reporters didn't know existed.

It was one of those late September days that felt like the long fingers of winter tugging the hem of New Hampshire — cold, bitter, with a biting wind. And yet, there still seemed to be a big crowd gathered on the front steps, which I could only just make out from where I was standing. A custodian pushed out the door and stood beside me to light up a cigarette. "What's going on up there?"

"Freaking circus," he said. "That case about the kid with the funky bones."

"Yeah, I've heard it's a nightmare," I muttered, and hugging my arms to stay warm, I picked my way to the edge of the group in front of the courthouse.

At the top of the stairs was a man I recognized from the news: Lou St. Pierre, the president of the New Hampshire chapter of the American Association of People with Disabilities. As if that wasn't impressive enough, he had a degree from Yale Law, was a Rhodes scholar, and had won a gold medal in the breast stroke at the Paralympics. Now, he traveled both in his customized wheelchair and in a plane that he piloted himself to fly kids around the country for medical treatment. His service dog sat by the side of St. Pierre's wheelchair, unflinching, while twenty reporters jammed microphones close to its nose. "You know why this lawsuit is so captivating? It's like a train wreck. You can't tear your eyes away, even though you'd rather not admit these kind of torts exist," he said. "Plain and simple: this topic is loaded. This is exactly the kind of lawsuit that makes your skin crawl, because we'd all like to believe that we might love any child that comes into our family — instead of admitting that, in reality, we might not be that accepting. Prenatal testing reduces a fetus to one trait: its disability. It's unfortunate that prenatal testing automatically makes the assumption that a parent might not want a child who's disabled, and that it implies it's unacceptable to live life with some sort of physical impairment. I know plenty of parents in the deaf community who would love a child just like them, for example. One person's disability is another person's culture."

As if on cue, his service dog barked.

"Abortion's already a hot-button issue: Is it okay to destroy a potential life? Termination takes that one step further: Is it okay to destroy *this* potential life?"

"Mr St. Pierre," a reporter called out. "What about the statistics that say raising a disabled child is stressful to a marriage?"

"Well, I agree. But there are also statistics that say it's equally stressful to raise a child who's a prodigy or an athletic superstar, and you don't see any doctors advising parents to terminate *those* pregnancies."

I wondered who'd called in the cavalry — Guy Booker, no doubt. Since this case was technically a malpractice suit, he wouldn't invite another attorney from outside his practice to cochair Piper's defense, but he made sure to stage this impromptu news conference all the same to stack his odds of winning.

"Lou," another reporter asked. "Are you going to testify?"

"That's what I'm doing right now in front of all you good people," St. Pierre preached. "And I'm going to keep on talking in the hopes that I can convince anyone who's listening never to bring another lawsuit like this to the great state of New Hampshire."

Excellent. I'd lost my case because of a guy who wasn't even a valid witness for the defense. I trudged back toward the loading dock door. "Who's talking?" the custodian said, grinding his cigarette butt underneath his boot. "That dwarf?"

"He's a Little Person," I corrected.

The custodian stared at me blankly. "Isn't that what I just said?"

The door banged shut behind him. I was freezing, but I waited before following him inside: I didn't feel like making small talk with him the whole way up the staircase. He was, in truth, the perfect example of the greased slope Charlotte and I were dancing down. If it was acceptable to want to terminate a fetus that had Down or OI, what about when medical advances made it possible to see your child's potential beauty, or her level of compassion? What about parents who wanted only a boy and learned they had conceived a girl? Who would be allowed to set the bars for access, and for rejection?

As much as it pained me to admit it, Lou St. Pierre was right. People were always saying they'd love any baby that came along, but that wasn't necessarily true. Sometimes, it really did come down to the particular child in question. There had to be a reason why blond-haired, blue-eyed babies got plucked out of adoption agencies like ripe peaches but children of color and children with disabilities might linger in foster homes for years. What people said they would do and what people actually did were two very different things.

Juliet Cooper had stated it clearly: there really were some babies who were better off not being born.

Like you.

And me.

Amelia

Whatever goodwill I thought might rain down on me from basking in my father's attention after he discovered my little secret quickly disappeared when I started to realize that I had created a new hell of my own making. I was not allowed to go to school, which would have been awesome beyond belief if not for the fact that, instead, I had to sit in a courthouse lobby reading the same newspaper over and over. I had envisioned my parents realizing how badly they'd messed up and falling all over each other to take care of me, the way they did for you when you had a break. But instead, they'd just yelled so loud in the hospital cafeteria that all the residents watched us like we were a reality TV show.

I wasn't even allowed to visit you during the long lunch recess, when Mom went to the hospital. I guess I had become, officially, *A Bad Influence*.

So I have to admit I was a little surprised when my mother showed up with a chocolate milkshake for me before court reconvened. I was sitting in this totally airless conference room, where my father had left me while he went over his testimony with some stupid lawyer. How my mother even found me in this building was a mystery, but when she stepped through the door, I was actually happy to see her.

"How's Willow?" I asked, because (a) I knew she expected it, and (b) I really did want to know.

"She's doing okay. The doctor says we might be able to take her home tomorrow."

"You kind of lucked out on the free babysitting," I said.

My mother's eyes flashed, hurt. "You don't really believe I think that way, do you?"

I shrugged.

"I brought you this," she said, and she passed over the milkshake.

I used to have a thing for chocolate Fribbles at Friendly's. I'd beg my mom to get one, even though they were three times more expensive than kiddie cones. Sometimes, she said yes, and we'd split one and rhapsodize about chocolate ice cream, something you and Dad never really understood, having the rare misfortune to be born loving vanilla as you both were.

"You want to share?" I asked quietly.

She shook her head. "That one's just for you. Provided it doesn't come back up again."

I flicked my eyes toward her and then back down at the lid of the shake, but I didn't say anything.

"I think I understand," my mother said. "I know what it's like to start something and have it suddenly grow out of control. And you want to get rid of it, because it's hurting you and everyone else around you,

633

but every time you try to do that, it consumes you again."

I stared at her, dumbfounded. That was *exactly* what I felt like, every day of my life.

"You asked me not too long ago what the world would be like without Willow in it," my mother said. "So here's what I think: if Willow had never been born, I'd still look for her in the aisles of the grocery store, or at the bank, or in the bowling alley. I'd stare at every individual face in a crowd, trying to find hers. There's this weird part about having kids — you know when your family is finished, and when it's not. If Willow hadn't been born, that's how the world would be for me — unfinished."

I slurped on the straw, on purpose, and tried not to blink, because then maybe the tears would reabsorb through osmosis.

"The thing is, Amelia," my mother continued, "if *you* weren't here . . . I'd feel the same exact way."

I was afraid to look at her. I was afraid I had heard her wrong. Was this her way of saying that she didn't just love me, which was a given for a mother, but she liked me? I imagined her making me open the lid of the shake to be sure I'd drunk it all. I would grumble, but deep down, I'd like that she was insisting. It meant she cared; it meant she wasn't going to let me go that easily.

"I did a little research today, at the hospital," my mother said. "There's a place just outside of Boston that takes care of kids with eating disorders. They have an inpatient program, and when you're ready, you get to move to a residential program with other girls who are going through the same issues."

My head snapped up. "Inpatient? Like, as in, live there?"

"Just until they can help you get this under control —"

"You're sending me away?" I said, panicking. This wasn't the way it was supposed to be. My mother knew what it felt like; so why didn't she understand that cutting me off was just like saying I'd never be good enough for this family? "How come Willow can break a thousand bones and she's still perfect and gets to live at home, and I make one little mistake and get shipped off?"

"Your father and I aren't shipping you off," my mother said. "We're doing this to help you —"

"He *knows* about it?" I felt my nose running. I had hoped that my father could be my last appeal; now, I found out he was a conspirator. The whole world hated me.

Suddenly Marin Gates stuck her head into the room. "We're ready to rock and roll," she said.

"I just need a minute —"

"Well, Judge Gellar needs you now."

My mother looked at me, her eyes begging me to cut her a break. "You have to sit inside the courtroom now. Your dad's testifying, and I can't stay here and watch over you."

"Go to hell," I said. "You can't tell me what to do."

Marin, who was watching all this, whistled long and low. "Actually, she can," she said. "Because you're a minor, and she's your mother."

I wanted to hurt my mother as bad as she'd hurt me, so I turned to the lawyer. "I don't think you're allowed to keep that title if you try to get rid of all of your kids."

I could see my mother flinch. She was bleeding, even if you couldn't see the cut, and she knew, like me, that she deserved it. As Marin unceremoniously deposited me in the gallery next to a man wearing a red flannel shirt and suspenders who smelled like tuna fish, I made myself a promise: if my mother was going to ruin my life, there was absolutely no reason I couldn't ruin hers.

Sean

On our wedding day, Charlotte made me forget all the vows I'd written and diligently memorized. There she was, walking down the aisle of the church, and those sentences were like fishing nets; they couldn't possibly hold all the feelings I wanted to present to her. Now, as I sat across from my wife in a courtroom, I hoped my words would transform one more time. Into feathers, clouds, steam — anything that did not have the power to land a solid blow.

"Lieutenant O'Keefe," said Guy Booker, "weren't you originally a plaintiff in this case?"

He'd promised me that he'd make it short and sweet, that I would be off the stand so quickly I barely felt it. I didn't trust him. It was his job to lie, cheat, and twist the truth into something the jury could believe.

Something I sorely hoped he'd be successful at, this time around.

"I was, at first," I replied. "My wife had convinced me that this lawsuit was in Willow's best interests, but I started to realize I didn't feel that way at all."

"How so?"

"I think this lawsuit's broken our family apart. Our dirty laundry is running on the six o'clock news. I've started divorce proceedings. And Willow, she knows what's going on. There was no hiding it, once it became public knowledge."

"You realize that wrongful birth suggests your daughter should never have been born. Do you wish that, Lieutenant O'Keefe?"

I shook my head. "Willow may not be perfect, but — well — neither am I. Neither are you. She may not be perfect," I repeated, "but she's one hundred percent *right*."

"Your witness," Booker said, and as Marin Gates got to her feet, I took a deep breath to galvanize myself, the same way I did before I ran into a building with the SWAT team.

"You say that this lawsuit has broken your family apart," she said. "But the same could be said of the divorce proceedings you initiated, isn't that true?"

I looked at Guy Booker. He'd anticipated this question; we'd practiced an answer. I was supposed to say something about how my actions had been a measure to protect the girls — not to drag them through the mud. But instead of saying that, I found myself looking at Charlotte. At that plaintiff's table, she seemed so tiny. She was staring down at the wood grain, as if she didn't trust herself to look me in the eye.

"Yes," I said quietly. "It is."

Booker stood up, and then figured he couldn't object to his own witness, I guess, because he sat back down.

I turned to the judge. "Sir? Do you mind if I talk directly to my wife?"

Judge Gellar raised his brows. "It's the jury that needs to hear you, son."

"With all due respect, Your Honor . . . I don't think that's true."

"Judge," Booker said. "May I approach?"

"No, Mr Booker, you may not," the judge said. "This man's got something to say."

Marin Gates looked like she'd swallowed a firecracker. She didn't know whether to ask me anything else or just let me hang myself. And maybe I was doing that; I didn't really care. "Charlotte," I said, "I don't know what's right anymore, except *admitting* that I don't know that. No, we don't have enough money. And no, we haven't had it easy. But that doesn't mean it hasn't been worth the trip."

Charlotte lifted her face. Her eyes were wide and still. "Some guys at the station, they said they knew what they were getting into when they got married. Well, I didn't. It was an adventure, and I was okay with that. See, you're it, for me. You let me take you skiing, and you never mentioned you were afraid of heights. You sleep curled up against me, no matter how far I move to my side of the bed. You let me eat the vanilla half of your Dixie Cup, and you take my chocolate. You tell me when my socks don't match. You buy Lucky Charms, because you know I like the marshmallows. You gave me two beautiful girls.

"Maybe you expected marriage to be perfect — I guess that's where you and I are different. See, I

639

thought it would be all about making mistakes, but doing it with someone who's there to remind you what you learned along the way. And I think we were *both* wrong about something. People always say that, when you love someone, nothing in the world matters. But that's not true, is it? You know, and I know, that when you love someone, everything in the world matters a little bit more."

Silence settled over the courtroom. "We're going to adjourn for the day," Judge Gellar announced.

"But I'm not finished —" Marin argued.

"Yes, you are," the judge said. "For God's sake, Ms. Gates, that's why you're still single. I want this courtroom cleared, except for Mr and Mrs O'Keefe."

He banged his gavel, and there was a flurry of activity, and suddenly, I was sitting alone on the witness stand and Charlotte was standing behind the plaintiff's table. She took a few steps forward, until she was standing level with me, her hands lightly resting on the wooden railing between us. "I don't want to get a divorce," she said.

"Neither do I."

She shifted nervously from one foot to the other. "So what do we do?"

I leaned forward slowly, so that she could see me coming. I leaned forward, and touched my lips to hers, sweet and familiar, home. "Whatever comes next," I whispered.

Amelia

My parents' oh-so-touching reconciliation was the talk of the courtroom. You would have thought the news media was *True Confessions* the way the reporters all lined up talking about this great romantic moment. The jury would fall for it unless they were a bunch of cynics, like me; the way I saw it, Marin could practically go home and break open the champagne.

Which is exactly why I was a girl on a mission.

While they were all swooning and sighing over the melodrama, I was sitting in that gallery, embarrassed as hell, and learning something new about myself: I didn't have to vomit for poison to come out of me. I could sweat it out, scream it out, and sometimes just whisper. If I was going to the bulimia camp in Boston, then I was going out with a bang.

I knew that the judge had deliberately played matchmaker and kept my mother and father in the courtroom together to work out Act Two of their drama, but that worked perfectly for me. I slipped out the back before Marin Gates could remember to come find me and ducked out of the courthouse without anyone noticing or caring who I was. I ran to the parking lot, to the mint green T-Bird.

When Guy Booker came out and found me leaning against his car, he scowled. "You scratch the paint job and you'll be doing community service for the next five years," he said.

"I'll take my chances."

"What are you doing here, anyway?"

"Waiting for you."

He frowned. "How'd you know this was my car?"

"Because it's so painfully subtle."

Booker smirked. "Shouldn't you be in school?"

"Long story."

"Well, then, skip it. It's been an even longer day," he said, unlocking the driver's side door. He opened it, hesitating. "Go home, Amelia. Your mother doesn't need to be worrying about where you are right now. She's got a lot on her plate."

"Yeah," I answered, folding my arms. "Which is why I figured you'd be interested in what I heard her say."

Marin

I had Juliet Cooper's address from the jury selection process. I knew that she lived in Epping, a tiny town to the west of Bankton. So as soon as court was adjourned for the day, I programmed the street into my GPS and started driving.

An hour later I pulled into a small cul-de-sac, a horseshoe of modified Capes. Number 22 was just to the right of the circle as you came into it. It had gray siding and black shutters, a red lacquered door. There was a van in the driveway. When I rang the doorbell, a dog started barking.

I could have lived here. This might have been my home. In another lifetime, I might have walked right through the door instead of approaching like a stranger; I might have had a room upstairs filled with horseback-riding ribbons and school yearbooks and the other detritus adults leave behind at their childhood residences. I could have told you where the silverware drawer was in the kitchen, where the vacuum cleaner was stashed, how to use the TV remote.

The door opened, and Juliet Cooper was standing in front of me. Dancing at her feet was a terrier. "Mom?" a girl's voice called. "Is it for me?"

"No," she said, her eyes never leaving my face.

"I know you don't want to see me," I said quickly, "and I promise that I will go away and never speak to you again. But first, you have to tell me why. What is it about me that makes me so . . . so repulsive?"

As soon as I spoke, I knew this was a mistake. Maisie at the family court would probably have had me arrested if she'd known I was here; every adoption search website strongly reminded adoptees *not* to do exactly this: ambush the birth mother, make her accept you on your time frame rather than hers.

"See, here's the thing," I said. "After thirty-five years, I think you owe me five minutes."

Juliet stepped outside, closing the door behind her. She wasn't wearing a coat, and on the other side of the door I could still hear the dog barking. But she didn't say a word to me.

What we all want, really, is to be loved. That craving drives our worst behavior: Charlotte's insistent belief that you would one day forgive her for the things she said in court, for example. Or my mad chase to Epping. The truth was, I was greedy. I knew that my adoptive parents wanted me more than anything, but it wasn't enough. I needed to understand why my birth mother *hadn't*, and until I did, there would always be a part of me that felt like a failure.

"You look just like him," she said finally.

I stared at her, although she still would not meet my gaze. Had it been a love affair that ended badly, with Juliet pregnant and my birth father refusing to support her? Had she gone on loving him, knowing their baby was somewhere in the world; had it eaten away at her even as she made a new life for herself with a husband and family?

"I was sixteen," Juliet murmured. "I was riding my bike home from school, through the woods, a shortcut. He came out of nowhere and knocked me off. He stuffed a sock in my mouth and pulled my dress up, and he raped me. Then he beat me up, so badly that the only way my parents recognized me was by my clothing. He left me bleeding and unconscious, and two hunters found me." She lifted her face, so that she was looking directly at me, finally. Her eyes were too bright, her voice thin. "I didn't speak for weeks. And then, just when I thought I could start over again, I found out I was pregnant," she said. "He was caught, and the police wanted me to testify, but I couldn't. I didn't think I could stand to see his face again. And then, when you were born, a nurse held you up, and there he was in you: the black hair and the blue eyes, those fists swinging. I was glad there was a family that wanted you so badly, because I didn't."

She took a deep, trembling breath. "I'm sorry if this isn't the reunion you'd hoped for. But seeing you, it brings it all back, when I've worked so hard to forget it. So please," Juliet Cooper whispered, "will you leave me alone?"

645

Be careful what you wish for. I staggered backward, silent. No wonder she had not wanted to look at me; no wonder she had not welcomed the letter I wrote that Maisie had forwarded; no wonder she only wanted me to go away. I'd want the same thing.

We had *that* much in common.

I started down the stone steps to my car, trying to see through the rush of tears. At the bottom, I hesitated, then turned back. She was still standing there. "Juliet," I said. "Thank you."

I think my car knew where I was headed long before I did. But when I pulled into the old white Colonial where I'd grown up, with the thicket of overgrown roses and the weathered gray trellis that never managed to tame them, I felt something burst inside me. This was the place where my photos were in the albums stacked in the front closet. This was the place where I knew how to work the garbage disposal. This was the place where, in an upstairs bedroom, I still kept pajamas and a toothbrush and a few sweaters, just in case.

This was home, and these were my parents.

It was dark out by now, nearly 9p.m. My mother would be wearing a fuzzy robe and slipper socks, and eating her nightly dish of ice cream. My father would be surfing the channels of the television, arguing that *Antiques Roadshow* was far more of a reality show than *The Amazing Race*. I let myself in through the side door, which we'd never locked the whole time I was growing up. "Hi," I called out, so that they wouldn't be alarmed. "It's just me."

646

My mother stood up when I came into the living room. "Marin!" she said, hugging me. "What are you doing here?"

"I was in the neighborhood." This was a lie. I'd driven sixty miles to get here.

"But I thought you were wrapping up that big trial," my father said. "We've been watching you on CNN. Nancy Grace, eat your heart out . . ."

I smiled a little. "I just . . . I felt like seeing you guys."

"Are you hungry?" my mother asked. It had taken her thirty seconds; surely that was a record.

"Not really."

"Then I'll get you a little ice cream," my mother said, as if I hadn't spoken. "Everyone can use a little ice cream."

My father patted the spot on the couch beside him, and I stripped off my coat and sank down into the cushions. They were not the ones I'd grown up with. I had jumped on those so often that they'd been rendered flat as pancakes; several years ago my mother had had the furniture reupholstered. These pillows were softer, more forgiving. "You think you're going to win?" my father asked.

"I don't know. It's not over till it's over."

"What's she like?"

"Who?"

"That O'Keefe woman?"

I thought hard before I spoke. "She's doing what she thinks is right," I said. "I don't think you can blame her for that." *Although I have*, I thought. *Although I was doing the same thing.*

Maybe you had to leave in order to really miss a place; maybe you had to travel to figure out how beloved your starting point was. My mother sat down beside me on the couch and passed over a bowl of ice cream. "I'm on a mint-chocolate-chip kick," she said, and in unison, we lifted our spoons, so synchronized that we might have been twins.

Parents aren't the people you come from. They're the people you want to be, when you grow up.

I sat between my mother and my father, watching strangers on TV carry in Shaker rockers and dusty paintings and ancient beer tankards and cranberry glass dishes; people and their hidden treasures, who had to be told by experts that they'd taken something incredibly precious for granted.

Amelia

I tried looking it up on the Internet, but there's nothing that tells you what you're supposed to wear to court if you're a witness. I figured, though, that I definitely wanted the jury to remember me. I mean, they'd had a parade of really boring doctors for the most part; compared to them, I planned to stand out.

So I spiked my hair, which made it look even darker blue. I wore a bright red sweater and my purple high-top Converses, and my lucky jeans, the ones with the hole in the knee, because I wasn't leaving anything to chance.

It was pretty ironic, but even last night, my parents hadn't slept in the same bed. Mom was overnight with you at the hospital; Dad and I were back home. Although Guy Booker had said he'd pick me up to go to court, I figured I could hitch a ride with my father and still make it look like I was unhappy to be dragged there. Guy and I had both decided that the longer we could keep my testimony a secret, the better.

My father, who had already testified, was now allowed to be in the courtroom gallery, which left me alone in the lobby, which was perfect. Shaking, I stood next to a bailiff. "You okay?" she asked.

I nodded. "Butterflies," I said, and then I heard Guy Booker's voice:

"The defense calls Amelia O'Keefe."

I was led inside, but all hell had broken loose. Marin and Guy were up at the bench, arguing; my mother was in tears; my father was standing up, craning his neck around to locate me.

"You can't call Amelia," Marin argued.

Booker shrugged. "Why not? *You're* the one who put her on the witness list."

"Is there a reason for calling this witness," Judge Gellar asked, "beyond simply rubbing the opposing counsel's face in the fact that you *can?*"

"Yes, Your Honor," Booker said. "Miss O'Keefe has information that this court needs to hear, given the implications of a wrongful birth lawsuit."

"All right," the judge said. "Bring her in."

As I walked toward the front of the courtroom, I could feel everyone's eyes on me. It felt like they were poking holes, and all my confidence was quickly leaking out. As I passed by my mother, I heard her whispering to Marin. "You promised," she said. "You told me it was just a precaution . . ."

"I had no idea he'd do this," Marin whispered back. "Do you have any clue what she's going to say?"

Then I was in the little wooden cage, like I was a specimen for the jury to scrutinize under a microscope. They brought a Bible over to me and made me swear on it. Guy Booker smiled at me. "Can you tell us who you are, for the record?"

"Amelia," I said, and I had to lick my lips because they were so dry. "Amelia O'Keefe."

"Amelia, where do you live?"

"Forty-six Stryker Lane in Bankton, New Hampshire." Could he hear my heart? Because, God, it was like a bongo drum in my chest.

"How old are you?"

"Thirteen."

"And who are your parents, Amelia?"

"Charlotte and Sean O'Keefe," I said. "Willow's my sister."

"Amelia, in your own words, can you explain to the court what this lawsuit is about?"

I couldn't look at my mother. I pulled my sleeves down, because my scars were burning. "My mom thinks that Piper should have known earlier that there was going to be a problem with Willow, and should have told her. Because then, she would have had an abortion."

"Do you think your mother's telling the truth?"

"Objection!" Marin shot up so fast it made me jump in the chair.

"No, I'll allow this," the judge said. "You can give your answer, Amelia."

I shook my head. "I know she's not."

"How do you know?"

"Because," I said, making the words as neat and small as I could, "I heard her say so."

★ ★ ★

I shouldn't have eavesdropped, but sometimes, that's the only way to find out the truth. And — although I certainly wouldn't admit this out loud — I was feeling sort of protective toward you. You had seemed so down after this latest break and surgery, and when you said *Mom wants to get rid of me*, it pretty much made me feel like my insides had gone to jelly. We all protected you, in our own ways. Dad blustered around, angry at anything that made life harder for you. Mom, well, she was apparently stupid enough to gamble everything in order to get more for you in the long run. And me, I guess I just lacquered a shell around myself, so that when you got hurt, it was easier to pretend I didn't feel it, too.

No one's throwing you away, my mother had said, but you were already crying.

I'm sorry about my leg. I thought if I didn't break anything for a long time, you'd think I was just like any other kid —

Accidents happen, Willow. Nobody is blaming you.

You do. You wish you'd never had me. I heard you say it.

I had held my breath. My mother could tell herself whatever she wanted to help herself get to sleep at night, but she wasn't fooling anyone — especially you.

Willow, my mother had replied, *you listen to me. Everyone makes mistakes . . . including me. We say and we do things we wish we hadn't. But you, you were never a mistake. I would not, in a thousand years — in a million years — have missed out on having you.*

I felt as if I'd been nailed to the wall. If that was true, then everything that had happened in the past year — this lawsuit, losing my friends, watching my parents split — was all for nothing.

If this was true, then my mother had been lying all along.

Charlotte

There's a cost for everything. You might have a beautiful baby girl, but you learn she'll be disabled. You move heaven and earth to make that child happier, but you leave your husband and your other daughter miserable. There is no cosmic scale on which you can weigh your actions; you learn too late what choices ruin the fragile balance.

As soon as Amelia finished talking, the judge turned to Marin. "Ms. Gates, your cross-examination?"

"I don't have any questions for this witness," she said, "but I'd like to recall Charlotte O'Keefe to the stand."

I stared at her. She hadn't said anything to me via whisper or note, so I stood up cautiously, unsure. Amelia was escorted past me by a bailiff. She was crying. "I'm sorry," she mouthed.

Stiffly, I sat down on the wooden chair. *Stick to the message,* Marin had said, over and over. But it had gotten harder and harder to remember what that message was.

"Do you remember that conversation your daughter was just talking about?" Marin asked. Her voice struck like a bullet.

"Yes."

"What were the circumstances?"

"We'd just brought Willow home from the hospital, after the first day of testimony here. She broke her femur so badly it needed surgery."

"Were you upset?"

"Yes," I said.

"Was Willow?"

"Very."

She walked toward me, waiting until I met her eye. And I saw in her the same veiled worry that I'd seen in Amelia when she stepped off that witness stand; in Sean, moments after the courtroom emptied the day before; in you, the night we'd had that very talk — the hidden fear that you might not be good enough for someone you loved. Maybe I felt that, too, and maybe that's why I had started this lawsuit all those months ago — so that when you looked back on your childhood, you didn't blame me for bringing you into a world full of hurt. But love wasn't about sacrifice, and it wasn't about falling short of someone's expectations. By definition, love made you better than good enough; it redefined perfection to include your traits, instead of excluding them.

All any of us wanted, really, was to know that we counted. That someone else's life would not have been as rich without us here.

"When you had that conversation with your daughter, Charlotte," Marin began. "When you said all those things right in the middle of this lawsuit . . . were you lying?"

"No."

"Then what *were* you doing?"

"My best," I whispered. "I was only doing my best."

Piper

"That," Guy Booker said, leaning closer to me, "is a slam dunk." He stood up, buttoning his suit jacket, and faced the jury to begin his closing. "The plaintiff," he said, "is a liar. She says this lawsuit isn't about the money, but even her husband has told you that it is, and can't support her in this lawsuit. She says she wishes that her daughter was never born, but then she tells her daughter the opposite. She tells you that she wished she had the choice to terminate her pregnancy, and she's pointing a finger at Piper Reece, a hardworking physician whose only sin, ladies and gentlemen, was having the poor fortune to become friendly with Charlotte O'Keefe."

He spread his palms wide. "Wrongful birth. Wrongful birth. It just makes you itchy to say it, doesn't it? Yet the plaintiff is saying that her daughter — her beautiful, smart, trivia-loving, beloved little girl — should never have existed. This mother discounts all of those positive traits and says they don't cancel out the fact that her child has osteogenesis imperfecta. Yet you've heard the experts — who admitted that nothing Piper Reece did as a physician was negligent. In fact, as

657

soon as Piper did see a complication during the plaintiff's pregnancy, she did exactly what she was supposed to: she called in someone who could take care of it. And for this, ladies and gentlemen, she's had her life ruined, watched her practice flounder, had her career and her confidence stripped away."

He stopped walking in front of the jury box. "You heard Dr Rosenblad say something we all know: terminating a wanted pregnancy is nobody's first choice. However, when parents are faced with the reality of a fetus who will become a profoundly disabled child, *all* the choices are bad. If you find in favor of the plaintiff, you're buying into her faulty logic: that you can love your child so much you'd sue a doctor — a close friend — because you believe she should never have been born. You're buying into a system that says obstetricians should determine which disabilities are worth living with and which aren't. And that, my friends, is a dangerous track to walk. What kind of message does that send to people who live daily with handicaps? Which disabilities will be considered 'too disabled' to be worthy of a life? Right now, ninety percent of patients whose fetuses are diagnosed with Down syndrome choose to abort, even though there are thousands of people with Down who lead happy, productive existences. What happens when science becomes more advanced? Will patients choose to terminate fetuses with a potential for future heart disease? Or those that might get Bs instead of As? Or those who don't look like supermodels?"

He began to walk back to the defense table. "Wrongful birth, ladies and gentlemen, presumes that every baby should be perfect — and Willow O'Keefe isn't. But I'm not perfect, either. Neither is Ms. Gates. Judge Gellar's not even perfect, although I'll admit he's pretty darn close. I'll even hazard a guess that all of you have some flaw, somewhere. So I ask you to think hard while you're considering your verdict," Booker said. "Look at this wrongful birth suit, and make the right choice."

When he sat down, Marin Gates rose. "It's ironic that Mr Booker would refer to choices, because that's exactly what Charlotte O'Keefe wasn't given."

She stood behind Charlotte, whose head was bowed. "This case isn't about religion. It's not about abortion. It's not about the rights of the disabled. It's not about whether Charlotte loves her daughter. It's not about any of those issues that the defense would like you to believe. This case is about one thing only: whether Dr Piper Reece provided the appropriate standard of care during Charlotte's pregnancy."

After all this time, all these witnesses, I still didn't know the answer to that myself. Even if I had looked at that eighteen-week ultrasound and found cause for concern, I would simply have recommended waiting to see what developed — and the outcome would have been the same. In that, I had saved Charlotte several months of an anxious pregnancy. But did that make me a good obstetrician or a negligent one? Maybe I *had* made assumptions about Charlotte, simply because I knew her too well, that I wouldn't have made with

659

another patient. Maybe I should have been looking more carefully for signs.

Maybe if I had, having my best friend sue me would not have come as such a shock.

"You've heard the evidence. You've heard that there was an anomaly during the eighteen-week ultrasound that suggested follow-up care, that flagged a fetal abnormality. Even if a physician wasn't sure what that abnormality signified, ladies and gentlemen, it was up to her to look more closely and find out. Piper Reece did not do that after the eighteen-week ultrasound, pure and simple. And that, ladies and gentlemen, is negligence."

She walked toward me. "Willow, the child who was born as a result, is going to have special needs her whole life. They're expensive, they're significant, they're painful. They're ongoing, they're cumulative, they're traumatic. They're overwhelming. They're exacerbated by age itself. Your job today is to decide whether Willow will be able to have a better, fuller life, with all the appropriate care she needs. Will she get the surgeries she needs? The adapted vehicles? The specialists' care? Will she continue to get therapy and walking aids — all out-of-pocket expenses for the O'Keefes, which have run them into significant debt? Today, these decisions are in your hands," Marin said. "Today you have the opportunity to make a choice . . . the way Charlotte O'Keefe never did."

The judge said a few words to the jury, and then everyone began to file out of the courtroom. Rob walked up to the bar that separated the gallery from the front of the court and put his hands on my shoulders. "You okay?" he asked.

I nodded. I tried to offer him a smile.

"Thank you," I said to Guy Booker.

He stuffed a pad into his briefcase. "Don't thank me yet," he said.

Charlotte

"You're making me dizzy," Sean said as I entered the conference room. Amelia was pacing back and forth, her hands speared through her electric hair. As soon as she saw me, she turned.

"So here's the thing," she said, talking fast. "I know you're thinking about killing me, but that wouldn't be the brightest move in a courthouse. I mean, there are cops all over the place, not to mention the fact that Dad's here and he'd be obligated to arrest you —"

"I'm not going to kill you," I said.

She stopped moving. "No?"

How had I never noticed before how beautiful Amelia had become? Her eyes, under the fringe of that ridiculous hair, were huge and almond-shaped. Her cheeks were naturally pink. Her mouth was a tiny bow, a purse string holding her opinions tight. I realized that she did not look like me, or like Sean. Mostly, she resembled you.

"What you did . . . what you *said*," I began. "I know why."

"Because I don't want to go to Boston!" Amelia blurted. "That stupid treatment facility. You're just going to leave me behind there."

I glanced at Sean, and then back at her. "Maybe we shouldn't have made that decision without you."

Amelia narrowed her eyes, as if she didn't quite trust what she was hearing.

"You may be angry at us, but that's not *really* why you told Guy Booker you'd testify," I continued. "I think you did it because you were trying to protect your sister."

"Well," Amelia said. "Yeah."

"How could I be angry at you, then, for doing the same thing I'm trying to do?"

Amelia threw herself into my arms with the force of a hurricane. "If we win," she said, muffled against my chest, "can I buy a Jet Ski?"

"No," Sean and I said simultaneously. He stood up, his hands in his pockets. "If you win," he said, "I was thinking I might move back home for good."

"What if I lose?"

"Well," Sean said, "I was still thinking I'd move back home for good."

I looked at him over the crown of Amelia's head. "You drive a hard bargain," I said, and I smiled.

On the way to Disney World, during an airport layover, we had eaten in a Mexican restaurant. You had a quesadilla; Amelia had a burrito. I had fish tacos, and Sean had a chimichanga. The mild sauce was too hot for us. Sean convinced me to get a margarita ("It's not like you're the one who'll be flying the plane"). We talked about fried ice cream, which was on the dessert menu and didn't seem possible: wouldn't the ice cream melt when it was put into the deep fryer? We talked about which rides we would go on first in the Magic Kingdom.

Back then, possibility stretched out in front of us like a red carpet. Back then, we were all focused on what could happen, instead of what had gone wrong. On our way out of the restaurant, the hostess — a girl with pockmarks on her cheeks and a nose stud — gave us each a helium balloon. "What's the point of this?" Sean said. "You can't take them on the plane."

"Not everything has to have a point," I replied, looping my arm through his. "Live a little."

Amelia nipped a hole in the neck of her balloon with her teeth and suctioned her lips over it. She took a deep breath, and then looked at us with a dazzling smile. "Hello, parents," she said, but her voice was high and reedy, that of a Munchkin, not Amelia's at all.

"God only knows what's in there —"

"Duh, Mom," Amelia trilled. "Helium."

"Me, too," you said, and Amelia took your balloon and showed you how to breathe it in.

"I really don't think they should be sucking in helium —"

"Live a little," Sean said, grinning, and he nipped a corner of his balloon and sucked in.

They all started talking at me, their voices a comedy, a bird chorus, a rainbow. "Do it, Mom," you said. "Do it!"

So I followed suit. The helium burned a little as I swallowed it, one great gulp. I could feel my vocal cords buzzing. "Maybe this isn't so bad after all," I peeped.

We sang "Row, Row, Row Your Boat." We recited the Lord's Prayer. And when a man in a business suit stopped Sean to ask if he knew the way to Baggage Claim, Sean took a long drag of his balloon and said, "Follow the yellow brick road."

I cannot remember laughing as much as I did that day, or feeling so liberated. Maybe it was the helium, which made me lighter, made me feel like I could close my eyes and fly to Orlando with or without the plane. Or maybe it was the fact that, no matter what we said to one another, we were not ourselves.

Four hours later, the jury had still not returned a verdict. Sean had driven to the hospital to check on you and had just called to say he was on his way back, had there been any news? Amelia was writing haikus on the white board in the conference room:

Help, I'm clearly trapped
Behind this very white board.
Please do not erase.

The rule for today
Is that there are no more rules.
Guess you're out of luck.

I headed to the bathroom for the third time since court had adjourned. I didn't have to go, but I ran the water in the sink and splashed some on my face. I kept telling myself this was not such a big deal, but that was a lie. You did not drag your family to the verge of dissolution

665

for nothing; to have gone through this with nothing to show would have been disastrous. If I had entered into this lawsuit to assuage my conscience, how could I reconcile an outcome where I left feeling even more guilty?

I patted my face dry and dabbed at my sweater, where it had gotten wet. I tossed the toweling into the trash just as there was a flush in one of the stalls. The door opened as I stepped away from the sink, and I inadvertently smacked it back against the person who was trying to exit. "Sorry," I said, and then I realized that the woman standing in front of me was Piper.

"You know, Charlotte," she said softly, "so am I."

I looked at her, silent. Of all the things to notice, I realized that she didn't smell the way she used to. She'd changed her perfume or her shampoo.

"So you admit it," I said. "That you made a mistake."

Piper shook her head. "No, I didn't. Not professionally, anyway. But on a personal level, well . . . I'm sorry that this is how things have turned out between us. And I'm sorry that you didn't get the healthy baby you wanted."

"Do you realize," I replied, "in all the years after Willow was born, you never said that to me?"

"You should have told me you were waiting to hear it," Piper said.

"I shouldn't have had to."

I tried not to remember how Piper and I had huddled together in the bleachers at the skating rink, reading the classified ads and trying to match up personal ads with each other. How we would take walks, pushing you in a stroller, punctuating the cold air with so many star-bursts of conversation that three miles passed in no time at all. I tried not to remember that I had thought of her as the sister I'd never had, that I'd hoped you and Amelia would grow up just as close.

I tried not to remember, but I would.

Suddenly the door of the bathroom opened. "There you are," Marin sighed. "The jury's back."

She hurried out the door, and Piper quickly rinsed her hands under the faucet. I could feel her a half step behind me as we walked toward the courtroom again, but her legs were longer, and eventually she caught up.

As we stepped in, side by side, a dozen camera flashes went off, and I could not see where I was headed. Marin pulled me forward by the wrist. I thought, although I could have imagined it, that I heard Piper whisper goodbye.

The judge entered, and we all sat down. "Madame Foreman," he said, turning to the jury, "have you reached a verdict?"

The woman was small and bird-like, with glasses that made her eyes seem overly magnified. "Yes, Your Honor. In the case of O'Keefe versus Reece, we find for the plaintiff."

Marin had told me 75 percent of all wrongful birth cases were found in favor of the defendant. I turned to her, and she grabbed my arm. "That's you, Charlotte."

"And," the foreman said, "we award damages in the amount of eight million dollars."

I remember falling back into my chair, and the gallery erupting. My fingers felt numb, and I had to work to breathe. I remember Sean and Amelia, climbing over the bar to hold me tight. I heard the uproar from a group of parents of special-needs kids who'd taken up residence in the back of the court during the trial, and the names they'd called me. I heard Marin telling a reporter that this was the biggest wrongful birth payout in New Hampshire history, and that justice had been done today. I looked through the crowd, trying to find Piper, but she was already gone.

Today, when I went to take you home from the hospital, I would tell you that this was finally over. I would tell you that you'd have everything you needed, for the rest of your life — and after mine ended. I'd tell you that I had won, that the verdict had been read out loud . . . although I didn't really believe it.

After all, if I had won this lawsuit, why was my smile as hollow as a drum, and my chest too tight?

If I had won this lawsuit, why did it feel like I'd lost?

Weeping: the release of extra moisture.

In baking, just as in life, there are tears when something's gone wrong. Meringues are only whipped egg whites and sugar; they are meant to be eaten right away. If you hesitate, water will seep between the filling and the meringue, and weeping — little beads that form on the snowy, white peaks — will occur. There are all sorts of theories on how to prevent this — from using only fresh egg whites to using superfine sugar, from adding cornstarch to precooking the meringue. Ask me, and I'll tell you the only foolproof method:

Do not bake while your heart is breaking.

LEMON MERINGUE PIE

I pie shell, blind-baked

FILLING

1½ cups granulated sugar
6 tablespoons cornstarch
Pinch of salt
1 ⅓ cups cold water
2 tablespoons unsalted butter
5 egg yolks
½ cup fresh lemon juice
I tablespoon grated lemon zest

Prepare the pie shell. Meanwhile, combine the sugar, cornstarch, salt, and water in a non-reactive saucepan. Mix until there are no lumps, and whisk as the mixture gradually comes to a boil. Remove from the heat and add the butter.

In a separate bowl, whisk the egg yolks. Add a small amount of the hot liquid mixture and whisk until smooth. Add the egg mixture to the saucepan and bring to a boil over medium heat, continuing to whisk as it thickens, approximately 2 minutes. Remove from the heat and stir in the lemon juice and zest.

MERINGUE

6 large egg whites at room temperature
Pinch of cream of tartar
Pinch of salt
¾ cup sugar

On low speed, beat the egg whites, cream of tartar, and salt until combined. Increase the speed and whip until they form stiff peaks. Beat in the sugar, 1 tablespoon at a time.

Preheat the oven to 350 degrees F. Add the filling to the pie shell and top it with the meringue. Make sure you spread the meringue all the way to touch the edges of the crust. Bake for 10 to 15 minutes. Let the pie cool for about 2 hours, then refrigerate to prevent weeping.

Or just think happy thoughts.

Willow

March 2009

In school we have Hundred Day. It falls in late November, and we have to bring in a hundred of something, anything. When Amelia was in first grade, she brought in a hundred chocolate chips, but by the time she made it off the bus, she was down to fifty-three. Me, I brought a list of seventy-five bones I've broken and the names of twenty-five more that I haven't.

A million is ten thousand hundreds. I can't even think of ten thousand. Maybe there are that many trees in a forest or water molecules in a lake. Eight million is even more than that, and it is the number of dollars written on the big blue check that has been on our refrigerator for almost six months now.

My parents talk about that check a lot. They say that pretty soon the van will officially wheeze itself to death and we'll have to use the money to buy a new one, but then they find a way to keep the old one running. They talk about how the registration deadline for camps for kids like me is coming up, and how they'll have to send in a deposit. I have the brochures next to my bed. In them, there are kids in every color who have OI, like me. They all look happy.

Maybe that's what happens to kids who go away somewhere. Amelia did, and when she came home, she had brown hair again and her own easel. She paints all the time — portraits of me while I'm sleeping, still lifes of coffee mugs and pears, landscapes in colors they'd never really be. I have to look really hard at her arms to see the silver scars, and even when she catches me looking, she hardly ever bothers to pull down her sleeves.

It was Saturday. My father was parked in front of the television, watching the Bruins. Amelia was outside somewhere, sketching. My mother was sitting at the kitchen table, playing solitaire with the index cards of her recipes. She had over a hundred (if only she was in the first grade!), and she'd decided to put them together in a cookbook. It was a compromise, because she didn't have to bake all the time anymore like she used to for Mr DeVille. He still stocked her pies and tarts and macaroons when she went off on a tear in the kitchen, but now her big plan was to publish the book, and give all the money she made to the Osteogenesis Imperfecta Foundation.

We didn't need money, because ours was all tacked to the refrigerator.

"Hey," my mother said, as I climbed onto a chair. "What's up?"

"Nothing." The mail, fanned out on the table like a bright scarf, caught my eye.

"There's something in there for you," my mother said.

It was a card — and inside was a picture of Marin with a boy who was probably around Amelia's age. He had buck teeth and skin the color of chocolate. His name was Anton, and she had adopted him two months ago.

We didn't see Piper, and Amelia and Emma weren't friends anymore. The sign in front of the building that used to be her office didn't have her name on it now. It said GRETEL HANDELMAN, CHIROPRACTOR, instead. And then one Saturday morning my dad and I went out to get bagels, and there was Piper in line in front of us. My dad said hello and she asked how I was doing, but even though she was trying to smile, it looked all wrong, like a wire that was bent out of shape and wouldn't ever really be straight again. She told my dad that she was working part-time at a women's free health clinic in Boston, and that she was on her way there right now. Then she knocked over the cup full of straws at the cash register, and she was in such a hurry to leave that she forgot to pay until the girl who had brought her her coffee reminded her it wasn't free.

I missed Piper, but I think my mother missed her more. She didn't really have any friends now. She didn't hang out with anyone but me, Amelia, and Dad.

It was kind of sad, actually.

"Wanna bake?" I asked.

My mother rolled her eyes. "You cannot seriously tell me you're hungry. You just had lunch."

I wasn't hungry, but I *was* bored.

She looked up at me. "Tell you what. Go get Amelia, and we'll figure out a plan of action. A movie, maybe."

"Really?"

"Sure," my mother said.

We could treat ourselves to movies now. And we went out to restaurants. And I was going to get a sports wheelchair so that I could actually play kickball in the gym with my class. Amelia said the reason we could spend money all of a sudden was the check that was still on the refrigerator. At school there were jerks who said we were rich, but I knew that wasn't really true. I mean, after all, my parents had never cashed the check. We still had a rusty old car and our little house and the same clothes. A lot of zeros didn't mean anything, really, except security — my parents could splurge a little, because if their funds ran out, there was a backup. That meant they didn't fight nearly as much, which wasn't something you could buy at a store anyway. I didn't know much about bank accounts, but I was smart enough to realize that checks didn't do you any good unless they were deposited. My parents, though, didn't seem to be in any great rush. Every few weeks my mother would say, *I really ought to bring that to the bank*, and my father would grunt in agreement, but somehow it never got done, and the check stayed tacked on the fridge.

I went into the mudroom to get my boots and my coat, my mother's voice trailing behind. "Be —"

"Careful," I finished. "Yeah, I know."

It was March, but it was still cold enough out for my breath to make funny shapes through my scarf: one that looked like a chicken and another that was a hippo. I started down the slope of the backyard carefully. There wasn't snow anymore, but the ground still crunched under the soles of my boots. It made a sound like teeth biting.

Amelia was probably in the woods; she liked to draw the birches because she said they were tragic, and that something so beautiful shouldn't have to die so quickly. I dug my hands into my pockets and tucked my nose under the edge of my scarf. With each step, I thought of something I knew:

The average woman consumes six pounds of lipstick in her lifetime.

Three Mile Island is really only two and a half miles long.

Cockroaches like to eat the glue on the backs of stamps.

I hesitated as I came to the edge of the pond. The reeds were nearly as tall as I was, and I had to work hard to push myself through them without tangling one of my arms or legs. Right now, for the first time in months, I had no healing fractures, and I planned to keep it that way.

My father told a story once about how he was out in his police cruiser when he realized all the cars in front of him were stopped dead. He slowed down and put the car into park, then opened the door to see what was going on. The minute he stepped onto the pavement, though, he landed flat on his back. Black ice; it was a miracle that he had even managed to brake safely.

The ice on the pond was like that: so clear that I could see the weeds and sand right through it, like it was a pane of glass. I got down carefully on my hands and knees, and inched forward.

I'd never been allowed on the ice, and like most things that you aren't allowed to do, it was all I thought about.

I couldn't get hurt this way — I was moving so slowly, and I wasn't standing up. My back was hunched like a cat's, my eyes staring down at the surface. Where did the fish go in the winter? Could you see them, if you looked carefully?

I moved my right knee, and my right hand. My left knee, and my left hand. I was breathing hard, not because it was so difficult but because I could not believe it was this easy.

There was a moan that rippled across the surface of the pond, as if the sky was crying. And then suddenly, all around me, the ice became a spiderweb, and I was the bug stuck at its center.

Grasshoppers have white blood Butterflies taste with their hind feet Caterpillars have about four thousand muscles . . .

"Help," I said, but I couldn't yell and breathe at the same time.

The water sucked at me all at once. I tried to grab for the ice, but it broke away in sheets; I tried to swim, but I didn't know how without a life jacket. My jacket and pants and boots were a sponge, and it was so cold, cold like frostbite, cold like an ice-cream headache.

An armadillo can walk underwater.

Minnows have teeth in their throats.

A shrimp can swim backward.

You would think I'd have been scared. But I could hear my mother, telling me a story before I went to bed, about a coyote who wanted to capture the sun. He climbed the tallest tree, and he put it in a jar and brought it home. That jar, though, it couldn't hold something so strong, and it burst. *See, Wills?* my mother had said. *You are filled with light.*

There was glass above me, and the runny eye of the sun in the sky, and I beat my fists against it. It was like the ice had sealed itself on top of me again, and I couldn't push through. I was so numb, I had stopped shivering.

As the water filled my nose and mouth, as the sun got tinier and tinier, I closed my eyes and curled my fists around the things I knew for sure:

That a scallop has thirty-five eyes, all blue.

That a tuna will suffocate if it ever stops swimming.

That I was loved.

That this time, it was not me who broke.

Recipe: (1) a set of instructions for preparing a dish; (2) something likely to lead to a certain outcome.

Follow these rules, and you will get what you want: it's the easiest prescription in the world. And yet, you can observe a recipe down to the letter, and it will not make a difference when the end product sits in front of you and you realize it's not what you wanted.

For a long time, I could only see you sinking. I pictured you, with your skin pale blue and your hair streaming out behind you like a mermaid's. I would wake up screaming, beating the mattress with my hands, as if I could reach through the ice and drag you to safety.

But that wasn't you, no more than the skeleton you'd been given was you. You were more than that, lighter. You were the steam that fogged the mirror in the morning when Sean dragged me out of bed and forced me to take a shower. You were the crystals painting my car windshield after a night's frost. You were the heat rising off the pavement like a ghost in the middle of the summer. You never left me.

I do not have the money anymore. It was yours, after all. I slipped the check into the silk lining of the coffin when I kissed you goodbye for the last time.

Here are the things I know for sure:

When you think you're right, you are most likely wrong.

Things that break — be they bones, hearts, or promises — can be put back together but will never really be whole.

678

And, in spite of what I said, you can miss a person you've never known.

I learn this over and over again, every day I spend without you.

WILLOW'S SABAYON, WITH CLOUDS

SABAYON

6 egg yolks
I cup sugar
2 cups heavy cream, whipped
½ cup light rum or Grand Marnier

Whisk the eggs and sugar in a double boiler. Once they are completely mixed, fold in the whipped cream. Remove from the heat, pass through a sieve, and add the rum.

CLOUDS

5 egg whites
Pinch of salt
⅓ cup sugar
2 cups milk or water

Place the egg whites and salt in a mixing bowl; on low speed, mix until smooth. Gradually increase the speed and sprinkle in the sugar. Beat until the whites hold a soft peak — this is meringue, the cloud I imagine you resting on nowadays. Meanwhile, simmer the milk or water. Take a spoonful of the meringue and gently drop it into the simmering liquid. Cook the meringue for 2 to 3 minutes and, with a slotted spoon, turn it over and continue cooking for another 2 to 3 minutes. Transfer the poached meringue to a paper towel. The clouds are fragile.

SPUN SUGAR

Cooking spray
2 cups granulated sugar
I teaspoon corn syrup

Spray a baking sheet with cooking spray, wiping any excess off with a paper towel.

Place the sugar and corn syrup in a saucepan and cook over low heat. Stir occasionally, until the sugar is dissolved. Raise the heat to high and bring the mixture to a boil, until a candy thermometer registers 310 degrees F (hard-crack stage). Remove from the heat and cool slightly. Let the syrup stand to thicken, about 1 minute.

Dip a fork into the sugar syrup and wave it back and forth over the baking sheet to paint long threads. The syrup will begin hardening almost immediately. With practice you can form the strands into lace, swirls, the letters of your name.

To serve, spoon some of the sabayon sauce into a shallow bowl or onto a large plate and top with 2 poached meringues. Gently place a few threads of spun sugar around the meringue, not on top, or it will deflate.

The outcome of this recipe is a work of art, if you can make it through the complicated preparation. Above all else: handle everything with care. This dessert, like you, is gone before you know it. This dessert, like you, is impossibly sweet.

This dessert fills me, when I miss you the most.

Author's Note

Willow's trivia came, in part, from *The Book of Useless Information*, edited by Noel Botham and the Useless Information Society (New York: Perigee, 2006).

If you'd like to learn more about osteogenesis imperfecta or to make a donation, please visit: www.oif.org.